TRAITOR'S SPRING

TRAITOR'S SPRING

BOOK 3 OF THE EISTEDDFOD CHRONICLES

SARAH JOY ADAMS

EMILY LAVIN LEVERETT

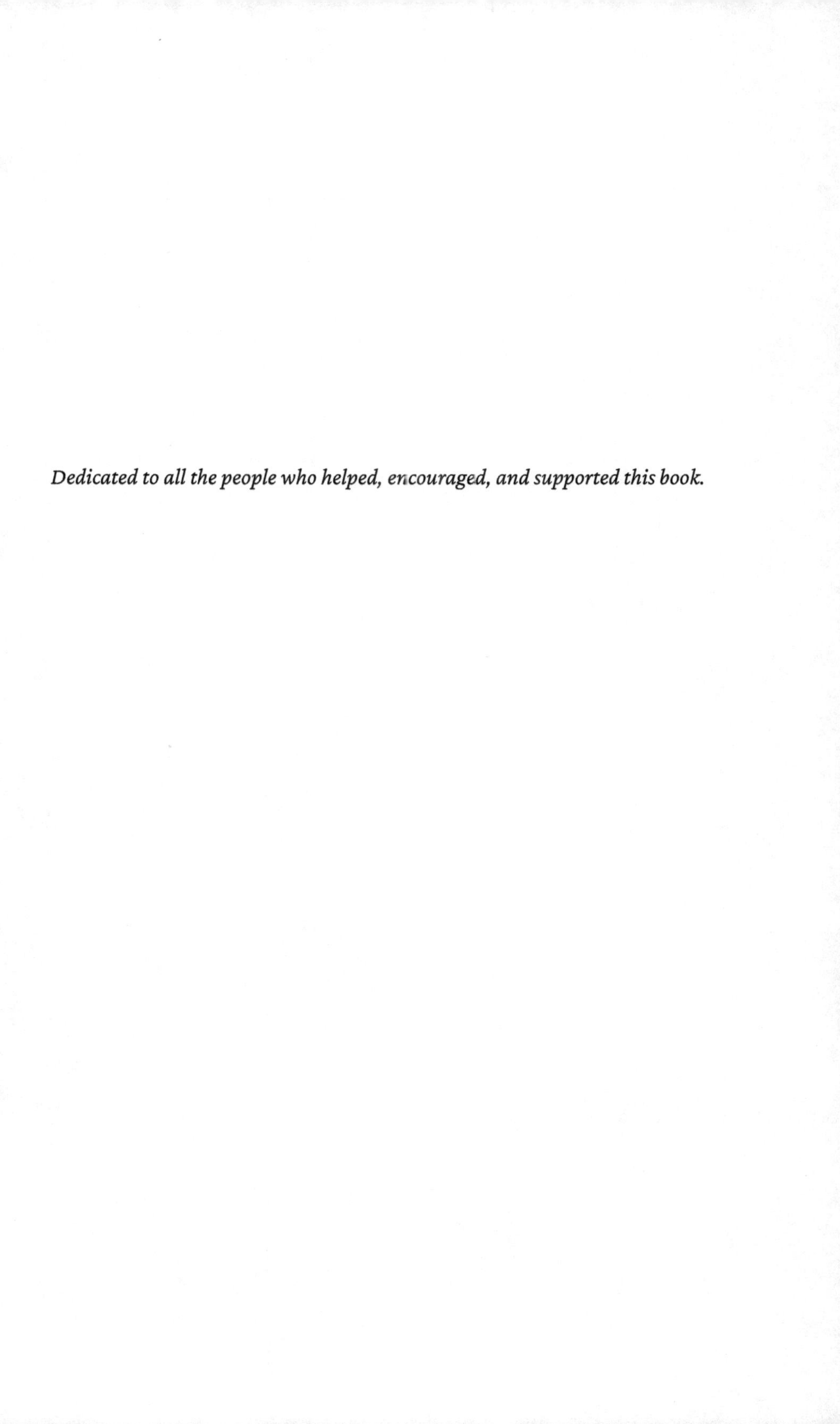

Dedicated to all the people who helped, encouraged, and supported this book.

WHAT CAME BEFORE

Changeling's Fall: Deor Smithfield is a changeling raised in the human world by her human grandmother. Forced to abandoned her career as a professor by mysterious and dangerous magic, she travels to the Winter Court to find the faerie who fathered her. There, she finds a job, a roommate, and a royal goblin boyfriend at Eisteddfod University. She also finds her magic worsening and her life in danger from all sides. Under close surveillance by the King's Sword of Peace and Justice, Deor struggles to find out her father's identity before her own magic kills her.

Rafe, Lord Farringdon is the devoted Sword to King Fionnleigh (Finn) and his appointed heir. He has agreed to undergo a painful magical adoption ceremony to make him the king's bodily heir. Each successive adoption ceremony drains Rafe of magic and leaves bloody gashes on his body, but no one knows why. In between these painful events, Rafe struggles to find out who is in the kingdom is attacking changeling women, leaving each one more psychically damaged than the last. Deor's all too convenient relationship with Geoff, the goblin Crown Prince, and her status as the sole material witness to yet another violent attack makes Rafe certain Deor is more than the innocent she seems.

Deor wrangles an invitation to the final Adoption Ceremony from Geoff, so that she might search for her father among the nation's nobility. As the ceremony begins, Deor is overwhelmed by magic. She realizes that she is the lost heir to the Winter Court, and Geoff plans to use her to murder the king. She breaks free from Geoff, interrupts the ceremony, and confronts the king about his affair with her mother. She then sits on the throne, proving that she is the rightful heir.

Winter's Heir: Deor is forced into the painful realization that her new role as heir leaves her incapable of pursuing her teaching. Forced to give up her job at the university, she struggles to master her newfound magic and wings while navigating a relationship with Fionnleigh. As Rafe is more and more convinced that his mother Madeline, a longtime enemy of the king, was behind the attempt on Finn's life, he finds an unexpected ally in his brother Victor, once a tool of their mother and now a supporter of princess Deor.

Fionnleigh demands a show of fealty from the nobility before opening parliament, taking place at the northern stronghold of Finn's loyalists. Rafe finds himself increasingly attracted to Deor, a problem that culminates in his fiancé, Genevieve, breaking off their engagement in an ugly public fight the night before the fealty ceremony.

Fionnleigh ignores Deor and Rafe's pleas that his actions are breeding resentment, leading people to support Madeline. As Deor and Rafe expected, Madeline attempts to steal the throne again, this time by enspelling Parliament with her powerful will magic. Deor, her newfound magic powers growing, confronts Madeline. Deor destroys the spell with a sword formed from her own magic. Order is restored, but Madeline and her retinue escape, leaving the other nobles dazed and confused.

The king is furious at Deor for making a public spectacle and is unconvinced by her explanation of what happened. Deor realizes that Finn now sees her as a rival for power. Rafe and Deor return to London on horseback, giving Deor a chance to see the wilds of the Winter Court, and giving them a chance to spend time alone. Unknown to Deor and Rafe, Finn has Rafe's brother Victor abducted and taken to a secret location.

CHAPTER ONE

Coming out of the highlands, Deor's horse ambled down the southbound road from Roger's castle at Northfalls, rocking her gently from side to side as it kept pace with the mounted soldiers around her. Finn and Astarte's much larger company parted from them at a crossroads miles back. Now it was just her, Rafe, and six others, Lt. Stephen Bolton among them. To her left a snow-covered field interrupted the forest through which they rode.

Over her other layers Deor wore a livery coat borrowed from Rafe's squire Gordie at the last minute. Since Gordie was traveling home in Finn's entourage of carriages, Deor borrowed it off him as she realized just how cold riding a horse could be. Even the beautiful winter clothes Astarte bought weren't enough to ward off the freezing cold of February in the very aptly named Winter Court.

As an added bonus, Gordie's coat left her enough room to hold Brand like a joey in a pouch, keeping both her and the puppy happily snuggled together. Trying to remember what Thea taught her about horses, Deor nudged at her horse until it was parallel with Rafe.

"How are you enjoying the ride?" he asked her from high up on his black charger, Sampson.

She pulled down the muffler that covered her face. "My toes are cold, but with all these layers, I'm pretty cozy. I think my leg muscles are going to hate me in the morning though. How much farther do we have to go?"

Rafe pointed ahead. "There's a village just over that next rise. Arthur and I often stay at the inn when we come here for the hunting. Best rabbit stew you've ever tasted."

Deor smiled, and her stomach growled. Their picnic lunch, eaten around a campfire on a rocky outcropping, happened hours ago. She pointed to the left. "What are those white things moving in the field? I can't quite make them out against the snow."

"Come see." Rafe urged Sampson off the road toward a gate in the hedge, signaling to the soldiers to wait for them on the road. In her coat, her brown, thick-furred puppy, Brand, poked his head out for a look and to lick Deor's chin. He was a Yule gift from Rafe, who bred Malossians, and the pick of the litter. She scratched his ear with one hand and kicked at her horse until it followed Rafe.

Once through the gate, Rafe led her into the field toward a pond half-surrounded by trees. The white shapes on the far side of the field moved toward them, carving paths through the ankle-deep snow. As they came closer, Deor realized that they were cows, massive, densely muscled cows of pure white with red ears. The lead cow, her short horns tipped with gold, wore a bell around her neck that clanged with every step.

Soon the animals stood around Deor and Rafe in a quiet semi-circle, chewing their cuds and staring up at them. Warm breath and the heat of a hundred cattle surrounded Deor. Up close, the cows had deep, liquid brown eyes fringed with long brown lashes. It gave them a friendly, doe-like expression. The lead cow lifted her head as if in greeting.

"The White Kine of the Faeries," Deor whispered in awe. "Just like in the stories." In her childhood reading and her grad studies she had read about the White Kine, the milk white cows that brought good fortune to the human lucky enough to find one or, even rarer, to be given one by a faerie ally. But woe betide the human who tried to steal one of the faerie creatures.

The belled cow pushed through the ranks of her sisters until her head was inches from Deor's knee. She stuck out a tongue like fat, pink boa and slurped Deor's boot from sole to knee. Deor shrieked, and the cow pulled back, hurt in its eyes.

"Uh, sorry. Good cow. Nice to meet you." She leaned out of the saddle and patted the cow on the crown of her head right between the gilded horns. The hair was softer and thicker than she expected. The other cows crowded closer in, a couple edging between Sampson and Deor's horse.

"I think they like me," Deor said.

"They're yours," Rafe said. "These are the King's Herd that can only be held by the royal family. Traditionally they belong to the Heir. All the income from the herd is yours to use for your personal expenses."

Deor sat back in her saddle, considering. "Funny that Finn never mentioned that. I have to ask him for money whenever I want to buy something."

"You should speak to the Exchequer about that when we get back to the Palace."

"Yes, I think I will." Deor reached out to pat the belled cow again. Brand wriggled and whined, trying to scramble out of her coat and jump down. "Not now, Brand," Deor said. "You'll get trampled."

Rafe chuckled. "He may need to go sniff a few trees."

"Um, speaking of 'sniffing trees,'" Deor said. "I could use a potty break myself. How far away from that town are we?"

"About an hour."

Deor groaned. "Great. Trees it is then. You wait here. I'll be over there," She gestured to the thick woods on the far side of the pond, "inspecting my royal forests. Come on, Brand."

With much heel kicking and tongue clicking, Deor managed to move her horse through the crowd of friendly cattle. She followed the cows' tracks around the edge of the pond toward a thick stand of bushes. The belled cow and a few others followed behind. Brand's whining grew more urgent.

"I know, I know," she said. "Just hang on and don't pee on me." Brand yipped and struggled to climb out of her coat. She urged her horse under the eaves of the forest.

Remembering that she'd needed a mounting block to get into the saddle that morning, Deor cast around for a large rock or a fallen tree she could use but saw nothing. Irked at the thought of having to trudge back across the field on foot to ask Rafe for a boost, Deor pushed a little further into the woods.

"Don't get lost," Rafe yelled from behind her.

"Yeah, yeah," she said, under her breath, peering around her. At least the snow was lighter here under the cover of the trees. The massive trees made a dense net of branches overhead, but none of the branches were low enough for her to tie up her horse. She glanced over her shoulder. She could still see the cows, all peering at her from the forest fringe, and beyond them a black shape that was Rafe on his horse.

"Really?" she said. "I do not need an audience for this."

She leaned out of the saddle as far as she could and let Brand jump down. Then she swung her leg over her horse and wriggled awkwardly to the ground.

Leading her horse, she ventured further in, headed toward a distant stand of bushes and gritting her teeth, while trying to walk with her knees clamped together. Brand bounded ahead of her, happily peeing on every tree and stump he came to.

"Easy for you," she said to him. She tied her horse to a bush and contemplated her options. Besides her hat and muffler, she was wearing two extra-long sweaters, stolen from Finn's wardrobe, under Gordie's double breasted livery coat, all of it layered over a pair of leather pants and silk long johns. If she crouched while holding onto the nearest tree, the tails of her coat were going to drag on the ground like a skirt. Splashing might happen. If she used her hands to hold everything up around her waist, she might lose her balance and fall over. Maybe she'd be okay if she held up her coat and leaned her back against a tree.

Yapping, Brand dove into the underbrush, no doubt chasing some small animal. She thought about running after him, but by now the situation was urgent. "If you tell anyone about this, I will kill you," she said to the horse. The horse stamped a hoof.

"Nothing ventured, nothing gained," she said. She headed for the nearest tree, gathering up the folds of her coat and sweaters.

As she braced her back against the tree and reached for the buttons of her pants, she heard a voice whisper, "Should we let him...?"

"Shut up!" another voice hissed as Deor turned in the direction of the voices. "Dammit. Now you've done it."

Magic moved in the air around her, fell over her like a net. The last thing she remembered was hitting the ground, her hands still fumbling with her buttons.

Chapter Two

Deor blinked her eyes open. The room was dark, but not pitch. Shadows danced on the walls and ceiling above her. A fire crackled and popped. She was on the floor, on a soft mattress. On her chest, she could feel the beating of Brand's heart against hers, and the rise and fall of his breath—he was alive.

Across the room, a door creaked open. Deor shut her eyes.

"Should I send word to him?" A male voice—adult, but not old.

"Not yet." A woman. "The lad won't wake up from the spell for a couple hours, so we've got some time. Wait about thirty minutes and send Sally to him."

"She's ten!" The man exclaimed.

"Yes," the woman's voice was impatient, but gentle. "He wouldn't hurt a child, especially a little girl, even if the message puts him off." There was a pause. "It's going to be okay, little brother. No harm is going to come to anyone, and that includes us. Now, go back to the inn and have a pint or two with the lads and lasses—keep everyone calm with your leadership."

The young man laughed. "They all know it's you who's really in charge."

"I know." The door opened. "That's part of what makes this work—they're scared of me."

"See you soon. Mirror if you need me."

"I will." A pause and the door clicked closed.

The scent of the fire filled Deor's nostrils. Under it, an earthy smell, like hay or grain. On the other side of the wall, a wind blew, but that was all she could hear. They couldn't be too far from civilization if the brother was going to a nearby inn. The spell comment helped clear up some fuzziness too. She went to the woods to pee, Brand made a noise, and she woke up here.

If she concentrated, she could feel the spell remnants all over her. No doubt the human part of her kept it from lasting as long as it was supposed to. Now the problem was that this woman thought she'd captured a young man—which meant she didn't know who the bundle in the corner really was.

A chair scraped the floor as it was dragged toward her. There was the sound of someone sitting.

Deor forced herself to stay still, to keep her eyes closed, even as she could feel the woman's gaze, and sense her leaning forward, reaching out.

The woman laid a hand on Deor's cheek. "Not too hot, not too cold," she whispered. "You'll likely be hungry when you wake, you and your pup, but there's nothing to do now but let you rest."

As fast as she could, Deor snatched the woman's wrist, opened her eyes, and sat up. "I've rested enough, I think."

The woman froze, mouth agape. Her fire-red hair was piled on her head. She wore a riding cloak with the hood back, supple leather pants and knee-high boots, like a forester. "The spell..."

"Should have held longer," Deor said. In her free hand, tucked down next to her side, she formed a knife. "Who are you and why have you kidnapped me?"

The woman pulled away, seemingly more annoyed than afraid. "You're not Rafe's page."

"No," Deor said. "Is that who you tried to kidnap?"

"Yes." The woman shook her head. "I mean, you haven't been kidnapped. Just ... detained."

Deor arched an eyebrow. As her eyes adjusted to the light, she recognized the woman. The lady with the arrow in her hair at Roger's. The one who looked like she'd stab Madeline through the heart if given the chance. "I know you," she said. "You were at the ceremony."

"I was." She leaned in. "Who are you? You're too small to be—"

"Stop." Deor set free the magic of the knife and held up her now-empty hand. She let go of the woman's wrist and hauled herself into a sitting position. "You don't want to know who I am. Trust me. You need to take me back where you found me."

"I couldn't do that, even if I wanted to," she said. She leaned back. "You're quite brave, you know."

Deor glared. "Take me back to the road."

"It's too late," the red-haired woman said. "It would be full dark by then, and you might freeze to death overnight or get eaten by a wildcat or unicorn. As soon as my brother gets back from letting Rafe know we have you, I'll speak with him, and it will be fine. I'm not going to hurt you."

"That's not what I'm afraid of." Deor dropped her head into her hands. "It's you who is going to get hurt. You and your brother." Deor pushed the hood that covered her face back and pulled down the scarf from her face. "Hello," she said with faux cheer, "I'm Deor. Princess of the Winter Court."

"Oh, shit!" The woman jerked up from her chair and stumbled back. "Oh, creator." She bolted to the door and grabbed the handle, then froze. She spun back around. "I didn't mean to kidnap you!" she insisted.

"I'm sure—"

"Please," she said, coming forward. "I will take you back right now. This was all my idea. I did it all. No one else is involved."

"Woah!" Deor held her hands up. "It's all going to be okay."

The woman stopped. "What?"

"Just take me wherever I need to go, and it will all be fine."

"There is no way this goes fine," the woman insisted. "I'll be hanged—I accept that. But not my little brother, not the people of this land, they don't deserve punishment for my crimes."

"You didn't mean to grab me. What were you doing?" Deor clambered to her feet, leaving the still-sleeping puppy on the mattress.

The woman crossed her arms and stared at Deor. "I was trying for the Sword's squire, Gordie. The Sword wouldn't talk to us when he escorted the king up here. All I want is a hearing. The land is sick—"

"You can say that again," Deor mumbled.

"What?" She demanded.

"Do you have a name?" Deor said with a sigh. The room was warm, and it made her drowsy. The spell was adding to that. All she wanted was to be at the Inn, to have some supper, to go to bed.

"Tess," she said. "Tess MacIntyre." She looked expectantly at Deor. As if she was supposed to know what that meant.

"Nice to meet you, Tess." Deor held out her hand. When Tess didn't respond, she dropped it. "So, yes, I know the land is sick. The nightmare the other day—"

"That story is true? You killed a nightmare?"

"No, Rafe and Victor killed it. I was just there." Deor wrapped her arms around herself. The room wasn't so warm in the face of the memory, and she shivered.

Tess pressed on. "They say you told your father the nightmare was his fault."

"Yes," Deor nodded, her arms still crossed over her chest. "It is his fault. I can't believe he killed all those people." She blinked as realization dawned. No wonder the woman looked so hostile at the ceremony. "This is your land, your people?"

Tess's shoulders slumped. She sat down in the chair and stared at the fire. "My mother was the Lord of the Manor's mistress. She was there when the king attacked, so she died with the rest of them. My brother and I—we survived because we were with our grandparents."

Tess picked up a poker and jabbed at the coals. "If that wasn't bad enough, the king let the land die. The poison he unleashed never went away—we've been withering ever since." Her mouth twisted, fighting back tears. "I just want the Sword to listen, to see if he can't convince the king to do something. At this point even giving the land to the Duke would be better than this!"

Deor sat back down on the mattress, gathering Brand into her lap. "You mean Roger? That duke?"

Tess nodded. "This land has no leader, no person to heal it and nurture it. It can't heal itself. The crops fail. Children get sick. Evil things— unicorns, wildcats, and nightmares run free, slaughtering cattle and attacking people." She wiped at her eyes. "I'm the eldest. It should be mine to care for. But I can't undo what the king did. Not unless I'm invested with the Lordship and the king or his heir releases the land from his anger. I don't care about the property," she snapped. She stared at Deor as if challenging her to say something. "I don't care if I'm never called Lady or given a seat in Parliament. All I want is to see the land to come back to life, the people thriving again."

"I believe you." Deor reached out and put a hand on Tess's knee. "I saw Mirrorvere for myself." She did not mention that she could feel the wound too. She did not know how far from Mirrovere they were, but it didn't matter. The land was all hers, in a way, and its pain broadcast through, loud and clear. "I'll do what I can when I get back to Caer Eisteddfod."

"What?" The woman gaped again. After a moment she barked out a laugh. "You're serious, aren't you?"

"Finn is stubborn and…difficult. But I'll do the best I can," Deor said.

Tess nodded her head. "Victor said you were like this."

"Victor Farringdon?" Deor asked. A memory flashed in her mind. Victor at Parliament, his voice amplified by a woman behind him—this woman in front of her.

"Yes," Tess said, chin raised. "He's a good man. He's not a traitor."

"I know," Deor said. "I trust him."

Tess squinted, annoyance clear on her face. "I thought he was wrong about you. But then at the ceremony. You apologized." She said it like she was saying Deor could raise the dead. "And you stopped Madeline."

"I didn't catch her though." Deor shifted and glared at the fire. A rage rumbled through her belly, and she knew from the halos at the edge of her vision that her eyes were silver as sharp steel. "I swear one day I'm going to kill that woman."

"Don't say things like that!" Tess snapped. When Deor turned back to her, she stepped back. "That sounds like an oath. Words can bind you. And Madeline is hard to kill."

"So am I," Deor said. "Was it Victor's idea to kidnap Rafe's squire?"

Tess snorted. "Don't be absurd. When I told him my plan, he tried to forbid me." She rolled her eyes. "He promised me that he would talk to Rafe, but when I heard Rafe was riding down here to stop at his favorite hunting spot, I couldn't miss the chance."

"Why not just go to the Inn and ask to talk to him?" Deor asked.

The woman gave her *a look* of the kind one used in place of saying something mean.

"Right. So, let's go back, and I'll talk to him. I'll explain everything."

"That I accidentally kidnapped you instead of his squire or page?" She sighed. "Please, leave my brother out of it, I don't want him to get in trouble."

"Why would he, or you, get in trouble?" Deor smiled. "I got lost in the woods, and you found me and brought me back to the Inn. Thank you SO much for your trouble."

Tess frowned. "You think Rafe will believe that?"

"No," Deor admitted. "But he'll accept it, so he doesn't have to arrest you and explain to the king that I was kidnapped on his watch. The two of us would be in so much trouble. Finn would probably never let me out of the house again."

Tess laughed. "Okay." She held out her hand. "I trust you."
Deor took her hand. "Great. Let's go."

THE PARLOR in the Inn was large. An L-shaped bar took up one third of the room, and the remainder of the space was a series of couches and comfortable chairs surrounding coffee tables. On one wall a roaring fire cast light and heat into the room.

"Tess!" a few people called as she walked in with Deor behind her. She waved.

A young man about a foot taller than Deor hurried over. "What are you doing? I haven't sent Sally," he hissed.

"That's fine, Ian," she cut him off. "Ian," she gestured at Deor and whispered, "meet Princess Deor, heir of the Winter Court."

"Hi." Deor cast back her hood and held out her hand.

"Oh god." The young man ignored her hand—she would have to stop bothering with handshakes—and drove his own hand through his long red hair. Now that Deor saw him, she saw the resemblance between the two siblings. By the stricken look on his face, he was clearly not the one used to problem solving.

"It's fine," Deor said. "I can't thank you enough for finding me when I was lost in the woods and keeping me safe!"

He gaped and looked between Deor and his sister. Tess gave him a meaningful look and a nod. After a moment he nodded back. "Right."

A small whine came from Deor. "Okay, okay," she said as she stripped off her coat. She loosened the bundle that held Brand and set him down on the floor. He shook himself from head to toe and sat down and yawned. "Could we get him some water?"

"Is that a Molossian?" A man came up. He didn't wait for an answer, just dropped down to one knee and scratched Brand behind the ears. "This is quite the pup." He looked up at Deor. "How did you get your hands on one?"

"He was a gift from Rafe," Deor said. She finished taking off her coat and scarf and hung them on a coat tree by the door. "For Solstice," she added. "His name is Brand."

The man's hand was still on the dog, but he stared at Deor, eyes wide. Suddenly he snatched back his hand. "Beggin' your pardon, miss, I mean

Your Majesty…" His accent was rough and thick, unlike the softer one of Tess and her brother.

"Don't worry about it!" Deor caught the man's hand and hauled him to his feet. "Brand loves the attention, see?" She glanced down at the dog, who was scanning the room, merrily wagging his tail. "So," Deor said, noticing that everyone in the room was silent and staring at her. "I got lost in the woods. Tess found me and brought me here. Isn't that lucky?"

Around the room, eyes widened, eyebrows raised. Neighbors exchanged scared glances.

"So," Deor said again, her voice firmer. "It's cold outside, and I'm tired. Could I get something warm? And some water for Brand? Whatever is cooking smells great too."

"O'course you can!" A voice boomed. A huge man came out from behind the bar. Tall and round and beaming like a cheerful cook from a children's story, the man had hands the size of frying pans. He bowed to Deor. "Whatever Your Majesty wants." He gestured toward a wingback chair in front of the fire, bowing again. "I expect Lord Farringdon will be here soon anyway. He called ahead earlier today to say he'd be stayin' here tonight and tomorrow," he said. "Said there would be two folks and wanted the room with a suite." He chuckled, a rumble that shook Deor and warmed her at the same time. "We had a little bet as to whether or not it was him and his fiancée tryin' to work it out, or him with some new lass, tryin' to forget his troubles."

"Looks like you were all wrong," Tess said. She leaned up and kissed the man on the cheek. "Now uncle, do you know where the Sword is?"

A harried servant in an apron bolted through the door. "The Sword is here, and he's in a state!" The skinny young man practically danced with nerves. "He's so mad there's near a snowstorm swirlin' round his head."

"I'll go talk to him," Tess said before anyone else could speak. She gave Deor a grateful smile. "You make yourself at home, Princess. My uncle, Callum McIntyre, will see to anything you want."

As Deor settled into the chair, Tess's uncle bowed again, saying, "Just give me a minute Your Majesty. I'll have a hot drink and a meal sent out at once. Your rooms are already in order if you'd prefer to eat in private."

Deor shook her head and stretched her booted feet out toward the fire. "This is lovely," she said. The large man bustled off toward the bar and the kitchen beyond it.

Around her, the room stayed frozen, half the patrons openly staring at her, the other half trying to look everywhere but at the royal person in their midst. No one spoke.

"So," Deor said in the bright voice she used on hostile classes, "I'd love to hear all about this place. On my way here, Rafe showed me the cows." They all still stared at her, and her mind raced as she tried to figure out something to say.

"Here you are," the owner bustled back in with a bowl and a steaming mug. "Some honey and warm whiskey for Your Majesty," he handed her the mug, "and some water for the pup." He set the bowl down on the floor. He pulled a hunk of meat from the pocket of his apron. "And a bit of venison, too." He dropped it on the floor next to the bowl. "Your meal is on its way from the kitchen."

Brand happily snatched the meat and began to chew.

"Thank you," Deor said.

"Happy to help, lass." He shooed a man out of the chair across from her and settled in. "So," he said, "what are you going to do about our nightmare problem?" He grinned. "I know you've faced one down, but what about the rest?"

Deor took a cautious sip of the drink. She could taste the magic, the sharp whiskey and the sweet honey too. It warmed her immediately but didn't seem to fuzz her brain. She leaned back in her chair. "I have no idea," she said. "You tell me what we should do."

The man stared for a moment and then burst out laughing. "You hear that, folks, the monarchy is taking suggestions!" He smirked and raised an eyebrow at her. "Right?"

She nodded. "Absolutely. I don't know that my father will listen to me," she shrugged. Around the room some faces turned glum. "But I'll do whatever I can to help you." Beneath all the cheer in the warm room, the building and the snow, the land thrummed. More distant from her than the palace, but still, in its way, her land. She looked the man in the face. "I promise."

CHAPTER THREE

Rafe shoved open the inn door and strode into the foyer, bellowing for the innkeeper. "MacIntyre! Get out here." At his feet, Jake barked as if to add his voice to his master's command. Sam whined and shoved his nose into Rafe's hand, but Rafe pushed him away.

Liam, the skinny serving man, popped out of doorway, wiping his hands on his apron. "Your lordship, how can I be of service?"

"Get me MacIntyre. And the head of the local Civil Patrol. I know he's in there propping up the bar at this hour. Move!"

As Liam skittered off to the bar, Lt. Stephen Bolton, the only member of the household guard Rafe completely trusted, cleared his throat at Rafe's elbow. "What's the plan, sir?"

Rafe's core burned hot with rage, drawing in all the available heat around him. "Search parties. Three of them. We'll get tracking dogs from the locals, recruit the local Civil Patrol, and go back out to the woods until we find whoever took her."

"Are you sure she was taken, sir? Perhaps she just wandered off."

Rafe lowered his voice and stepped closer, his mouth near the Lieutenant's ear. "She can't fly yet, Bolton. You saw the spot—the snow was swept by wind, and there were no tracks leading away. Someone knocked her out, picked her up, and made off with her. I'd bet my head on it." With one hand in his pocket, he turned his mirror over and over as he spoke. Creator help him, as soon as the search parties were organized, he needed to notify the king. After that he'd be lucky if his head didn't end up hanging over Tower Bridge, even if they did find her safe and sound.

He shook the thought away. Find the princess before she was harmed. That was all that mattered. He'd take whatever punishment Finn wanted to mete out, so long as they could get Deor back.

The door to the bar opened, but instead of the hulking innkeeper, his red-headed niece Tess emerged.

"Welcome, Lord Farringdon—" she started to say, but Rafe cut her off.

"Good, it's you. I'm conscripting you, your brother, and your uncle. And any other poaching friends you may have. It's an emergency."

Tess MacIntyre blinked at him and folded her hands together. "It's not poaching if it's your own land."

Rafe waved off her objection. "I don't give a damn. You can kill every deer between here and Wellhall if you make yourself useful tonight. The...someone from my party is missing, and we need to find her."

Tess smiled, a bright pretense of ease, but her knuckles were white. "The princess, sir? She's right in there, having her supper." She gestured behind her toward the bar.

Rafe blinked at her, twice. Then he charged past, nearly knocking Tess over as he threw the parlor door open with a bang and strode into the room. Everyone in the room turned toward him, including MacIntyre, who was just setting down a plate of bread and cheese in front of a large, wing-back chair before the fire. With a happy yelp, Brand came bounding toward him and bounced straight into Jake.

"Where is she?" Rafe shouted.

Deor peered around the edge of the chair, a mug of whiskey in her hand. "Don't shout like that, Rafe. It's not polite. Come and have some food, and I'll tell you all about the adventure I've been having." Every face in the room swiveled in unison to look at her, then at him. Deor leaned a little further out of the chair and waved the mug at Bolton. "Hello, Stephen! Come and eat with us. Where are the rest of the men? They aren't still out in the cold, are they?"

Rafe felt a strange spasm in his chest, a combination of rage and relief that twisted his lungs together. "You pint-sized, smooth-faced truant! Where the hell have you been?"

The faces watching them pulled back, eyes widening.

Deor cocked her head at him. "I got lost in the woods. And then Tess helped me get unlost." She pointed behind him. Tess gave him a too bright smile, her hands still clenched together.

"Really, Rafe," Deor said in a more reasonable tone. "You're blowing cold air all over the place. My feet are just starting to thaw out, and you're not helping. Stop grinding your teeth and come over here. I'll explain everything." She beckoned at him with her whiskey glass.

Rafe rubbed a hand over his mouth. The tips of his fingers burned. "Bolton," he said in an altogether too steady voice. "Tell the men to stand down. You're dismissed."

"Yes, sir." Bolton saluted smartly and marched out of the room.

Forcing himself to breathe slowly, Rafe unclenched his hands and approached Deor. MacIntyre hastily pulled over another comfortable chair and positioned it next to Deor's. He stepped aside out of Rafe's path. "Stew, sir?"

"Whisky," Rafe said.

"Have some stew too," Deor said. "You were right. It's really good. Bring him some stew, would you?" MacIntyre hustled away toward the kitchen.

Rafe lowered himself into the chair and fixed Deor with a glare. Then he turned toward Tess. "You. Don't go anywhere." She nodded and stayed standing by the door.

He turned back to Deor, casting a privacy spell around the two of them. He flicked his fingers, sending a dispelling cantrip at her to dissolve any hidden spells of compulsion on her. Deor frowned at him and waved at the spell, as if it were a gnat flying into her face.

"Don't. Touch. It," he said. He took another deep breath and composed himself, leaning forward so that their knees nearly touched. "What really happened?"

"I went looking for a bush, you know for privacy, and I...went astray."

Their eyes locked for a long minute. Deor's face was solemn, without a hint of the levity from before. Slowly, Rafe nodded.

"I see. And how did she know where you were?"

"She didn't. She thought I was your lost squire."

"My lost... Oh. Of course. And she would help him find his way back to me so that she could speak to me."

"Tess was very kind to me."

"And what was the price of her 'help'?" he asked, his anger still palpable.

"There was no price, Rafe. I'm not being extorted. I'm not hurt." She looked around the room. "But the land here is hurt. I can feel it. People need help."

He shook his head. "There's nothing I can do about that."

"Yes, you can. You're the Sword of Peace and Justice. What kind of peace and justice is there in a land where crops die and monsters proliferate? You have to help me talk to Finn about this. If Finn restores the land's magic and gives it back a proper heir, the people will thrive again."

"He won't listen."

"He has to! That's his whole job as king—to keep the kingdom alive. If he can't even do that, what good is he?"

A blur appeared on the edge of the privacy spell. Rafe lowered the spell for a moment, allowing MacIntyre to set a bowl of stew and a glass of whisky on the small table. "Thank you, MacIntyre. See that my men are fed and given rooms for the night as well, will you?"

"Of course, my lord," the big red-headed man said.

"Tell your niece to relax. And thank her for her help."

MacIntyre's shoulders sagged with relief. He hurried off.

"Thank you," Deor said, her voice low.

Rafe shrugged. "Your wish is my command, princess."

"Don't be like that. You know this is the best way," she said.

Rafe took the whisky and sipped it, staring into the fire. Deor picked up Brand and cuddled him on her lap, her eyes still on Rafe. Rafe took another sip of the whisky. Finally, he set the glass down, turning back to Deor. "I'm sorry I didn't watch over you more carefully."

"Oh, please. It was my fault. You told me not to go too far into the woods," She leaned forward, a conspiratorial grin on her face. "I will tell you one thing—I don't care what kind of earth faerie I am, I don't ever want to have to piss in a bush again."

They both laughed, breaking the last of the tension between them. The firelight danced over her face and hair, gilding her dark hair. Her grey eyes shone. He wanted to reach out and take her hand in his, to pull her close and press his cold lips against her warm mouth. Instead, he looked back at the fire and took another drink of his whisky.

Chapter Four

Deor waved goodbye to the room full of Scots and followed MacIntyre through the lobby and up the stairs. He opened the door to the suite. "Here you are, Your Majesty, your lordship."

"Thanks, Callum," Rafe said and slapped the man on the shoulder.

"Breakfast at dawn for hunting?" the large man asked.

"No," Rafe shook his head. "We'll have breakfast at nine and then head on down the road to the garrison at Loch Lomond. We'll be portalling from there."

The man nodded and smiled at Deor. "Not much of a hunter, Your Majesty?"

"Not at all," she beamed back at him. "And thanks again for the lovely meal and whisky."

He nodded and doffed an invisible hat at them before closing the doors.

Rafe flicked the lock, even though there would be a rotating pair of soldiers there for the night. Deor also suspected that the Innkeeper would sooner die than let anything happen to her or to Rafe.

Brand gave a small bark and hurried away from her to flop in front of a crackling fire where Jake and Sam waited, having woken at the opening door.

"Your room is to the right," Rafe said. "Bedroom and bath. I'm sure your things are all waiting for you. Do you need a maid to help with your long johns?" He grinned.

"I think I've got it," Deor returned the smile. "I'm going to change into jammies."

He laughed at the word. "Jammies?"

"My night clothes," she said. "Or at least the clothes I'm wearing between taking off my outside clothes and putting on what I'll actually wear to bed. Lounge-wear. You know, like those black pants you favor."

"Ah, of course." He kept the smile and gave a small bow.

As he headed toward his room Deor bit her lip and then called, "I'll call if I need any help."

He waved but did not turn around to face her.

Dammit, she thought. Perhaps that interrupted kiss in her bedroom was a fluke, something he regretted, and now he was happy to avoid her. He certainly wasn't dense, and her suggestion of needing help was likely far more blunt than many faerie women he'd encountered.

She sifted through her clothing. Nothing that even remotely qualified as lingerie. It was more aptly named skivvies. Oh well. She tugged off her boots and began the rather arduous task of shedding layers until she was naked, her clothes in a pile at the foot of the bed. She wandered into the bathroom and was thrilled to find a hot bath already drawn. No doubt magic kept the water warm, and she eased into it with a sigh.

She let her body soak out the cold and the sore muscles from riding. She had thought perhaps she wanted to ride the whole way home, but her aching thighs proclaimed that it wasn't a good idea.

After the water cooled, Deor dragged herself out and wrapped herself in a towel. She moved to the door to the parlor and listened—she didn't hear anything. Perhaps Rafe was already asleep. *Dammit, again.* The room was warm enough for her to sleep naked if she chose, but she wanted to go out and get Brand, so she pulled on panties and one of Finn's long, baggy sweaters.

She took the pins out of her hair—she'd kept it up and out of the bath—and let it fall around her shoulders. She shook her head at her reflection. The sweater was baggy enough that the neck hung off one shoulder, and her hair was softly curled from being worn up all day, followed by the steamy air. She looked right out of *Flashdance* or some other 1980s flick. She tamed her hair with her fingers a bit, still impressed by the speed at which it now grew—magic again—and went to find Brand.

Out in the parlor, Jake, Sam, and Brand were curled in a pile by the fire, snoring quietly. She'd leave her door cracked, then, in case Brand wanted her, but if Rafe's dogs were sleeping out here, then the puppy would want to as well. He was increasingly happy being part of the pack.

"Hello." A voice, soft in the low burning light of the fire, startled her. Rafe sat on the couch in his black lounging pants and nothing else, sipping a dark brown liquid from a rounded glass.

"Hi," she said. "What's that?"

"Cognac. Want one?" He pointed at a set of bottles and glasses on a table against the wall. "They always have some of my favorites for me." He smiled. "There's a wine that Genevieve favors too. No doubt they were expecting her."

"Ouch," she said.

He shrugged. "I'm sure it wasn't meant for spite."

"What is it?" she asked.

"It's a pinot gris. It's a soft wine, with a bit of raspberry."

Deor shook her head. She poured some cognac into a glass and sat on the far side of the couch from Rafe, sipping her drink. "I see why you like it."

"Never had it before?"

She shook her head, curling her feet under her and draping the baggy sweater over her knees. She often sat that way, keeping the chill away, but she always left her feet bare, even here, far from the palace. "So," she said. "Sorry about today."

"What about it?" he said.

"Oh, you know. Going off to pee. Getting kidnapped by a hostile political figure. Chatting with the locals. Making promises I might not be able to keep."

He sighed. "You promised to try to help them. That's what you'll do."

"Do you think I'll actually be able to help?" she asked.

"No," he said. He swallowed the rest of his drink. "But I don't really want to talk about Finn right now. Do you?"

"Definitely not."

He stood. "Do you want another?"

Yes. "No. I shouldn't. Faerie alcohol always affects me way more than human alcohol, so that's my limit for today. Too much and I start saying things I shouldn't."

"That happens only after you drink?" He poured himself another and sat back down on the couch, his body turned toward her. He took another sip.

"It gets worse." She shoved her hair out of her face and wished she'd brushed it more carefully—okay, at all. He was handsome, with his moon-shadow blue skin and vivid blue eyes. His straight black hair fell loose over his broad shoulders. Even the thin scar from under his left eye, across his cheek, and finishing in a small nick in his left nostril made him more attractive. She could see faint scars on his chest, too. She wanted to trace each one with her finger and ask him about them.

When they first met, the one on his face was glamoured, but she saw through it—she saw through most glamours if she tried. She'd since learned that doing so was rude—the equivalent of running around splashing women with makeup remover. Now, they lived in the same part of the palace, shared a suite even (delightfully referred to as the home of the heir and the spare). Her father referred to them as brother and sister.

She did not think of him like a brother.

She could have another drink and use it as an excuse. But he was a good guy. The kind of guy who wouldn't use alcohol as an excuse, or let a woman use it as one, either.

Rafe took another sip.

"So," she said, after drawing a deep breath. "Would you like to have sex with me?"

Rafe coughed, nearly spitting out his drink.

"Are you okay?" Deor leaned forward, but he waved her away.

"I'm fine." He set the drink down. "You did just ask me if I would like to have sex with you, right?"

"Yes." She nodded, her face flushing a bright red. She thought it would feel less ridiculous to say it out loud than to hint around it. She was wrong.

"Tonight? Here?"

"Yes." Her voice shrank a bit, and she considered making a sprint for her room and locking the door behind her.

"Right." He stared at her for a moment. "Yes. I would very much like to have sex with you. Tonight. Here." He paused. "Or perhaps in the bedroom. Away from prying eyes." He gestured toward the dogs, all three of which were staring at them expectantly.

"Bedroom it is," Deor said before her confidence waned. "Yours or mine?"

"Mine has a bigger bed," he said and stood up. In a single swift moment, he bent down and scooped her up into his arms, bouncing her slightly to catch her under her knees and behind her back.

She gasped and giggled, throwing her arm around his shoulder. "I can walk, you know," she said, laughing.

"After a long day's ride?" He shook his head. "I wouldn't dream of putting you to the trouble."

She barked out another laugh when he kicked the door closed behind them as he carried her into his bedroom. The bed certainly was bigger in here—longer and wider. He lightly tossed her into the center. She bounced and flopped backward, staring at the top of the canopy. The four-poster bed was hung with a deep blue canopy and drapes.

The room was dim, the only light coming from one lamp on the nightstand and the low burning fire, casting shadows.

Rafe cocked his head to the side and looked at her, a small smile quirking the corner of his mouth. "I think I have wanted to have you in my bed since you stopped the adoption. I wasn't particularly honest about it, of course, until much more recently."

"I'm a big fan of honesty," she said, letting her gaze wander over his body again. "You are one of the most beautiful men I have ever seen." She flicked her gaze back up to his and caught a look of pleased surprise. He must know he was attractive, but perhaps people didn't tell him enough. If whatever this was went on past tonight, she would certainly let him know.

Honesty cut both ways, though. She had a small moment of panic in the face of his hungry look. What if she wasn't as pretty—*Stop it* she told herself. *You're being stupid. He's here. He didn't say yes because he was being polite.* Still, she dropped her gaze and felt her cheeks flare red again as she grabbed the hem of the sweater and hauled it over her head. She tossed it off the bed. She still wore panties, but other than that, she was naked, with nowhere to hide.

She could have grabbed a pillow from behind her, and covered herself, but she wasn't a teenager. And the bed was made, covers all tucked away, so no wrapping up in a comforter, either. So, she faked her confidence. She stretched out her legs and crossed one ankle over the other. She leaned back, propping herself up on her hands.

"You're beautiful," he said. "I suppose turnabout is fair play." He tugged free the tie at his waist and slipped his thumbs under the waistband of his pants.

Deor bit her lip, ready for the show, but a bolt of panic shot through her. The last time a guy disrobed in front of her, she laughed.

"Wait!" she said at the exact moment he started to slip his pants over his hips.

He froze. After a moment's pause, he said "We don't have to…"

"No!" She held up a hand. "I mean," she said. "No. Don't stop. But wait."

Gah. His expression drifted from puzzlement to mild concern. Time to break the cardinal rule: do not bring up sex with other guys when you're naked, and about to have sex, with a new guy. "When I was with Geoff—"

His eyes widened. "Is this the best time …?"

"No." She shook her head. "It is not. But I don't want the same thing to happen."

He arched an eyebrow. "I seriously doubt there is much past the bare minimum that Geoff and I have in common when it comes to sex."

"I don't doubt that," Deor said. Was it her imagination, or did his pants seem slightly less snug across his pelvis? She shoved the thought away and stared at a point on the edge of the bed about three feet in front of her, avoiding his face. "Look, when I first slept with Geoff," the words came tumbling out, "I turned the lights on, then he turned them off, then he took off his pants, and I screamed and laughed because he glowed in the dark and that startled me, and I don't know about you …"

"Wait," he said. "You pointed and laughed at Geoff's dick the first time you saw it?"

Deor's cheeks burned. "Yes," she barely managed to say. He was going to toss her out. She knew it.

He laughed. "I would have paid good money to see that."

When she met his gaze, she saw the bright laughter in his eyes. "It was kind of funny, especially looking back on it. I didn't want the same thing to happen with you."

"I don't glow in the dark. Most faeries don't."

"I figured that, but I don't know if there's anything else …" She waved her hands a bit, as if that helped.

"Are you trying to ask if there is something … unique about my body?"

"Yes." She sighed, relieved.

"I don't believe so," he said.

"So, no extra wings or anything?"

"Extra…? Oh!" He laughed again. "No." He slipped his thumbs back into the waistband. "Here. It's easier to show you." He dropped his pants. "Anything worth laughing about?" He put his hands on his hips.

He was impressive, stunning even. The blue of his body didn't change at all, neither darker nor lighter. The flickering of the fire accentuated the muscles of his legs and the sharp vee of his pelvis. His body belonged in one of those artsy issues of sports magazines, where the whole point was the diverse glory of the athletic human form. He could be the front page—or the centerfold.

Deor swallowed hard. "Perfect," she managed.

He eased forward, resting his hands on the bed before crawling on his hands and knees, his hair dropping over his face and swinging over his shoulders as he stalked toward her.

Instinctively she scooted backward until she hit the pillows and stopped, knowing the headboard was only a few inches away.

He caught her ankles, one after the other, and pulled her toward him, quickly but gently, so she slid onto her back, and he loomed over her. He leaned down and brushed her hair out of the way before cupping her face in one hand. He brushed his lips across hers and then kissed her cheek and down to her ear, where he closed his teeth around her earlobe, drawing a gasp from her.

"You're perfect too," he whispered, breath hot on her neck.

Chills ran down her body.

He cupped her breast with his other hand and stroked her stiffening nipple with his thumb, kissing his way down her throat and her breastbone to take it into his mouth.

She arched her back and slipped her fingers into his hair.

"Do you like this?" he asked, his voice husky against her flesh.

"Mmmhmmm," she managed.

He shifted his mouth to the other nipple, and the chill of the air made her gasp again. She squirmed under his tongue, biting her lip and trying not to cry out, though there was no reason for quiet. She kept one hand curled in his hair and with the other, she clutched his shoulder. She turned her face toward his hand and kissed his palm.

Slowly he kissed his way down from between her breasts to her stomach, teasing her navel with his tongue, and further down still, stopping at the edge of her panties. "I want to taste you," he said.

"Yes," she moaned.

He slid both his hands down her sides and caught the delicate lace, curling his index fingers into the waistband and pulling them down. The chill of the air skimmed across her torso as he lifted himself off her to slide her panties down her legs and off of her, tossing them to the floor. He sat back on his knees and looked at her for a long moment.

Deor's cheeks burned and the flush rushed down her whole body, a caressing heat that made her body glow. She wanted to close her eyes, but she couldn't—she couldn't take her eyes off him, the lazy grin that spread across his face as she locked eyes with him.

He rested his hands on her knees for a moment and slid them up her thighs, pushing her legs apart with delicate firmness, leaning forward as he did so. He kissed her again, first the inside of one thigh, then the other, and then his tongue was between her folds, flicking across her clit, swollen with desire, and she cried out as pleasure shot through her. He didn't stop, and when she arched her back and slipped her fingers into his hair again, he moaned softly.

Tension built inside her, tight, aching pressure rising as she writhed under his mouth. He slid one finger into her, and another, and she cried out, her body clenching. She bit her lip again and turned her face to the side, pressing it into the pillow and closing her eyes as he moved his fingers in and out, never stopping the flicking of his tongue.

"Oh, god." She gasped and let go of his hair, sliding her hands down to clutch his shoulders. "Rafe," she cried as the first orgasm shot through her and she tightened her muscles around his fingers. He didn't stop, or slow down, until she called his name again, voice shaking with her body's shuddering pleasure.

He slipped his fingers out of her and kissed his way back up her body. She cupped his cheek and, still breathing heavily, stared into his eyes. "That was," she shook her head. "I don't know." She leaned up and kissed him and pulled him back down as she rested her head on the pillow again. She slipped her tongue into his mouth and tasted her own desire. He deepened the kiss, slipping his tongue into her mouth.

She wrapped her legs around his waist and rocked her hips upward. His erection pressed against her, and she rocked again, the pleasure of her orgasms lost in the desire to feel him inside her. She broke the kiss and pressed her lips to his ear. "Please," she whispered.

"Please?" he said, his own breath coming in jagged gasps. He wanted her as much as she wanted him, she knew. He pushed his body off hers, held himself over her and looked down at her.

Deor slid her hand between them and stroked him. He closed his eyes and drew a deep breath. He threw his head back and rocked his hips in time with her rhythm until he suddenly caught her wrist and pulled her hand away. He opened his eyes and looked down at her.

"I want to come inside you," he said.

"Yes." Deor nodded. She twined her arms around his neck and leaned up to kiss him. "Now."

He shook his head. "I'm not fertile, are you?"

She blinked, taken aback by the question. No one ever asked her that before—but the conversation with Finn flooded back—faerie fertility cycles. Rafe wasn't fertile, so they should be fine. On the other hand, that line of thinking went badly for her mother.

"I ...," she said, and closed her eyes again. *Am I?* "No," she said, suddenly, like it was coming from somewhere deep inside her body, not her brain. She wasn't. She knew, though she couldn't say why. "I'm not fertile," she said with a grin. She rocked her hips up against him again. "Please," she repeated.

He grinned at her. "As my lady requests." He covered her mouth with his. He shifted his hips back and eased forward.

She gasped as he entered her and pressed her face to his shoulder. She closed her eyes and savored the feeling of him filling her, slowly, gently.

"Are you okay?" he whispered in her ear.

"Perfect," she said. She wrapped her legs around his waist again. She looked up at him and took his face in her hands. "I'm not delicate, Rafe," she said softly. "You won't break me." A smirk crossed her face. "You're welcome to try."

Laughter filled his eyes. He eased back and thrust forward once, and again, picking up speed and finding his rhythm. She wrapped her arms around his neck and clung to him as another orgasm built. She held it off as long as she could, savoring the weight of his body on top of hers, the power of each thrust, the way he filled her, covered her.

She cried and shut her eyes out as another orgasm shuddered through her, and he gasped as she clenched her muscles around him. He cried out, too, as he came, catching her in his arms and holding her body against his until he trembled, spent.

He released her back onto the bed, and she let go of him, cupping his face in one hand and kissing him tenderly. She dropped her legs from around his waist and chuckled at the trembling her thighs were doing. He kissed her one more time and dropped onto his side next to her.

"That was splendid," he said.

"Very."

Rafe got up and pulled the covers back. He scooted them out from beneath her and slipped into bed next to her. He tugged them back up to his waist. He propped his head up on his elbow and smiled at her. "Stay the night with me?" he asked.

"Sure." She snuggled down stared up at him. "Oh," she said. "Except that we have to let Brand in." She giggled. "He'll paw at the door all night and whine if I don't let him sleep with me."

"No problem." Rafe cast off the covers and got up. "Do you mind if Jake and Sam are in here too?" He looked vaguely nervous about the request.

"Not at all. It certainly will help me keep warm," she said.

"Great." He opened the door to the parlor. Sure enough, all three dogs were sitting in the doorway, in a row, waiting to be let in. Brand hurled himself into the room and, after three starter attempts, managed to scramble up onto the bed. Sam followed but landed on the bed with one jump. Jake, on the other hand, paused long enough to sniff Rafe all over and give a snort, whether of approval or derision, Deor couldn't be sure, before he settled onto the bed too.

"Shoo," Rafe waved Jake out of his spot next to Deor and climbed back into bed. "You sure you don't mind this?" he asked as he settled onto his back.

"It's perfect," Deor said, rolling onto her side and snuggling up against him. "I can't think of a better way to spend the night."

Rafe turned off the light on the nightstand, and the room fell into a comfortable darkness. The fire burned down to mere embers and gave off a subtle glow. Outside the window, flurries of snow spun past. The ride tomorrow would be through a Winter Wonderland. Tomorrow would also bring to light the reality of their actions.

Rafe's breathing slowed as he drifted off to sleep, falling into a soft, steady rhythm. Deor watched his silhouette as his chest rose and fell with each breath. They hadn't talked about what any of this meant. And that was fine with her. They both could use a bit of fun, with no complications. They were friends—getting to be good friends.

He would never talk about her to the press. He would never brag about his conquest to his friends. Of all the people in all the world, he was probably the safest person to have an affair with.

A consequence-free tryst—just what they needed.

Chapter Five

True to Deor's expectations, the next morning Rafe did not suggest they rehash the previous night's events, except for a brief lesson on how to not get kidnapped.

Though chilly, the ride through the countryside to the garrison was beautiful. The night's snow dusted everything without causing too much in the way of snowdrifts to slow their progress. Rafe even paused once to point out a unicorn through a patch of dense trees. Its white body blended in with the snow-covered branches. At a distance, it was stunning, and far less terrifying than when one tore through the woods right at her, nearly spearing off her head.

Rafe bent close to whisper to her about the habits and behavior of unicorns and other fae creatures of the forest. While the biology lesson was interesting, the sound of Rafe's voice low in her ear sent thrills up and down her spine.

The garrison was a simple fort and a portal—mostly a waystation for the king's journeys up and down the nation. Just like her first long distance portal trip, this one left her feeling stretched and disoriented for a few seconds. The reception at the palace, however, was far more uncomfortable.

As soon as she showered and changed, Deor went to say hello to Finn in his parlor. His brows were furrowed and his eyes a steely grey—a quick step from angry silver. She blinked rapidly, shoving down any response in kind. He did not smile, nor did he rise to greet her.

"Deor," he nodded. He was alone in the room. From his tone, he was still displeased about her apology to Parliament and her challenging Madeline. "The press is having a field day with what happened at Roger's." He rose and put his hands on her shoulders. "I should be very cross with you for diverting all the attention." It was clear from his expression that he was teasing her, or at least he thought he was, but Deor felt the threat. "But you seem, once again, to come out the other side a heroine. Several people who were there swear that Madeline was trying to control them, and you stopped her."

"Does this mean she can be arrested?" Deor sighed in relief. Knowing that woman was out there, somewhere, was the kind of thing that kept her up at night.

"If someone would officially come forward," he said. "But no one will. They won't cross her. Even with witnesses, it would be incredibly difficult to prove, and I'm not sure a court would convict. That would be worse than nothing at all. With luck she and her family will crawl back to Wellhall and not bother any of us again."

"Well, the less trouble she can cause the better."

"True. For the next few weeks, be careful what you say and do in public." His gaze rolled over her, and his expression showed little satisfaction. "The Summer Court is spreading lies that you are not my child through their press. Don't behave in a way that supports such rumors."

"Of course, Your Majesty—it won't happen again."

He nodded, holding eye contact until Deor realized she needed to speak again.

She needed something safe, something cheerful, something non-scandalous. "It was a lovely ride back to the palace," Deor said suddenly. "I see why Rafe likes MacIntyre's Inn." She sat down in the armchair across the coffee table from him. "Oh!" she added as the thought came to her. "Rafe showed me the cows. The White Kine?"

Finn's face softened. "Those are yours," he said. "They are lovely, sweet things."

Deor nodded. Cows seemed a safe subject. "They came up around me—the one with the bell even licked my leg." She felt ever more like a city girl—excited at the notion of cows.

The storm clouds around Finn seemed to vanish. "I remember the first time my father took me to see them. They were huge—I was only about six or so—they were beautiful. Like you, I saw them first in the winter—some of them made the snow look dingy." He beamed at the memory. "I used my first profit from them to buy my first set of clothes on my own." He shook his head. "Bless my mother for letting me choose, but the suit was hideous. Loud and obnoxious, with far too much flounce."

"That sounds adorable," Deor said, well aware she was flattering him, and pleased that he preened himself as she said it. "I was wondering about the money part."

"Do you need some?" Finn looked concerned.

"Oh, no. I don't need anything," Deor shook her head. "The last time I gambled, at Delaney's party, I came away ahead." She grinned, and when he seemed pleased, she continued. "But I would like my own money," she said. "It feels strange, like a burden to you, to always come about clothes and other things."

Finn nodded. "I do admit you have made excellent choices in clothing. The dresses for Roger's were entirely appropriate for a princess." He grimaced slightly and Deor braced herself for a lecture. "I do believe I ought not have pressed you into going with Genevieve. Her dress was lovely, but it would not have done your beauty justice."

Deor smiled at the compliment. "Thank you," she said. "So, should I speak to the exchequer?"

"No." He waved his hand dismissively. "I have to meet with him later today, and I will tell him you need to be set up with accounts. Do you want credit in the human world?"

"I hadn't really thought about it," Deor lied. She thought about it a lot. The ability to buy a one-way ticket to America, or possibly the Moon, seemed like a good idea. "But you know, there are some things I can only get there—and I'd like to be able to go see London. I do love the city. Perhaps you and I could go to a show or dinner sometime?" *Slow down, there. Don't lay it on too thick.*

"That would be delightful!" He slapped his hands onto the arms of the chair and stood. "I hope your hearing this doesn't make you sad," he said, a softness coming into his features, "but I did so enjoy those experiences with your mother."

A lump caught in Deor's throat. "It does make me a bit sad," she said. "But I'd love to hear you talk more about her. Good or bad, I miss her every day and want to know more." Deor rose as her father approached.

He leaned down and kissed her on the forehead.

Deor stood and hugged him, even though she flinched as she did. "I plan on staying at home, mostly, though I might go out with Rafe sometimes. I like Rodney and Clarissa, and they seem very low key."

Her father hugged her back and let go. "They are. They would make excellent allies and friends." He let a condescending smile crawl into his features. "I think I would avoid the Lady Genevieve for awhile."

"Right," Deor said. "I know when to head back to the lair, hide, and lick my wounds."

"Excellent." He gestured to the door. "Why don't you get some rest? I'll speak to the exchequer, and he'll contact you if he needs anything, or when he has made the arrangements. Perhaps then you might go shopping? It might do the public good to see you out and about in non-political ways."

"Yes, Your Majesty." Deor gave another small bow and followed him out, headed for her room. Political dancing was never her favorite, but she was stuck with it.

Back in her suite, she sat down on the couch. It was nice to be home in the quiet parlor, with the crackling fire and Brand wagging his tail at her feet. Underfoot, the Palace's stone floor softened and raised, supporting her feet as if to welcome her back. She wriggled her toes and gave a mental hello to the Palace.

The sun shone bright outside, though it began to dip toward the horizon. The days were still short, though they were on their way to spring. Winter in Caer Eisteddfod, unlike in Bakersfield, California, was still in full force in February, and would be well into March—there was a reason it was April showers and May flowers.

Deor leaned her head against the couch back and closed her eyes. Her legs ached, as did her back, a bit. She knew better than to think it was merely the two days of horse riding. At least, she knew that with persistent exercise, she'd get stronger, and the pain would stop. She let go of any riding puns or jokes, and let her mind wander back to the previous night, and to the way Rafe touched her—

"Nope!" Deor stood. It did her no good to fantasize about that right now. If he were interested in more than a one night stand, he'd let her know. She rested her hands on her hips and drummed her fingers. She needed to do something between now and dinner to keep her mind occupied, and further study of *The Noble Babee's Noble Book* sounded awful.

Sitting on the coffee table was her mirror. She snatched it up and settled herself in one of the wingback chairs in front of the fire.

"Bill?" she asked, swiping her fingers across it. "Grandma? Are you there?"

The mirror faded to black and flashed Bill's face. He was smiling at her.

"Deor!" He waved. "Good to hear from you! We were starting to get worried!"

She hadn't spoken with them since before the trip to Roger's. She'd been so overwhelmed at the time that she thought it better to wait. Now, with Bill staring at her, and her grandmother waving behind him, she knew she should have worked up what to say before calling.

"What's up with you?" she asked, stalling for time.

"It's morning," her grandmother said. "We've just finished breakfast, actually. Later Bill is going to teach—," she glanced at him. "What is it again?"

"I'm adjuncting for the Philosophy department at Cal State. I'm teaching a course on death and dying."

Of course, he is. Deor smiled. "Sounds fun. Do you like your students?"

"Very much," he nodded. His eyes were brighter, maybe, than when she left, but not much—and might only be a trick of the light, or, even more likely, forced enthusiasm. Her mother had done that too— "getting herself up for Deor," her grandmother called it. Hiding the sick. Bill was still pale, though, with dark, haunted circles under his eyes, and a washed-out, almost lost expression when he dropped the façade. "What about you? How is the new semester?"

"Well," she said, deciding just how much to lie, "I took this semester off." *True.* "It was a lot of work, and I want some time to explore who I am." *Also true! Go me!*

"And your father?" Her grandmother's voice was cold, her eyes narrow and judgy as they peered at her over her reading glasses.

"He's okay." *Kind of true.*

"He's not trying to hurt you or anything, is he?" Her grandmother leaned closer to the mirror and peered at her. "He's not using any magic on you?"

"He's not trying to hurt me!" Deor scoffed, waving her free hand. "He's fine." *Mostly true—not quite lying yet.*

"Will you be home anytime soon?" Bill asked, voice strained with hope.

"Sure." *Okay, that's a bald-faced lie.* "I'll try."

Bill nodded. "Meet anyone interesting? What about that guy you told us about before? The policeman?"

"Rafe." Deor smiled. "We've gotten to be good friends." Her gaze slipped from Bill and her grandmother, over the rim of the mirror, to the door to his room.

"I see." Her grandmother's voice was sharp, and when Deor looked back, she saw her grandmother's eyebrows raised.

"Grandma," she started.

"I'll bet he's handsome too. Right?" She scolded. "Don't you go making the same mistakes your mother did. Don't you fall for some faerie man who will break your heart. He doesn't have a wife, does he?"

"No!" Deor frowned, her own sharp anger at the suggestion startling her. "He's not seeing anyone right now." The mirror jolted in her hands as Brand hopped up into her lap, ducking under it to snuggle against her. She lifted the puppy up with a bright smile. "This is Brand. He was a Christmas gift."

"From your father?" Bill eyed the dog skeptically. "It's not some kind of death herald, is it?"

"No. It was from Rafe, and they're companion dogs. Sometimes used for hunting, but mostly for protection and companionship." She scratched him behind the ears for a moment.

"Mmmhmmm." Her grandmother eyed her. "Well, he's adorable," she relented. "I've got to get ready for my bridge group," she said. "I love you!"

"I love you too!" Deor waved at her as she moved out of frame.

"So," Bill said after watching her grandmother leave the room. "Have you had sex with this Rafe yet?"

"Bill!" Deor snapped.

"Oh, my." He grinned at her. "So, it was recently?"

The door to their shared parlor opened, and Rafe came in. He saw her holding the mirror and waved but didn't say anything at all.

Deor bit her lip. "I can't really say, Bill."

"He's there, isn't he?" Bill grinned at her, shifting to a laugh as he watched her fumble for something to say. "Well, I'll let you go then. Have fun." His smile faded a bit. "Love you; miss you."

"Love you; miss you, too, Bill." Her heart ached. She wanted to tell him she'd be home soon, to visit, or even to stay, but those were lies. She had no idea when she could leave. The MacIntyres's land still tugged at her, even so far away, and the rest of the kingdom did too. The thought of leaving sent rumbles through her, like the land itself were quaking. "We'll talk again soon. Mirror anytime."

"Okay." He nodded, but she saw the skepticism. "Bye!" The mirror went black.

Deor set the mirror on the coffee table and flopped back.

"Everything okay?" Rafe asked, concerned.

"Yeah." She forced a smile. "They just miss me. And worry about me. And I miss them."

He nodded. "Well, we can find a way for you to visit soon...maybe. Or maybe they can come here?"

"I'm not bringing them within a thousand miles of Finn, Rafe."

"Right." He came over and took her hand. "I'm sorry—I know it is hard being away from them. I wish I could help."

Deor shooed Brand off her lap and stood. She leaned up and kissed him, and not a peck on the cheek either. Her grandmother's warning still rang in her ears, but she ignored it and wrapped her arms around his neck when he let go of her hand and took her in his arms. She broke the kiss. "Any plans for between now and supper?" She grinned at him.

"Not until just now," he smiled. "My room or yours?"

Chapter Six

A few days later as he eased back into his routine, Rafe settled once more into his office in the Tower. He rapped his knuckles on the giant oak desk. Stephen Bolton, standing stiffly at parade rest before his desk straightened a little more, and Arthur settled into the couch by the wall, one foot draped on the couch, the other on the floor. The dogs by the fire didn't so much as lift their heads.

"Alright, gentlemen," Rafe said. "Let's get the new year underway. Stephen, have a seat." Stephen sat, his hands on his knees.

"Stephen, you first," Rafe said. "How are the Houseboys looking these days? Have you weeded out the last of the Michael's supporters?"

"I think so, sir," Stephen said. "Though, I'll be honest, there are a few I don't entirely trust yet even so. But I suspect their problem lies more with me than with their loyalty to the king."

"How so?" Arthur said.

Stephen turned in his chair so he could address Arthur without fully turning his back on Rafe. His Cornwall accent broadened as he spoke. "I'm an upstart, sir. Not one of them. Promoting someone from the peerage would have pleased them better."

"Monjoie, for example?" Rafe said.

"Exactly."

"He has been with the Household Guard longer than almost anyone else," Arthur said. "They may feel you passed over a good man for the newcomer. That's bound to create some resentment."

Leaning back in his chair, Rafe drummed his fingers on the desk. "I knew they might feel that way. If they're all so scalded at being passed over, they should be asking themselves why they didn't realize there was a traitor in their midst. Still, I have an idea for the situation. I'm going to give Monjoie greater control over the daily ins and outs of the Houseboys at the Tower because I want you at the Palace more, Stephen."

Before he could continue, Arthur coughed from the couch. "I think you might have asked me about that before you made a decision, Rafe. I am acting Shield."

Rafe smiled and waved his hand, bowing as elaborately as the desk would allow him to. "Alright, Acting Shield Arthur, do you object to me making Stephen the princess's personal guard?"

"I don't object, per se," Arthur said. "I do have a few questions." He rose from the couch and walked toward the desk to stand over Stephen, his hands behind his back as if about to deliver an examination.

Rafe blinked in surprise. "Very well," he said. He frowned at Arthur's unexpected display of authority, but Arthur ignored him, his eyes intent on Stephen.

"How exactly would you describe your relationship with the princess?" Arthur said.

"Pleasant enough, sir. She's taken notice of me a time or two, but she notices everyone. She's very kind to underlings."

"And why do you want this position?" Arthur continued.

Stephen didn't look away from Arthur's gaze, but he did pause before answering. "I never asked for it, and I wasn't expecting the Sword to offer me the job, but I won't deny I'm eager for it. Being in the Household Guard has been a life ambition of mine. I'm not going to pretend I'm too modest to take it. Right now, I'm the best you've got, by a long shot. I'm fitter, fresher, and more alert than anyone else in the Houseboys. She's the heir to the entire kingdom. That means there's no one in the world more important than she is. You'd be a fool to let one of them guard her instead of me."

"What about Monjoie?" Arthur said, a smile curving across his face. It was the smile that always reminded Rafe of a cat that has spotted a mouse.

Stephen didn't flinch. "I'm better. And I don't like the way he looks at her dog."

Arthur drew back a bit at that. Rafe leaned forward. "Stand down, Arthur. He's not a prisoner for you to interrogate."

For a moment, the two men locked eyes. Slowly, Arthur nodded and took a step back. Instead of returning to his chaise lounge, he pulled up a chair and sat facing Rafe.

Rafe continued, "Stephen, you're hired. From now on, you're with her every waking moment even if she's inside the Palace walls. Don't restrict her movements, but don't let her out of your sight unless she's safe inside the Household itself. If she objects, let me, or Arthur, sort it out." Arthur shifted in his chair.

A delighted grin spread across Stephen's face, and his chest swelled. "Thank you, sir. Both of you. I won't fail you. Or her."

"I don't expect you to. Go on and start your duties now. Arthur and I have other matters to discuss."

Rising from his chair, Stephen offered Rafe a bow that managed to take in Arthur as well and marched out of the room. As soon as he was gone, Arthur glared at Rafe. "He doesn't know the first thing about court behavior. The last thing the princess needs is someone to egg her on. She's far too proud of her commoner roots as it is."

"Deor has nothing to be ashamed of," Rafe snapped. "And neither does Stephen."

"He's a shepherd."

"*Was* a shepherd. Who earned every promotion he's ever gotten," Rafe countered. "And she likes him. More importantly, she trusts him, which means in a crisis she's more likely to listen to orders if they're coming from his mouth. And since when do you gainsay me in front of subordinates?"

Arthur shifted in his seat, turning his face away from Rafe. "That's a grey area. The Houseboys answer to the Shield, not the Sword."

Running his hands through his hair, Rafe sighed in frustration. "It's a damned mess, is what it is. Finn has got to appoint a real Shield and soon. It's not safe for him or the kingdom not to have someone invested with the full power of the office." He cocked his head at Arthur. "Do you want the position? For real, not just as the extra duty you're pulling now? It would mean coming out of the shadows, making yourself prominent. Damned hard to be a spy if everyone knows your face. And I'm sure Parliament is ready and waiting with a list of politically expedient candidates, but if you want the job, I'll stand for you."

Arthur gave him a broad smile, the old boyish smile of their squire training days. But he said, "Don't trouble yourself about it. I'm sure the king will appoint someone in due time. I can manage until then."

"I've no doubt of that, my old friend," Rafe said, returning the smile.

"You could manage anything if you put your mind to it. Speaking of anything, have you heard any whispers about my brother? He's not answering my mirror calls."

Shaking his head, Arthur said, "Odd. I thought the two of you came to an understanding."

"So did I. That's why I'm worried. With Finn looking at him suspiciously and our mother none too pleased with him either, I'm more than a little afraid for his safety."

Arthur laughed. "You're far too trusting, Rafe. Depend on it, he's gone running back to Mother Darling for his allowance and a pat on the head. If they ever were at odds to begin with, which I doubt. It was likely a ruse to get closer to the princess."

"Still," Rafe said, rising to pace back and forth between desk and fireplace. "I'm worried. Find him for me, will you?"

"Of course. I'll let you know the minute I hear anything."

Rafe turned to face Arthur. "Thank you. You're a good friend." Arthur returned his smile.

"Now that we've got domestic matters settled," Arthur said. "What about the Summer Court?'

Emitting an exaggerated groan, Rafe flung up his hands. "What can we do? His majesty has hamstrung us at every turn.'

Rafe gathered magic into his fingers and wove a glamor in the air between himself and Arthur, a detailed map of the Winter Court and their adjoining countries. He pointed toward the northeastern borders. "Finn forced us to reduce the garrisons to a sliver all along the eastern border. And we must consider the Goblins as potential hostiles from now on."

Arthur chuckled. "Certainly, we do after what the princess said to Geoff on the dance floor." The two men shared a companionable laugh over the memory of Geoff's face as Deor told him exactly what she thought of his precious "purity" ring.

As they stood contemplating the magical map, Arthur reached out a finger, adding details to it. "The Summer Court garrisons here and here are larger than we originally thought," he said, indicating points along the Winter Court's southeastern border. "At least ten thousand strong all together."

"Great Creator," Rafe swore. "That's right on the edge of Wellhall."

"True, but the Summer Court Sword D'nath has to know he'll never get them by your parents. With your mother's magic and your father's tactical genius, they could hold Wellhall against twice as many for a hundred years."

"Unless someone let them in," Rafe said.

Arthur looked at him skeptically. "Surely you don't think your mother is that much of a traitor. She wants to rule the Winter Court, not hand it over to a foreign power."

Nodding, Rafe agreed. "You're right. She's a mad bitch, but not a stupid one." He crossed his arms and propped his chin on his hand. At the fireplace Jake shook himself, yawned, and padded over to sit next to Rafe in front of the map. Rafe patted him absentmindedly on the head. "What about the vampires?"

"Not enough money in the treasury to afford them."

"Still, a hint to Donovan that we'd appreciate their help might not be a waste. He and his father might be more open to it now that things have soured between him and Geoff."

The two men nodded together.

"The dwarves are no good," Arthur said. "They haven't the faintest interest in coming above ground these days, and even if they did, they wouldn't lift a finger to help either us or the Summer Court."

"Who could blame them?" Rafe grunted. He poked a finger at Scotland. "What about reinforcing Northfalls? If the goblins let the Summer Court through, that would be their best point of attack. We could tell Finn there's suspicious 'human activity' across the border."

"It might work. The humans are doing Creator only knows what to the sea floor on their side of the veil up there. Roger has said that it's disturbing the sea life."

Rafe sighed and rubbed a hand over his face. "Good enough. Finn won't question it if Roger agrees. I know you just came from there, but I'd like you to go up there and oversee the defenses in person."

Arthur shook his head. "That would make Finn take too much notice. Better to keep me here."

"I suppose you're right." He scratched behind Jake's ears, contemplating the map. Somehow, by hook or by crook, he must expand the army and strengthen the garrisons. Waiting until the Summer Court invaded would be too late, even if they declared a general impress and snatched up every able-bodied faerie who could hold a weapon or toss a spell. War was coming, no matter what Finn or the diplomats said.

Beside him, Arthur shifted his feet.

"Yes?" Rafe said.

"There is one more domestic matter to mention. Now that Robbie's returned to the Caer, I doubt she'll wait long to start agitating with her university friends again. What are we going to do about them?"

"I suppose 'nothing' would be the wrong answer," Rafe said.

Arthur widened his eyes and tilted his head as if to say, "Oh you think so?"

Rafe sighed. "Alright, I'll talk to Robbie about keeping things quiet for a while. She needs her rest still. But let Lord Overton handle the Sons of London. They'll listen to him because he listens to them." He patted Arthur on the shoulder and dismissed the map with a wave of his hand.

Chapter Seven

The following days went peacefully enough and waking up with Deor curled into the crook of his arm and Jake's massive head draped across his feet was enough to make him forgo his normal morning run. But if he did that Arthur would ask questions. So, Rafe planted a gentle kiss on Deor's still sleeping face and slipped out of the bed with his dogs to run the long route along the top of the Palace's outer wall. He'd been pleased to see that Stephen was already on duty outside the heir's apartments as he left.

Once settled into his pace, he'd stretched his legs and breathed deep. The crystalline February air awoke all his senses and brightened his eyes.

"Want to fly the last two laps?" he'd shouted to Arthur, and before his friend could answer, he spread his wings and leaped into the air. Whooping, Arthur followed suit, and they raced, dodging and looping around one another until they alit, neck and neck, just inside the great gate, laughing at one another.

"You're getting slower," Arthur said. "You're out of practice."

"I am," Rafe agreed. "We ought to fly more often." He clapped Arthur on the shoulder. "Let's get more flying on the Houseboys' training roster too. What do you say?"

Before Arthur could answer, both men's pocket mirrors buzzed. As Rafe opened his, Jameson, his valet's face, appeared. "Forgive me for bothering you, sir," Jameson said. "A message from the King has arrived at your quarters. His majesty intends to address Parliament today and wishes for his entire household to be in attendance."

Eyes widening, Rafe glanced over at Arthur who was evidently receiving the same message from his valet.

"What the hell for?" Rafe said. "And why the short notice?"

"I have no information in that regard, sir," Jameson said, his cultured tones indicating exactly what he thought of people who sent urgent and imperious summons without a moment's notice. "I have laid out your dress uniform and jewels."

"Thank you, Jameson. I'll be up shortly," Rafe said before the significance of that statement sank in. Jameson was in his quarters already. Deor was asleep when Rafe left. She might still have been there when Jameson arrived. There was no earthly way to find out without being even more indiscreet.

Rafe shoved his mirror into his pocket. "See you back here," he shouted to Arthur as he spread his wings and leaped straight for the sky. No point in running back into the house and taking portals when he could fly straight to his own balcony.

Behind him Arthur shouted, "What are you in such a hurry for? We're not due to leave for another two hours." Rafe ignored him.

A few minutes later, Rafe alit, panting, on the balcony outside the parlor he shared with Deor. The sweat prickling his scalp was as much anxiety as exertion. As he came through the glass doors, Deor, barefoot and wrapped in a fluffy bathrobe, waved to him cheerfully from the parlor couch. Jameson was just serving her a steaming cup of tea, and Stephen, still very much at attention, sat in a parlor chair opposite her, a cup of tea already in his hands and a china plate with a scone on it balanced on his knee.

"Come and have breakfast," Deor said. "Melanie and Jameson are all in a dither about getting us presentable for the king, but I refuse to do anything until I've had my tea and a muffin."

"I trust your morning run was invigorating, sir?" Jameson said. "Would you care for some tea?"

Rafe gaped at the trio. He had the uncomfortable feeling of having stumbled into some sort of farcical play—at any moment his mother would pop out from behind a curtain and deliver a witty pun.

"Tea, sir?" Jameson prompted.

"Um, no. No, thank you. I should bathe first. I'm not fit for company."

"Good idea," Deor said. "We don't want you to be stinky for the king." She sipped her tea, her eyes twinkling at him over the rim. Whatever happened between his leaving and returning, she was enjoying his discomfiture enormously. Jameson's face was as impassive as ever. Stephen's attention was on Brand, who he slipped a piece of scone.

"Right," Rafe said. "I'll just go shower." He walked off, wondering when his parlor became the social hub of the Palace.

Less than two hours later, washed, dressed, and suitably bejeweled for the occasion, Rafe stood with Deor and the rest of Finn's retinue at the great gate, preparing to portal through to Parliament. The dogs were in the kennels for the morning.

Rubies glowed red in Deor's hair and in her ears, her grandmother's jewels. She nudged Rafe with her elbow. "What is all this about?" she whispered.

He shrugged. "Your guess is as good as mine. Whatever it is, I'm sure it will stir up the Winter Court like an anthill poked with a stick."

Ahead of them in the entourage, Astarte glanced over her shoulder at them and shook her head slightly. She didn't know either.

As the portal opened trumpeters blew the opening notes, signaling that the king was arriving. Through the portal, Rafe could faintly hear the Speaker of the House gaveling the House of Lords to attention and the bailiff calling for the assembly to be upstanding for his majesty Sweordmund VIII.

"Wings out," Astarte said.

"Ugh. Do I have to?" Deor whispered. She gave a little shrug, and her wings unfurled behind her, a glorious profusion of deep, velvety red that put her rubies to shame. Rafe smothered the urge to sweep her up in his arms and fly off to someplace private. Instead, he fixed his eyes forward, shoulders back in parade formation, and put out his own wings as all around him the rest of the king's retinue followed suit.

"When we get into the chamber, just follow Astarte to the king's box," Rafe said to Deor. "And if anything strange happens, stay with Stephen. You'll be fine." She nodded, stepping forward as Finn and Astarte began to move.

Once they arrived in Parliament, Rafe and Arthur separated from the king's party to take their seats as Sword and acting Shield near the Speaker's podium facing the three-sided rows of benches that held the assembled Lords. Deor and Astarte were ushered to the King's box, while Finn was escorted in person by the Speaker to the royal seat before the Speaker's podium.

Rafe scanned the room as he sat. Parliament was packed—not an empty seat, a much more common occurrence since the princess arrived—and they were filled with the holders of the seats themselves, not their heirs or proxies. There were seven duchies. In the west were Northfalls and the Royal Duchy which surrounded and included the capital city—technically the source of the heir's "Duchess" title. Then Ireland, where the were-wolves lived, and finally Wales in the south. The eastern part of the Winter Court was made up of Wellhall in the north, and then Normandy across the center and Aquitaine in the south.

His mother sat in the Wellhall seat, one that should, someday, be his, but Victor was nowhere to be seen. Wellhall, Normandy, and Aquitaine often supported one another in politics and law, especially if one of the bordering nations got feisty. Overall, the area was well governed, and the Farringdons, especially, were loved by the people who lived there. Today, though, they took matters a step farther. Every seat displayed its own banner, and the three duchies had combined theirs into one. Not quite a direct affront to the king, but definitely a statement.

No question, today was going to be fun.

As the Speaker of the House took her seat, the Chamber Guard called out the ritual opening of a Parliamentary session. The second the Speaker's gavel struck, multiple people leaped to their feet, demanding the floor. Rafe counted Ama Nefasta, Rodney, and, oh balls, his mother Madeline, all of them clamoring to be heard first.

"Quiet!" The Speaker banged her gavel on the podium, her face pinched with irritation already. "This is not a riot. We will recognize the member of the Bardic Council first. Everyone else sit down."

Ama walked forward to speak, carrying a curved silver sickle tied with a sprig of mistletoe. Technically it was a tool, not a weapon, so it passed the strict rule against bringing an instrument of destruction onto the Parliament floor, but even so, Rafe wondered how many throats it could slit, if the holder were so inclined. Even from where he sat, he could see that the sickle's blade gleamed sharp.

Ama inclined her head to the Speaker and to the rest of the chamber, then drew a scroll out of her robe. "I have come to speak on behalf of all the werefolk of the Winter Court. The Bardic Council unanimously condemns the banishment of the werefolk and urges this Parliament to do the same. Sweordmund must behave as a gracious and just ruler to *all* his subjects, not only the faeries. Until such time as the werefolk are made safe in the Winter Court, the Bardic Council will continue to offer them safe passage through the portals of Eisteddfod University and give sanctuary to any who ask for it." She paused to look around the chamber, glaring at each of the assembled nobles in turn. "Speaking for myself, it is a disgrace that all of you have failed to make this motion on your own. You should be ashamed of yourselves, pretending to speak for the people of the Winter Court when not a one of you has made a peep on behalf of the werefolk. My own partner, Reynard, has not been able to set foot off campus grounds since this ridiculous ban started. How long will you let your king's petty grudges run this country into ruin?"

The gallery went wild. The commoners stamped, whistled, and shouted in support as some nobles shuffled their feet and looked ashamed. An equal number of commoners and nobles booed and sneered, rolling their eyes.

Clarissa, of all people, rose to her feet to applaud. "Hear, hear!" she shouted, her normally soft voice almost drowned by the ruckus in the galleries above her. Rafe recalled that a substantial number of werefolk lived in her portion of the Winter Court. In fact, now that he thought of it, one of her chief vintners was a were. Clarissa continued to stand, clapping even as the Speaker gaveled for silence. Slowly, other nobles rose to stand with her.

"Enough," the Speaker said. "The Bardic Council's position is duly noted and entered into the record. Next item of business."

"Vote! Vote! Vote!" commoners in the gallery chanted. Some members of Parliament shouted the same. Genevieve and Delaney were not adding to the shouting, but they both continued to clap from their seats.

The Speaker hammered the podium again. "I said, enough! If a Member of Parliament wishes to bring a motion regarding the werefolk, they are welcome to do so. Moving on ..." She consulted her notes. "The House recognizes Duchess Madeline Farringdon."

Madeline rose from her seat, her husband Edgar behind her. "My son is missing," Madeline said. "And I have reason to believe that those two," she pointed at Rafe and Arthur, "know where he is. What have you done with your brother, Rafe?" More murmuring and shuffling broke out, both in the galleries and among the parliamentarians.

The Speaker was shouting again, trying to reach over the sounds of people shouting in agreement with Madeline. A familiar red-haired woman, a green feathered arrow worn prominently through her piled up hair, clapped and shouted from the gallery along with her brother and their supporters. Rafe shot a glance to his left before he rose to answer Madeline, but Arthur's impassive face told him nothing.

"I'm sorry, Duchess Farringdon," Rafe said. "I have no information on the location of your son. He was hale and healthy the last time I spoke to him, which was in Northfalls. If he were in my custody, his arrest would be a matter of public record."

Shouts of "Liar!" broke out from the gallery.

"I don't believe you," Madeline said. "Show us the proof that you do not have him."

Rafe spread his hands and laughed. "I can't prove an absence. What do you want from me? A personal tour of every room in the Tower?" That got a laugh from some at least, though not many. A few people shouted back "Yes!"

Rising in irritation, the Speaker's voice said, "Does anyone have a *proper* motion to put before this body? There are procedural rules you know."

Rafe sat back down. As he did, Arthur passed him a mirror set to show the outside of the Parliament. Rafe's eyes widened in surprise. Despite the February chill, crowds of people were gathered outside as if for a holiday. Word of Finn's planned announcement must have gotten out. Rafe spotted a Sons of London banner toward the back of the crowd, but for the most part the assembled people seemed to be in a jolly, anticipatory mood. He slipped the mirror back to Arthur.

Before the Speaker's podium, Finn rose, his hands clasped before him and waited for the noise to die down.

"The King wishes to speak! Let there be silence before the King!" the Sergeant at Arms shouted.

"You grace us with your presence, sire." The speaker bowed her head. "The floor is yours."

Graciously, Finn nodded his head to the Speaker, then perused the room, his smile taking in all sides, including the gallery. "My people," he said. "A new year has begun and a new era. With the arrival of my long absent daughter," here he indicated Deor, who gave him a too bright smile back. "We ought to rejoice. As a nation we have a renewed hope, a renewed vigor."

This earned some sporadic claps and cheers along with some foot shuffling and confused murmuring. Deor's arrival was hardly news at this point. From across the room, Genevieve, seated with the Overton family, caught Rafe's eye and raised her eyebrows.

Finn went on. "As spring approaches, bringing with it a time of burgeoning life and joy, we ought to proclaim our nation's greatness, our unity as a people, with a great celebration." Slightly more enthusiastic cheers. "Therefore, it is our deep pleasure to announce that, one month from today, we will hold a Tournament Royale!"

One month! Rafe gripped the arms of his chair in shock as thunderous applause broke out. Everyone was on their feet, shouting, cheering. Winter Court flags appeared among the gallery spectators and were waved. Collecting himself, Rafe rose to his feet and clapped along with everyone else, not wanting to seem tardy with his enthusiasm. Only Ama Nefasta sat, her face sour enough to curdle new milk and her sickle clutched tightly in her hand.

Even as he clapped, Rafe's mind was racing as he struggled to encompass the scope of what a Tournament Royale would mean for security and safety as hundreds of armed participants swarmed into Caer Eisteddfod. He'd need to double the Civil Patrol, re-assign some units of the military to street duty. Registration of arms. He'd need to start recruiting immediately.

The word "recruiting" repeated itself in his brain and a wicked grin spread across his face. Yes, indeed. A Tournament Royale would be the perfect opportunity to recruit for the army. This stunt of Finn's was going to be a logistical nightmare for every member of the Palace and Tower staff, but some good might come of it after all. If he could use it to swell the ranks of the army and navy, they might have a better chance against the Summer Court. His grin widened, and his clapping increased.

Before the cheering crowd of nobles, Finn stood with his arms outspread, bathing in the adulation.

Chapter Eight

When they arrived back at the palace, Deor headed back to her rooms—everyone else was going to a special meeting about the tournament. There were all sorts of planning decisions to be made. Folks would start pouring in from all over the Winter Court. Apparently, Deor's job in all this required no meetings. She would sit in the King's box and watch. She would smile at the winners and the losers, cheer in a respectful manner, and wave to the crowd. She figured she could manage.

The uneasy atmosphere at Parliament rattled her a bit. A lot of people were upset about the were-creature ban, a completely rational response in Deor's opinion. When Finn announced the tournament, though, the weight on the crowd seemed to lift. Everyone, even the most dour Madeline, seemed to brighten a bit. Maybe Finn was right, and maybe this would work. A show of all the good bits of the Winter Court. Plus, there would be jousts and swordfights. Folks in armor.

If she was being honest with herself, Deor was so excited she could hardly stand it.

The excitement, though, didn't quell her own flush of shame at her behavior at Roger's. Yes, she'd apologized successfully for being an ass at his ball, but most of the people barely remembered their encounter with Madeline, let alone realized they had been enspelled. No one, she was sure, forgot the embarrassing tongue lashing she got from Genevieve, nor her eloquent and razor-sharp breaking of her and Rafe's engagement.

Sitting pretty in a box at the tournament wouldn't fix that.

The solution, though, was obvious and easy. Learn about the Winter Court. Learn the things that she didn't know, that she should, and learn about her history. It struck her how much she knew about the United States wasn't learned in school, not really, but by osmosis. Just existing in the space, reading articles and op-eds, talking politics with folks.

She didn't have time for osmosis.

She'd head for the library.

The moment she thought of it, knowledge of the library's location flashed in her mind. The palace unfolded like a vision, and she could see the library aglow, marked like a spot of interest on a video game map. Third floor. East wing. Off she went.

She stepped into the hall, Brand at her heels, and ran into Stephen, who seemed to be hanging around outside her rooms. He stood at parade rest and smiled when he saw her.

"Hey," Deor said. "Are you looking for me?"

"Yes, actually." Stephen gave a small bow as he relaxed. "I wanted to talk to you about my new assignment."

"Okay," Deor said. "I'm heading for the library—mind if we walk and talk?"

"Of course not, Princess." He gestured for her to walk, and she did. He fell in step with her. "We haven't yet talked about my new position as your bodyguard. Even in the palace, where you go, I go, unless you're in your own rooms," he said.

Deor stopped and faced him. "Does this mean you're spying on me?"

"Absolutely not." He went on before she could cut in. "We think we've gotten the traitors out of the Houseboys, but we're still taking precautions. My job is to protect you, not to report your behavior." he said, his eyes twinkling. "Unless you're being assassinated, I have no opinions about how you spend your time or who you spend it with."

Deor stared at him a long while. She liked Stephen—she had from the moment she met him at Immigration. He'd been with Rafe and his men when they showed up in Eisteddfod to rescue her from goblins once she'd been outed as the princess. "Okay," Deor said cautiously. "But I want to know more about you." She started walking again. "You're from Cornwall, right? Sheep family?"

He laughed. "You remember. I'm flattered. Yes. I grew up in the gentry, the third son of a sheep farmer. I bolted as soon as I could—joined the military on my thirtieth birthday."

"Hated home that much?" Deor asked.

"Yep." He smiled, and his voice was cheerful—mostly. There was underneath a current of something: anger, disappointment. Whatever it was, home was not a happy memory.

She changed the subject. "Excited about the tournament?"

"Completely!" He beamed at her. She thought he was downright perky before, but he lit up like a Christmas tree. "I'm not a nobleman, so I wouldn't be able to compete, but I'm a Houseboy, and that confers a kind of automatic knightly status. I can participate in the melee."

"The melee." Deor gaped.

Stories of melees were rampant in medieval European literature. Massive fights of sometimes hundreds of knights, and the last man standing won. Sometimes they were divided into teams, but often the fight fit its name perfectly. A bunch of mad people swinging swords and shields and whatever they could get their hands on, making brief alliances only to shatter them in hopes of an advantage. They were not to-the-death fights, though. Often the weapons were blunted, sometimes people even used pillows stuffed with sand or grain.

"Yes!" His grin didn't waver. "I'll be allowed to participate in the first match on the day before the tournament officially begins. Something like 500 people being cut down to 50. Then the final round will be the first event on the last day."

"So, 50 people will fight for one prize on the last day?" Deor could hardly imagine it.

"No," Stephen shook his head. "There are 50 spots reserved for anyone who is noble who is high enough ranked as a fighter and can buy their way in. There will be 100 fighters in the final."

"And you're not going to buy your way in?" Deor asked. That seemed easier, albeit a bit like cheating.

He laughed. "No, I haven't got that kind of money." He shrugged and leaned in. "I know the tournament is supposed to be this grand, nation-uniting affair, but it is only nobility and soldiers who have earned knighthood via service that can participate. And the soldier-knights only can do the melee."

"That sucks," Deor said, unsurprised. "Can commoners watch?"

"Oh sure. There'll be a lot of places to watch, especially because a lot of the events and early rounds will happen around the city—not on the palace grounds. The three main events will be at the palace with the finals of each on the last day. First, the melee, then the dagger-and-hand, and then the broadsword."

"Got it." She resumed her amble toward the library.

"I hope I make it—I can't wait to show some of those soft, poncy, noble lads what it means to brawl. Not some tourney fight—no—a real melee brawl." The grin in his voice was clear. "But," his cheer dropped, "I don't have any of the fancy armor those nobles have."

"You've got weapons, right?" Deor asked as they reached the staircase. "You're not going in unarmed?"

"Everyone is," he said, "if you mean weapons. This is a magic fight. Whatever magic you have, you can use. So, folks like you—thankfully not many—can make their own weapons. I'm an air faerie."

"So why do you need fancy armor? Protection?"

"Nah. Armor—more like a uniform—can be designed to enhance and focus magic."

"You don't have any? Is it expensive?"

"Very. Usually custom made." He gave a dismissive shrug. "But I'll be fine. You don't see it so much in the qualifier—most of the folks will be gentry, like me." He grinned at her.

They paused in front of a huge set of double doors. "Here we are." He gestured at them. "The library." He bowed.

The doors were carved to look like massive bookshelves lined with tomes. Each handle was a brass book with the eight-pointed Aethelwing house star on it. She grabbed them and pulled. The doors swung easily, and she stepped inside.

Deor's jaw dropped. Next to her, Stephen whistled. Brand darted inside and began to sniff around. The room was two stories high. On either side of the room, spiral staircases spun upward. Bookshelves lined three of the four walls, floor to ceiling, with tall ladders on rails waiting to be slid to the correct spot and climbed. One wall was covered by floor-to-ceiling windows. Winter light filtered in through a cloudy grey sky, reflecting off the snow.

At the far end of the room in a massive stone fireplace, a low fire burned. The main floor had shelves, too, though fewer and no more than seven or so feet tall. Under the windows, two long tables. Each table had five comfortable-looking stuffed chairs on each side, and lamps as well. Above the fireplace on the second floor was an alcove in which five pedestals stood.

"I could spend decades in here," Deor said quietly. There was no one else in the room but them, and still, it felt wrong to speak in a normal voice.

"You've got the time," Stephen responded, equally quiet. "Do you want me to wait outside?"

"No," Deor shook her head. She gestured around the room. "Find something entertaining to read?"

He laughed. "Maybe, but too much of that isn't doing my job. You go on."

Deor crept forward. In the center of the room was a desk and an apparatus on it that reminded her of the search-engine in the Eisteddfod library. She approached it. A surface and a quill, much like a human tablet, waited. She pulled out her own mirror and stylus and set them next to the slate. She jotted down search terms like *Winter Court Political History* and *Winter Court Families* and *Politics of the Winter Court*. When the list returned was overwhelming, Deor limited it to the reign of her father. That was a bit more manageable.

She spent at least an hour gathering the various books from different sections. Inevitably, at each section, she'd find the one book she wanted easily but then spend a ton of time looking at other books on the shelves.

Finally, with a stack of about twenty books in front of her on a table, Deor sighed. There was enough here to keep her busy for a long while. Not that she'd read all cover-to-cover. Nonetheless, it was a good starting place —an introductory class on the current Winter Court.

"Stephen?" she asked, and he was at her side in an instant. "Would you mind helping me carry these back to my room."

He looked at them. "Not at all, but why don't you just stamp them?" He pointed at a stamp on the table. He went and grabbed it and brought it to her. "See?" He spun the wheel, much like a date-marker on human stamps used in libraries in the past century. He stopped on *Heir's Quarters*. "Just stamp them, and they'll show up in your room."

She took the stamp from him. "I love faerie technology." She stamped the first one, and it popped out of sight with a blur of magic. Nineteen pops later, she was ready to leave.

Back in her quarters, she settled in on the couch with a general introduction, her mirror, and her stylus. "Are you going to stay in here with me?" she asked Stephen. "You're more than welcome."

"No," he smiled. "These are your private rooms. I'll be out in the hall. But if you need me, call. I'm magically connected—that is, I'll hear you no matter where I am." He stared at her thoughtfully for a moment. "Two requests: don't lie to me and don't sneak off. I need to know where you are. So long as you're in the palace, especially the private quarters, that's all I need to know. But if I ask you a question for your safety, I need the truth, okay?" He looked at her, his eyes serious and warm.

"Got it," Deor said. "I won't lie; I won't sneak; I won't hide. I promise."

He smiled, relieved. "You're the kind of person who keeps their promises." He bowed to her and left the room.

Deor set down the book and picked up her mirror. She opened a blank page and began to write:

Dear Wham! And Thorsen, I am writing to inquire about the possibility of armor for an air faerie for the melee part of the tournament. Is it possible to have such a thing designed? Are there other items that would be necessary or beneficial to the fighter? I would like to order armor and anything else for the air faerie, Lt. Stephen Bolton, should he make it out of the qualifying round and into the final melee. Please let me know if you can do this as soon as possible. Put it on my account and deliver it to Lt. Bolton when it is time. Much thanks, Deor.

She made a few more taps, and the note disappeared. Within five minutes, a reply came that, of course they could do what she asked and were more than happy to do so. They also informed her that they would be delighted to make his tournament ball suit, and her gown as well. With a quick stroke of her stylus, she agreed and returned to her Winter Court studies.

Chapter Nine

In the Amber Room, Rafe ran both hands through his hair in frustration, trying to calculate the number of soldiers he'd have to withdraw from the border in order to keep Caer Eisteddfod from descending into chaos during the tournament. He and Arthur were dispatching orders as fast as they could write them. Beside them, the Exchequer was clutching his hair and whispering furiously to a number of underlings. Across the room, the Chief Butler was whispering soothing things to the Head Steward who was shrieking. "One month? I have one month?!" Astarte sat impassively at the foot of the table, observing it all while Finn grinned, clearly enjoying the fray.

All around Rafe courtiers and servants buzzed back and forth. The half-eaten remains of a hastily laid out cold luncheon were scattered around the table, pushed aside to make room for tablets, note paper, and mirrors. Aides hovered around the edges of the room, taking mirror calls and repeatedly murmuring variations on, "Of course I will relay your concerns to His Majesty / The Princess Consort / The Sword / The Acting Shield" or, in the case of inquiries from the press, "More details will be forthcoming soon." Servants ran in and out of the room, delivering messages, clearing plates, and taking orders. Every few minutes a mirror call from some remote part of the kingdom would be deemed important enough for an aide to whisper in Finn's ear before Finn took the call in person. On the other side of the mirror, Roger gushed with excitement and approval.

"I don't give a wyvern's left testicle what Roger wants," Rafe shouted after the mirror call was over. "We are not staging a full-scale naval battle on the Thames in the middle of March."

VARIOUS COURT FLUNKIES HOVERED like flies around Finn's chair, buzzing with flattery and suggestions for the tournament.

"This tournament is a brilliant idea, sire, simply brilliant," one of them said, pouring Finn some more wine. "How ever did you think of it?"

"It came to me this morning," Finn said. "I woke up, and there it was, as clear as day. A tournament. There hasn't been a Tournament Royale in the Winter Court since I achieved my majority. It was a glorious event. People talked about it for years. It's high time we held another one."

The flunkies twittered with delight. In the corner, the Steward moaned and wrung her hands.

All at once, Astarte rose, rapping her knuckles on the table. Silence fell. "Your Majesty," she said. "I think we can all agree that at Tournament Royale is an excellent way to bring the nation together." Finn nodded graciously and smiled at her. "Still, I have one pressing question. How exactly are we going to pay for all this?"

Finn blinked at her mildly and sipped from his wine glass. "Taxes," he said.

"Sire, if I may...," the Exchequer began.

"I'm sorry, my dear. I don't quite understand. Do you mean that you intend to levy a new tax to pay for the tournament?" Astarte said. "Or do you anticipate funding the tournament from taxes already collected?"

Finn waved his glass at the Exchequer, a grey-haired man with powdery grey wings to match. "You explain it to her," he said.

Every eye in the room turned to the Exchequer. Astarte gave him an encouraging smile. The Exchequer cleared his throat nervously. "Well, your majesties, that's actually a very good question. We *don't* have a reserve fund of this sort in the annual budget. Indeed, I'm not even sure what portion of the budget the money ought to come from." He clasped his hands together on the table and addressed Astarte directly. "You see, Your Majesty, there are a number of problems involved with even calculating the cost of a Tournament Royale, not to mention the question of funding it. First of all..."

As the Exchequer talked about reserve funds, tax brackets, the fluctuations in agrarian markets, tariffs and trade imbalances, and the difference between the king's personal income and the kingdom's tax base, Rafe's eyes began to glaze over, but he struggled to stay alert and listen carefully. Astarte nodded along and asked the occasional question that sparked even more explanation from the Exchequer. At the head of the table, Finn yawned and sipped his wine.

Rafe leaned over to Arthur and whispered, "It's been quite a while since John Dell tried to teach me to manage my allowance, but am I hearing this right? The treasury is perilously scant of money because the king has been ill for decades?"

"Yes," Arthur said. "That's about the shape of it. Rather puts a crimp in our plans to recruit more soldiers if we can't afford to pay them."

Rafe glared at the tablet in front of him, flicking his stylus back and forth between his fingers. "Perhaps. Or we could take a page from Finn's book and let someone else worry about that." He tapped the tablet's surface, and his message to the commander of the Rouen garrison disappeared on its way.

From the head of the table, Finn stretched and yawned. "That was a delicious lunch," he said. "I think I'll retire to my rooms and take a nap." He stretched once more, kissed Astarte on the forehead and strolled from the room. Everyone else watched him go in silence. As the door closed behind the king, a collective breath went through the room. Then everyone started arguing at once, voices rising over voices as each person scrambled to be heard.

"Enough!" Astarte stood. "The king has decreed that we will have a Tournament Royale, and so that is what we will have. Even if we have to move heaven and earth to do it.

"Exchequer, I want you to meet with Lord Overton to determine what portion of cost can be borne by the city of Caer Eisteddfod. People are going to flood into this city and bring their money with them. Get the Master of the City to set a special tournament tax on every luxury meal and hotel room and national flag sold within the county. Put a tax on new weapons and armor. Or some such thing. Set the tournament entry fees as high as you think can be borne by the participants. Do not levy fees on bread or other necessities. Then come see me and the Head Steward about what the King's household can contribute."

She turned to Rafe and Arthur. "You two draw up the rules and list of events. I want them done by tomorrow morning, along with a list of people who can serve as Masters of the Lists. Consult the histories and the College of Heraldry at the University for precedent. And Rafe? I'm sorry, but I'm going to involve Genevieve. We'll never get through this without her help.

Alright everyone, we have a Tournament to prepare for. Let's not let it catch us napping." She paused a moment on her way out the door and turned back toward Rafe. "Didn't Deor say her education was concerned with knighthood and performances of chivalry?"

"Yes," Rafe said slowly. "She reads a lot of chivalric romances, I believe."

"Good. See if you can't give her something useful to do as well. We'll need every hand we can manage." With that she swept out of the room, dictating a list of tasks to the Steward as she went. Rafe caught the words "...and call the Rangley family immediately. We'll need all the wine they have. Perhaps Clarissa will give us a good price because she's friends with Rafe."

Rafe slumped back in his chair and stared at Arthur for a moment. "Melee?" he said finally.

"Of course, a melee," Arthur said. "Jousts, wrestling, broadsword, and dagger-and-hand, too, I presume."

Head tilted back toward the ceiling, Rafe closed his eyes and tried to picture what it would all look like. Pageantry. Gallantry. Prowess and courtesy. Glittering armor and rich clothes on gorgeous display. A tournament was all about the display. That's what Finn wanted, wasn't it? A giant, national display of prowess, with himself right at the center, presiding over it all. Rafe slid a bit further down in his chair and rubbed his temples.

"Well?" Arthur prompted. "What are you brooding about? This is the sort of thing we used to dream about as squires—a chance to show off our skills before an adoring nation."

"Right," Rafe said, his eyes still closed. Arthur was right. He had always wanted to compete in a tournament, a real tournament like the grand old days of Finn's youth. But something else was niggling at the back of his brain, an idea for making this tournament into more than just an orgy of self-congratulation. "Let's have a division for the squires. Everyone under the age of forty who was in training to be a knight by New Year's Day of this year is eligible. No jousting or jumping contests though. If Gordie gets a lance through the eye, I'll never forgive myself."

"Fair enough." Arthur's stylus scratched at his tablet.

"What if ..." Rafe spoke slowly, the idea forming even as he spoke. "What if we invite the Werefolk to participate?"

"They're banished."

"I know, but what if this were Rufus's chance to redeem himself?" Rafe sat up. He could see it now, as bright as crystal. "Rufus is as keen a swordsman as I've seen. I'll petition Finn to let him enter the broadsword competition to make his obeisance before the throne. Finn will get to be suitably gracious to him, *noblesse oblige,* and Rufus will make a display of accepting the prize from his sovereign."

Arthur frowned. "The broadsword is your event, Rafe. No one is going to beat you at it."

Rafe grinned back at him. "You never know. It might happen." He stood up. "You finish working out the eligibility details for the entrants. I'm going to ask Finn right now, while he's still thrilled with himself over this idea. If I start working on him now and get Astarte to agree, he's bound to say yes in time for Rufus to register."

Shrugging, Arthur said, "You go right ahead and try if you think it's worth it."

"Good man. I'll be back in an hour to help you with security matters."

Rafe left the room with a spring in his step. Perhaps he could wear Deor's favor as he fought in the tournament.

Chapter Ten

Two weeks later, Deor stood in the parlor of her suite, arms crossed, staring at the mirror. On it, a group of people stood outside the gates of the palace. Probably fifty people, if that, stood in front of the main marketplace gates. Clearly it wasn't organized, as they milled about. A few carried signs, and a few more were scuttling about making them.

What was clear: they were angry.

The good will that had blossomed at the announcement of the tournament had collapsed like a deflated balloon. Pure fury rose in its place.

"Volume?" she called to the mirror.

A flurry of voices filled the room. It was hard to make out all of what they were saying, but the gist was clear. They were furious that there would be no competition but the melee for those not already of noble status. Toward the side of the group, an older man lectured a few students. Deor caught snatches of "in my day" and "tournaments used to be a way to become a knight!" The students nodded sagely, though Deor was reasonably certain that they had no intention, regardless of their class, to swing swords at one another.

Deor shook her head and closed the mirror.

Why was Finn so bloody tone deaf? It was all one step forward, two or more steps back. He didn't seem to grasp the concept that his people, *all* of his people, wanted a chance to participate in their world. Maybe this fury would blow over by the time the tournament rolled around, but right now, it felt to Deor a bit more like Marie Antoinette telling them to eat cake than it did a grand Fourth of July celebration.

"Stephen?" she called.

The door to the hallway opened, and Stephen stuck his head inside. "Yes?"

"Come in here," she said, taking a seat in one of the wingback chairs. She tucked her feet up under her. "I've got a couple questions for you."

He came in and sat. "Yes?" He leaned down a scratched Brand's head as the puppy charged over and sniffed him, putting his front paws on Stephen's knee.

"He likes you a lot." Deor smiled. "So," she turned serious, "what do you think of the protestors out there? Do you think they're right?"

Stephen's eyes widened. "I don't talk politics, Princess," he said carefully.

Deor rolled her eyes. "Try."

He sighed and leaned back in his chair. "I could have told you it was coming. People are insulted not to be allowed in. The melee isn't enough. It's generally considered the lowest skilled event." Stephen glanced up at the mirror. "You were watching the gate?"

"Yeah," she said. "Why not just let everyone in?"

"Logistics, mostly," Stephen said. "You can't have all the eligible folks come here. There's not enough room, enough event space. Something that large would take months, maybe years, to organize. Nobles-only solves that."

"Seems to cause worse problems," Deor noted.

Stephen shrugged. "Possibly. The king isn't going to give them a House of Commons," he said flatly. "The people don't see it as taking power from him, though. They see it as ensuring that someone will listen to them." He paused and seemed to consider continuing. "The folks who are supposed to listen aren't doing the best job."

"What do you mean? Like the Overtons?" Deor had met both the younger and older Delaney Overton, and the youngest son, George, and none of them struck her as particularly offensive. True, the youngest seemed like a twit, but no more so than anyone of his age. A bit spoiled, perhaps, but not bad.

"The Master of the City and his sons are a bit of an exception, actually. From what I've seen, anyway. The senior actually meets with common people, and his heir does too. But back in Cornwall, ugh." He shook his head. "I don't ever remember our Countess holding any kind of town hall meeting. I don't think she even lives there. Or is from there. I think a lot of folks feel that way about the king too."

Deor listened, keeping her face schooled in careful neutrality. She'd been reading up on governance, and the nation was divided into Duchies with Counties and other sections in those. Theoretically the noble in charge should take the interests of his or her people to heart, and then come to Parliament to speak for them. That didn't seem to be working. There was little incentive for the count or duke to really listen. Tess MacIntyre and her family were a prime example of what could happen without an effective and caring ruler.

"Is there anything I can do?" Deor asked.

Stephen laughed. "If anyone can, I imagine it's you." He jerked his head in the direction of the stack of books on the table. "That given you any ideas?"

"None so far," she shook her head. "But I'm still trying to get my bearings and figure out how all this works, who the important families are, etc."

"Planning on scoring better on Genevieve's next quiz?" A small smile quirked the edge of his mouth.

"Yep." Deor picked up one of the books. "Thanks. You told me what I wanted to know. I don't know how, or even if I can fix it, but I'll try my best."

Stephen stood. "I don't doubt it." He bowed and left the room.

Deor spent the rest of the day studying in her rooms. Neither Rafe nor anyone else contacted her, busy, she assumed, with the preparations.

THE LIGHT of the afternoon sun had faded enough that Deor suspected she should get ready for dinner. She made a note of where she was in her particular book—a semi-interesting account of political machinations of the Wellhall area for the past hundred years—and stood.

She was halfway through a stretch when the parlor door bounced open. "Your Majesty?" Stephen held it with one hand, mirror in another. He stepped into the room and closed the door behind him. "You've got to—" He stopped and shook his head. "You'll want to see this, I think." He tapped his mirror a few times and flicked his hand toward the massive one over the fireplace. It lit up with a flurry of motion that Deor couldn't quite understand.

"Volume!" Stephen said.

"Monjoie! Over there!" a voice called. Deor thought it might be Arthur. Whoever held the mirror turned, and Deor caught a glimpse of the room. A large meeting hall, maybe, with a Sons of London poster hanging, half ripped, on the far wall. A fallen podium lay in front of scattered chairs as faeries of varied ages scrambled away from their seats, apparently fleeing. Wings and limbs crowded together, making it hard for Deor to discern faces. Many of the running people wore rough, work-a-day clothes, but black scholar's robes mingled with them. Here and there she caught the flash of silk and velvet though Deor couldn't make out if the wearers were noble or simply more richly dressed. Members of the Civil Patrol tackled fleeing faeries, wrestling them to the ground.

"What the hell?" Deor said. More than one of the guardsmen wore the badge of the king, their insignia marking them as members of the House-boys, Finn's elite personal guard.

Monjoie, the highest-ranking member of the Household Guard now that Michael was gone, came into frame dragging a young man in scholar's robes. Deor caught her breath as she recognized his prisoner as Aiden, one of Robbie's friends from her Shakespeare class. The outspoken young man struggled in Monjoie's grip, a trickle of blood from his split lip visible even against his flame red skin. Monjoie thrust the kid into another soldier's waiting arms and spun again. His dark teal skin flushed with excitement. Whatever he was doing, the bastard was enjoying himself.

"Let go of me!" A woman's voice came from off screen.

"I'll handle that one!" Monjoie leered a bit and strode forward.

"I think not!" A sharp voice, Rafe's. The mirror, she realized, was from his point of view. He was there. Monjoie backed away with a frown and turned, heading for another mass of troops manhandling people. Arthur, meanwhile, was striding forward.

"You can't interfere, Rafe," he snapped. "We're arresting everyone here. No exceptions. King's orders."

"Fuck the king," Rafe growled, and both Deor and Stephen gasped.

"Yeah!" A girlish voice added to the fray. "Fuck the king!"

Deor saw Rafe's hand dart out and drag a person into view, so that she was standing in front of him. Robbie, of course. Wearing her, "I don't give a fuck who your daddy is!" T-shirt.

"Don't you ever, ever say that, sister." he snapped. His breath and hers blew white with cold.

"But," she started.

"No." Rafe cut her off. "I'll handle her, Arthur. No one else lays a hand on the Consort's daughter—do you hear me?"

Arthur frowned. "Fine. But she goes in the cart with the rest of them." He cast a glance to the side. "You wouldn't want her little boytoy to be lonely." Before anyone could respond, Arthur headed off screen.

"We're going back to the Tower," he said to Robbie.

"Of course, we are!" she snapped. "I don't need you to tell me that!"

"I know that," Rafe said softly. "Now let's go. Don't make this worse. We should reach the tower in about thirty minutes, maybe less." The mirror went dark.

"Was that last bit for us?" Deor asked.

"Pretty sure," Stephen said. "My mirror lit up all of a sudden. I knew it was Rafe, but he didn't say anything at all directly to me. Only a faint 'if only the princess could see this.' And then he left his mirror on."

"Was that Mayor Overton I saw getting hauled off, too?"

"Seemed to be."

"Okay," Deor said. "Let me get my shoes, and we go to the Tower."

Stephen saluted. "Yes, ma'am."

When Deor and Stephen arrived at the tower, the prisoners stood in huddled groups just inside the wide entrance to the ancient prison. Guards stood on all sides, their weapons drawn.

"You can't do this!" Robbie was standing with a group of students, some of whom Deor recognized. Aiden hovered right behind her, a swelling bruise rising around his right eye. Cuts, scuffs and other signs of rough treatment showed on other prisoners as well. "It was a peaceful gathering. There was nothing illegal about it. I know the law!"

"Easy," Stephen said behind Deor, gently laying a hand on her elbow.

She was about to protest when she noticed the swirling cloud of sparkles growing around her. She blinked a few times, but a persistent silver halo edged her vision, making whatever she focused on sharp and crisp.

"My eyes are silver, right?" she asked.

"Heading that way." Stephen jutted his chin in the direction of the gate. "There are Rafe and Arthur."

Deor nodded and blinked a few more times. She straightened and strode toward the two men. Rafe looked angry, while Arthur merely looked pleased with himself. "What the hell is this?" Deor demanded as she stormed up to Arthur.

"Seditious activity," Arthur said. "We broke up a meeting where they were discussing ways to disrupt the tournament."

Rafe rolled his eyes. "You know as well as I do that Delaney Overton Sr., may well be the least seditious man on the face of the planet!"

"Then what, exactly, was he doing there?" Arthur smirked, and Deor wanted to hurl a tiny spike through his eye. The arrested people were shivering cold, having obviously not been allowed to grab their coats, hats, and gloves on the way out.

Rafe spun toward the crowd. "Let's go ask him, shall we?" He made long strides toward Overton, leaving the three of them to catch up. "So, Lord Overton, may I ask what you were doing at the...event?"

Overton, the Master of the capital city Caer Eisteddfod, stood among the first group of prisoners, his hands behind his back and his posture upright, despite his age and the cold. Behind him stood Holman Redfern, also bound. Deor knew he was a senior guildsman—the rope-makers, she thought, from her recent readings.

Rafe approached Overton, laying a hand on the man's shoulder. "How did it come to this, sir?"

Lord Overton lifted his chin defiantly. "The Sons of London requested I address their meeting to discuss how best to *peacefully* approach the king about the tournament," he glanced over his shoulder at the others behind him, "as well as any other concerns. I went in good faith, as it is my duty to hear the needs of the city's people. I neither spoke nor encouraged sedition." The old man turned his glare to the guards next to him, his gaze lingering on Arthur. "The king will hear of this." Holman nodded along enthusiastically.

"He already has, sir," Arthur said, his smirk never slipping.

Deor scanned the crowd. College students, some in scholar's robes, and working men and women in the outfits of their trades. A fair number of them appeared to be apprentice age, but there were a few heads of guilds—the grocers and silversmiths in particular. Robbie, her golden hair tangled around her tear-streaked face, shivered in just her t-shirt and pants. Aiden huddled close behind her, trying, even with his arms bound, to shield her from the wind.

Deor glanced toward the gates where reporters peered around the guards, their mirrors flashing. There was no way this wasn't going to make the evening papers, including pictures of her here. Rafe watched the crowd, soldiers and all, and Arthur was now huddled over his mirror whispering furiously. Next to her, Stephen stood alert but unobtrusive, his eyes consistently scanning back and forth.

Rafe raised his arm over his head, sending blue sparks up into the air. "Now hear this! I am releasing each of these prisoners on my personal recognizance. I will stand bond for their good behavior until this matter is sorted out. Those of you who were arrested today are not to leave the city without first informing my office, but you are free to go. Officers, release them."

A ragged cheer went up from the prisoners and a few of the reporters. Guards' eyes widened, and they looked back and forth between Rafe and Arthur, hands gripping their weapons.

"But sir," Monjoie said, "If we release the students, they'll just scuttle back to the university. We'll never get them back out."

"Did I ask for your opinion, Monjoie?" Rafe roared.

Robbie whooped.

Arthur, his mirror in hand, strolled over. Without a word, he held up the mirror and cast a privacy spell around the two of them. On the mirror, Finn's face showed livid. Rafe met his look with equal fury.

"Rafe, are you conspiring to defy my direct orders? And what is Deor doing there? Defying me as well?"

"Not conspiring, sire. Just doing my job to maintain peace *and justice* in this realm."

"When I sent you and Arthur to break up the seditious meeting, I did not give you leave to make bail for any of the prisoners!" Silver rimmed Finn's eyes, and he glanced over Rafe's shoulder at Deor frequently. "You will do as I say!" The edges of Finn's lips were white with fury.

Rafe took a deep breath. Deor rested her hand on his back, out of sight, trying to offer support without being obvious. "Sire," Rafe said, "it is within the scope of my duty to release prisoners who present no ongoing threat to the nation. You've made your point by having them arrested. What possible gain is there in locking up a bunch of workers and students?"

Finn bit his lower lip and looked to the side, not meeting Rafe's eyes.

"Some of these people earn a daily wage, Your Majesty," Rafe pressed his point. "If they don't go home to their families tonight, others may go hungry."

"Very well," Finn snapped. "Let the rabble go. But the ring leaders are detained at the king's pleasure. Arthur?"

"Here, sire." Arthur turned the mirror so that he could be seen in it.

Finn spoke. "Lord Delaney Overton, Holeman Redfern, Roberta

Gemmelsdottir Ellington are to be confined in the tower immediately. Along with anyone else you feel should be detained. It is entirely at your discretion."

"Of course, Your Majesty. My duty and pleasure." Arthur bowed. Deor struggled not to snort and roll her eyes.

"As for you, Rafe," Finn said, "you and my daughter keep out of my sight for the rest of the evening. It concerns and wounds me deeply that the two of you would so conspire to support those who would ruin the tournament—those who would be a threat to our national unity." He shook his head sadly. "I encourage you to think on your duties." The mirror went black.

"I've been trying to warn you, Rafe," Arthur said, with the look of a disappointed older brother. "And, Princess," he went on, "I don't know how you discovered this event, but you would do well in the future to stay out of things that are not your concern."

"Fuck you, Arthur, you creepy toady," Deor said. She turned away, searching for Robbie in the huddled crowd. Deor found her fellow changeling near Aiden, her lips blue edged and teeth chattering. Like Deor she seemed to feel the cold more sharply than the Winter Court faeries around her.

Rafe joined them, stripping off his coat. "Take this," he said, slinging it around Robbie's shoulders. Deor took Robbie's hands in her own, trying to warm them.

Not far from where they stood, Arthur relayed the king's orders to the surrounding guards. Here and there, a student was unchained and sent to stand apart from the rest. Those staying were far more than Deor had hoped there would be.

"We can't leave Robbie here," Deor insisted.

"We must," Rafe said. "I'm sorry. If we try to stop it, it will make it worse for her." He wrapped his arms around Robbie and hugged her to him. "Be strong, little sister. I'll get you out as soon as I can."

He turned to Deor. "King's orders. We have to go back to the palace and 'stay out of sight.'" He mimed quote marks and rolled his eyes.

Deor clenched her jaw and sighed but nodded. She gave Robbie one last hug. "Hang in there, kiddo. We've got your back."

Stephen bowed at Deor, and she fell into step with Rafe, headed back to the palace. Behind her, Arthur barked orders.

Chapter Eleven

Deor was certain that she would never quite get over the size of Rafe's bed. The frame was dark, polished wood carved from a single tree. It was at least seven-by-ten feet, and nearly three feet off the ground, which meant there was no way for her to get in without climbing. The four posts were carved to look like thin trees, with the branches intersecting and twining to form the canopy frame. The massive headboard, too, was carved to look like branches and leaves.

She leaned back against the headboard, supported by a pillow. Over her panties, she wore another of Finn's castoff sweaters, her now-usual choice for sleeping.

Rafe laid on his back, his head in her lap, staring up at her. "It was like I was set up," he said. A chill buffeted off of him, but she said nothing. His eyes were closed, and his brow furrowed.

Deor stroked her fingers along his temples and back through his hair, and he sighed.

"I know," she said.

Her own rage at the arrests, especially Robbie's, still simmered, but for now she could put it aside for him. She'd never loved Finn, never been eager to please him, never burned with the desire to be his real child. To her, the king was nothing more than a selfish, childish bully. He claimed to care for his people, but he was cruel and vindictive at least as often as he was compassionate and merciful. He was quick to anger, and, worse, immediate with unforgiving punishment. The were-creatures were still banned from the Winter Court—a state that didn't seem likely to end any time soon.

"I feel helpless," Rafe said. "Finn won't listen to me. The insane part is that the people seem to love him for it." He waved his hand at the pile of newspapers next to him on the bed. In the evening editions of all the major papers only one, a paper put out by the guilds, was even mildly critical of the king. "What was it the *Times* said? *It's time to come together—these protests can wait for another day.* And even the *Herald*, the one that loves to quote my mother? Their lead editorial went on for a page and a half about how appreciative the *rabble* should be for the boost in the economy."

"Yes," Deor said. "It's like every concern about him evaporated in a cloud of rose-colored jingoism." Her father basked in the praise, and no doubt now he was busy strutting around his room telling Astarte how fabulous he was. Even after he'd thrown her daughter in jail.

Even in his good moods, though, he frightened her. When he hugged her and talked about loving her, there was something off. There was an anger there, hovering just below the surface, focused solely on her. He hated her in a way, she was sure of it. And that hate was dangerous. What could she do? Every fiber of her being told her that saying yes to the needs of her newfound people meant saying no to Finn.

Suddenly, from somewhere above them, there was a thump. Loud, like the collapse of some huge piece of furniture. A door slammed.

"What the hell?" Deor gazed upward.

Rafe jerked up into a sitting position, eyes locked on the canopy.

"Is someone up there?" Deor asked.

"Finn and Astarte have the suite upstairs," he said as he scrambled out of bed, keeping his head tilted toward the ceiling. He glanced down long enough to find his pants.

Deor hopped out of bed and pulled on a pair of pajama bottoms, too. "Do you hear them often?"

"Never before," Rafe said.

She opened her mouth to ask another question, but he held up his hand, silencing her.

Through their ceiling—Finn and Astarte's floor—she could hear shouting. They were moving. Both Deor and Rafe crept along the same path, eyes upward. Whatever was happening, it was angry.

"You don't think someone's broken in, do you?" she asked.

"I don't know." He made his way out into their shared parlor, and she followed. Brand, Jake, and Sam dogged their heels, Brand whining softly and sticking close to Deor.

Another loud bang made both of them jump.

Rafe flicked his hand at the mirror. "Look in: the King's Suite."

The mirror fuzzed and cleared. Finn stood in front of the bedroom door pounding on it. The ebony door bore the king's eight-pointed star inlaid in pale white wood. Twining around the door grew two beautiful rose bushes, flowering even in the dead of winter. Finn wore a pair of long black lounging pants, like Rafe often wore, but dotted with the eight-pointed star of the Aethelwing house. A matching robe hung open, flapping around him.

"Dammit, Astarte! You cannot lock me out of my own room!" He turned the knob hard, and the door swung inward.

"You are not sleeping in here!" her voice boomed from the bedroom. "You are NEVER, EVER touching me again!"

"This is politics! I had no choice!" he yelled back at her.

Astarte came through the door like a Fury, driving Finn back. Her golden hair flew loose behind her, and her eyes, normally a rich, soothing brown, were violently lit with magic, burning an amber so fierce it was almost red. Her golden skin crackled with power, and her translucent, opalescent wings glittered, edges sharp as shattered glass. "You always have a choice," she said, her voice a vicious whisper. "That's what being the king means—you are the one with all the choices."

"Fine," he said. "Then I choose to share our bed with you."

"No," she said.

He took a step toward her.

"Don't you dare." She held up her hands.

"Oh, creator in heaven," Rafe said and turned toward the door. "I can't let him lay hands on her!"

Deor reached out and snatched his arm. "Don't," she said. "Wait."

Rafe tugged a bit but relented, turning back to the mirror.

"This is my house, woman."

"I thought you said it was *our* room," she spat back at him.

"Mine, ours, it's the same." He put his hands on his hips and looked down his nose at her, like she was a petulant child. "Now, let me in and come to bed."

"What a fool," Deor whispered.

"Yes." Rafe shook her hand from his arm and caught it in his own. He squeezed her hand gently. "This is a mess. Robbie is her only child, how can he...?" He trailed off, unable to answer his own question.

"This isn't just about Robbie," Deor said. She saw the anger, the hurt, the betrayal in the Consort's eyes. Robbie's arrest was the match on a wood pile built from years of disappointment, suffering and abuse. The spark on Finn's pyre. "This is about everything."

"Do not take another step, Fionnleigh!" Astarte commanded.

Deor and Rafe both winced at the power. Finn didn't even flinch. He didn't take another step either.

"Woman," he said. "You belong to me."

"I belong to no one," Astarte said.

Finn suddenly lunged forward, as though he meant to barrel through her into the room. He didn't get the chance.

Astarte screamed, a war cry from the bottom of her soul, and threw out her hands, magic pouring off them.

The rose bushes exploded to life. In an instant, faster than Finn could advance two steps, they shielded the door, becoming a thicket of heavy branches, with beautiful red blooms surrounded by sharp, wicked thorns several inches long.

"Gah!" Finn hurled himself backward, out of the reach of the expanding wall. Soon, the opening was completely hidden behind a thick, thorny hedge.

"You cannot keep me out!" Finn hollered.

"Try me!" Astarte's voice, nearly a screech, made it through the thick brush.

"Dammit, woman," Finn said to himself. He flicked his wrist, and a broadsword appeared—a gleaming, single piece of magic silver metal whose diamond-sharp edges glinted in the soft light. He settled both hands around the hilt, raised the thing above his head and slashed it down, hacking in a single blow through the entire length of the rose bush shield. He raised his sword and slashed again, and again, hacking away at the hedge until he made a gap wide enough to enter.

Panting, he lowered the sword and stepped forward.

With a harrowing hiss, the branches shot forth anew, reforming, driving Finn backwards, but only after catching and tearing his billowing robe.

Finn cursed in frustration. He dropped the sword, its magic dissipating even as he let it go, and stripped off his shredded robe. His nearly-alabaster skin was taut over sinewy muscles. He flexed his fingers, and the sword materialized in his hand again. He lifted the sword again, driving it through the new foliage, snapping thorns and sending them flying, ignoring them when they ricocheted back on him, nicking his chest and face.

"Should we try to stop them?" Deor asked.

"No," Rafe said. "If Finn ordered me to stop Astarte..." His voice trailed off. "We should shut off the mirror and go to bed."

"Yes," Deor agreed. "We should." She gripped Rafe's hand even tighter.

The horrific cycle repeated itself over and over, roses growing and twining into place even as Finn hacked and slashed. Deor leaned hard into Rafe's shoulder, his hand squeezing hers as they watched. Hours passed.

Eventually Finn was left panting, dripping with sweat and blood. He staggered back a few steps, leaning heavily on his sword. "Astarte? My love?" he called.

Golden light flared behind the massed branches. "Don't you dare!" Astarte's voice rang out, loud and clear. "Do. Not. Sweet-talk. Me." Each word was steel, but the voice was rough, panting.

An hour after dawn, Rafe and Deor rose from the couch and stretched. Finn finally collapsed, unconscious but breathing, in front of the ever-regrowing rose bush. The thorny hedge still held, though only barely. All its blossoms lay on the ground, wilting, and gaping holes appeared between the branches. Through the openings, Rafe and Deor could see Astarte, also collapsed and also breathing, on the other side.

Rafe turned to Deor, her hand still clutched in his. "That," he said, "was horrifying."

Deor nodded. "I think I might skip marriage."

Rafe did not reply but gave a small nod, his face glum. "I need a couple hours sleep. You?"

"Yes, but..." She leaned up and kissed him on the cheek, dropping his hand. "I'm going back to my room."

For a moment, Rafe looked distressed, but the look passed, and he nodded. "Good ... good morning, I suppose."

"Good morning," Deor responded as she scooped a sleeping Brand up from his spot curled in front of the near-spent fire. She smiled, a tight quick expression, almost a grimace, before leaving for her own room, her face buried in the comfort of Brand's fur.

Chapter Twelve

When Deor woke around noon the next day, her head ached from staying up too late, from being so very angry, and from haunting, ugly morning nightmares of silver swords slashing downward through a pile of papers—her dissertation, as she sat helplessly behind the table at her defense, heavy with the fear that, once he finished with the book, and then the table, he was coming for her.

"Ugh." She stretched as she sat up, arching her back and reaching her arms to the sky.

From the floor next to the bed, Brand barked and then scrambled up to lick her. She hugged him close and laughed. "You slept some last night," she said. "I didn't."

He squirmed from her arms and leapt off the bed to run into the parlor. Barks and growls followed.

Deor flung on her robe and headed out—Brand never growled except when he was chewing on a bone or tugging a particularly recalcitrant rope, and these sounds didn't sound like play at all.

Out in the parlor, Brand pointed at the coffee table, eyes fixed, ears perked up. He didn't even move when she came in.

In the center was a stone statue that certainly hadn't been there when she went to bed. It was winged, with rounded feathers. It had a stocky, almost square body, and an oval face with a beak, like a bird, but also a bit like a human. It had talons on its feet, too. She circled the table, eyeing the thing. The coloring was unclear—in a certain light it seemed grey, like the castle's stone. In another, a greenish marble, another a limestone.

"Hello there," Deor said. Perhaps her father or someone sent it to her? "What are you?" She leaned in to pick it up. It was heavy for such a small thing. No larger than a robin, it felt like it was made of solid lead. She held it up to her face, studying it.

"You're kind of an ugly creature," she mused. "In a so-ugly-you're-cute kind of way."

Cute kind of way? it echoed. *Cute? Cute? Cute?*

"Gah!" Deor dropped it, and it hit the coffee table with a loud *thunk*. Brand darted up to the table where the creature was righting itself, having landed on its side. Brand barked furiously at it.

Bark! Bark! A near perfect imitation of Brand sounded in Deor's head. The creature—a gargoyle now that Deor thought about it—was watching the dog, its head tilted to one side. It swiveled its head to look at her—a bit like an owl might. *Cute?* It blinked wide, pupil-less eyes at her.

Deor shook her head, trying to dislodge the echoing voice. It rang in her ears, and she both understood what it said and stumbled over the words in her own head.

"*You're speaking Faerie*," she finally got it.

Faerie! Faerie!

"*Yes*," Deor said. She thought hard. She understood it when it was spoken, and, if she didn't think too much about it, she could bypass her conscious brain and react in Faerie, too. But composing sentences, working through translations bit by bit, was tough work. "*What are you?*"

Are you! Faerie! Faerie! What! What? The creature stretched out its wings, unfolding them until they were full spread—about a foot in wingspan. *Aethel. House of Aethel. Winter Court. Winter Court.*

"*Yes*," Deor said. "*You're in the Winter Court. I'm Deor. The heir to the house of Aethelwing?*"

Aethelwing! Heir! Heir!" The creature fluttered up off the coffee table toward her, bouncing madly in the air in front of her. She cupped her hands and held them out—it lifted itself up a bit before dropping back down with the weight of a brick into her hands.

She almost dropped him. "Woah there, little guy," Deor said. "*Do you have a name?*"

Aethel!

"*No*." Deor shook her head. "*That's my name. I'm Deor Aethelwing.*"

Deor! it crowed.

Deor held the thing up in the air, inspecting its underside. She turned it round and round in her hands, trying to find seams, trying to see some sort of magic on it. But nothing. It was a hunk of stone. It felt like holding the castle itself—

"Are you the palace?" Deor said suddenly. Since she arrived, it felt like the palace spoke to her. Finn knew about it, felt it too. *"Have you spoken to the king?"*

It shook its head. *No voice. No voice. No ears. No ears. No king.*

Deor sat down on the couch. *"Okay, little guy, you don't need to repeat everything. You haven't spoken to the king? Or the king doesn't hear you?"*

The creature cocked its head one way, then another, like it was evaluating her. The eyes, circles carved into a rock, swiveled, taking her in.

"Do you have a name?" Deor asked.

Palace.

"Why are you here? Why are you talking to me? What do you want?"

You listen. You hear. It hopped out of her hand into her lap and snuggled up against her body. *You save us.* It seemed to settle down there.

Brand lifted up, putting his paws on her thigh, and sniffed at the thing. It lunged forward at him, gently knocking noses. Brand jerked back on all fours and began a furious litany of barks.

"Easy, Brand," Deor said stroking his head with her free hand. "It's not going to hurt you." As Brand calmed down, Deor soothed, "Good dog."

Good Dog! it said in Faerie.

She stroked its stone head. "You look like you came off the front of a gothic cathedral. Some kind of watcher, or waterspout."

Gargoyle watch out for the palace. You keep the Winter Court safe.

Deor scooped up the creature and held it in front of her face. *"I hear you. I'll keep the Winter Court safe. It belongs to me, now."* She gasped as soon as the last of the words left her mouth. Even to her own ears it sounded like treason. She couldn't take them back, even though she wanted to. The land was broken. The wound cut her to the quick—its pain was her own. The creature was right. The land needed saving, and her father wasn't going to do it. He might not even feel the suffering anymore.

"You can't talk to Finn, can you?" she asked.

Finn? Finn? Finn? It shook its little head back and forth, like it didn't understand.

"The king," she said. *"I'm the heir."*

Talk to you. Protect you.

"Protect me?" Deor laughed. "Well, that's a gargoyle's job, I guess." She scratched it under its chin, and it tilted its head back; a small rumble like a purr coming from a stone cat thrummed out of it. "You sound like a content kitten."

The rumble grew louder, and the creature began to change. Deor yelped and scooped it up, holding it out in front of her. The stone sculpture receded, dulled, until it was a lump of rock in her hand. Slowly, molded by some invisible hands, it took shape. Wings like a bat's spread out from its body, which shifted into something lean and sinuous. A tail curled out from its body, and the head formed. A sleek muzzle and two pert, triangle ears, and two pointed fangs peeking out from the mouth. Last, whiskers sprouted from its face. A small, ferocious, winged cat.

You like me?

"*I like you very much,*" Deor assured it.

My name?

"You want me to name you?" Deor picked up the winged cat and held it cupped in her hands. She raised its body so she could look it directly in the eye. "Hmmmm," she said as she studied it. "*How about* Beukeboom? *I'll call you* Boomie."

Bo-o-o-o-mee.

"Boomie," Deor repeated.

Boomie leapt from her hands into the air and whirled around the room on its stone wings. *Boomie!* it called out.

Brand yelped and began to chase it, running under it as it circled the room, barking in delight. Boomie swept down and skimmed over the puppy who nipped at it in the air. Eventually the creature landed, and Brand skidded to a halt in front of it. He wagged his tail and dropped into a play bow, rubbing first one side of his face and then another on the rug before letting out another sharp bark.

The cat-faced creature barked back, a near perfect echo, and pushed off again, swirling into the air.

For ten minutes the two creatures played together, Deor laughing all the while. Brand took to leaping into the air, trying to catch Boomie. Once he succeeded, and landed with a crash on the ground, spitting the gargoyle out so that it bounced across the floor and landed at Deor's feet. Before she could gather it up to see if it was okay, Boomie was off in the air again, dive bombing Brand, but never hurting him.

Finally, Brand gave out, and flopped down on the rug next to Deor on the couch.

Boomie landed on the back of the couch and then climbed onto her shoulder.

"So, Boomie, what can I do for you?"

The creature frowned. *Fight. Screaming. Magic. Violence.* He shook his head.

"Do you mean last night? The fight between the King and his Consort?"

Yes! He fluttered about, never quite taking off, in a kind of agitated wing-bound pacing.

"I'm sorry," Deor said. *"I don't know how to fix it. The king is..."* She trailed off. Was it treason to give her opinion of the king to the palace itself? It must know her feelings. In fact, when she really concentrated, she could feel the angst all around her. Boomie was the focal point—the manifestation, but the palace, perhaps even the Winter Court itself, was afraid.

Bad at his job. You too. You have a job.

"I know that!" She snapped. She didn't need a chunk of rock to tell her she wasn't doing what she needed to do. Robbie and Aiden in dank cells somewhere in the Tower were enough to do that.

The creature shook its head. *You don't know. Heir job. King job. Sword job. Shield job. Consort job.*

"We all have jobs?" That made a certain kind of sense. *"Do you mean like Merlin? Some humans think he wasn't a person named Merlin, but maybe that was some kind of office?"*

Boomie blinked at her. *Books,* he repeated.

"Books. Right. Back to the library."

Boomie took to the air, and Deor stood. Despite the gargoyle's persistent chittering, Deor dressed, donning a comfortable but suitably formal grey day-dress, and then twisted her hair up into a bun and pinned it. She didn't bother with shoes, her preference when she was in the palace. *"Let's go."*

Boomie settled on her shoulder, and Brand paced with her out the door.

Outside her shared rooms, Stephen was at his normal post in the hall. He bowed slightly when she emerged. "Princess."

"We're on our way to the library," Deor said.

He nodded and fell into step next to her, the same side Boomie was on. She waited for him to ask about the weird, winged, stone cat on her shoulder, but he never mentioned it. When they stepped through the massive doors to the library, Boomie took off, shooting from her shoulder up to the second floor to the alcove with the pedestals.

"Ouch!" she said and rubbed her shoulder. His push-off hurt.

"Are you okay?" Stephen glanced around. "Did something hurt you?"

Above them, flying in wide circles, was Boomie. Next to her, Brand watched the stone creature, his head moving in small rings in sync with it.

Stephen glanced at Brand and then up toward the ceiling.

"You don't see it, do you?" Deor said. "The stone cat-gargoyle thing flying up there? It was on my shoulder when I came out of my rooms?" She couldn't be crazy, because Brand saw it too.

Stephen looked around the room and then at her for a long moment. "No. I don't see anything. What is it?"

Deor bit her lip. He didn't seem to be humoring her, so she went for it. "It's a small gargoyle about yay high," she demonstrated with her hands. "It looks like a cat with bat wings. It speaks to me in Faerie, in my head, and says it is the manifestation of the palace. I'm supposed to help the country, and it wanted me to come to the library so I could learn to do my job."

Stephen stared at her for a long moment, and then glanced down at Brand. "He sees it too?"

"Yep."

"Does it have a name?"

"Boomie. It asked me to name him. There's this hockey player I liked as a kid—you know what, never mind. Yes. It has a name."

There was a screech above them, and Deor looked up in time to see a book tumbling out of the air toward them. Stephen followed her gaze and snatched it right before it smacked him in the head.

Do. Your. Job.

Deor ignored it. "Are you okay?"

Stephen held the book, staring at the cover. "*A Soldier's Etiquette.*" He read the title. "Okay, so the palace talks to you through a magic stone gargoyle." He set the book on the nearest table. He shrugged. "I've always heard stories of royal magic being weird. Do you think it is going to hurt you?"

Boomie hovered in the air over Stephen, its tail flicking furiously.

"No," she said. "Not so long as I do my job, apparently. Which means looking at the pedestals, I think."

"Off you go then." Stephen pulled out a chair and sat. "Unless you want me to come up there with you?"

"No," she shook her head. "There's nothing that's going to hurt me here, I think." She followed Boomie up a spiral staircase and to the alcove.

When she arrived in front of the pedestals, sconces lighting the alcove flared brightly to life. At the center of the arc, a bowl burned with white flame, bathing the space in the whiteness of pure sunlight.

Each pedestal seemed designed to hold a book, with a high, slanted platform with a lip at the bottom, perfect for setting and reading a tome. She walked around so that she could stand in front of the first one. No book, but an elaborately carved shield sat in the middle. The next pedestal was a pair of hands, open, palms up. The third, an elaborate crown. The fourth a smaller crown. The final pedestal, a sword. Each of the pedestals also bore an eight-pointed star—the symbol of the Winter Court.

Little Crown; little crown.

Deor nodded and stepped up to the pedestal with the smaller crown. She took hold of the pedestal on both sides. *"I am the heir,"* she said, though she wasn't sure why.

The sconce behind her flared and sparked, and a tome appeared on the pedestal before her. She gasped. The book was huge—at least a foot long by two feet tall, and several inches thick. A heavy cover of dark, blood-brown leather bore the same symbol as the pedestal, and stamped in gold, *The Heir*.

Deor opened the book. It yielded to her touch. The first page repeated the elaborate iconography of the cover. The next was blank. The third page was a table of contents. The words danced and shifted, unreadable. The quivering soon settled and plain, American English graced the ancient book.

"What is this?" she asked.

Book! Bards! Book-bards!

She scanned down the contents and realized what she now held: a complete history of the heirs of the Winter Court. She read name after name—there were dozens of them, stretching back millennia. Even though the alphabet stayed her American one, the names were an unreadable mishmash of letters, combinations that didn't even form sounds in English. Slowly the names started making more sense until she found Finn's, and then her own.

She noted the page number and flipped to her section.

Deor, daughter of Susan Smithfield and his Majesty, King Sweordmund Fionnleigh the VIII, of the house of Aethwing. There was a birthdate. And nothing more.

"Why isn't there more about me?" she asked.

Not time! Boomie insisted. Before she could ask what he meant, Boomie settled on her shoulder, nipped at her ear.

"Ow!" Deor swatted at him.

He swatted back, grazing her hand with his stone claws. *Read job. Read rules!!* He hissed in her ear.

Brand growled low and barked once.

"*Fine.*" Deor flipped back to the Table of Contents and found the historical section on the structure of the monarchy. It laid out the five pillars of the monarchy: the crown, the heir, the consort, the shield, and the sword. The king or queen was to lead the Winter Court. He or she was to love and cherish it, to care for it as if it were a child, and to seek prosperity and, above all, justice for the land. *Duh*, Deor thought. Of course, they were.

The Sword was the leader of the military—the protector of the kingdom, monarch, and royal family from threats abroad. The Shield, the protector of the kingdom, monarch, and royal family from threats at home. Sometimes, of course, those lines got fuzzy, but overall, both jobs emphasized justice and care over any kind of violence.

It struck Deor that the Sword and Shield in Finn's court didn't seem to follow that design. There wasn't a Shield at all, and from what she gathered, Rafe and Arthur together functioned more like the Sword and Shield combined than Michael and Rafe had ever functioned separately. She wasn't surprised at the dysfunction. The two, the book assured her, should never, ever be the same person. They were not the same office. The protection of the people from enemies abroad was different from the assurance of peace at home. Interesting.

The consort, she learned, was rarely a lover. There was a role for the spouse of the monarch, and a powerful one at that, but the consort was something else. The description was brief and made little sense to Deor. *A keeper.* That phrase was repeated over and over. But a keeper of what? The finances, perhaps? Astarte certainly seemed to run the household. Later in the passage, the consort was described as a *giver*, and as the *restorer*. Deor shrugged and kept on—a consort was the last thing she needed to worry about.

Unsurprisingly, the description of the heir was the longest. There was, the book made very clear, no necessary structure of succession—the monarch could choose or could defer the choice to all of the Aethelwings, including nieces and nephews, siblings, or cousins. There was even a way for Parliament to interfere, to elect a new heir if the monarch either failed to produce one, or the possibilities, such as they were, were unacceptable. The book was unclear on what that standard was.

For the first time, Deor worried that she could be disinherited by Parliament. She understood that a vote of no-confidence would be bad for the nation—it could spur open rebellion and possible coup attempts—but she hadn't realized that she could be, essentially, unmade. It had been possible to make Rafe into an heir. So why should she be surprised that she herself could be unmade?

While each description made clear the Winter Court was the highest value, not the physical monarch, it was in the description of the heir that this came most to bear. The heir, not merely any child, but the person selected to be the next monarch, must protect the nation, too. The heir's voice was to be one of support in public, but, more often than not, challenge in private. To question every decision, every choice, every possibility: that was the heir's vocation. For as much as the Sword and Shield guarded the nation and the consort backed the monarchy, the heir stood alone.

The body of the heir was the last line of defense.

The conscience of the heir was the final stay of judgment.

The heir, once named, was the voice of no.

Deor reached up and scratched Boomie under the chin. *"This is what you wanted me to see, right?"*

The heir is the no.

Robbie, Aiden, Holman, Overton—they were imprisoned, wrongly. Rafe could not stand up to Finn—he didn't have the power. Astarte, whatever her role as Consort was, didn't seem to be able to control Finn either. There was, as far as Deor knew, no Shield at all.

That left her.

She closed the book and stepped back. It disappeared.

She wondered, could she read the others?

She stepped in front of the Sword's pedestal. A book appeared, as expected, and she opened it. As she flipped through the pages, she found it was like reading a redacted letter from some intelligence agency. Much of it was blurred and fuzzy.

"Most of this is just for the office holder, then."

Go now. Boomie said. *Help them! Your job!*

"In a moment." She moved to the monarch's book.

It, too, appeared and opened. It, too, looked heavily redacted. But she found Finn's section, the last in the book, and opened to that page. The first page had another, smaller, table of contents, and she jumped toward the bottom, to find details of her mother. But the last entry was "The Fostering of Raphael, Lord Farringdon."

"Why is this it?" she asked Boomie.

Books lag behind. A century. Maybe more. Maybe less.

"Ah." She thought about reading the story of Rafe's separation from his parents, but that felt too intimate and personal. If he wanted her to know, he could tell her. There was nothing to be gained for her own troubles now with Finn from that.

Then an entry caught her eye: "The Seduction of the Summer Court Heir."

Deor started to flip the pages.

Boomie leapt from her shoulder to the book. *No time for silly stories! Your job!*

"*I want to know!*" She tried to shoo him off, but he darted away and hooked the book with a talon, knocking it closed and to the floor. When it hit the ground, it vanished. "*Silly … cat—bird—whatever you are!*"

Now! Fix the problem!

Deor moved away from the books. She'd come back later when her companion wasn't quite so earnest. She was dying to know how Finn managed to convince Astarte to give up a kingdom for him. Especially after that fight last night. "*Alright. I'll see what I can do, but I'm not sure how to get him to change his mind. It's not like I could sneak into the Tower and release them!*"

The palace map flashed in her mind again, and another pathway lit up.

Follow! Help you!

"*Okay, I'll follow along.*" She might as well. Maybe there was some other document, something else that would convince Finn that what he was doing was not only wrong—unjust—but inane and more likely to cause rebellion and treason than quell it. "*Lead the way.*"

She made her way down the spiral staircase and over to Stephen.

"Find out anything interesting?" he asked as he rose.

"A lot actually. But now he's got something else to show me." She sighed. "I've got a kind of map in my head of the palace," she said. When he quirked an eyebrow at her she shook her head. "I'll explain all of it on the way."

"Off we go then!" He opened the door for her. He grinned. "It will be an adventure."

THE PALACE WAS silent as Deor closed the door to the library and her troop headed off down the hall. Boomie remained on her shoulder, Brand at her heels, and Stephen companionably kept pace with her.

She paused at a window in the long hallway. The sill came up to her chest, making her feel like a little girl. Brand whined at her feet, so she lifted him up and set him on the sill. "You want to see, too? Okay." Frost crystals collected around the edge of the frame. Outside, the grounds were covered in pure white snow. No tracks of any kind from the back veranda of the second floor of the palace down to the inner wall of the courtyard. Past it, the last defense, were rolling hills of gardens and forest surrounded by the outer wall. The palace was on a far edge of the city. While the front gate was on a main square, the lands themselves trailed miles behind. She could just make out the top of the Tower.

Her mind flooded with information, and she set Brand on the floor. "Come on, let's go!" Down the hall, down stairs and more stairs until she was below ground level. She followed the magic directions in her mind. The upper halls she had seen before, either on her own wanderings or with Finn. They walked through a set of doors that led to the back of the house —the hallways and passages servants used. A sharp left turn and more stairs—these stone—down into darkness. The grey stone grew darker with frost as she took each step.

"I knew the palace had a lot of underground rooms," Stephen said, "but no idea it was like this."

"Yeah," Deor said. She wished she knew where she was leading all of them, but Boomie seemed to like the direction she was going, and her brain-map was clear.

The spiraling stone staircase was dimly lit—and the light seemed to come from the walls themselves, no sconces. As they passed, it faded behind them. She kept her hand on the wall until she got to the bottom. She blinked, and there was some light, but not much. As her eyes adjusted, she stepped forward, dragging her fingers along the wall again, heading toward a small pool of light.

Brand whined and pressed himself next to her, almost tripping her a couple times until she finally picked him up.

"Here," Stephen said, gently taking Brand from her and tucking him under his arm. "You lead, I'll take care of him." He stroked the pup under his chin. "It's okay, Brand," he leaned down and spoke to him.

The stone floor beneath her feet was cold as ice, but otherwise comfortable and smooth to walk on. More like marble than the rough stone it appeared to be. She wondered if the palace was somehow doing that on purpose. Still, she wished she had bothered to put on shoes.

Once she was close enough, she saw the small pier. Stephen caught her arm as she moved to test whether it would hold her weight. "Me first," he said. Before she could argue, he'd stepped out on the pier and taken a few paces. When it held, he waved for her to follow.

It went on for a dozen yards before breaking out into a larger dock. She still wasn't in the sun, but the opening was large enough for a good-sized ship to pass through. The walls and ceiling were bedrock, the same that drove deep below the castle. Outside the mouth of the cave, the Thames waited. While from upstairs it appeared a solid ribbon of ice, she saw now that large and small floes jostled together as they made their way down the river. As they rocked through the current, she saw some that must have been a half a yard thick or more. Certainly enough to hold her weight. Not that she was going to try.

This part of the river, she knew from the map in her head, would lead her either to the Tower, in one direction, or, in the opposite direction, to an escape from the palace.

Go to the Tower! Boomie said.

"*Oh, hell no!*" Deor said aloud. She suddenly realized why Boomie brought her down to the river. "*I cannot go break people out of the Tower. Even if I can get in and find them, I don't know that I can open the doors. If I could get them all the way out, all hell would break loose, and things would be worse than they are now!*"

Boomie readjusted his position on her shoulder and fluttered his wings.

"That thing wants you to break prisoners from the tower?" Stephen demanded. "As you said, *oh, hell no.*" Stephen seemed to be up on his faerie swearing, too.

"I'm not going to," she said. She took Boomie off her shoulder and held his face near to hers. "*I'm sorry. This isn't the way to do my job. But I promise— I promise—I will stand up to him. I will say no.*" Boomie eyed her but said nothing as she settled him back on her shoulder.

She turned from the edge of the pier and led her small crew back. A smaller pier jutted out deeper into the darkness of the cave, and when she squinted, she could make out some kind of craft. A small, single masted sailboat big enough to hold maybe a half a dozen people at most. She certainly wasn't going to get into it.

She shivered in the cold. Her toes were numb while the bottoms of her feet screamed with cold. She built an image of her parlor, soft rugs and warm fire, in her mind and waited for the palace to tell her where to go. She followed the palace's nudges back up the main pier. She got ready to make the long hike back up the stone steps but paused at a noise.

A creak cut the hushed air, and a piece of the rock swung back—a door. She ran her fingers down the yard-thick stone. It wasn't a carved door, not that she could see. The door seemed to have broken from the bedrock itself, following small fissures or lines of ore.

"That's interesting," Stephen said, stepping past her to peer inside. "It goes up. No surprise there." He stepped in and gestured her to follow. The door quietly closed behind them, plunging them into darkness.

Deor spun around and pressed on the wall, but it refused to budge. She imagined the pier again, and still it didn't move. Slowly, the black room grew lighter as crystals on the walls came into view, urging them up the hallway. They followed the light, crystals winking on a few feet ahead and fizzling out after they passed. The ground was stone, but smooth, and much warmer than outside in the cave. Hand cut marble from a master craftsman would not have been as flawless, and yet she was sure that it was natural—or at least not made with tools.

The hallway climbed upward, curling round and round itself, steep enough to tire her after some yards. Thousands of years ago, perhaps the first Aethelwing had stood at the end of this tunnel, at that point a hunk of solid rock, and willed it aside, magicking the floor and walls smooth, and drawing out the light-giving crystals.

Finally, the ground flattened, and they came to an open space with three doorways. One path continued straight, one to the left, one right.

"How do we choose?" Stephen asked. "Do you know where we are?"

"No idea," she said. "Though we've got to be somewhere near the main part of the palace by now, right?"

The crystals along the left hallway lit up.

She looked behind her. The tunnel vanished into black darkness within a few feet. The ground was so smooth that she probably could go back to the pier, even without any light.

As if it read her mind, the stone around her rumbled, a building vibration until the walls around her rocked and the ceiling above her cracked. A long fissure traced itself around the tops of all four openings. A gust of wind blew up from the pier below, and Stephen grabbed Deor and pulled them both back to the center of the tunnels, shielding her and Brand from any falling rock.

A crash made the both of them drop to the ground and cover their heads. They crouched there as all around, the scraping of stone and the patter of falling rocks filled the air. A cloud of dust billowed up and settled as the space stilled to silence.

She and Stephen stood cautiously. All around, three of the entrances, the ones forward and back, and the one to the right, had been closed off. Piles of rock completely blocked the doorways. She reached out and touched the stones, expecting them to be jagged and rough against her hand. They were smooth, like the floor. She leaned in and could see a crack at the edge of the cave-in, one that she traced up one side, across the top, and down the other. Like the one at the pier, a door, not a cave-in.

"Okay," she said to the space. "We can take a hint. Left it is."

They followed the path again with the crystals leading the way. She passed another door, this one wooden, but like the doors below, it seemed perfectly fitted to the frame. She doubted she could get a single sheet of tissue paper between the wood and stone. She continued around the long curve, until the door behind her was out of sight. She came to another wooden door. She squinted down the tunnel ahead of her but couldn't see more than a few yards.

The wooden door swung inward silently, like its hinges were perfectly oiled and used every day. The crystals around the doorway blinked out, and they stepped into the dim room. The door swung shut. Deor moved forward a few steps. On either side of her there was something on the walls —some kind of hanging plant, maybe? Pieces fluttered when the door closed behind her. She stepped forward a bit more, and her legs hit something. She almost pitched forward but flailed and caught herself. One side of the thing was higher than the other. She groped for the far side, clutching what felt like smooth wood, until she hit the edge, which was about even with her knees. Fabric? She ran her fingers over a soft curve, the texture like a brocade.

"Lights?" Stephen asked.

She blinked as light flooded the space. She stood next to the fainting couch in the middle of her closet. The plants? Racks of her clothes. She laughed and spun around. The chest of drawers containing her scarves, gloves, and handkerchiefs was in place. She grabbed it on each side and tried to shake it. It didn't budge. She ran her fingers along the wall where the seam of the door should be. Nothing.

"This is your closet," Stephen said.

"Yep," Deor agreed. "I wanted to go back to my nice, warm parlor, and it took me here."

Stephen nodded and, like Deor, inspected the area that must be the door. "I wish I knew how to open it again," he said.

"Why would they have something like that?" Deor asked.

"Escape," Stephen shrugged. "I'll bet those other doors led to the other parts of the royal household. Maybe there are even some on the lower floors. Doors that open when needed to get the royal family out. I wonder if Rafe or Arthur knows about them."

"No one has mentioned it to me, but that doesn't mean much." Deor took Brand from Stephen and set him on the ground before she opened the door into her bedroom. "But it's good to know it's here."

"Indeed," Stephen said absently as he continued his inspection of the room. He reached for a rack of clothes and froze. "Sorry," he said. "Do you mind if I keep poking around in here?"

"Just don't rearrange anything," she said with a smile as she left him behind. "My maid might have a stroke."

In her own room she gathered Boomie from her shoulder and held him. "That's enough for today," she said. "Okay?"

Enough. Okay. He flapped his wings and leapt from her hands, swirling around the room and taking up a post in the corner. After a few seconds, he disappeared, as if he melted back into the stone of the palace itself.

"Neat trick," Deor said to herself. "I wish I could do it."

Chapter Thirteen

The tension between Rafe and Finn had not waned in the week since the arrest of Robbie and the others, but for the moment, he could forget about it. Rafe gazed up at Deor from the deep pillows of his bed as she sat astride him, her hands braced against his, the covers kicked down to the end of the bed. She leaned in to kiss him, and he raised his head, eager to meet her mouth with his.

As they broke the kiss and his head sank back against the pillow, he said, "You know, this is rapidly becoming my favorite time of the day."

She laughed, a small, cheerful chuckle in the back of her throat and bent to kiss him again, a longer, more searching kiss this time, their tongues darting against each other until little thrills of pleasure ran like electric lines down the inside of his mouth to his chest, and his breathing deepened. His hands tightened around hers.

Pulling out from the kiss, she brushed her mouth against his and whispered, "Any special requests?"

"Put your wings out for me?"

She sat back on her heels, the smile wavering a bit from her face. "Okay."

But she didn't move. They stared at each other a moment, and he said, "Too much?"

"No... it's just," she didn't meet his gaze. "I don't put them out when I don't have to."

"I've noticed," he said. He pulled himself upright against the head-board, sliding his legs out from under her. She held her arms crossed protectively under her breasts. "Why is that?"

She frowned, thinking. "I just can't get used to how big and conspic-uous they are. Like giant flags, screaming *Look at me!* It's like when I went through puberty and suddenly had *these*," She gestured at her chest, "bouncing and drawing attention every time I stepped out of the house. And they're so sensitive!"

He crossed his legs, nodding.

She looked up with a wry smile. "Not wanting to put them out probably makes me some sort of faerie prude. Although, I notice you don't put your wings out much either. Why?"

In his back, his folded wings twitched at the mention. He opened his mouth to say something vague about their size, the danger of scraping a wing on doorways. But she was sitting there before him, naked and unabashed, with an inquiring smile on her face.

So instead, he said, "I had a bad experience with my wings when I was younger. So now I appreciate the freedom not to put them on display if I don't want to."

"I'm sorry." She put out a hand to stroke his face. He smiled and leaned his cheek against her hand.

Deor sat back on her heels, mischief in her eyes. "How about this? You show me yours, and I'll show you mine? And if it's not fun, we'll stop. Because if this isn't fun for both of us, I don't know what we're doing here."

He laughed and bowed as elaborately as he could while sitting naked in a bed. "An excellent suggestion, your highness."

"Ah sir, your gallantry overwhelms me." She pressed the back of her hand to her forehead, sighing before she collapsed into infectious giggles. Laughing with her, Rafe fell on her, tickling her until they both pushed back to catch their breaths. When the laughter subsided a bit, he pushed himself upright onto his knees. She lay stretched out in his bed, one hand resting on her ribcage as she watched him.

"Alright," he said and closed his eyes. He flexed his shoulder blades, feeling his wings unfurl behind him, scraping across the pillows and sheets. He grimaced and sat a bit further forward as the bottom part of his left wing caught on the sheet.

"Oooh!" Deor's eyes lit up as his wings spread out over the two of them. She put out a finger. "May I?"

He nodded at once, though an all-too-familiar urge to pull back surged through him. He swallowed and held still, his wings quivering slightly behind him.

A look of concern came over Deor's face, and she pulled back her hand. Raising herself on one elbow, she said, "It's okay to say no to me, Rafe. For any reason. Or no reason at all."

He breathed again, fanning his wings behind him. "It's not that exactly." He fell silent, biting his lip. He'd put his wings out for other women before her, pushing past the moment of discomfort for the sake of good bedsport. And yet here was this woman, unwilling to tease him past his hesitation.

She sat up, her head slightly to one side. "Would it help if I put my wings out too?"

He nodded. She put out her hands and took his hands in hers. "You're lovely," she said. "Even more beautiful up close."

The tips of her fingers were cold in his, so he ran his fingers over hers and raised them to his mouth to kiss.

She blushed and smiled as he did so. Then she squinched her eyes shut, held her breath, and shrugged her shoulders. Gorgeous folds of velvety soft red wings edged in silver emerged behind her, blossoming outward until their shadow fell across his face.

For a moment, he could say nothing, he was so taken with her beauty. He stared, slowly drinking her in. He wanted nothing more in that moment than to reach out and run his finger tips across her wings, to see her shudder in delicious pleasure at the sensation.

Slowly, he took his hand from hers and reached over her shoulder. He felt her breath quicken with anticipation, and his heart beat faster in his chest. He brushed her hair out of the way. She rolled her shoulders, leaning toward him with her own hands outstretched.

The bedroom door banged open, and Arthur said, "Rafe, we need to...Holy hell, what is going on here?"

Deor shrieked, clutching her hands over her chest as she turned toward the intruder. Her wings vanished. Instinctively, Rafe pulled her against him, wrapping his arms around her as if he could shield her with his body. Then sense took hold, and he dove for the covers, pulling them up around the two of them.

Arthur stood in the doorway, mouth agape. At his back stood the three dogs, tails wagging. Rafe shook himself, shouting. "Why are you still standing there? Get out."

Arthur managed to close his mouth. "What... what on earth is she doing in your bed? Have you lost your entire mind?"

"Oh my God," Deor said and covered her face with her hand. She started to slide toward the edge of the bed. "I'm just going to get my robe and go."

Rafe grabbed her wrist. "No. There's no need for you to go." He looked pointedly at Arthur. "You're not the one who's intruding."

Ignoring Deor, Arthur took another step into the room. "Rafe, you cannot be doing this. The king is already angry with you. You have to regain his trust. Do have any idea how much angrier the king will be when he finds out about this? This could ruin you."

"Ruin me?" Rafe looked from Arthur to Deor and back again. "Don't be absurd."

Arthur advanced farther into the room, his hand held out in a pleading gesture. Deor pressed herself back into the pillows and held the blankets up to her chin.

"This is ridiculous." Rafe flung himself out of the bed and snatched his lounging pants off the chair where he tossed them. Pants in hand, he took Arthur by the arm and brusquely shoved him out the bedroom door into the parlor. "Stay. Guard," he said to the three dogs and shut them inside the bedroom.

Shutting the door behind him, he rounded on Arthur. "What? What is so important that you have to interrupt me now?" Still glaring at Arthur, he yanked on his pants and tied them at the waist. Hands on hips, bare feet planted on the carpet he towered over his friend, not bothering to pull back the swirls of cold he knew were emanating from him.

For once, Arthur was at a loss for words. His mouth opened and shut, and he kept looking back toward the closed bedroom where Deor lay.

Finally, he said, "Why didn't you tell me?"

"It was none of your business."

"But you tell me everything. You told me when you were going to propose to Genevieve."

Rafe rubbed his forehead with one hand. "That was different."

"She is going to ruin you."

Rolling his eyes, Rafe said, "Are you auditioning for a role in a melo-drama? Get a grip on yourself, man, and tell me what you came here to say."

Arthur could not be distracted. "When the king finds out, he'll cut off your...head."

"He's not going to find out, because you're not going to tell him. I'm not going to tell him. And Deor sure as hell isn't going to tell him. No one is going to tell him."

Fury twisted Arthur's features. "I will not betray my duty to my king. Not even for you."

Rafe seized him by the shoulders and shook him. "Betray your duty? Finn does not have an inherent right to know who I'm sleeping with. Having an affair with the princess is not treason. It's not even a misdemeanor. She is perfectly free to take any lover she chooses for as long as she chooses. And for the moment, she's chosen me."

"And what about when she's done with you? What then?"

Rafe spread his hands in a shrug. "Then I'll be sorry to see it end. These things happen."

"I know you better than that, Rafe."

Rafe took a step back, regarding his friend for a long moment. In the fireplace, the embers cast a low, red light over the scene, making the lines of Arthur's face sharp and harsh. "Do you?" Rafe said. "Do you know me so well? Then you know I mean her no harm. She is perfectly safe with me."

"It's not *her* I'm worried about, you fool!" Arthur turned away, pacing the room. "Ever since she arrived you've been fascinated by her. She's changing you, turning your head. You aren't yourself anymore."

Rafe folded his arms over his chest. "On the contrary. I feel more like myself every day."

Red and yellow light flickered off Arthur's face from the embers in the fire. His eyes were pits of black shadow. "Do you? I never realized how much you longed to be some royal woman's pet."

Rafe lunged at him, knocking a chair out of the way. Arthur flinched but did not step back. His breathing harsh in his throat, Rafe said, "Call me that again, Arthur, and I'll meet you on the field."

"You really think you could take me in a fair fight?"

"I don't think you'd know a fair fight if one came up to you and presented its card."

Arthur lifted his chin and stepped toward Rafe. Rafe stood his ground, glowering down at his friend. Even in his bare feet, the difference between them was obvious.

Finally, Arthur, speaking through clenched teeth said, "When this comes out, and it will, I may not be able to save you. Just remember that I tried." With that he turned on his heel and left, slamming the door behind him. The impact shook the walls and rattled the windows on the French doors.

For a long time, Rafe stared after his friend, the red firelight flickering in his eyes. Then he turned and made his way out onto the balcony. He stood, feet planted on the cold marble, savoring the late winter chill on his skin and looking up at the diamond stars above him. Each point of light seemed to prick and sting his eyes.

After a long while, he heard the shush of silk on stone. Turning his head, he saw Deor coming toward him, one of his dressing robes around her. Its skirts spread out around her feet and trailed behind her as if she wore some rich court gown. She said nothing; just came up and tucked her hands under his elbow, leaning her head on his arm. She heaved a soft sigh and brushed her cheek against his skin.

Eventually, he felt her shiver. Uncrossing his arms, he cast one arm around her shoulders, tucking her against him and drawing heat to keep her warm. She snuggled closer, holding his hand as it draped across her shoulder.

"Tell me what he said that has you out here staring at the stars so that you don't cry."

Rafe blinked in shock and looked down at her. "How did you know?"

"I've pulled the not blinking so I don't cry trick a few times myself," she said. "Most women have. So, what did he say?"

"He called me your pet. I haven't been called that...in a very long time."

"And who first used that word on you?"

"The Queen of the Summer Court. When I was her prisoner." Now that the words were spoken, the old story came flooding out, the story everyone in the Winter Court knew, but none ever had the courage, or lack of courtesy, to allude to. "I was young, a banner boy in my first foreign campaign. Full of guts and glory stories, and no common sense. When the signal to retreat came, I stood my ground, waving the flag. Of course, I was captured at once. She—the Queen—recognized me among the other prisoners, and so when they were ransomed, I was not."

Deor squeezed his hand tighter. "She kept you as her prisoner?"

"As her pet. Chained to her throne by a golden leash so that Finn and Astarte could see me at her feet while they negotiated for my release. She liked me to keep my wings out."

"Oh. I'm so sorry." Deor turned to wrap both her arms around him and squeeze him tight. They stood together for a long moment in each other's arms, her face pressed into his chest.

Then she pulled back and looked up at him. "Rafe, look at me."

He turned his face down to stare into her steel grey eyes, streaked with silver. "Someday," she said. "I will kill that woman for you." As she said it, the stones of the Palace trembled beneath their feet with the resonances of her words. For a split second, the spark of throne magic shot between them, just as it had done on Deor's first night in the Palace after the Adoption.

"I believe you," he said. At that moment, he would have bent the knee to her and kissed her hands. She stood up on tiptoe and kissed his mouth, her lips cool against his warmth.

"Come to bed," she said. "That's enough excitement for one night."

Arm in arm, they walked back into the warm haven of his bedroom and climbed back into the massive bed. Deor snuggled down with her head in the crook of his shoulder, and he drew up the covers over them. The dogs took up their places across the foot of the bed, tails thumping sleepily now that their persons were back where they belonged. The posts of the bed enclosed them like a grove of trees. Rafe lay against the pillows and watched the firelight warm the pale contours of his lady's face.

CHAPTER FOURTEEN

Deor's alarm—Brand having to pee—went off promptly at five-thirty in the morning. Brand knew how to whine softly, so Rafe was still asleep. He had flung the covers off in the night, and his wings had come out. Deor wondered if he were dreaming. All she wanted to do was reach out and stroke the blue wings, wake him up, kiss him and have sex with him until the wretched memories he had shared with her the night before vanished, if only for a few moments.

Instead, she crept quietly out of bed and out of the room with Brand.

Back in her own quarters she brushed her teeth and dragged her hair into a severe bun. Afterwards she put on a black dress that made her look like a villain in one of those horrid nineteenth-century British boarding school novels. She even put on matching boots.

After letting out Brand and securing him back in her suite with Jake and Sam, Deor let the map in her head lead her straight to Arthur's room. She was surprised to find that he lived on the first floor with other household guard soldiers. Arthur's quarters were a private suite, but still it seemed a bit like being a college RA. Surely this couldn't be required of the Sword's right-hand man. He must choose to live here rather than in the upper floors with people of his rank.

It was just after six, and Deor leaned in to listen—but she couldn't hear much of anything. Around her, other soldiers were up and bustling around in their rooms. The few that spotted her in the hall froze at attention until she passed. She doubted Finn ever came to this area of the palace.

She knocked a few times, as loud as she could manage, and waited.

In a few moments, the door opened.

"Yeah?" Arthur asked, as though the person on the other side would be some soldier. He was dressed in a pair of green lounging pants and nothing else. His dark brown skin was tight against his lean form. The muscles of his arms, chest, and abs were well formed. They were the kind of muscles men got from a combination of real work—riding horses, swinging swords, running—and working out with weights. "Your Majesty!" A look of genuine shock spread across his face.

"May I have a word, Captain?" Deor didn't wait for his reply but stepped past him into his room. It reminded her of her graduate student apartment. There was a small parlor and a hallway that doubtless led to a bathroom and bedroom. A low fire crackled. Above the fire was a large mirror, and Thea, the woman she hunted with at Northfalls, in a bathrobe and curlers and holding a stick, looked out from it, clearly surprised.

"Lady Thea," Deor said. "It is nice to see you again."

"You as well, Your Majesty." Thea managed a curtsey-ish motion without actually standing.

As Deor got closer, she saw that Thea held a riding crop. Interesting. She was, apparently, *very* into horses. Deor turned back to Arthur, who had closed the door and followed her in. "I am sorry to interrupt, but I do need to speak with you."

"Of course." His eyes were glittering with anger, and his tone stiffly polite. "Thea," he said, addressing the mirror, "I shall call you later?"

She smiled warmly. "Of course." She glanced at the princess and gave another nod before the mirror went black and again reflected the room.

The room was an altar to tidy simplicity. There was nothing on the walls and only a few pictures on the mantle and on a side table. At a glance, they seemed to be family and military. There was an adorable picture of him giving a piggyback ride to a young girl who must have been his little sister. In a silver frame, another picture showed him and Thea. In the picture, he held her stirrup as she smiled down from atop her horse, riding crop in hand.

"What do you want, princess?" Arthur's voice lacked the normal faux deference he had mastered, instead offering a low-grade hostility.

Deor sat on his couch, without asking. "I want to speak to you about last night."

Arthur rolled his eyes. "It was nothing I haven't seen before."

Deor arched an eyebrow. If he was trying to shame her out of the room, it wouldn't work, but that was quite the stab, the implication that Rafe had so many partners distinguishing between them was tedious work, and that she herself was not particularly remarkable.

"Oh?" She smiled. "You've seen me naked with my wings out? How did that happen? Through one of your security spells?"

"What? No!" He flailed a bit. "That's not what I meant." When Deor waited for him to elaborate, he simply repeated, "What do you want?"

"I want you to apologize to Rafe," she said.

"For entering his rooms? I have permission as his—"

"No." She cut him off. "That was actually an understandable, if rude, mistake." The image of Rafe's anger, his hurt, when she found him on the balcony flashed in her mind and rage rose inside her. "Apologize for that dig about him being some woman's pet."

"You were listening?" He seemed smug, like he had caught her out.

"No. He told me." Though she didn't want them, images of what Rafe must have looked like chained to the throne in the Summer Court flashed up in her mind. Someday, she and that woman would have words... Deor blinked hard and refocused. The edges of her vision were fuzzing with a silver glow, and Arthur was no longer looking so smug.

"So?" Arthur said. "He is making an incredible mistake sleeping with you. You will ruin him, possibly be the death of him."

"I'm not going to kill him," Deor snapped. She was about to lay into Arthur when a thought crossed her mind. He, too, was angry. She could see the fire in his brown eyes building. He was furious at her—a response that seemed...out of proportion, unless... "Arthur," she said, "answer me honestly. Are you in love with Rafe?"

"What?" He started back as though she had slapped him. "No. He is my friend. My dearest friend. We have been friends—"

"For seventy years," Deor finished for him. "I know. Why were you so cruel?"

"I... I... The truth sometimes is cruel." His eyes held a flicker of doubt for an instant, and then it was gone, covered by condescension. He was never going to even tolerate a hint that he was wrong.

She stood. "Look, I care about Rafe, deeply. We're both adults. We both have the same expectations about this affair—we're enjoying each other's company. No more. No less. I certainly have no desire to put him on some sort of leash. When he is done, we're done. So put your mind at ease about that." Deor ambled up to him, close enough that she had to tilt her head back. "But hear me on this, right here, right now. If you do not apologize, if you do not make it right, you will lose your friend. If you do such a thing again, if you hurt him again, I will do everything in my power to ruin you. And I have an excellent memory, Arthur. I might forgive sometimes, but I do not forget."

"Are you threatening me, Your Majesty?" Arthur mocked her. "That would be unwise. Your position here is not as solid as you may believe it to be."

"I am well aware of my position, Arthur, as well as my duty." She reached up and pinched his cheek, grinning as he glared at her, but made no move to touch her. "Don't think of it as a threat, Arthur." She let go of his face. "Think of it as a promise."

She headed back the way she came, nodding at various soldiers she passed. As she rounded a corner, she nearly ran into a tall young man. "Oh," she said. "Hello, Gordie."

"Your Majesty!" He fumbled a bow at her.

"Have a good day," she said, patting his arm and stepping around him. As she moved down the hall, she heard his friends gather around him and ask him questions.

She made her way back to her suite and peeked into Rafe's room. He was gone, as were Jake and Sam. Probably out for his morning run before breakfast. Deor headed back to her room and stripped off her clothes. She would grab a shower and then go down to face Finn. Perhaps there was some diplomatic way to help the people in prison.

Do your job! Boomies voice trilled.

Deor glanced up and saw him perched on top of one of the bedposts, blinking down at her. *"I'm working on it, you silly creature! The king isn't easy to talk to."*

Dangerous king, Boomie cautioned and flapped his wings. *Careful, careful.*

Deor sighed. *"I know, Boomie."* She headed for the bathroom.

He could hurt you.

Deor froze. *"What did you say?"* She turned around and looked back at the gargoyle.

Boomie flapped his wings and took off, heading for her. Deor held out her cupped hands for him, and he landed gracefully, though still heavy as a stone, in her hands. *He can hurt you. He hurts people.*

Chills ran up and down Deor's spine. She knew it was true, she'd seen it happen. Confirmation that the palace knew it, especially considering how much the palace had seen, made it all the more real. Deor stroked Boomie's rough head, and he nuzzled at her hand. *"I'll be careful, Boomie. But I have to do my job."*

Do your job, he echoed softly. He leapt into the air again and swirled around the room a few times before landing on the bed and tumbling in somersaults until he rolled into Brand, who barked cheerfully at him.

Deor left the two of them to wrestle and play on the bed and headed for a long, hot shower.

Chapter Fifteen

As the final few days before the tournament counted down, the mood in the Palace soured. By the end of each day, Rafe longed to retreat to his parlor with Deor and the dogs. He turned down invitations to card parties and dances among the glittering set, not, as the papers presumed, because he was nursing a broken heart and a bruised pride after the dramatic breakup with Genevieve, but because nightly dinners with the king had become a command performance. Finn was determined to have his family fall in line. Arthur frequently joined them.

One night as the footmen were setting down the second course, Arthur mentioned that a new trio of prisoners had been brought into the Tower. "More charges of sedition, sire," he said.

Rafe put down his fork. "Why was I not informed of this?"

Arthur looked up, eyes innocent. "I didn't think I needed to bother you with it. You were in meetings most of the day."

"Yes, with the Overton brothers," Rafe said. "They are eager to see their father again." He looked significantly at Finn, who continued to eat his terrine. Rafe turned to Astarte, who sat quietly at the opposite end of the table, her face downcast.

"Who are the prisoners?" Deor asked, her tone a touch too bright. "Anyone I know?"

"I doubt it, Princess," Arthur said. "A brother and sister from the north and their uncle. The siblings have been a thorn in the flesh of local law enforcement for some time now, and their uncle was long suspected of aiding them, but they were caught and charged with sedition last week. I had them brought down to the Tower."

Deor gasped and clutched her fork, looking to Rafe.

"The MacIntyres?" Rafe managed to say. "Arthur, you know them. You've stayed at their inn with me a hundred times on hunting trips."

Arthur resumed eating. "No one is above the law, Rafe. I can't exempt people just because they make a good stew. Which was probably made from poached rabbit." He chuckled.

"Monster," Deor whispered. She turned toward Finn. "Tess and Ian are not seditionists. I know them. They just want their father's land restored so that the people will survive."

"It's true, sire," Rafe chimed in. "I'm well aware of who these people are. They are not disloyal, and their petitions have merit."

Finn frowned and motioned for a footman to take away his plate. "MacIntyre? Are they children of the Lord of Mirrorvere?"

"His bastards, not his legitimate heirs," Arthur said.

Deor shot him a poisonous look.

Rafe repressed the urge to freeze Arthur's wine. "They are the only members of that family line left. By rights, Tessa should be restored to her father's office so that she can heal the land."

"By rights," Finn said, "they should have perished with their father."

Rafe slammed his hand down on the table. "They were children, Finn!"

At the far end of the table, Astarte jumped and clutched her napkin. Her shoulders heaved as she pressed her lips together. Slowly and deliberately, Deor reached for her water glass and took a sip.

Setting it down, she said, "We rode through that region on our way back to the Palace, Finn. I could feel the land suffering. I'm sure as king you felt it too. Wouldn't it better for the kingdom if the land was restored?"

Finn frowned at her. "This is not an area of policy you have had time to study, daughter."

"True," she said. "Although after our return, I did some digging around in the library and found newspaper accounts from that period. I quite understand why you felt the Lord of Mirrorvere needed to be," she paused, searching for a word, "made an example of. But now that the example has been made, I don't see why innocent people should have to suffer."

Leaning toward Finn, Rafe added his voice. "Speaking as your Sword, I have to agree with the princess. It is not in the best interests of national stability for a region, even a small one such as Mirrorvere, to be left in such a desolate state."

Finn's eyes narrowed. He sat back in his chair, looking from one face to another. "Oh, you have to agree with the princess, do you? So, this is a planned course of attack? What else have you two conspired about?"

"Finn," Astarte said in a strangled voice. "Listen to yourself. No one is conspiring against you."

Picking up her fork, Deor said with a brittle smile, "I'll admit that it was Rafe who introduced me to the best rabbit stew I've ever had. But I don't think that rises to the level of conspiracy. Unless you think the rabbits are in on it, poor things."

As she spoke, Rafe looked around the room. The servants in their white gloves and black suits stood still against the wall, their faces blank. There might have been no conversation at all from their reaction. Yet the chief butler by the door made no move to signal the service of the next course.

"Do not mock me, daughter," Finn said. Even through his boots, Rafe felt the faint tremor of angry magic run through the palace as the king spoke. Deor continued to smile, but the lines of her jaw were tight.

"It's true, I met Tessa and her brother Ian at the Inn. We talked about the state of the land, and they asked me to speak to you on their behalf." She held up a hand as Finn opened his mouth to object. "Which I agreed to because it's the king's job to protect the land, and it's the Heir's job to point out when he's not doing it. There's no sedition in any of that."

Finn harrumphed and toyed with his fork, stabbing it into the remains of his terrine. "Why is this mess still in front of me?" he demanded. "Take it away."

A servant leaped to remove the plate from in front of the king. Hands extended like a conductor, the butler motioned for the other servants to bring in the next course. Rafe held out his wine glass for it to be refilled and immediately drank off half the vintage. From the corner of his eye, he saw that Astarte's plate was removed with her food still untouched.

Bowls of richly sauced noodles scattered with crispy lardons were placed in front of the diners. A bright, lemony aroma scented with garlic rose from the bowl. Rafe reached for his fork, but as he did so, Finn said, "What is this?"

Hurrying over to him, the butler said, "Bucatini, sire, with lemon carbonara."

"This is a summer court dish," Finn snapped. "Take it away and bring me something from my own land."

"At once, sire." The butler whisked the offending dish away. He motioned for the servants to remove the rest of the plates.

"I'm sorry, Finn," Astarte said as a servant took her bowl. "I thought you would like it."

Before the hapless footman could take his dish, Rafe stabbed his fork down into it. "I like bucatini," he said, "and I've had a long day. Leave it."

The servant snatched back his fingers as if stung, looking fearfully from Rafe to the king to the butler. The butler made discreet waves with his gloved hands for the servant to back away. Rafe took a defiant mouthful, eyes locked on Finn.

As another servant approached Deor, she put out her hand, saying "Thank you, I'm not quite finished with my pasta." She took a forkful into her mouth.

Arthur looked pointedly at Rafe, giving a small shake of his head. When Rafe ignored him, he rolled his eyes and waved a servant over to take his pasta.

Finn glared at them all but said nothing. Faces set, Rafe and Deor methodically ate their pasta as the servants brought in the next course, presenting it to the king for approval before serving it to the other diners.

When, after three more excruciating courses, dinner was finally over, Finn rose from the table. "Would anyone care to join me for a drink?" he said.

"That's very gracious of you, Your Majesty," Arthur said. "I think I shall."

Astarte murmured something about having a headache and left the room.

"I need to wash my hair," Deor said and walked out after her.

Finn turned to Rafe. "And you?"

Rafe met the king's eyes, wanting above everything else to escape back to his own rooms, throw on a pair of lounging pants and stretch out on the parlor couch with the dogs until Deor finished whatever she was really up to. But as he opened his mouth to speak, he thought about how much time Arthur spent with the king lately, how often he seemed to have orders directly from the king that came to Rafe's attention only after the fact.

"I'd be delighted to join you, sire," Rafe said, forcing a smile. "I have a bottle of dwarven brandy I think you might like to sample."

Finn beamed at this offer. "Excellent. This way, gentlemen." He led the way out of the dining room and into the parlor.

Deor hurried down the stone corridor, Stephen following behind, her bare feet padding on the cool floor. Boomie flitted along beside her, surging forward in nervous spurts and then swerving back to hover at her shoulder.

Do job! Do job!

"*I'm trying to,*" she hissed at him through gritted teeth.

The Houseboys at the doors snapped into salutes and stepped aside every time she approached a door. She half expected to be challenged as she entered the king's private rooms, but no one said a word. Stephen nodded at them and at her, signaling that he would wait in the hall with the guards.

Astarte was not in the sitting room, but the door to the bedroom was closed. Gashes and nicks still marred the bedroom's doorposts, and the rose bush hadn't fully recovered its blooms. Hesitating a moment, Deor knocked.

She heard a faint gasp behind the door. Astarte's voice, but roughened, said, "Come in, Finn."

Deor eased open the door, peering around it. "It's me, not Finn. Is it okay if I come in?"

Astarte sat at her dressing table, still in the long-sleeved gown she had worn to supper and clutching a handkerchief. Deor caught sight of glamours edging her sleeves where they drew back over her wrists but resisted the impulse to peer past the spells.

Tucking the handkerchief into her palm, Astarte turned toward Deor. "How can I help you, Princess?"

"Please don't call me that. You shouldn't have to defer to me in your own house." Deor crouched down next to Astarte. "How are you doing?"

"I'm quite well, thank you. Just a slight headache."

Deor raised an eyebrow. "You're safe with me, you know. I will never report our conversation to Finn. I know about the fight."

Astarte gasped, and her eyes brimmed. She clamped the handkerchief over her mouth to stifle sobs.

"I'm so sorry." Deor stood up and put her arms around the older woman's shoulders. "I'm so, so sorry."

Gradually, Astarte let her head rest against Deor as she cried, hands still clamped over her face as if she feared to be heard. Deor held her close, rocking Astarte the way her grandmother used to rock her when the pain of missing her mother had been too much.

"I don't even know if she's still alive," Astarte managed to gasp out.

"You mean Robbie?"

Astarte nodded. Deor crouched again, one arm still around Astarte. "I think… I think if he had killed her, he would have made a public show of it," Deor said. "As a warning to others."

Still sniffling, Astarte nodded. "That's what I'm hoping. I'm so afraid for her."

"Me too." Deor patted Astarte's hand. "If we got her out, do you think we could send her to the human world? Maybe to my Grandmother? She'd probably be safe there."

Astarte flung herself into Deor's arms and sobbed again. Eventually, she composed herself, pulling back from the embrace. As she did so, Deor's fingers slid over her wrist, snagging the glamour around it. Deor gasped. Too late Astarte hid her wrist, covering it in her lap with her other hand. Deor saw the bruises.

"What else has he done to you?" she demanded.

Shaking her head, Astarte couldn't meet Deor's eyes. "It's not that bad."

"It's abuse! He has no right to treat you this way." Deor stood up, but Astarte grabbed her sleeve.

"Please, you'll only make him angrier," Astarte said.

A memory came flooding back—the same posture, the same words, long ago in the human world. A student had come to her for help on an essay, hiding bruises under long sleeves even in the heat of June. "He has no right to do this," Deor said. "You are a wonderful, valuable person, and no one has the right to hurt you."

Tears brimmed in Astarte's brown eyes. "If I make him angry, he may hurt Robbie."

Deor swallowed hard, pushing down her anger. The Consort was right. And where were the domestic violence shelters for the wife of a king?

"Is there anything I can do to help?" Deor said.

"Just get Robbie out. I don't matter. Just help her."

"You do matter." Deor clutched the Consort's hand. "I promise, I will do whatever I can to help Robbie and all the rest of them."

Astarte's look was more than thanks enough. "You should go," she whispered. "He may be back soon. I don't want him to see I've been crying."

Deor nodded. Skirts swishing around her, she padded over the deep carpet of the king's bedroom. At the door she turned to look back. Astarte was already brushing her hair and cleaning up her face in the mirror. Deor pulled the door shut as softly as she could and headed back toward her own rooms. Boomie flew ahead of her, bobbing sorrowfully in the air.

IN THE KING'S PARLOR, Rafe lifted a brandy snifter and swirled the liquid before inhaling deeply. His feet extended toward the fire as the three men sat around it, each in their own deep armchair. Around the room, lamps cast a yellow glow over the room.

Finn sipped his brandy slowly, and said, "You were right, Rafe. This is an excellent distillation."

"Thank you, sir." Rafe settled his back against his chair, trying not to think of the fire in his own parlor, the dogs snoozing in front of it, Deor perhaps emerging from the shower.

"Ah," Finn said. "It has been too long since we men enjoyed each other's company like this."

Rafe lifted his glass in salute and forced a smile. Across from him, Arthur did the same. Silence reigned in the room. Rafe crossed and uncrossed his legs. He sipped his brandy. Inside his boots, he wiggled his toes, an old trick he'd learned to keep from falling asleep while standing watch as a member of the Household Guard.

Arthur spoke first. "Do you mean to bring our prisoners to trial soon, sire?" he said.

Finn swirled his brandy in his glass and shook his head. "Let them cool their heels a while. There's no rush to proceed with formalities."

Rafe clenched his jaw and took another sip of brandy. "Do you intend on addressing Parliament about this matter? I expect George and Delaney Overton will be presenting a petition soon for their father's release."

"Pah. Their father knew what he was doing when he went down to that meeting. Addressing a bunch of rabble rousers, lending them his countenance. I should keep him longer than any of the others," Finn said.

Arthur nodded. "Quite right, sire."

"The city needs him," Rafe said.

Finn waved a hand dismissively. "What for? The Civil Patrol can maintain order."

"There's more to running a city than patrolling the streets," Rafe said.

"Then let Arthur see to it," Finn said.

Arthur blinked a moment, then bowed his head. "If you wish me to, sire."

Leaning forward, Rafe narrowed his eyes at Arthur. "Since when are you a politician? You don't know any more about running a city than I do."

"No," Arthur conceded. "But I can learn. I serve at the king's pleasure."

"Quite right," Finn said, and drained his glass.

Rafe ran his tongue over his lips and tried again, "My point, sire, was that there are other, better prepared people to supervise the running of Caer Eisteddfod. Delaney Overton comes to mind. I need Arthur for other matters to which he is better suited." As he said this last bit, he shot Arthur a pointed look.

Arthur shrugged. "If the king needs me more urgently, I'm sure some of my underlings can assist you."

Rafe clenched his fingers into the padded arm of the chair. "That wasn't quite what I meant."

Finn stretched his legs further toward the fire and gave Rafe an indulgent look. "What exactly did you have in mind, dear boy?"

Ignoring the sting of the old affectionate term, Rafe cast about for something to say. "My brother," he said. "I haven't heard from him since Roger's party. None of my friends have mentioned him to me, and as far as I know he wasn't caught up in one of Arthur's sedition arrests." He looked over the rim of his glass at Arthur. "Unless he was and you forgot to tell me."

Arthur shook his head, a sympathetic smile on his face. "I certainly would have told you that."

"Forget about your brother, Rafe," Finn said. "No doubt he's skulking at Wellhall with your parents, as usual."

"Perhaps, sire." For lack of anything better to do, Rafe reached for the brandy bottle and refilled his snifter. "I had hoped better of him."

"Sometimes people disappoint us," Finn said, gazing into the fire.

"Yes, that is certainly true," Rafe agreed.

A silence settled over the room once more, the men sipping their brandy and watching the flames. Boredom grew, dulling Rafe's mind more than the brandy could. He wriggled his toes and checked his periphery, making a conscious note of what he saw to keep his mind from wandering. Same black granite mantelpiece. Carved wyvern andirons on either side the fire. A door just out of sight behind him, and one across from him on the other side of the fire. Finn, resting his chin on one hand, staring into the fire. A contented, homely look on Arthur's face that he recognized from evenings after a successful hunt. Rafe wriggled his toes again and wondered if Deor were asleep by now.

The door to the parlor opened, and Deor came in. "Do you mind if I join you all?" she asked. A sour look passed over Arthur's face.

"Not at all, my dear," Finn said. "I'll ring for a servant to get you a glass."

"Oh no, don't bother with that," Deor said. "It's just I've had an idea, and I thought I would see if you approved." She stood in front of him, her back to the flames and her hands folded together in front of her, as if she were a schoolgirl about to make a presentation.

Finn settled back in his chair, a benevolent smile on his face. "Say on."

"Thank you." She gave each of the men a smile in turn. "With the exception of one trip to the theater with Rodney and Clarissa, I've been out of the public eye ever since the events at Roger's. The press is starting to wonder where I am. If I'm not seen fairly soon, rumors will spread."

Finn nodded along as she spoke. Rafe regarded her over the rim of his glass, but Arthur leaned forward in his seat, eyes narrowed as he studied her. She ignored him, her eyes fixed on Finn. "I don't want to give any credence to these nasty rumors the Summer Court is spreading about me," she continued. "So, I thought, what if I gave a press conference this week? I could answer the press' questions and talk a bit about what I've learned since becoming Heir. Make myself visible and available, but not too available. I wouldn't be in any danger, as I was at Eisteddfod." She ended with another smile in Finn's direction.

"An excellent idea." Finn slapped the arm of his chair and stood. "Now you're beginning to think like a princess instead of a school marm. I'll have my Press Secretary set one up for tomorrow afternoon."

Deor held her smile as the king stood to kiss her on the forehead.

"Thank you, Your Majesty," she said. "Well, in that case, I should probably be getting to bed. I'll see you all at breakfast?" She smiled again at Arthur and Rafe in equal measure and padded softly out of the room.

Finn turned to Arthur and Rafe, his hand on his hip, and raised his glass. "Now we're getting somewhere. Rafe, I think you should attend the press conference with her. You can help her out if she gets into deep waters with the press or they become impudent."

"I think she can manage impudence all on her own, sire," Arthur said. Finn laughed and slapped him on the shoulder. Rafe re-buried his face in his glass, squeezing the short stem so tightly he feared it might break under his fingers.

"A toast," Finn said. "To the princess."

Rafe raised his glass along with the other two and allowed Finn to top up his glass for the third time.

Eventually, Finn stretched and yawned. "Well, gentlemen," he said. "I thank you for your companionship, but I must get to bed."

Both Rafe and Arthur rose, bowing. "Good night, sire." They watched the king leave the room before departing out the side door. Side-by-side they walked down the corridor to the portal that would take them to their own quarters.

As they reached the portal, Arthur slapped Rafe on the shoulder, and said, "We should do this more often."

Rafe turned to him, one eyebrow raised. "Should we? I should think you would have more self-respect than to spend time with some woman's pet." He stepped through the portal, away from the shock on Arthur's face and into the corridor leading to his own rooms.

Once alone in his home, Rafe's pace increased, his stride lengthening. He threw a quick salute to Stephen, who stood watch at the door to the apartments and closed the doors behind him.

The shared parlor was dark except for the fading embers of the fire. To his surprise, no furry bodies hurled themselves out of the dark to greet him. Pulling off his boots, he looked around. The door to his own rooms was closed, just as he had left it. But the door to Deor's rooms stood half open, a faint light shining from it.

Dumping his boots at the edge of the carpet and stripping off his uniform jacket, Rafe followed the light into Deor's bedroom. A single lamp burned on her nightstand. Three furry shapes encircled Deor in her bed. One raised his head and greeted Rafe with a muffled woof.

"Shhh, Jake." Rafe tiptoed closer to pat his dog on the head. "Stay, boy."

Deor turned over on her pillow, blinking. "How was it?"

"Excruciating," he said.

She patted the bed beside her and shoved Sam to one side. "You can tell me all about it in the morning."

Chapter Sixteen

Deor sat quietly at her vanity, three sets of jewelry in front of her. She had her dress laid out, a black one she had ordered from Wham! and Thorsen before going to Northfalls in case she had to do some sort of public appearance. Long-sleeved and falling nearly to the floor with a conservative neckline to boot, it was perfect for a press conference.

Melanie, her lady's maid, came out of her closet with two different pairs of boots. "These," she said holding one pair up, "are taller by about an inch, but they are probably less comfortable than these," she held up the other pair. "But you're only walking from here to the second balcony, and I don't think standing in either for an hour or so will hurt."

Deor studied them. "Let's go with the taller ones for the press photos." Rafe would be right there, standing behind her, giving his silent support. He'd offered to make a speech, too, but Deor had refused. While the Sword certainly should say *no* to the king, those were closed meeting refusals. A public statement needed to come from the Heir herself.

With the boots and appropriate stockings set out, Melanie returned to the vanity. "What about makeup and hair?"

"Makeup is easy," Deor said. "Plain, with nothing too attention-getting. Natural, I guess."

"I figured, majesty." Melanie pulled out a particular tray from the elaborate cosmetics case she had compiled for Deor. Most faerie women wore magic rather than actual makeup. But no matter how many times Deor and Melanie tried, it slid off. Especially if Deor was at all stressed. Her human side, though carefully tucked away beneath the faerie, rejected magic rapidly and ruthlessly. It was great for will spells attacking her, but when it came to things like makeup or getting jewels to stay in her hair, it was the human way or no way at all.

Deor smiled at the contents of Melanie's tray. The various foundations, blushes, eyeshadows, and so on would make a quiet, faerie version of the infamous smokey eye. Apparently, this had been all the rage in the Winter Court for so long it had moved from passé to dowager and on to the ultimate in conservative non-statement. The kind of stuff you wore to be taken seriously.

The jewelry, on the other hand, Deor had picked to make a statement. She had narrowed her choices to three crowns, two in the platinum the Aethelwings favored and one in a brilliant yellow gold. She ditched the yellow gold first. That left the other two. The first was not a full circle, but a partial ring, with branches formed in platinum wire and scattered with tiny diamonds like light reflecting off snow. In the center, a beautiful sapphire the size of the last joint of her thumb glittered, surrounded by petals made of platinum. She put that one aside, too.

The last crown was a favorite of Finn's mother. Melanie explained that the queen had used it when she was displeased with her audience or, on rare occasions, her husband. A full circle of platinum sprouted forty-seven pointed platinum bars inlaid with multiple diamonds, increasing in size around both half-circles to form a peak in the center two inches tall. Diamond spikes of increasing size were interspersed between the bars. The tiara was a crown of glittering sword blades and spikes. Perfect.

"This one," Deor said. She put on diamond stud earrings as Melanie curled her hair into long waves down her back then gathered the front of her hair and pinned it where the base of the crown would rest. Deor chose a thin, single-strand diamond choker for her necklace.

Melanie went about putting on Deor's makeup and then helped her into her dress, lacing the bodice up the back. She helped Deor with the boots. Finally, Deor took a seat again in front of the vanity and Melanie placed the crown on her head. Deor gasped at the glittering sight. She looked regal and felt so wrong—the inside did not match this woman in the mirror. That woman was fearless.

There was a knock at her door, and Rafe entered. He was in his Sword's uniform, wanting the Winter Court to see the office itself support the Princess.

Deor stood. "Ready?"

"Yes," he managed. "You look amazing." He smiled at her. "You look like a Queen."

"Princess," Deor corrected.

"I didn't misspeak." He offered her his arm and smiled.

Deor took it. Stephen joined them as they left the suite, dogs following along behind. Deor caught a glimpse of Boomie out of the corner of her eye, fluttering along, unseen to everyone but her and the dogs.

THE PALACE PRESS conference took place on the terrace overlooking the garden. The monarch at the edge of the terrace with the press looking up from below. The March sky was a brutal grey as late winter continued its grip with cold snow. A stiff, chill wind blew through the garden, catching Deor's hair so that it fluttered behind her like a flag. The crown had been secured twice, once with near invisible pins and again with magic. Both seemed to be holding.

Rafe kept hold of Deor's arm, and she stayed close as the Press Secretary announced the order of business, which was a single item: a statement from the princess. Deor squeezed Rafe's arm, happy to have him nearby, thrilled at the magic he used to keep them warm.

Next to her, Brand whined, and she knelt a bit to scratch his head. "It's okay, sweetie," she said. "This won't take long." Brand was smart, sweet, quick to learn, and eager to please, so, like his older packmates Jake and Sam, he didn't need a leash. Still, Deor had chosen to use a collar and a leash today. She wasn't sure why—or at least she didn't want to admit that once she had said what she had to say, the ensuing chaos might cause them to be separated.

She looked to Stephen, "Take him, please?" She handed him the leash.

Stephen nodded. "C'mon, Brand." He clicked his tongue, and the dog trotted along as he stepped out of sight of the crowd.

She gave one more glance at her dog and turned away, striding toward the podium where the Press Secretary was finishing his introduction with the very firm assertion that the princess would not be taking questions. A few steps to the side Arthur stood, as grim as though he were supervising an execution.

As Deor approached the podium, she recognized many of the faces in the crowd—press she had seen at the Adoption, at Roger's or at Parliament. None seemed openly hostile, though many looked impatient or tense. Deor stepped up to the podium and cleared her throat. A magic spell in front of her amplified her words. "Good morning," she said. "Thank you all for joining me today." The crowd murmured their responses and clutched a stylus over their mirror or held them out like microphones. "In the past few weeks, several members of the Loyal Sons of London, along with others who might support them, have been arrested and charged with varying levels of sedition. It is my understanding that they are agitating for better representation, both at the tournament and in Parliament, for non-noble and non-faerie citizens of the Winter Court."

A few of the reporters rolled their eyes—this was not news.

"I believe that it is very important for a nation and its people to work out problems together. We all want what is best for the Winter Court. Certainly violence, rioting, and threats to the king, to anyone, are not acceptable. The leaders of the group—at least those suspected of being the leaders, including Aiden Kirby, Holman Redfern, Lord Mayor of the City Delaney Overton Sr., and Roberta Gemmelsdottir Ellington are among the ones arrested some weeks ago. Others have been arrested and have joined them in the Tower.

"I do not need to remind any of you that the Tower of London is a legendary keeper of traitors. Even in the human world where magic is relegated to children's stories, the haunting and grim history of those stone walls is still spoken of in hushed and fearful tones. Treason and sedition are indeed the highest and gravest of crimes. Both in my capacity as the Heir to the throne of the Winter Court and as a citizen of my own human nation, I cannot condone either. Traitors seek destruction. The destruction of my land is something I cannot bear.

"I feel the nation beneath my feet. When my toes curl on the marble floors of the palace, my soul senses the bedrock below. When I ride the countryside, the magic of this land surrounds me. When I travel to the broken, suffering areas of this kingdom, my heart breaks as well. The Winter Court from the hearts of its people to the very center of its being longs for healing, for comfort, and for peace. My job as heir is to seek that peace."

Members of the press nodded along. Some even seemed moved by her words. She could simply stop there, and dismiss them, leaving them to write pleasant articles about the dutiful and loyal heir. She drew a deep breath.

"It is because I seek the peace and comfort of my people that I cannot condone the recent actions of my father, King Fionnleigh the Eighth. First, his ban on the werecreatures is cruel and unnecessary. Many families have been torn apart by the separation, and our nation is weaker for the loss. Second, these so-called seditious leaders are no such thing. In each of their hearts burns the same desire I have: to heal, to comfort, and to make us all better tomorrow than we are today. Treason is synonymous with destruction, and these loyal sons and daughters of this kingdom desire no such thing.

"The cries of the people are sacred. The monarchy would do well to remember that."

Deor trembled. Tears were forming in her eyes, and not from the stinging wind. As she spoke, she felt the living, breathing bodies of those in the Tower, and their suffering. "My heart and my voice go out to those wrongly charged with and imprisoned for treason. I demand that they be released, without prejudice and without record. Anything short of this is a failure of justice."

She scanned the crowd again. Those who had begun with bored expressions were nearly frozen in shock. Many were scribbling furiously on tablets, whispering frantically into their mirrors. "Thank you," she said, "for taking time to come hear me today." She gave a small bow and turned away from the podium, returning to Rafe's side. Out of the corner of her eye she saw Arthur glare at her and then hurry away, no doubt to the king.

"Come on," Deor said as she took Rafe's arm. "I imagine that the king wants to see us."

"I imagine so," Rafe said as he led her toward the palace. "You were perfect." He patted her hand. "This moment will go down in history."

"Good or bad," Deor said with a shrug, "I suppose you're right."

Chapter Seventeen

When Deor passed through the doorway from the terrace into the palace, she blinked in the darker room. As her vision cleared, she saw Arthur, furious.

"The king wants to see you both. Now. In his quarters." Arthur turned on his heel and marched away.

Deor glanced over her shoulder at Lt. Bolton. "Take Brand to my rooms, please."

"Jake and Sam too," Rafe added. "Follow Bolton, boys." He nodded to his dogs who reluctantly did as they were told.

"Yes, Your Majesty," Bolton nodded at Deor, "and sir," he nodded at Rafe. "I'll keep them safe." He turned and led the dogs away.

Deor pulled her arm free of Rafe's and clasped his hand, giving it a tight squeeze before letting go and following Arthur to the portal. They stepped through into the King's household, into the same parlor that Astarte had led her to after the Adoption. The same crackling fire, the same couch and chairs. Not the same emotional feel.

The tension was thick enough to feel along her skin. Not tension, Deor realized, but magic. The king was giving off a kind of residual magic that filled the room. One deep breath in and Deor trembled—will magic, whether intentional or not, coated her throat and burrowed into her mind. The king was angry, furious, and the only option was to fling herself at his feet and beg for mercy. Mercy she did not deserve.

Deor nearly snorted her derision but managed to stave it off. The whole thing reminded her of her faceoffs with Madeline. What was it about these people, these great practitioners of magic, that made them focus on making their prey feel small and weak? Madeline had first told her she was a good girl, and so to prove her wrong, Deor punched her in the face. Of course, at the time she hadn't known who the woman in the alley was, nor that she herself was the princess. Their next encounter was far less subtle as Madeline tried to will all of Parliament into rebelling against the king. Deor had none of that, either, and with a sword made of her own magic, she shredded the winding ropes of will spells that Madeline had created.

Now, here was Finn, his magic demeaning everyone around him. Deor's response? She wanted to scream at him, to curse him, to swear that she would never, ever succumb to such nonsense. He was the monster, he was the creature that deserved no mercy, not her.

He was facing the fireplace, his back to them—another gesture meant to minimize them. He would speak to them when he was ready, and they would wait as long as he wished.

Astarte sat on the couch, her face blank, eyes staring off into the distance. The mirror from above the fireplace lay broken on the hearth. A jagged pattern of cracks splintered out like lightning bolts from a hole in the center. A slit. Perfect for a magic-made knife. Right where Deor's own face must have been as she talked.

Deor looked to Rafe, whose expression showed deep concern. He stared at Astarte and suddenly moved as if to go to her. Arthur caught his arm and shook his head. Rafe jerked his arm away but did not move again. Finally, Finn turned around. His eyes were solid silver disks in his face, flat and non-reflective; they sucked light out of the room. He flicked his gaze from person to person, and though she was not looking at him, Astarte flinched when his eyes briefly settled on her.

Memories of the bruises on Astarte's arms made Deor flinch herself, a small jerk forward before she could stop herself. Anything to get his eyes off that poor woman.

Her movement worked. Finn's gaze snapped to her and remained there. She held it with a simple, expectant expression. Despite the thundering weight of his will—this was his home, his palace, his kingdom, after all— demanding that she crumple before him, she did not look away. The pressure grew. The ambient magic of his will had shifted, he was pushing it at her now, working to break her.

The faerie side of Deor trembled, shuddered, and her knees threatened to buckle, to collapse her into a groveling kneel on their own. A few silver sparkles spun away from her, a weak defense that fizzled into nothingness before making it halfway across the room. She was certain he could see her about to break when he smiled—a half smile, a quirk of one side of his mouth. It made him look cruel and wicked.

Inside Deor, the human part of her was clawing at her, trying to dig its way to the surface, even if that meant coming out through the skin. At first, she pushed it away, slamming down on it and keeping it from escaping, but she paused. In the alley and at Roger's, it was her humanity that saved her. Flickering between faerie and human had disrupted Madeline's magic. She had kept her human side hidden for weeks—mostly because it felt so much more natural to be a faerie in this place. She still felt the magic of the world on her skin, but it wasn't uncomfortable, unnatural, like it was when she was human.

Deor set free her human side, and it exploded to the surface. The will that had piled up on her, layer upon layer like coats of plaster, cracked and shattered. Now broken, it was visible. Fine, gossamer threads of silver magic, floating to the floor.

Finn gasped and staggered back, as if a rope in his hands finally snapped. His will had hooked to hers, hauling her mind toward his, and, like a clever fish, she had cut the line.

Around them, the rest of the people seemed to wake. They had been neither the recipient of the will spells, nor any kind of participant, simply a frozen audience. Deor wasn't certain whether they had witnessed the struggle or been lost to a void.

Now, though, Rafe caught her arm. "Are you okay?" he whispered.

"I'm fine." Deor focused on Finn. "So, is that it? I'm not bending on this, Finn. Not now. Not tomorrow. Not ever."

Finn's eyes flashed again, the dullness a veil for the will spell earlier. Now that his energy was no longer focused on controlling her, anger rolled off him in waves. "How dare you defy me! You promised you would not speak against me in public."

"I broke that promise," Deor admitted. "But I never should have made it. I didn't understand then what I do now. I must protect the Winter Court. Even if I'm protecting it from you."

Shock crossed Finn's face. "I know my nation! I protect it."

Deor shook her head. "No. You control it—or try to. People are hurting, and you do nothing to help them. You arrest Tess, Ian, and MacIntyre. You arrest Robbie and use that to torture your wife. You arrest Overton, an old man and the epitome of loyalty. You arrest children and workers, people with limited power. Worst of all, you lie to yourself. You aren't protecting anything but yourself, and you aren't acting out of anything but fear."

"So," he threw up his hands, "I'm a bad king. Is that it?"

"Yes," Deor said. She shook her head and relented a little. "You're not a bad person, Finn, but you have to stop acting badly."

"And you?" Finn glared at Rafe. "You stood there behind her, like you agreed with this nonsense."

"It's not nonsense," Rafe said, voice flat. "I do agree with her. You cannot keep arresting people for disagreeing with you, for speaking out against you. If nothing else, from a strategy standpoint, it makes you look weak." He looked at Deor and back at the king. "She looks strong for standing up to you. That's why people are rallying behind her."

"You," he pointed at Deor. "Are you amassing people against me?"

Deor's jaw dropped. "Of course not! I stood out there and made my statement alone. I'm not trying to turn anyone against you. Frankly, you don't need any help from me."

"You've turned my boy against me," he said and turned to Rafe, "hasn't she?"

"I am not your boy!" Rafe yelled. He drew a deep breath before continuing. "She hasn't turned me against you."

"Don't lie, Rafe," Arthur snapped, drawing everyone's attention. "Do not lie to the king."

"What are you talking about?" Rafe spun to face Arthur, lurking across the room.

Arthur stared at him for a moment. "Make a choice. You tell him or I will."

"Don't you dare," Rafe said.

"Dare tell me what?" Finn demanded. "Rafe, what have you done?"

"Your daughter," Arthur said before Rafe could speak.

Rafe closed his eyes and shook his head. When he opened them, he set his jaw. "Arthur, you—"

"Rafe, look at me!" The king demanded, and Rafe's head snapped to attention.

Deor winced but said nothing. Nothing she could say could make this better, and a lot could make it worse. The will magic Finn used on Rafe, and his compliance, made her want to scream. She wanted to leap in between them, make a sword, and keep Finn away from her lov—from her friend.

"Is Arthur saying you have been having sex with my daughter?"

"Yes," Rafe nodded. "That's what he's saying."

"Is it true?" For a moment the king seemed more baffled than angry. Deor wondered what exactly confused him. Was it Rafe would sleep with her, that he would want her, or that she would want him?

"Yes," Rafe said. "She and I are completely consenting adults. It certainly isn't treason. It isn't even illegal. The heir may do whatever she likes."

Finn went white with anger and turned on Deor. "You are sleeping with him?" he demanded.

"Yes."

"Finn...," Rafe warned.

"No!" Both Finn and Deor said at the same time. "Let him ask whatever he wants, Rafe." Deor added.

"You are sleeping with my Sword?" Finn demanded.

"Having sex with my friend, Rafe, yes." Deor confirmed, raising her chin in challenge. "And I will not stop until he and I wish it."

"See?" Arthur said, spreading his arms out in a pleading gesture to the king. "I told you that she was turning his head."

"How long have you known, Arthur?" Finn asked.

"Not long," Arthur said. "I was hoping Rafe would come to his senses, especially after we had drinks the other night. I thought he was starting to see things our way. I was wrong."

"Oh, for god's sake—" Deor had enough of the melodrama.

"Silence, daughter!" Finn yelled. The walls trembled.

Up in a corner of the room, Boomie appeared, hissing with his fangs bared. No one else saw him.

"Arthur, see Rafe to his quarters, where he will remain until I summon him."

"Yes, sir," Arthur said. He turned to Rafe and smirked. "I warned you."

Rafe said nothing.

"Monjoie!" Finn demanded.

"Yes, sir!" The soldier stepped forward from his position near Arthur, his eyes forward, hands behind his back, apparently looking at nothing.

"Take my daughter to my office," Finn said slowly, articulating every word. "I will deal with her there."

Rafe moved to intercept Monjoie. "If you lay one hand one her—"

"It's fine, Rafe," Deor interrupted him. She stepped toward Monjoie. "Let's go," she said. She threw a backward glance at Finn and gave Rafe a small smile. "I'll be fine."

"This way, Princess," Monjoie said, reaching for her arm.

"Don't," Deor said, remaining perfectly still. "Do not put hands on me."

Monjoie looked to the king, who nodded. "As my lady says," he said and bowed low after opening the door to the hallway.

"Thank you," Deor said and swept out of the room.

Chapter Eighteen

Deor walked ahead of Monjoie toward Finn's office, her head held high. At that moment she missed the cheerful bouncing of her dog at her feet, but she was grateful she had handed him over to Stephen for safekeeping. It might be a while before she saw Brand again.

Her boot heels clicked in rhythm on the floors, sending little shivering echoes along the polished black stone. Boomie swooped and pirouetted in the air ahead of her, casting worried glances over his shoulder. She longed to reach up and pluck the little gargoyle out of the air, tuck him onto her shoulder, but Monjoie was watching. All around her the Palace stones trembled with Boomie's anxiety.

"In here, Your Majesty." Monjoie opened one of the carved wooden doors that led into Finn's office. She passed through without so much as a glance at his face. Chairs stood in front of the massive oak desk, but Deor preferred to stand. She rested one hand lightly on the back of the chair, its cool leather and brass rivets comforting sensations under her fingertips. She forced herself to breathe slowly, calmly through her nose, remembering the bruises on Astarte's wrists. Whatever Finn had in mind for her, it would end.

Nothing lasts forever.

Monjoie took up his post at the door, feet wide and arms crossed over his chest as if to block any attempt at escape. Turning her back to him, Deor walked to the window and looked out.

Snow blanketed the gardens, broken only by the occasional evergreen bush wearing its own cap of white. In the distance, bare trees lifted their black branches against the pale grey sky. To her California-bred eyes, the trees appeared dead, ravaged by fire. She had to remind herself that the spring would bring back their green.

Time passed, measured by the beat of her heart. Neither she nor Monjoie spoke. From time to time, she glanced at his reflection in the window, checking that he had not moved from his place. She would not give him the satisfaction of looking him in the face. Inside her boots, she wiggled her toes, longing to take them off and sink down onto the comforting stone floor, to be grounded in the Palace's bedrock. Instead, she kept her upright posture, waiting. She allowed herself to rest one hand on the stone window frame, marble and porphyry.

Boomie watched her, crouched high in a corner of the room.

At last, the doors swung open. Monjoie stepped aside, saluting. Finn strode in, followed by an entire retinue of retainers and servants. So, there was to be an audience for whatever followed. Perhaps he would be less likely strike her where others were watching. Perhaps.

Astarte followed directly at Finn's heels. Behind them came more Houseboys, Asphodel the healer, and for some strange reason, her maid servant Melanie, carrying a dark bundle of cloth. Melanie was shivering and clutching the bundle to her chest. Her eyes widened, and her lips trembled as she met Deor's eyes.

Deor gave her a quick smile and turned to Finn. She schooled her face into careful blankness, neither defiant nor submissive, not angry nor afraid, only expectant. If she could maintain that look in the face of three hours of her dissertation committee's hostile grilling, she could maintain the look in the face of an angry king.

The look Finn gave her in turn was still furious as before, but the fury had simmered down into a collected, calculating rage. He motioned Monjoie toward him and handed the guard a scroll.

"Read aloud this," Finn said.

Monjoie cleared his throat and read, "Deor Aethelwing, daughter of Sweordmund Fionnliegh Aethelwing, 8th of his House, you have been found guilty of sedition and gross insubordination toward your father and monarch."

Deor quirked her mouth into a smile. "What, Finn? Verdict first, trial afterward? Will there be heart shaped tarts for tea?"

"Quiet!" Finn snapped at her.

Deor tilted her head in what might have been mistaken for a bow. Monjoie read on. "You are hereby sentenced, in accordance with the law, to be flogged. In consideration of the prisoner's stature, execution will be done upon her by the Shield to the Crown of the Winter Court. Sentence is to be carried out immediately."

A stifled sob broke from Melanie, who covered her mouth with the bundle in her arms.

Deor blinked a few times. "Are you serious?" She looked to Finn. "This is barbaric."

He crossed his arms and glared down at her. "Do you recant your recent actions?"

She pulled herself straighter. "Not one word."

"Proceed." Finn waved a hand to the retinue waiting around the edges of the room.

Asphodel, the red-haired healer who had tended to Deor after her encounter with the throne, came forward. She placed two fingers on Deor's throat over her jugular vein. Magic flowed from her, spreading down Deor's body inside and out. Deor braced herself for pain but felt only a slight tingle. Asphodel withdrew her fingers. Her mouth was set in a thin line, and worry creased her eyes as she looked into Deor's face.

"The princess is in fit health to be flogged," she said.

Deor snorted. Against her better judgment she said, "So, everyone must be whole before they're broken."

Asphodel withdrew to a place against the wall by Astarte. The two women said nothing to each other, but Asphodel stood very close to her lady.

One of the Houseboys gave Melanie a shove toward Deor. "You. Dress the prisoner."

Melanie stumbled forward, trembling visibly.

"I am not taking off my clothes in front of all these men and you," Deor said to Finn. He merely turned his head and nodded at Monjoie. One hand raised, Monjoie sent a screen of magic to encircle Deor and Melanie. It blurred the air around them so that the figures of the others in the room could be seen, but dimly as if through frosted glass. The screen extended from Deor's shoulders down.

Deor took a deep breath and lifted the crown off her head. She set it on the windowsill. She unfastened her diamond earrings and necklace and laid them inside the circle of her crown. Turning to Melanie, she held out her arms so the other woman could undo the elaborate buttons of her dress.

Melanie's fingers slipped and fumbled as she worked. "I'm so, so sorry, Your Majesty," she whispered, her voice choking. "Please forgive me."

Deor turned and seized her maid's fingers. She bent her head, whispering back. "It's not your fault. There's nothing you can do to stop this. Don't make any silly gestures that will get you hurt."

Tears pouring down her face, Melanie nodded and continued stripping Deor's clothes. When Deor finally stood fully naked, her long hair tumbling down around her face and shoulders, a chill breeze blew across her body, and she shivered involuntarily. She took a deeper breath and steeled herself, willing herself not to shiver despite the goosebumps that prickled across her skin.

"Please, Your Majesty," Melanie choked out. "Put out your arms."

Deor complied, and Melanie slipped a white shift over Deor's arms and fastened it in the back at her neck. Still feeling a breeze, Deor turned her head to look over her shoulder. The shift lay open, leaving her back and upper buttocks fully exposed. Only the sleeves, from shoulder to wrist, and the garment's hips held it in place on her body.

"How...clever," Deor said. She looked around the room, scanning the faces of those who watched. The soldiers were, for the most part, carefully blank, their gaze fixed on some invisible spot a hundred yards away. Asphodel glared at the floor, clenching and unclenching her fists at her side. Beside her, Astarte never took her eyes off Deor, her golden skinned face schooled into a look of grief and resolve. Tears streamed unchecked down her cheeks.

Settling a warm garment somewhere between a dress and a cloak over Deor's shoulders and wrapping her snugly in it, Melanie whispered, "At least this will keep you warm until you get there." Deor squeezed her fingers and tried to give her a smile.

Melanie turned to the king, unable to look him in the eye. "I'm done, sire."

Finn nodded, and Monjoie swept the privacy screen away. He stepped aside, bowing to the king.

Finn signaled to Monjoie and another Houseboy. "Escort the prisoner."

The two men fell into step beside Deor, putting out their hands to take her by the elbows. She stepped forward before they could do so and fell into step behind Finn, not turning her head to the right or left.

Chapter Nineteen

Rafe paced in his parlor, whipping back and forth in front of the fire. He had already flung his jacket onto the couch and rolled up the sleeves of his starched shirt. Splinters of ice flew off his body, some landing in the fire and steaming. The dogs were shut up in his bedroom with Brand where the splinters couldn't hurt them.

Finally, the door opened, and he spun to face who he hoped would be Deor.

It was Arthur.

"Come on," he said. "Put your Coat of Office back on. Now."

"Where?" Rafe grabbed his jacket from the couch and caught up with Arthur before he made it out of the room. He grabbed Arthur by the arm and spun him around, slamming him into the door. "Where are we going?" He held Arthur's shoulders.

Arthur planted his palms on Rafe's chest and shoved back. "The king needs the Sword of Office," he said. "That's all you need to know."

"No." Rafe stepped away. "Go if you like, but I am not moving until you tell me what is going on."

Arthur glared at him like he would slap him. Finally, his face cleared, a calm neutral expression. "The king sees fit to punish his seditious daughter and would do so in front of the Sword and Shield, as is customary."

Rafe tossed his jacket on the sofa. He wasn't going anywhere without an explanation. "What do you mean punish?" A pit formed in Rafe's stomach. He had found himself on the wrong end of Finn's punishment a few times in his youth. The memories could still make the flesh on his back and legs crawl with remembered pain and humiliation. The last time, the worst of it, in his twenties when Finn had taken off his belt and beaten Rafe until he wept despite himself, and Astarte had begged Finn to stop.

But none of it had ever been public.

"She is to be flogged." Arthur said as if it was nothing. "Ten lashes."

"What?" Rafe lunged for the door. He had to find the king, convince him not to do this.

Arthur snagged his arm, and in a deft little move they had practiced together when they were soldiers, he flung Rafe to the floor, sending him sprawling onto his stomach. Arthur put one foot on either side of Rafe and dropped onto his knees, planting one in the center of Rafe's back. From the bedroom, Jake and Sam began barking.

Rafe's breath left him, and he gasped. To Arthur's credit, such a move could damage kidneys or break ribs, and Rafe didn't feel nearly enough pain for either of those. Arthur grabbed a handful of Rafe's hair near the skull, turned his head to the side, and slammed it into the floor. Again, hard enough to hurt, a lot, but not enough to do damage, though Rafe might have a bruise in the morning.

"Listen carefully," Arthur leaned forward and hissed in Rafe's ear, "because I'm only going to tell you this once. The king has charged his daughter with sedition. Nothing will change this. Nothing will move him away from his course. Frankly, she deserves even worse for her little public performance."

"Dammit, Arthur!" Rafe shoved his palms into the floor and heaved up, trying to dislodge Arthur. Jake's barking turned to a roar, and the bedroom doors shook as the dog flung himself against them. Arthur spoke a word and the bedroom door's lock clicked.

Arthur let go of Rafe's head and snatched both of his arms above the elbow and hauled them backwards, jerking Rafe's body back in a painful arc. Arthur slammed him forward again, and Rafe barely turned his face aside in time to avoid a broken nose. Arthur shifted, putting both knees on Rafe's back.

Rafe grunted. There were ways to dislodge Arthur, but any would escalate the violence, and that wouldn't get him any closer to stopping Finn. He doubted the king would have the patience to wait. He relaxed the muscles in his arms and waited.

"There you go." Arthur eased back a bit. "The king wants his Sword present at the flogging. Go down to the armory. Your squire is there waiting with a clean uniform, as I suspected this might happen. We wouldn't want you to appear rumpled." He let go of one of Rafe's arms and patted him on the shoulder. "If I let you up, are you going to behave, or do I need to have Houseboys escort you?"

"I'm fine," Rafe said.

"Right." Arthur hauled himself off Rafe's back and stood.

Rafe flipped around to see Arthur's hand extended. Refusing it would be petulant. So, he reached out, clasped Arthur's hand by the wrist, letting Arthur haul him to his feet.

Arthur jerked Rafe forward into a hug and spoke low in his ear, "I'm telling you this as a friend, both of you and the princess. If you so much as twitch while she is getting her due, Finn will add blows. She's small, Rafe, it won't take long for the flogger to run out of real estate, and that's when permanent damage can occur."

Rafe shoved Arthur away from him, eyes prickling. "I understand," he said softly. "I give my word." His mouth was dry, and he wanted more than anything to punch that smug look off Arthur's face. "We've known each other a long time, Arthur," he said. "You know I keep my word."

"Good." Arthur nodded and let go of Rafe's hand, "Let's go."

"I'll follow," he said. When Arthur raised an eyebrow, he gestured at his bedroom door. "I want to check on the dogs first."

Arthur rolled his eyes. "Don't dawdle," he said, and left.

Rafe waited for the door to close before heading for his room. He undid the magic holding the lock shut and swung open the door. Jake and Sam flung themselves at him, whining and sniffing while Brand ran in frantic circles barking and yelping.

"It's alright, boys," he said, ruffling their heads. "I'm not hurt." Sam leaned his massive paws on Rafe's chest and licked his cheek, whining, his liquid brown eyes full of worry. "Stay here and take care of the youngster," Rafe told them. "I'll be back soon."

As he jogged out of the apartment toward the nearest portal, he took his mirror out. "Stephen, where are you?" he hissed.

"On my way to the Tower. Monjoie just informed me I've been relieved of my bodyguard position with the princess and sent back to the Tower. Smug bastard. I assume it's because the captain thinks I'm too loyal to the princess."

Rafe swore. "I'm telling you that you're still her guard, regardless of whatever those fools say. She'll need you. Don't draw attention to yourself or say anything until then."

"Aye, sir." Stephen's Cornish accent broadened into what Rafe realized was his country bumpkin persona. He wondered who might have come into the room. "You'll not hear a peep out of me. I know my duty, sir." The mirror went blank.

Time was passing. Too much time. As he leaped through the portal, Rafe shuddered with rage and horror at what was to come. He let a blast of cold magic fly off him, sending shards of ice in a fountain around him. Might as well get them out now.

As he made his way from the Household to the armory, he couldn't get the image of Arthur's smug smile out of his mind. He knew his best friend had skill, and even a talent, for interrogation, but he hadn't let himself believe that Arthur would ever enjoy punishment. Perhaps Arthur really did believe this was justice? No. It wasn't justice Arthur loved, it was order. He was right about Deor—she was a force of chaos. And Finn was warping the law, bending it, to break her.

Rafe snorted as he arrived at the doors to the armory and pushed them inwards.

Deor would never capitulate to bullying. Whatever effect this event had on her, Rafe was certain it would not chill her resolve.

When he arrived at his stall, Gordie was already there. Rafe's fresh uniform was hanging on the rack, and his sash of office was there as well.

"Well done, Gordie," Rafe said, forcing a smile.

"Thank you, sir." The kid's voice cracked as he spoke—that hadn't happened in awhile. No wonder, though. His normally ruddy olive complexion was washed out. He looked like he might be sick at any moment.

"You've heard what we're about to see?" Rafe stripped off his rumpled shirt and began buttoning the new one as fast as he could.

"Yes, sir." Gordie bent to polish Rafe's boots. "I will perform my duties and stand at your right hand, sir."

"Of course, you will, lad." He jutted his chin at the uniform jacket, with its eight-pointed star brooch that would hold his sash in place. "Let's get this finery on. We do not want to keep the king waiting."

Gordie nodded and took the jacket from the hanger. As Rafe turned his back to the boy, Gordie slid the jacket up his shoulders and on. Rafe buttoned it while Gordie got his sash. Gordie draped it over Rafe's head and over one arm so that it hung across his body from his right shoulder to his left hip. Once he had affixed the pin, Gordie stepped back, allowing Rafe to see himself in the mirror.

"Right," Rafe said, drawing on his black gloves. "Let's go get that behemoth sword out of its case."

The Sword of Peace and Justice—the actual sword—was primarily used for pomp and circumstance, not actual violence. It was technically a broadsword but too big for even one as tall as Rafe to wield in battle. It was the perfect size, though, for intimidation and, according to history, quite good at separating traitors' heads from their shoulders.

Rafe drew it from the case in which it stood, its tip resting on a small piece of black velvet and its pommel supported from above by two platinum cords. He took it out and turned to Gordie, who had put on gloves of his own. Rafe laid the sword across Gordie's open palms.

"Are you ready?" Rafe asked.

"Yes, sir." Gordie licked his lips and looked like he might faint.

Rafe put a hand on his shoulder. "This will be every bit as awful as you expect. But you must do your duty, for the princess's sake. Stand firm. Don't flinch. Don't even twitch a muscle. Any distraction you provide will only make things worse for the princess." He couldn't manage a smile, but he gripped the lad's shoulder more tightly. "She'll be furious if you were to get in trouble on her behalf."

Gordie gulped hard and nodded.

"Come on." Rafe led the way to the portal that would take them to the Tower Green. Before laying his hand on the doorway, he offered a final piece of advice. "Don't watch, if you can help it. You already know how to fix your eyes on nothing. I recommend it. And, if you can, let your mind go somewhere else."

Gordie nodded. "Thank you, sir."

"Onward then." Rafe said and tapped the portal to open it. He gestured Gordie to precede him. Even with his thoughts fixed on Deor, Rafe's heart broke a bit for Gordie too.

Despite what he had told Gordie, Rafe knew the young man would never be able to forget what was about to happen—the slap of the flogger on flesh, the involuntary cries, the blood. No matter how devoted the young squire might remain to his king, he would know, deep inside, that this was unjust, and he would carry that with him forever.

Rafe knew, too, that he would not be taking his own advice. He would not find someplace else to look, to let his mind wander. If he could not stop the cruelty, he would bear witness, and sear into his memory every indignity, every stroke, every drop of blood. Someday, he would have a reckoning, and the king and his flunkies would pay in full.

Chapter Twenty

The entire party walked after Finn, following the king down the long corridors of the Palace. As Finn led the way, a distressed Boomie buzzed and dive-bombed his head, skimming within a razor's width of the king's face but never quite connecting. The little gargoyle jibbered frantically at the king, darting between him and Deor. Finn gave no indication he could see or hear it. Under her bare feet, the Palace floors softened and rippled as if to ease her path the only way they could. Deor wished she could put out a hand and pat the walls of the building, but her guards on either side prevented her.

It was only when they passed through a portal to the Tower that Deor realized they were headed for the Green. At last, they emerged into the thin March light. An even larger crowd of reporters stood clustered together at the edge of the grass, their handheld mirrors raised high to catch sight of the parade as it made its way across the grounds. Around the perimeter, full length mirrors stood ready to catch every detail of what was about to occur.

In the center of the Green was a wooden frame like two letter As leaning together. Shackles hung at the peak and the base of the frame. Next to it stood a small table on which lay a long, split cane and a pair of scissors. Fizzing sparks of magic spat off Deor despite her best efforts to control them. Her nails lengthened and grew silver as her heart beat harder.

The king and his retinue took up their places beside the whipping frame, Finn closest to it, with Astarte at his side. Her tears were dry now, and she stared straight ahead.

On the other side of the frame waited another noble crowd. Deor spotted the younger Delaney Overton, the Speaker of Parliament, and Rodney, Roger's nephew and his paramour Clarissa. Rafe, his blue face paled nearly to grey with fury, stood at full attention in the very front of the crowd, still in his uniform of office, the great Sword of State clasped upright before him. Gordie, his eyes bulging, stood just behind Rafe's elbow.

Beside Rafe stood Arthur, holding the Shield of State, the full-sized replica of the carving Deor had seen on the Shield's book in the library. A diamond glittered in the center of the white eight-pointed star that covered the glossy black shield. Over his uniform, Arthur wore the same sash of office that Michael had worn. So, this was the Shield who would carry out her punishment.

Her two guards led Deor to stand in front of the wooden frame. "Face the crowd," Monjoie told her.

At the king's signal, Arthur handed his shield of office to a nearby squire and stepped forward to take the scroll from Monjoie. In a loud voice, he read her sentence to the waiting crowd. Gasps went up from the reporters.

Turning to Deor, Arthur said in a loud, carrying voice, "Do you recant your seditious actions and ask your sovereign for mercy?"

Deor turned her head to look directly at Finn. "I do not."

Finn gave Arthur a nod.

"Prepare the prisoner for punishment," Arthur said. At once, the two guards on either side of Deor seized her outer garment and ripped it off her body. The cloth tore with a long shredding sound and fell into puddles at her feet. A gasp went up from the crowd. A bitter east wind blew straight up Deor's shift and she shivered in spite of herself. Silver sparks poured off her.

Methodically, Arthur stripped off his sash and uniform jacket, then his shirt, leaving him in just his pants and boots. His face calm, intent on his work, he approached the small table. He pulled on the leather gauntlet. It fit smoothly, covering his arm up to the elbow. Then he took the scissors and approached Deor.

Against her will, her eyes widened as he raised the scissors. With quick, methodical strokes, he cut off her hair just below the ears. There was no unnecessary pulling or ripping, just the silent fall of her locks to the ground.

"Keep your wings in, if you know what is good for you," Arthur said. He replaced the scissors on the table and took up the cane.

The guards held Deor by the wrists and turned her around to face the frame. In her back, Deor's wings jumped and twitched, ready to burst out silver-sharp to slash at her enemies. She clenched her muscles and willed her wings to stay where they were. As the guards pushed her against the frame, magic poured over her, suppressing her own magic. Her nails shrank back to their usual shape and size. Her defensive sparkles stopped. Through her feet, Deor could still feel the magic of the Palace, but her own magic was dampened, held down by spells woven into the shackles.

With straps of leather lined with iron, the guards bound Deor's hands above her head and fastened her ankles to the frame's base. Out of the edge of her sight, Arthur lifted the cane and snapped it through the air, a cracking sound that resounded off the Palace walls. Deor's breath came shorter and faster. Her back cringed.

Pain is temporary, she told herself. *It's not going to last.* She pressed her tongue tight against the back of her teeth, and clamped her mouth shut.

"The prisoner will receive ten lashes," Arthur announced. More gasps and murmurs went up from the reporters.

One brave soul shouted, "Too much!"

In the corner of Deor's vision, Finn raised his hand. "Proceed."

Deor shut her eyes. For a split second her mind threw her back to childhood, a visit to the doctor's office, a nurse saying, "Just a little pinch."

Just a little pinch, Deor told herself, though she knew it was a lie.

"One," Monjoie said.

The cane whistled through the air. Crack. Heat spread across her lower back, then sharp pain as her skin split. Air rushed out of her lungs, but she did not scream.

"Two," Monjoie called out.

Again, the whistle, the crack, and the pain. This time the blow landed just above the first. The pain spread outward to all her limbs. Deor panted and dug her nails into her palms.

"Three." Monjoie's voice reverberated.

The third blow fell. A faint, high pitched groan escaped Deor's throat. She held her breath and clenched her eyes shut. "A third done. Only seven more to go," she told herself. Tears forced themselves out from under her eyelids.

"Four." The cane landed again, working its way up her back.

Her whole body was on fire. The pain radiated it ways through every vein in her body. She sagged, her knees giving cut, thighs shaking despite her best efforts.

"Don't scream. Don't scream," she repeated over and over to herself.

More blows fell across her back, each one perfectly aimed, splitting her skin straight across from side to side. The crossbar of the A dug into her hips as she sagged against it, her breath ragged. She could no longer tell where one cut began and the next left off. Warm blood trickled down her buttocks and over her thighs. It ran down around to her front, sticking the thin shift to her body. Wind whipped across her legs, freezing her so that every inch of her skin burned.

"Ten."

The last blow landed. Deor's head hung down between her arms, too heavy for her to lift it. She tried to rouse herself, to pull back up to her feet, but all her limbs shook with pain and cold. Tears and snot froze on her face.

Finn was saying something to the crowd, but she couldn't make it out through the throbbing pain. More blood trickled down one leg to her ankle. She looked down. Three drops of red dotted the grass at her feet. Rough hands unshackled her. Holding her by the upper arms, the guards held her upright and forced her to face the silent crowd.

Deor raised her head, fighting to focus. A sea of wide-eyed faces and upheld mirrors shone before her. Her head drooped again. Finn was still talking. Why must he still be talking?

She caught "...to the Tower..."

Asphodel approached her and laid her hands on Deor's back. Deor hissed as the healer drew her hands slowly down over her raw and bleeding flesh.

"This will stop the bleeding," Asphodel whispered. "I know it hurts now, but you'll be all better in a day or two."

The guards led her away. Down through the parting crowd they led her, still barefoot, over the snowy pathway. Her feet stung and throbbed with cold. Her toes were already numb. A slow drop of blood traced the same path as before down her thigh, around her knee, and over her shin.

An open carriage waited for her, the king's own royal conveyance with his insignia emblazoned on the door.

"What," Deor rasped, her voice as dry, "No tumbril cart?"

Monjoie and the other guard ushered her into the carriage and seated her gently on the wide, padded bench. Ahead of her the driver chirped to the horses and with a jerk that slammed her wounds into the seatback, they began a tour around the Market, to demonstrate to the people the cost of sedition.

Chapter Twenty-One

Incandescent rage glowed deep inside Rafe as Deor was led away. Red smeared her back and streaked the white linen of her shift. Every fiber of his body urged him to heft the sword of office in both hands and cut down the two men dragging her past the crowd toward the waiting carriage. The muscles of his own back ached in sympathy with the pain she must be in. Never in Rafe's lifetime had Finn served Rafe as he had just done with Deor. Crystals of ice grew outward from his hands, creeping down the sword's hilt and onto its blade.

The reporters followed after the carriage, hand mirrors outstretched, but eerily silent. No shouted questions followed the princess. She sat upright in the carriage, dead pale, swaying a little. With a whip crack that sent a flinch through the crowd, the carriage moved off.

The party on the Green held still, statues frozen in place until the king's command might release them. At Rafe's elbow, Gordie sniffed in short, jerky gasps as the youngster tried with all his might not to blubber.

Finn stepped forward, his hand raised. "My Shield, my Sword, and my Consort will attend me in my chambers. All the rest may go about their business." He turned to go, and the group unfroze. Arthur stripped off his gauntlet and reached for his shirt, a workman putting away his tools for the day. Soldiers dismantled the whipping frame.

Rafe took his first deep breath since Deor had appeared. Turning to Gordie, he saw streaks on the young man's face. There was no time for comfort, no space to say what he might have said without so many watching eyes. He pressed the sword of office into his squire's hands. Fighting past his own anger, he said as gently as he could, "Put this away for me, would you? And when you are done, would you look in on my dogs in the kennel? It's been far too long since I went and saw to them. You might take the pack for a long run in one of the fields." Of course, the kennel master had plenty of helpers to keep the pack in good trim, but he would make no objections if the Sword's squire arrived with special orders. And if any tears fell into their thick dark coats in the process, well, dogs were excellent secret keepers.

"Yes, sir." Gordie's eyes brimmed. He cast a glance past Rafe in the direction Deor had gone. "I wish it had been me, sir."

Rafe gave a quick shake of his head. "If anyone, it should have been me. Go on now."

The lad gave Rafe a look of pure hero worship and hurried off with the sword. Rafe flexed his fingers at his side, trying to release the tension. If only the boy knew how little Rafe deserved his admiration.

No time for brooding now, though.

The king could not be kept waiting.

When Rafe arrived in the king's parlor, Astarte and Arthur were already there, Arthur standing at ease next to Astarte, who sat on a settee, her hands folded in her lap. Rafe stopped just inside the door to spare Astarte the cold he knew was pouring off him, and to make it easier not to put his hands around Arthur's neck. Finn stood facing a window, hands clasped behind his back.

"I'm here, sire," Rafe said.

Finn turned toward them, looking intently at each of their faces before he spoke. "I realize that my long illness has had a deleterious effect on the kingdom. Matters to which I should have attended have escaped my attention. Discipline has become lax. Lines of duty and loyalty have become blurred."

Astarte licked her lips. "No one in this room is disloyal to you, Finn."

"I hope that is true, my love," Finn said. "But I think there are some who have forgotten their places." He looked at Rafe.

Rafe returned his look without flinching. "As your Sword it is my duty to guard the kingdom against all threats."

"And was it your duty to be led about by your cock?" Finn shouted. "To be blinded by a pair of pretty eyes and a saucy tongue?"

As Finn spoke an image of Deor laughing and tossing a pillow at him flashed into Rafe's mind. Deor standing firm before the rack and the cane, refusing to ask for mercy. He would follow that woman to the ends of the earth.

"You have no idea what you are doing, Finn," Rafe said. "You are leading this country to rack and ruin. Your own people are suffering because of you."

Finn strode toward Rafe, a hand raised, but before he could reach Rafe, Astarte rose from her seat. "Please, Finn. He's overwrought. He doesn't know what he's saying." She placed a hand on Finn's chest. "We're all upset at what happened today, you most of all. You… I know how much Deor's behavior has wounded you. She's cut you to the quick. But don't take it out on your son." Astarte turned toward Rafe, her hand still on Finn's chest. "Rafe, apologize to your father. Immediately."

Her tone rang with power, a remembrance that she, too, came from a line of kings and queens, and her eyes glinted with golden light.

"Mother, I…" Rafe started to protest that he meant every word he had said, and Finn could tie him in the public square and flog him from morning to night, but he would not change his mind, but Astarte's look caught him up short. It was a sharp, commanding look, a look that clearly said, "don't be a fool." She mouthed the word "Robbie," at him and realization crept in, pushing back the edges of Rafe's defiance. The more he dared, the worse it would be for others less able to defend themselves. Any show of bravado in this moment was selfish pride, not courage.

He swallowed hard and said, "I apologize, sire. I spoke out of turn."

Finn's hand lowered. He nodded his head. "You did indeed. I am glad to see my Consort can still bring you to listen to reason."

Forcing himself, Rafe bent his neck. "I will do better, sire."

"Indeed, you will. From now on you will restrict your activities to those within the scope of your duties. The Civil Patrol is the purview of the Shield, not the Sword, and the Tower falls under his jurisdiction. You are not to go there, save on my orders, and you are not to meddle with civil matters, such as the prisoners within the Tower. Do I make myself clear?"

His eyes still on the carpet, Rafe said, "Yes, sire. Perfectly clear."

"Excellent." Finn took Astarte's hand. "It's time things returned to normal around here. Arthur, Rafe, you may go. I will see the two of you again at supper. Come, Astarte." Kissing Astarte's hand, Finn led her from the room.

For a split second, Rafe's knees buckled. He steadied himself against a chair back, his loose hair falling about his face. Ice crystals froze on his hair and lashes.

"I know this is a sharp lesson," Arthur said. "But once everyone has found their place, once things are settled and calm again, it will be better. You'll see."

Rafe looked up in amazement at his friend. "I suppose next you'll tell me it hurt *him* more than it hurt *her*," he said.

A wry smile quirked one corner of Arthur's face. "I wouldn't go that far. But she'll recover. I'll make sure the Tower healer looks in on her tonight just to be doubly sure. And someday, when she's Queen, she'll understand. The king can't let the Heir of all people go about undermining his reign. It would be chaos. Give her some time to reflect and cool her heels, and she'll understand her duties better. You might want to do a bit of reflecting yourself while she's in there."

Rafe gave Arthur a slow nod and shut his open mouth. "I'll take that under consideration, oh, Shield of the Realm. Thank you for your insight."

Arthur spread his hands. "I would have told you the king had invested me with the office, but he wanted it kept quiet."

Drawing himself up, Rafe tried and failed to force an understanding smile onto his face. The best he could do was to draw back some of the cold that poured off him. "Of course. You couldn't disobey the king. Do excuse me. There are some hours between now and dinner. I think I shall go reflect on my duties."

Rafe turned on his heel and left the room. It took all his self-discipline not to make an obscene gesture in Arthur's direction as he went.

His first impulse on leaving the king's parlor was to go for a long run. Running would clear his head and ease the furious tension in all his muscles. But when he got to his apartments, he found Melanie seated on the parlor couch, sobbing. A half circle of three dogs stood guard around her, whining and thumping their tails on the floor.

At the sight of him, Melanie scrambled to her feet, mopping her face with a sodden handkerchief. Rafe waived off her apologies and handed her his own handkerchief, which only made her sob harder. All three dogs looked to him expectantly.

"It will be alright," he said.

Melanie muffled her face in the handkerchief, shoulders shaking.

"We can't sit around feeling sorry," Rafe said, as much to himself as to the hapless maid. "We have to do what we can."

"What can we possibly do, sir?" Melanie choked out.

"Pack something for her," Rafe said. "Clothes, warm ones. She'll need something to put on once her back is healed." He looked around the parlor, searching for ideas. "And books. She always wants her books. Pack her something interesting to read. And pack Brand up too. Whatever he needs —bowl, leash. Send it all to Lt. Stephen Bolton of the Tower Guard."

Melanie lifted her head. "Yes, sir. And what are you going to do, sir?"

"I'm…" Rafe looked around the room again, taking in the shelves full of romances, histories, and law. An idea struck him. Perhaps Arthur was not entirely wrong. He would follow in Deor's footsteps. "I'm going to the library. Jake, Sam, come on. No, Brand, you stay." He left Melanie behind, staring after him.

As the idea grew in him, Rafe's pace quickened. He practically leaped through the portal from his quarters to the floor where the library was, barely holding the portal open long enough for his dogs to follow.

Once in the library, he put out his wings and kicked off from the ground, shunning the stairs to fly up to the alcove where the five podiums stood. As he placed his hands on either side of the podium bearing an etched sword, a book appeared. He sighed and opened it. Finn had brought him here the day after his investiture as Sword and showed him the book, but truth be told he had spent little time up here since. Too busy doing the job to read about it, he had thought.

Now he opened the smooth leather cover and scanned the chapter headings. He opened to the first page, rereading the chapter titled The Commission of a Sword.

It is the duty of the Sword to protect the kingdom, monarch, and royal family from threats abroad, the text read. So, the ongoing threat of the Summer Court was his job, whether Finn agreed with him or not. He read on. *A wise Sword will not stint in his efforts on behalf of the kingdom, always bearing in mind that it is no part of his duty to participate in factions, nor to amass power to himself. He will lead the armies in times of war, but he will hone his sharpness in times of peace. He will not seek out war but do his utmost to prevent warfare from breaking out. It is a false and foolish Sword who seeks out glory for himself on the battlefield at the expense of the people's lives.*

A true Sword is no mere weapon in the hands of the king. He owes his sovereign his loyalty, even his very life, but moreover he owes his sovereign wisdom. It is the duty of Sword to know what threats stand upon the kingdom's borders and to warn the monarch in due time. If the ruler will not be warned, or if the other members of the monarch's council be unwise, then the Sword must still do all he may within the scope of his power to protect them and the rest of the kingdom, for they are his sacred charge.

The words of the commission running through his head, Rafe flipped the book's pages, scanning for the names of Swords past. Some he remembered from his history lessons. Others were less familiar to him. He paused on one history, a shorter chapter than some others, from the time of Finn's great-great-great-grandfather.

And then Lady Brocca contained her wrath against the King, for she saw he was besotted with ill council and would not hear reason. She sought no more to say the king nay, but always to win his trust so that she might do as she list. For she did not cease from striving after the kingdom's good. She sought alliance from whom she could and practiced deep magics in secret, even while great with child, so that when the dwarves broke out against the Winter Court, they found the kingdom's defenses far stronger than they had surmised.

When Lady Brocca came to be delivered of her child, she left the babe in the care of a keeper of the king's White Kine, for her armies were in the field and she would not wait, not even to name her child. And so, the keeper named the child Brigid and fed her on the milk of a white kine with red ears. In the meanwhile, Lady Brocca poured out her hoarded wrath on the kingdom's enemies.

As Rafe read, he idly ruffled the hair around Jake's head and ears. The dog leaned his shoulder against Rafe's thigh.

"Lady Brocca," Rafe said. "I bow to your superior example." He placed the red silk bookmark so that he could return to his predecessor's story.

Whistling to his dogs, Rafe headed for the nearest exterior portal. He had two hours until he needed to dress for supper. Time enough to pour out some of his own hoarded wrath on the practice fields.

Chapter Twenty-Two

The slow progression around the Market and back to the Tower reminded Deor of the Rose Parade floats she had watched on TV with her grandmother. Should she wave? Crowds lined the route. Like during the flogging itself, they were silent. Thankfully, none threw rotten fruit or rocks, but the eerie silence made her feel utterly alone, trapped in a silent bubble.

A stream of upturned faces went by, a blur through the tears that Deor couldn't stop trailing down her cheeks. She wasn't crying—at least not in any way she ever had before. If she had she didn't remember—her body seemed to be doing it on its own.

Perhaps that was because she was empty.

Pain throbbed through her body, but even that was distant.

A gaping hole seemed to be all that remained of her chest. Her breath came in ragged gasps, the kind that shook her whole form.

The emptiness, the weariness, the exhaustion that overcame her were familiar, though distant. In the hours after her mother had died, Deor had sobbed. Sobbed until there were no more tears. When she had worn herself out, she had felt this way, shaky and lost. She shivered, but not from the cold. The sky was grey and bleak, and the only color she really saw was the red of the trickles of blood running down her legs.

The Tower loomed over her as she passed again through the main gates and into the empty courtyard. Two ravens sat on the green, staring at her.

"Princess?" A voice drew her attention.

Deor focused on the person opening the cart's door. He looked up at her expectantly. "Stephen," she said.

He offered her his hand. "Let me help you down."

Behind him Monjoie frowned and glared directly at her. The rest of the household guard had found other places to look.

Deor took Stephen's hand and rose. When she lifted her foot to take the first step, her other leg gave and she fell. Deftly, Stephen caught her by the hip, avoiding her cuts, and swung her down, setting her gingerly on her feet. "Are you steady?" he asked softly, not letting go of her.

Deor eased weight onto her legs and then nodded. "Yes, I think so." She held her head up high and scanned around her. When Stephen let go, her knees buckled again.

Stephen caught her and swept her up into his arms. "I'm sorry," he said. "This hurts your back, I know."

"My pride more," Deor said. "But thank you."

"The prisoner is to move of her own volition!" Monjoie snapped. "If she cannot walk, she can sit here until she is able."

"Is that straight from the king's mouth?" Stephen said. When he didn't respond, Stephen sneered. "I didn't think so." Holding Deor, he headed for one of the main buildings of the Tower. He touched the portal and stepped through.

They were in a small anteroom. If she hadn't known they were still in the Tower—its stones still ringing beneath her—she'd have thought they had stepped into the entryway of a city townhouse. Except for the two heavily armed guards on either side of the door.

Each wore full armor, though it was more supple and less clangy than the medieval armor she had seen. They had helmets, too, and visors that covered their faces. Again, the material seemed to both be and not be metal. Magical, likely.

Monjoie joined them in the room, glaring at Stephen. "The Shield will hear of this," he muttered. He pounded on the next door, and it opened.

Stephen carried her inside to a space between two iron covered doors. More guards opened the last door, and he carried her through.

Iron surrounded her—she could sense it—in the hallway between the antechamber sand wherever she was going. The weight of it was insistent, though not painful. "Sorry about the iron room, Your Majesty. I know it must hurt," Stephen said.

"It's fine—" she began.

"You don't have to say that," he cut her off. "Iron hurts all of us faeries, even when we're not touching it. You don't need to pretend to be strong." He arched his eyebrows at her.

Pain throbbed, and she couldn't quite make out what he was trying to get across. Iron hurt faeries and blocked their magic, she knew that, but her human side kept it from hurting her. Her mind revolved slowly. Oh, of course. If the guards knew that she wasn't affected they might take other measures to keep her docile. "Looks like you're still my bodyguard," she managed. "Thank you."

He nodded.

Monjoie joined the armed soldiers at the far end of the room. He unlocked the door and the two soldiers stepped inside. Monjoie turned to look at her. "Your Majesty, this way please." He gave a mock bow. "Your home for an as yet undefined amount of time. Do enjoy."

Deor said nothing. She imagined that on the other side was a stone room not unlike her first experience in the Tower the day she came to the Winter Court. There would be iron bars, perhaps a drain in the center of the floor—or a hole for her "business." Probably a grubby grey mattress filled with rancid straw, if any mattress at all.

Stephen carried her through the door into a cell that was...not what she expected.

They entered a square room about the size of the living room at the flat she had shared with Penny at Eisteddfod. The bare stone walls let in light through a handful of slim windows glazed in magic instead of glass. Instead of straw and chains, she saw a sofa and two chairs, with a coffee table and end tables, before a crackling fireplace. There were plush rugs on the floor. There were bookshelves, mostly empty except for a few volumes and a pile of newspapers. There was a desk on one side of the room, and a table set for four on the other.

Deor blinked in surprise, not quite taking it all in.

The room also was not empty. Three men were seated in the small parlor area. One she did not recognize. He was an old man, dressed in a white monk's robe and holding a rosary, the first she had seen in the Winter Court. His mane of white hair and neatly trimmed goatee surrounded his face, and he offered her a look of compassion as their eyes met before closing his eyes and whispering, *"Sancta Adelieda, ora pro nobis."*

The two other men she recognized. One was Delaney Overton senior. His eyes widened as he saw her, and he came to his feet, bowing as Stephen carried her in. The elderly gentleman looked tired, but otherwise in good health. The final person looked anything but. Victor Farringdon's blue face was grey tinged, wan and pale, and his black stubble suggested he hadn't shaved for days, though he looked clean otherwise. His long black hair hung loose and untidy around his shoulders. His clothes also looked worn, though not dirty, a suit he might have worn one night at Roger's. His eyes were puffy and swollen with deep, dark circles under them. He struggled to rise from the couch where he had been lying.

"Is this where the king is putting me?" Deor asked.

"It is!" Monjoie sounded pleased with himself. "Take her to her cell."

Stephen carried her across the room through an open doorway. There were four doorways off a short hallway, each with metal bars across them. None of them were fully closed. The last one on the left was open, and Stephen stepped inside.

The room was stone, like the one before it, and had a single window. There was a bed with what seemed to be a perfectly suitable mattress with clean blankets and sheets. An extra wool blanket lay folded at the bottom. Two pillows, too, though the bed was about the size of a twin. A wooden desk and chair stood under the window. One wall held a small wardrobe and chest of drawers.

Stephen set her down gently on the bed. "Here you go, Your Majesty." He pointed out the door. "The bathroom is shared, I'm afraid. The door at the end of the hall. The metal doors to the individual sleeping chambers can be locked, but rarely are, as far as I understand. You can come and go as you please, as far as the outer chamber."

"So, this is the prison?" Deor asked, incredulous.

"I'm afraid so."

Deor barked out a laugh that sent spikes of pain through her body, and she winced and gasped.

"Are you alright?" Stephen asked, concerned.

"No," she shook her head. "I'm bleeding again, and I hurt like I've been beaten with a stick." She looked around. "But this is not what I was expecting from the Tower—the most terrifying place in all of England's imagination." She looked at him. "Frankly, Stephen, my first dorm living experience in college was smaller than this."

Stephen smiled. "That parlor out there is bigger than my parents' parlor and dining room combined," he said. He shook his head. "Nobles."

Deor wanted to laugh but suppressed it. She could push aside her weariness for a moment in favor of curiosity, but now that she was on a bed, it slammed into her with a vengeance.

"Excuse me, Your Majesty?" A young man hovered at the door. He looked vaguely familiar, but she could not place him. He carried a rather large case. He stepped in the room. "I'm Root," he said. "The Tower healer. The Shield asked me to see to you." He set down the case. "May I?"

Deor hesitated, staring at him. Then her memory found his face. His was one of the many she saw flitting by the night of the Adoption and in the days that followed. "You're a healer?" she asked.

He nodded. "I see that you've started to bleed again. That's not unusual with the ride to the Tower. You need to clean your wounds and have them sealed again." He frowned. "Do you need help?"

"I need rest," she snapped. The thin material of the penitential shift clung to the clotting blood on her back—she could feel it tug and pull every time she moved. When she did take it off, it was going to hurt something fierce. Leaving it on, though, wouldn't solve anything. Still, she wished that red-headed healer who had looked after her before and after the flogging were here. "But I need to get cleaned up too," she relented.

Root nodded. He was dressed in a loose tunic, rather like a monk's outfit. It certainly gave him freedom of movement. His brown hair was close cropped. His skin brown, too, though lighter than his hair. He moved furtively, with small jerks here and there as ideas struck him, rather than in the confident, smooth ease of an experienced physician.

"Is this your first job?" Deor asked.

Root stiffened over his bag. "My first formal appointment," he said, not looking up. He opened his bag and began to neatly unfold it, the way Melanie had her makeup case. "But I did my training here before I took this position," he said. "I've been here for two years."

"That's nice," Deor said for lack of something to say.

"Here," he said, standing up. He handed her a small bottle that looked to hold about one shot of some liquid. "This is a tincture to help ease the pain. I'll do some local work, too, when I look at your back and seal off the bleeding. It shouldn't make you drowsy."

Deor popped the cork off the bottle and drank it. There was no use fighting this, and it wasn't actually uncommon in civilized nations to take care of prisoners. Make sure the prisoner was not broken, break them, fix them—to be broken again, if necessary. The liquid was cool and eased the rough ache of her throat. Soon, a calm rolled down her limbs easing the aching over her whole body. The stinging of the wounds remained but was lessened. She liked this faerie magic thing. "Thank you."

"You're welcome." He frowned. "We need to get that shift off you and cover your back with something suitable."

Stephen stepped in front of her and crossed his arms. "I don't think you're the one to be doing that," he said softly.

Root gasped and actually pressed his hand to his chest. "Of course, I'm not!" He glared at the lieutenant. "What do you think I am?"

"Apparently, a good healer," Stephen said and eased his position. "So, who do we get to help?"

"Me." A small voice came from the doorway. Melanie stood there, her eyes red rimmed, but her face scrubbed and her hair back in a neat braid, a tote bag in one hand and a traveling bag in another. "I have brought the princess some things."

A look of relief swept across Root's face. "Excellent. Can you take her to the bathroom and help remove her shift? Did you bring something she can wear that will leave her back open for me to examine?"

"I did." Melanie set the bags down and opened up the tote. She drew out a pair of loose pants with a drawstring waist and a tunic that tied at the back of the neck, but that left open her back. "I brought several of these."

Stephen helped Deor to the bathroom and Melanie gently bathed her, first loosening the fabric from her wounds with water, and then washing all the blood away. "Root is a good healer," she said as she delicately dabbed at Deor in the bath. "He sometimes helps the servants in the palace too. Not just the soldiers."

Deor leaned over the side of the tub and let Melanie pour warm water over her wounds. It stung, but the tincture Root had given her had eased the pain and disconnected it. She knew pain was happening, but it felt like it was far away, perhaps happening to someone else. For now, it was wonderful. When she was cleaned up, Melanie dressed her in loose pajama pants and a shirt that slipped over her arms in front of her and left her back bare.

"Once Root has treated you," she said, "I'll put on your tunic."

Deor nodded again.

She lay on her bed and closed her eyes as Root worked. His touch was gentle, and he was swift in his work. After what seemed like only a few moments, he stood. "That should do it." He smiled down at her. "Take it easy. I've left extra bandages here if some come loose, but after tomorrow you shouldn't need any at all."

"Tomorrow?" Deor said, sitting up. "That seems fast."

Root shook his head. "Not particularly. I mean, you won't be healed completely for a couple weeks and may have some residual pain for up to a month. But the beating was skillfully done. You won't have any scars."

Deor was skeptical, but she knew little about faerie magic, so he was probably right. "Thank you," she said. She stood and turned her back to the room while she changed into the loose tunic that Melanie had brought her. After she was dressed, she hugged Melanie. "Thank you too."

Root gathered his things and hurried out, while Stephen and Melanie escorted her to the parlor.

Monjoie stood, arms crossed, in front of the door. "Is the princess all snuggled in and cozy?"

Deor wanted to slap him but said nothing.

Monjoie gestured the two out the door and stepped out himself. "Have a lovely night," he added before slamming the door.

Deor looked around for a moment and settled her gaze on her new companions, who regarded her with open-faced wonder. Finally, the man she didn't know spoke.

"Come here, my child. Sit with us." He patted the seat next to him. "My friend Delaney there has made fresh tea. And there are biscuits." He pointed at the table.

"Thanks," Deor said. She moved slowly to the group and perched on the edge of the couch.

"Oh here," Victor said as he stood up. "Take the chair so you can lean on the arm and not hurt your back. And it's closer to the fire."

She thought about politely deferring, but her back throbbed in pain, and she wouldn't have to perch on the edge of the wingback chair. "Thank you." She switched places with him.

"Sugar?" Delaney Sr. asked her.

"Please," she said.

He passed her the cup, and she sipped.

All three stared at her.

"So," she said. "What shall we talk about?"

"Your father is a monster!" Victor hissed.

"Shush, my son," the old man said. "The walls have ears."

"They know what I think!" Victor shouted. "I don't care who hears me say it!"

Delaney Sr. patted Victor on the arm and leaned toward Deor. "How are you faring, Your Majesty?"

"Pretty horribly. I was beaten today, he had me flogged—"

"We know," Victor cut her off. "We watched it." He pointed at a mirror over the fire.

"Then you know how I am." She looked at Victor. "How long have you been here?" she asked. "Rafe and I have been wondering about you. He's been trying to find you."

"He doesn't know I'm here?" Victor looked startled.

"Not that I know of," Deor said. "He would have told me. Unless, did he arrest you?"

"No. That was the new Shield, Arthur. I was arrested at Roger's right as I was about to leave."

"You've been here weeks!" Deor said, indignant. "On what charges? Do you have a trial date? What about a lawyer?"

The old man laughed. "Oh, Victor, you were right about this one."

"No trial. No formal arrest. I'm being held for questioning 'at the king's pleasure.'" He mimed the quotation marks.

"Have you been tortured?" The anger was rising in her again. If she had known, she'd have told the press—which was why she hadn't been told. Her or Rafe. He wouldn't have stood for this either.

"I've been interrogated." Victor said. "I don't have much to tell that they don't already know."

"This is awful." Deor shook her head. "I'm sorry." She turned to Delaney Sr. "To you too. I'm so sorry. If there is anything I can do..."

He shook his head. "Oh, no, Your Majesty. None of this is your fault. Your father, I fear, is not well."

"He's fine," Deor snapped. "Absolutely fine. Except for being a fucking narcissistic, sadistic bastard. Those aren't illnesses."

Delaney Sr. jerked back slightly.

"You are a breath of fresh air in that family," the old man added.

"I'm sorry," Deor said, shifting slightly to look at him. "Who are you?"

The man stood and bowed slightly. "My name is John Dell. I am a bard." He held out his hand. "Pleased to finally make your acquaintance."

Deor shook his hand, frowning. The name was familiar, she'd heard it or seen it somewhere. "John Dell!" She said suddenly. "I took your class when you didn't show up to teach it!"

He nodded. "Alas, I was detained just before the Adoption also 'at the king's pleasure' and without the privilege of writing a letter. I'm afraid I rather vociferously disagreed with Finn about his choice for heir. Not that Rafe isn't a good lad, he is. But he would not make a good king and certainly didn't want to be one. Finn was not in agreement with my assessment, and when I said I would speak my mind to Ama and the other bards, he took umbrage."

"That fool." She drew a deep breath in and tried to keep her anger down. The anger only made her aches and pains worse. But every new thing she learned about that man made her more furious.

"You were very brave today," Delaney Sr. said. "In your speech and in your refusal to capitulate to your father. You give me hope for the future."

"Thank you," Deor said, and felt tears welling in her eyes. "I can't agree with him," she said, and the tears started to roll down her cheeks. "I just can't. He's hurting the kingdom..."

Victor handed her a handkerchief and she accepted it, dabbing at her eyes.

"There, there," Delaney Sr. said. "It is nothing that cannot be fixed," he said. "I'm sure your father will see reason."

Victor snorted. "He won't. The only hope we have is that he dies sooner rather than later."

"Victor! That's treasonous," Delaney insisted.

"It is not," he said. "Is it, Dell?"

Dell seemed to consider it. "No. It is, I'm sure, a statement that would be upsetting to the king, but that does not make it treason. Though I'm not sure the king currently sees the difference. I'm not even a Winter Court citizen. I'm a bard. That did not stop him from incarcerating me. So, things being as they are, Victor, I would not say such things in the palace, for everything in the palace is within the hearing of the king, especially since he is now well."

Deor nodded. "Yes. Be careful, Victor. He needs only the slimmest of excuses to put you to death, so don't give him one."

The other gentlemen agreed, and the topic turned to other events of the day. Apparently, there was to be some kind of palace exclusive in the *Winter Court Times* tomorrow, according to a statement they had made the day before. She sighed and rolled her shoulders, trying to stretch out some of the tension. She winced as a short but sharp stab of pain shot through one of the wounds on her upper back. Root's draught seemed to be wearing off rather faster than he had promised.

WITH THE MORNING sun slipping into the window and onto her face, Deor awoke. For a few moments she lay in bed, groggy. The small room, the warm blankets, the twin bed, for a split second she thought she was in college, in a small dorm room, with the California sun filtering in through the dirty window. An attempt to roll over drove the fuzz from her brain in stabs of sharp pain and a wave of aching muscles.

She was on her stomach and slipped her hands under her and pushed up, wincing as she did so. Her wings throbbed, but she didn't release them, no matter how much she wanted to stretch them. Pushing her wings out through the torn muscles of her back would be agony, far worse than a cramp.

After sitting up and taking a few deep breaths, Deor stood. The rug covered stone floor thrummed with magic and was rife with hostility. She could feel the built-up rage of something—perhaps the king. Was he still mad at her for yesterday? Or had something new been brought to his attention?

She stepped to the edge of the room, off the rug and onto the stone. There, the rolling emotions were easier to decipher—they weren't only from the king. His anger was faint compared to the dread. The very bones of the Tower itself seemed to be upset. The thought of this heaping pile of stones being angry on her behalf cheered her slightly. She opened the door and listened. There were voices already in the parlor, so she was likely the last one up. She slipped into the bathroom.

In the mirror she could see that blood had begun to seep through several bandages. At least Root had left more. She pulled on new pants and a tunic—a halter top—made of a single piece of cloth. Each half wrapped around the front of her body and the corner connected on her opposite shoulder, leaving her front covered and her back almost entirely open. She gathered the medical materials that Root had left in her room, pausing to down another of the tinctures he gave her yesterday, and headed for the parlor.

"Good morning?" she said.

The gentlemen turned from their places at the dining table and greeted her. The smell of fresh bacon and warm biscuits drew her to them. She was famished. Before she sat, she forked a couple pieces of bacon onto her plate and grabbed a scone. Once seated, she poured herself some tea. She had cut a piece of bacon and was raising it to her lips when she noticed that all of the men were staring at her.

She glanced down. She was fully dressed. She popped the bit in her mouth and chewed and swallowed. "How are you all this morning?" She aimed for chipper. If this was Tower life, confinement still sucked, but compared to the American prison system? She'd take it.

"So," Victor said cautiously. "How are you feeling this morning?"

Deor rolled her shoulders. "I hurt. A lot. But the potion Root gave me takes the majority of the pain out. Some of my bandages have bled through, so if someone could help me after breakfast, I'd appreciate it." She smiled. "Otherwise, I'm fine I suppose. Surprisingly, no nightmares last night." She looked at them. They seemed to be waiting for something. "How are you?"

"Give it to her, Victor." Dell said. "She seems fine."

"What do you mean I seem fine? Give me what?" A small flare of panic rose in her chest. Had something happened to Robbie? To Rafe? To Brand? "What is it?"

Victor gave Dell a distinct side eye before handing Deor the *Times*. "Oh," she said. "The story you mentioned yesterday." She unfolded the paper.

Cost of a flogging? A tuppence! Read the headline.

The story detailed Deor's affair with Rafe. A "palace insider" reported that the two had been secretly... Deor paused, eyes widening. She didn't think they'd use that word in print. Most of it was accurate, if sensationalized. There was no question who the source might be. The vivid description of her and Rafe being found, naked with their wings out, was a perfect recounting of how Arthur had found them. Right down to the color of the sheets.

"Ugh." She threw the paper over her shoulder.

"So, it isn't true?" Delaney Sr. said quickly. "What a relief."

"Oh, no." Deor opened her scone and began to butter it. "It's totally true. Right down to the smallest detail. That's the night Arthur found out. I'm sure that creepy tool is the palace source." She added a small bit of jam to the scone and took a bite.

"You and my brother were having an affair?" Victor tried for neutral but sounded more strangled.

"Yes," Deor said before taking a sip of tea. She clutched the cup tight to keep from shaking. At least there weren't pictures, not that the article needed them. Arthur had a great memory for detail and quite the capacity for description. All in all, it wasn't *that* bad of a description, though Arthur and the reporter would pay for the snide little aside about how much bigger her wings seemed given her small body—followed by the comment that, even compared to Rafe's, they were impressive. *The color of fresh spilled blood,* the article had said. She wondered how they would compare to her back now.

When no one spoke again, Deor continued on with her breakfast in silence.

Finally, Delaney Sr. asked, "Is that why he had you beaten?"

"Probably played quite a big part," Deor said. "I think he's mad I corrupted his boy." She tried not to spit that last word with venom but failed. She threw her napkin down and stood. "I think I've lost my appetite." She scanned the three men. "Dr. Dell, do you think you could help me? My back is bleeding again, and I need to change a couple bandages."

"Of course, young lady." He stood. "And please, do call me John." He rose and dragged his chair away from the table. "Why don't you sit here, facing the back. It will make it easier to see your wounds."

Deor handed him the bandages that Root had left and sat.

As Dell gently pulled off the used ones, he drew in a breath between his teeth.

"Creator's heart," Delaney said and whistled. "Those have come open again. What kind of healer does the king have here? It's a disgrace."

"Root is quite good," Victor said.

"Oh?" Deor asked through gritted teeth. Dell was being gentle, certainly, but as he cleaned up the blood and pressed the seams of the wound together, it still hurt.

"He's fixed me up a few times after a particularly long interrogation session with Arthur and the king."

Tears formed in Deor's eyes and slipped down her cheeks. She didn't want the men to see. They'd think it was from the pain in her back. That added to it, but the idea that her father, her flesh and blood, tortured people enough that they could speak to a healer's prowess made her physically ill.

"All done." Dell stood. "I do think that you should let Root know that you are having problems when he comes to see you today."

"Of course," Deor said.

The cell door opened, and Stephen came in, Brand in his arms. "Good morning," he said as though he were greeting her in her own parlor.

"Brand!" Deor bolted up, wincing and hurried across the room.

Stephen set the dog down, and he ran to her, jumping into her arms and licking her face.

"Oh Brand." She scooped him up and cuddled him. "Thank you," she said over the wriggling dog. "How did you get Arthur or my father to agree to this?"

"I didn't ask them," he said. "Malossians are known for their emotional connections. It might have really hurt him to be away from you." He shrugged. "I helped raise sheepdogs on the farm. They were similar."

Deor nodded, not buying for a moment Stephen's sweet, but dumb, story, but she didn't challenge it. She had Brand, and she wouldn't forget his kindness.

Chapter Twenty-Three

Back in his rooms at the Palace, Jameson had laid out Rafe's dinner jacket but was uncharacteristically scarce. Rafe didn't bother summoning him. He could put on his own pants and quite probably the man was in the servants' quarters, comforting his daughter Melanie. Rafe wondered how many linens would be scorched, how many soups under seasoned, or dusting spells go unrenewed in the following days. Servants had ways of making their displeasure known, and he would be very surprised if Deor were not already popular with the below stairs set. Jameson and Melanie held a place of high prestige among the other servants as well. As their mood went, so went much of the Palace.

Rafe bathed and dressed, pausing before his jewel cabinet. Rarely had he felt less like dressing for dinner. Still, he slipped on his ring of office. That felt right, at least.

"Conceal your wrath," he said to himself. He took moonstones from the cabinet – they reminded him of Deor coming out to the balcony as he stared at the moon—and wove them into his hair. Last he picked a diamond earring in the shape of the Aethelwing star and hung it in his ear. That should please Finn.

Fully outfitted, he turned to the full-length mirror and studied his own face. Grim. He looked decidedly grim. Finn was likely to call him sullen if he appeared looking like that. He squared his shoulders and looked himself in the eye.

"Buck up," he said to himself. "If Astarte can do it, so can you." He concentrated on his magic and his anger. The rage from this morning was still there, settled deep inside his bones, but growing the closer he got to dinner time. A cold wind blew about his face.

With a shock, he realized that at ninety years old, he had never really learned to control his temper. Oh, he could hold his tongue when he had to, but when had he ever had to contain the freezing cold that poured off him when he was displeased? No one needed a word from him to know just how angry he might be. As a child he'd frozen the bathwater solid just to put out a nanny he disliked and now here he was, a grown man who behaved just the same. Deor was the only person who had ever told him to stop.

"I'm as bad as Finn," he said aloud. The thought knocked him off his feet, and he sat down on the edge of the bed with a thump. Jake and Sam trotted over to place their heads on his knees. Sam licked his hand until Rafe petted him back.

"If I can't do this," he said to his dogs, "she and Robbie will suffer. The kingdom will suffer." The dogs thumped their tails on the carpet in chorus.

Calling in the ice magic that flowed off him in his anger, winding it up into a ball inside himself, Rafe stood and tried again. He practiced until the dinner gong sounded. He was the last to take his place at the dinner table. Deor's place was not set.

"You're late," Finn said, placing his napkin on his lap.

"I apologize for my tardiness, sire," Rafe said. "It won't happen again." He glanced at the menu beside his plate. Sweet Creator, it had five courses listed. He picked up his soup spoon and tried to smile across the table at Arthur.

From the other end of the table, Astarte set the conversational tone, talking brightly about the Tournament's progression, about how helpful everyone was being, especially Genevieve and Pookie, who were just invaluable.

"And how are the lists shaping up?" Finn inquired. "Plenty of entrants scrambling to get in, I imagine."

Astarte's smile faltered for a moment before she could restore it. "The lists are not quite full. Yet," she managed. "I'm sure they will be, though. You know how these things go. People need time to assemble the entrance fee and make sure all their equipment is in suitable condition."

"About half full, sire," Arthur said. "We have plenty of room for more entrants. Indeed, we may have to cancel the broadsword. There aren't enough competitors to fill out the brackets and just this afternoon three of those who had registered dropped out."

Finn glared as the footman hastily took away his soup plate. "Who?"

Arthur buttered a roll. "Delaney Overton and two of his household knights."

Finn slammed his hand down on the table, his fingernails glinting sharp with silver.

"I'll speak to him, sir," Rafe said. "I'm sure he can be persuaded to change his mind. And," he forced a lighthearted laugh, "I haven't officially registered yet myself, but you know I wouldn't miss the broadsword for all the world. Unless Your Majesty prefer I not compete?"

Finn eyed Rafe for a long moment, harrumphed and dug into his next course, a roast boar, muttering about traitors and sedition. "Go ahead and register," he said after a few mouthfuls. "People ought to see that you're still in fighting trim. I won't have people saying I've damaged you with the Adoption."

"No one is saying that, Finn," Astarte said.

"They are!"

Astarte flinched. It was the merest flick of muscle and skin, but Rafe saw it. "Well, we'll prove them wrong, won't we, sire?" he said, his voice sounding too hearty to his own ears. "I was out practicing just this afternoon." Across the table Arthur shot Rafe a warning look. Rafe pretended not to have seen it. "And what's your event, Arthur? Surely you'll be competing as well."

"Dagger-and-hand, of course. You know that," Arthur said. "Always assuming Your Majesty doesn't prefer I stick to my duties as Shield."

"No, no, I wouldn't keep you from the pleasure of competition," Finn answered. "It won't do you any harm to be taken notice of by the public either." He smiled broadly at Arthur. "No more hiding in Rafe's shadow for you."

Rafe couldn't wipe the smirk off his face at that and so was forced to hide it in his water glass. Arthur might find it much harder now to carry out his precious spying operations with his face plastered across the morning papers and a shiny new badge of office pinned to his chest. No one cared about a drab secretary carrying a sheaf of papers through the halls. Everyone would want the ear of the new Shield.

An idea grew in Rafe's mind. He might be edging out onto thin ice with it, but time was short. Only two weeks to go before the Tournament began and he, the Winter Court, needed every ally they could assemble. Slowly, as casually as he could manage, he said, "What about allowing some of the werewolves to compete, sire? As a gesture of your magnanimity and good will toward all your people. If I recall, Rufus also loves the broadsword. It would be a pleasure to cross swords with him in the lists."

"Why should I reward those who defy me?" Finn said. "King Gregory is still fuming over the loss of his ambassadors. You have no notion of how much work I've had to do placating our allies in the Goblin court to assure their continued alliance."

Rafe faltered. "I'm sure you have, sir. The Goblins..." Mouth dry, he turned his eyes to Astarte. Diplomacy had never been his strong suit.

Smiling serenely, Astarte beckoned to the butler. "That was excellent," she said. "Do convey our thanks to the cooks. Would anyone care for a digestif? Finn, my love, you've had a difficult day. Do allow me to serve you one of my herbal liqueurs—I have a decoction of valerian and angelica that will ease your mind and your stomach."

At his place, Rafe's stomach clenched. What was Astarte doing, babbling about herbals at a moment like this?

However, as the butler set tiny crystal glasses of a pale green liquid in front of each diner, Finn's scowl eased. He sipped the drink with an air of faint suspicion, but then raised his glass in a salute. "Excellent," he said. "I feel it doing me good already. You always do take such good care of me."

From her place at the foot of the table, Astarte smiled fondly at him. She rose, setting her napkin to one side and came down the long table to stand by Finn's chair and kissed him lightly on the cheek, bending to whisper something in his ear. "I'll leave you gentlemen to your conversation and go tuck my plants into bed before I retire," she said. "Good night, Rafe. Good night, Arthur. Congratulations on your promotion." With that she sailed out of the room. Finn watched her go, eyes softening.

Silence reigned over the table while they drank. The liqueur did something pleasant to Rafe's insides, unknotting some of the pain growing just below his rib cage. He held his silence until Finn had finished his drink and wordlessly led him and Arthur into the adjoining parlor for brandy and cigars.

Rafe accepted the slender black object and the offer of a light from a footman who was a fire faerie. Arthur leaned back in his chair, blowing smoke rings. Rafe fantasized briefly about chucking his lit cigar across the table and catching him right in the eye with it. Instead, he took a deep drag on the cigar and slowly let the smoke out his nostrils.

"Pixie grown, are these?" Arthur said to the king as the butler poured out snifters of brandy for each of them and shooed away the footmen. Finn confirmed that yes, the cigars were from the pixies. Through the cloud of smoke around his head, Rafe watched Finn and Arthur.

"Well, Arthur," Finn said, "you might as well tell us. How is she doing?"

Rafe's chest tightened.

Arthur waved the cigar. "She's right as rain. Sore, of course, but that's to be expected. She made rather a show of not being able to walk, so one of the soldiers carried her in. Once she was in her new quarters, Root gave her the once over just to be sure she was well."

Swallowing hard in an effort to pull back the cold that surged from him, Rafe said in a strangled voice, "How are you sure it was all a show?"

Arthur gave him a look of pure condescension. "I know my work, Rafe."

"So does Asphodel. But the princess was still bleeding when you took her away." Rafe's voice rose. "Did it occur to either of you that she might not be as strong as she makes out to be?"

Finn lowered his cigar and gave Rafe a hard look. Rafe's fingers tightened around his own cigar, stomach clenching. He decided discretion was the better part of valor. "If you'll excuse me, Your Majesty," he said. "I've had rather a long day. Arthur."

He stubbed out his cigar and exited the room as quickly as he could, grateful that the butler was there to open and close the door. If Rafe had had to close it himself, he might have slammed it off its hinges.

The second he was alone in the hall, he let the cold pour off him. Frost followed in his footsteps. He made his way to the nearest balcony and jumped off, wings stretching into the freezing cold night.

After a few hard loops around the gardens, Rafe lowered himself down to where a light still shone in Astarte's greenhouse. Knocking, he let himself in. Damp heat and the smell of wet earth enveloped him. Wading through the thick, waxy leaves of orchids, he called out, "Hello?"

"I'm back here," Astarte answered him.

He found her at a workbench, a sturdy apron covering her dinner gown. She had rolled up her sleeves to the elbow and stood over a potted white rose, her fingertips buried in the dirt. The rose blossoms pulsed with magic, a glow like sunrise leaking out between the tightly packed petals. Tiny streaks of red grew up the petals' veins. Rafe drew up a stool and watched her work. He didn't understand the earth magic she did, but watching her plants evolve had always fascinated him as a child.

This night, something else caught his eye. Bruises, layered purple and green and yellow over her wrists and forearms along with small, half-moon shaped cuts. Rafe held his tongue, not wanting to disturb her concentration, and stared at the cuts. As an experiment, he wrapped one hand around his wrist and pressed his own fingernails into the skin. They left the same indentation, though without drawing blood.

Astarte finished whatever working she was performing on the rose and withdrew her fingers. Looking up, she hastily drew down her sleeves, leaving dirt smudges on the cloth.

"How long has he been hurting you like that?" Rafe said.

Instinctively, Astarte pulled her arms in, covering one wrist with her hand. Without looking up, she said, "Since the night Robbie was arrested. Though he's done it off and on before when we quarreled. It's never been this bad before."

"Can't Asphodel do anything for you?"

"I prefer that she not know." Astarte ran her hand over her forearm. "And they are a reminder to me that worse may happen if I'm not careful."

Shards of frost crystalized in the air around Rafe as she spoke. The cooled air swirled, whipping his hair into his eyes.

"Rafe, don't," Astarte said. "You'll frostbite my plants."

"I'm sorry." Once again, he struggled to pull back his rage, guiding the magic into calmer lines through his body instead of letting it rush off of him. When he finally had it under control he slumped on his stool. "I don't know how you do it all the time. How do you not strangle him where he sits with a creeper vine or something?"

She turned her wrist over, examining the layers of bruises. "I brought this on myself when I abandoned my kingdom for him. I should have known better. I was the Heir—I should have done my duty to my people no matter what I wanted for myself."

Rafe reached out to take her hand. "No. You don't deserve this." She shrugged and looked away, but she didn't let go of Rafe's hand.

After a few minutes, she said, "Wait a day or two until Finn brings up the werewolves on his own. He'll most likely allow you to invite them then."

"How do you know?"

"Because I reminded him that all comers must do obeisance to the king and finalists receive their reward from his hand. In the unlikely event that Rufus bests you at the broadsword, it is a chance for him to be suitably cowed and for Finn to receive him back on his own terms. And if Rufus loses...." she shrugged, "the whole world will see the Alpha's son chastened. But don't press the matter. Let Finn change his mind on his own."

Rafe's fingers tightened on Astarte's. "You always teach me to be wiser, mother," he said.

He headed back to his rooms, cold filling the air around him. He held back just enough that he didn't leave frost on the windows or trail frost ferns on the stone floor, but the guards outside his quarters looked visibly chilled even before he reached them. He nodded at both as he entered his quarters, letting the door shut behind him.

"I've been waiting," Arthur spoke from his place on the couch where he stared into the low burning fire. "Where have you been?" He shifted position, turning to look over the back of the couch.

Rafe drew a deep breath in and tried to rein in the cold. "I was out for a walk."

"Oh?" Arthur waved him over. "A nice evening stroll?"

He nodded and took a seat in one of the chairs near the couch. Both Jake and Sam lay in front of the fire, watching Arthur. "I went to see Astarte in her greenhouse," he said. As he stared at Arthur he wondered how many times something he had said off the cuff, not thinking—or rather thinking that the only thing more sure of its secrets than Arthur was the grave—and how much of what he had said had gotten to Finn's ears, in one way or another.

"I'm an earth faerie," Arthur said, shaking his head, "and I have no idea how she does what she does."

Rafe shrugged. "So," he said. "What do you want? It's been a long day."

Arthur arched an eyebrow. "I wouldn't want to keep the Sword from his beauty sleep."

"Then hurry," Rafe said, uninterested in playing any kind of teasing game.

"As his lordship wishes," Arthur drawled, with a flick of two fingers to his forehead. He didn't pause. "The princess is fine. A healer sees her every day and makes sure that she is doing well."

"I didn't ask—"

"You didn't have to. But I didn't come to tell you that. I came to tell you to knock the wounded hero shit off. The truth is, you should have been the one on that scaffold, not her. And you know it. You had to know that the king wouldn't damage his precious boy."

Rafe cut him off. "So help me, Arthur, you call me his boy again—"

"And what? You'll punch me? Funny how you never had a problem being his 'boy' before *she* got here." He raised a hand before Rafe could interrupt. "And your opinion on it is beside the point. You knew how he felt about you, so were you really surprised he chose to punish her? And then you have the nerve to get angry at me? She would never have been in the situation if you'd had the sense to keep your dick in your pants—"

"Arthur—" Rafe cautioned.

"I'm not finished!" Arthur snapped. "You can, for once, sit there and shut up when I'm talking."

Rafe gaped. He'd never not valued Arthur's opinion, until recently anyway. He closed his mouth and stared at him.

"Great." Arthur nodded. "As I was saying, you never even considered that you were putting her in danger. That your desire to play some kind of romance hero was going to end with her in chains. Oh, no. You'd created the massive fantasy in your head that she was some kind of Guinevere, and you Lancelot, but when the time came, the king was going to burn her— not his favorite knight. And there was nothing you could do to stop it."

Rafe slumped down. "You're—"

"Right. I know." Arthur glared at him. "I'm not finished. You caused this problem more than the king or anyone else did. You. And then you have the nerve to be angry at me. To blame me for her suffering."

"You did hit her with a stick..."

"Yes. I did." He paused. "*I DID*. Me. Not someone else. Not someone who was, perhaps, less skilled and more enthusiastic. Or someone weaker willed, who would have pulled his punches, and led to the king requiring more lashes, or decided to add more himself. Ask yourself what shape she would be in then."

"So, you want some kind of award?" Rafe said, though without much venom. Arthur was right. All of this was his fault.

"Maybe," he said. "I know my work, Rafe. I've said it before. I am precise, and she will be fine. It hurt, of course, that's the point. But I don't think I've done a more precise job."

"Again, I'll make sure I nominate you for torturer of the year."

"It isn't torture!" Arthur shot to his feet. "We've both taken a beating in our time and been better for it." He paused, a brief flicker of doubt crossing his face. "Or at least, we survived. She will too. And even if it were torture," he said, drawing a deep breath, "it's still safer for her that I did it."

"Wonderful!" Rage swelled inside Rafe, but he drew a deep breath instead of shouting, or showering Arthur with shards of ice. "You're right," he whispered.

"I'm sorry?" Arthur sounded genuinely confused.

Rafe looked up at Arthur—a man that until recently he considered his best friend in the world. "You're right that what happened to her is my fault. And you're right that my anger at you has been part of that. But you also made it worse than it needed to be. And you know it."

"No," he said. "If it hadn't come out then, it would have at an even worse time. He was mad, he punished her, it's over. She has the best healers, Rafe. I swear. She is fine."

"Arthur," Rafe sighed, "she's not a faerie. She's a changeling. That matters."

"She's fine," Arthur insisted. "I see her, I get reports, all of it." Arthur stood. "Just stay out of it. For her sake, if not for yours." Arthur patted him on the shoulder as he passed and left without another word.

Rafe sat for a few minutes, staring into the fire. Finally, he stood. "C'mon boys," he said. "Let's go to bed." He led the way and the dogs followed. He didn't think that he'd sleep, but he had to try. Each day with his majesty was a loyalty test and failing would hurt everyone but him.

Chapter Twenty-Four

By the end of the first week in the Tower, Deor understood the real pain of confinement: boredom. That, and helplessness. The plans for the Tournament were going on apace. Astarte had even made two speeches about it to the press. Bright-eyed, cheerful, excited about the coming events. She promised neutrality in her opinions of the events, but jokingly hinted at her appreciation of the broadsword. She made no mention of Robbie whatsoever.

How did Deor know all of these things? The king insisted that the tower prisoners be kept up on events. Several papers arrived daily—all pro-monarchy, of course—and the mirror would come on whenever something deemed interesting enough happened. Who made that decision, Deor didn't know. She didn't think it was the king himself, but perhaps. More likely it fell to Monjoie. Whoever it was selected things designed to upset or irritate someone in the room.

The papers said nothing about more arrests, but neither did they mention any of the people in the Tower being given their day in court. At least no one else was condemned to a public lashing. Deor hoped this meant that the others were safe in the cells.

All of these thoughts wandered through her mind as she sat facing the back of a chair—as she had every morning—and Root examined her wounds.

"I just don't understand it," Root said as he gently inspected her wounds. The magic that flowed into Deor didn't hurt, per se, but it wasn't pleasant either. "These should be sealed. They're finally scabbing over, but it is clear they still bleed often. Your bruises, along with the deep muscle damage, are healing, but slowly."

"So, you expected me to be healed by now?" Deor asked. "Is that normal?"

"More or less, yes. Certainly, your condition is not normal." He refixed some of her bandages. "You're a changeling, and that's having some effect. I'll return in a bit with the other healers, and we'll take a look again. We'll fix it." He was speaking more out loud to himself than to her. His tone, the staring off at a point in the distance...whatever was wrong with her, he took it personally and aimed to fix it. Comforting in one sense. In another, it meant she was a sample to be studied, less a person and more a case. If it got her healed, she was fine with it.

After Root left Deor made her way to the couch where she sat down next to Dell. He had the Bible open in his hands.

"Do you read that every day?" Deor asked.

"No," he shook his head. "I've read it several times, cover to cover, and I find it to be a comfort. It is also great to read aloud from it when the soldiers are listening in. A few chapters of *Numbers* and they're off. If they are particularly persistent, I sermonize on the ills of wine and women." He grinned. "That runs them off in a hurry too." He set the book aside.

"I'll bet. You're a human then?"

"Yes. Bards come from all species, including human. Around puberty I started hearing voices. Either God or the devil was speaking to me, so I became a monk. My brothers were quite understanding, but when a lovely lady stepped out of a tree to talk to me, I finally knew that whatever I was, it wasn't going to work in the human world. So, I came to the Winter Court with her, and she planted herself at Eisteddfod so we could be married. Over time I've taught a lot of things, but I've always kept touch with the human world."

"You married a dryad?" Deor asked. "So, what kind of monk were you?"

"Benedictine—the tenth century."

"You're over a thousand years old?" Deor gaped.

"Fae lives are longer than human," he said. "And yes, I am. Though I'm not sure exactly how old I am. Then again, at this age, I don't think it matters. I've seen a lot of changes in my beloved Wessex over the centuries."

"Do you still speak Old English?" Deor asked. "Can you say something? I want to know what it sounds like from someone who actually speaks it!"

Dell crossed himself and intoned, *"Fæder ure þu þe eart on heofonum, si þin nama gehalgod. Tobecume þin rice. Gewurþe ðin willa on eorðan swa swa on heofonum."*

Deor clapped, delighted. "That's awesome!" She paused. "Wait, did you know my father when he was a child?"

"Yes, I did. I watched him grow up, from Eisteddfod. I tutored him some when he was young, as I did Rafe. And I performed his wedding ceremony."

"And what do you think of him?" Deor asked.

"I think that you should decide how you are going to spend your time in the Tower. I'm happy to teach you some things—a bit about your history, your magic. And I'm sure both Delaney and Victor would be happy to help."

Deor shrugged, to the extent that she could. "I hadn't thought about it. I didn't think I'd be here that long. I'm not sure why, but I figured he'd have me back in the palace within a few days."

"Faeries often have a different sense of time than humans," Dell said.

Deor looked around. Delaney and Victor both watched the two of them. "Would you be willing to teach me things?" Deor asked.

"Of course!" Delaney beamed. "There's so much to know about Caer Eisteddfod!"

"Okay," Deor said. She looked to Victor.

"If I had a knife, I could teach you to fight," Victor grinned. "That's about all I'm good for, but I'm very good for it."

Deor laughed. "I do need to know how to fight." She stood. "Quick lesson right now?"

Victor laughed and stood up. He took a fighting stance, hand clutched around an imaginary hilt. "En garde!"

"Here," Deor said. "Let me just make one." She closed her eyes and imagined the weight of the blade's hilt in her hand. Moments later, she opened them, and clutched a pure silver knife, a blade of honed magic. "Okay. So how do I hold it?"

Victor gaped at her. "How did you do that?" He asked.

"It's just the magic I can do. Finn can do it too. I think it's an Aethel-wing thing." She looked at Overton, who also seemed stunned. Dell, on the other hand, had a sly smile on his face.

"We can't do magic in here!" Victor said.

"Oh!" Deor shook her hand, dissipating the knife into dozens of small, silver sparkles that floated in the air for a moment and faded. "Will they be able to tell? Did I get you in trouble?"

Delany came closer, his voice low and his eyes on the door. "It isn't a matter of permission, Princess. It is a matter of ability. Can't you feel the iron embedded all around us? We are in an iron box—and faeries cannot do magic in iron."

Deor looked back and forth between Victor and Delaney, seeing again the dark circles under their eyes. "That's why you both look so rough, isn't it? It's why they don't bother to keep you chained." She looked back at Dell. "What about you?"

"Iron doesn't hinder me. But my magic isn't really weaponizable. I can talk to all living things. The moss growing on the stones outside can't be persuaded to do much except grow a touch faster, I'm afraid."

Victor scrubbed his hands over his face. "The iron is exhausting. It isn't enough to physically wound us—like pressing an iron bar to our flesh or something—but it limits magical power to nearly nothing. I could throw one or two punches, but not enough to escape or anything like that."

"What about the soldiers outside?" Deor asked.

"That's why they wear such heavy armor and don't come in often. Monjoie and Bolton were only in here a short time. But iron really doesn't bother you?" Delaney Sr. asked.

"Not at all. I can feel it, just like I can feel any other kind of metal and recognize it, or at least know it is different from the stuff around it, even if I can't name it. But my magic isn't neutralized at all in here."

"Keep that quiet," Victor snapped. "You mustn't let them know. Especially Finn—there's no way he could know that and let you in here without some sort of magical restraint. If they find out," he shook his head. "It will not go well for you."

"Got it," Deor said.

"But, it will make it easier to teach you to fight. Now stand up." She did as she was told. John Dell took up a place by the door, one eye on the guards outside. Victor led her to a small open space behind the couch. "Make a knife and try to stab me."

She closed her eyes and made another knife. This took a bit more effort, given the last one she'd lost. She opened and closed her hand around the hilt and stared at Victor. It was ridiculous of her to think she could hurt him. He had decades of experience and was apparently one of the best with bladed short weapons in the nation. Even at half-strength, he could defeat her easily.

Deor lunged at him, slashing at his body. He dodged and snagged her wrist. A sharp stab of pain, and he had her dagger. He stepped forward and pressed the blade tip to her belly.

"You're dead, or wounded," he said. "I could gut you."

"Okay." Deor laid her hand on Victor's wrist and jerked it forward, driving the blade through her tunic and deep into her body.

"Gah!" Victor screamed and hurled himself back, hand empty. "What did you do?"

Deor laughed. She held the blade part way into her stomach. "Don't freak out," she said. She pushed it in all the way to the hilt, and a shower of silver sparkles cascaded up and around. "My own magic blades don't hurt me," she said.

Dell and Delaney Sr. burst out laughing.

"It's not funny!" Victor shouted. He was visibly shaking.

"I'm sorry," Deor said. She walked over and put her hand on his arm. "I should have told you. That was cruel."

He drew in a few deep breaths. "It's good to know," he said. "How did you learn to do that?"

"I didn't," she said. "It is a royalty thing, so Finn says. He can pull the magic back into his body too. I can't quite do that. Though it would be nice. Making swords takes a lot out of me."

"I imagine," Victor said. "Okay. So, I won't worry about stabbing you with your own knives." He grinned. "That will make training a lot more exciting and, frankly, less stressful for me."

"I'll bet." Deor smiled at him. "Shall we try again?" She made another dagger.

Victor took a couple steps back and held out his hand to her. He flicked his fingers up a couple times. "Take your best shot."

Chapter Twenty-Five

To Rafe's surprise, though just as Astarte predicted, three days later, Finn announced over breakfast that he had decided to open the Tournament lists to werecreatures who were Winter Court citizens. Their banishment was not rescinded, but any and all entrants would be given special passes for their attendance at the Tournament. After that, they "could see how it all went." Rafe and Astarte congratulated him on his decision.

Finn had a further announcement as well. Arthur would be moving up from his present rooms in Officers' Quarters to the suite designated for the Shield. Astarte didn't even sigh as she promised to send Palace servants to complete the move immediately.

As Arthur thanked Finn for the consideration, he shifted uncomfortably in his chair.

"Something the matter?" Rafe asked.

Grimacing, Arthur tugged at his shirt cuffs. "I don't know what kind of devilry has gotten into the laundry these days, but all my uniform shirts seem to be as stiff and rough as unplaned boards. It's like wearing a hair shirt."

Astarte tsked sympathetically and poured herself more tea.

"You should speak to your valet about that," Rafe said.

"I have spoken to him," Arthur snapped. "Do you think I'm a simpleton?"

"More bacon?" Astarte passed the platter.

"Why thank you, mother," Rafe said. He took several rashers and chewed happily at Arthur, noting the thin red scrape of irritated skin growing at his friend's collar line. "Off to the Tower this morning, are you, Arthur?"

"Yes. What of it?"

"Nothing at all. I've no business with the Tower. Not part of my duties." Rafe stood, beaming at everyone. He inclined his head toward Finn. "If Your Majesty will excuse me, I do have other work to do. And sword practice, of course. I want to make you proud at the finals."

Finn waved a hand dismissively, his mouth full of scrambled quail eggs. Rafe bowed and kept up his jaunty air until he'd reached the Household's outer portals. Only then did he allow his shoulders to sag. Gordie was waiting for him at the great gate with a two-seater carriage.

There was no concealing that he was leaving the Palace grounds, so the next best thing would be to have an easily recognizable and unexceptional destination. If anyone asked where he'd been and what he'd been up to, he'd have a ready and truthful answer for them.

"Off to Eisteddfod we go," Rafe said. "I need a book from their library."

As Gordie clucked to the horses and shook the reins, Rafe took out his mirror. "Stephen," he said. "Are you free a moment?"

Stephen's face appeared. "Only for a moment. I've just delivered the prisoners' breakfast."

"How are the lambs faring in your parents' flock? Recovering well, I hear."

A confused frown creased Stephen's face for a second. "I don't really talk... Oh yes! The lambs." His tone lowered and his Cornwall accent drawled broader. "All's well as can be expected. Though they'd benefit from sunnier pastures for sure. There's one ewe lamb not doing as well as the healers predicted I'm afraid. She's a bright and feisty little thing, but she's been off her feed for the past few days. I think that big ram might have done her more harm than was first thought on. I saw blood on her wool just yesternight."

"Yes...," Rafe said, frost growing outward from his fingertips around the edge of the mirror. "Dangerous things, rams. Can your family get a healer to tend to her?"

"Aye, we've got a local fellow. He's competent."

"Do better than competent!" Rafe shouted. "Get a healer who knows what the fuck they're doing with a... a lamb as unique—*a mixed breed*—as this one."

"I'm doing what I can, sir," Stephen said. He glanced at someone or something outside the view of the mirror. "Well, lad, it's good to hear from the old country. Wish I could be there to help with the lambing season. I'll see the lot of you when you're down for the tournament, sure. Tarra till then, duck." Rafe's mirror went dark.

Beside him, Gordie snickered. "I'll wager you've never been called 'duck' before, sir."

Rafe settled back in the carriage, stowing his mirror in his pocket. "You'd be surprised what people have called me over the years."

Once arrived at the gate of the University, Rafe engaged in a tense conversation with the brothers Bernie and Bob who made their displeasure with the king and anyone even remotely associated with him abundantly clear. After several long and aggravating minutes and a call to Ama Nefasta, Rafe managed to convince the brother bears to allow him onto campus "for research purposes related to the Tournament."

"It's not like you to lie like that, sir," Gordie said, his voice tentative, as they left their carriage at the gate and walked up the central path of the broad, snow-covered oval between the University's front gate and the library at the far end. They stopped in front of the stone circle marking the path's halfway point.

"Who said I was lying?" Rafe took a slip of paper out of his pocket and handed it to Gordie. "Take this list of books to the library and find them for me, would you? I'll join you shortly. And if I take a little longer than you expect, just make yourself comfortable and wait. Get lunch in the student commons or something."

Taking the paper, Gordie looked over it in some confusion. "*Principles of Sword-Craft*, sir? Heimholtz *On the Way of the Blade*?" He furrowed his brow. "Er, do you want me to look around the shelves for any other books like this? Perhaps get the librarian to suggest others?"

"Yes, that would be very helpful. Take your time. No rush at all."

"Yes, sir. Understood, sir." Gordie drew himself up straight as if being handed a suicide mission. "I'll do my very best, sir. Oh, and Lord Farringdon?"

"Yes, Gordie?"

"I hope whatever you're doing helps the princess."

"Me too, lad. Now off you go." Rafe waited until Gordie was out of earshot before he stepped up to the Portal and said, "Ireland."

Rafe stepped through the portal into a rainy meadow in Ireland, the grey sky lowering over him. Unlike the faeries, the were-creatures preferred to keep their portals apart from major urban areas, the better to protect themselves in the event of a breach. This particular portal was marked by a ten-foot stone, carved in swirling lines and known as Clochafarmore, or Cuchulain's Stone. Legend had it that a hero of the Irish wolves had died here, tying himself to the stone so that he would remain upright against his foes even in death.

Rufus and Penny, along with a loose contingent of Rufus' siblings and cousins stood nearby to receive him. From the crossed arms and unsmiling looks, this was not to be a warm welcome. Four wore their wolf form, standing on all fours among their bipedal relatives with fangs bared.

Bowing, Rafe said, "Thank you for allowing me to visit you, Lord Rufus. I hope your father is well?"

Rufus nodded. "As well as can be. Allow me to introduce you to my wife, Lady Penelope." Penny held out her hand with a slight inclination of her head.

Rafe almost replied that of course the two of them had met, before the word "wife" sank into his consciousness. Finn would be less than pleased at the news—it was no surprise that the two of them had finally tied the knot, but the timing was hardly a coincidence. The daughter of a local faerie lord marrying the Alpha's son was a statement of solidarity. Rafe took Penny's hand and bowed again, kissing it. "Congratulations, Lady Penelope. May the two of you have a long and happy life together."

"Thank you, Lord Farringdon," she said.

"You know my kinfolk," Rufus said, waving a hand at the dozen men and women grouped behind him.

"I do. My greetings to you all." Heads nodded, along with hostile looks. Not a tail wagged. Rafe held out his arms. "You see that I come alone and unarmed. I've not even brought a servant with me. I hope that tells you I come in peace."

"We'll see about that," Penny said. "Let's get in out of this rain first." She took Rufus's arm and turned away, not looking back to see if Rafe followed. He fell into step behind them and the pack of Rufus's kin came after, forming a loose semi-circle around him. His fingers itched to touch the hilt of his sword, but he had none with him. Well, if worst came to worst, he was surrounded by water. That would give him plenty of material to work his magic on. The heavy drizzle continued to fall.

LATER, after the formalities were through and lunch eaten, Rufus, Penny, and Rufus's father, Angus, gathered before a large fire in the great hall of the Alpha's manor.

"I'll admit," Angus said. "This is not the kind of embassy I expected from the king."

Rafe laughed. "Were you expecting something more along the lines of an invasion?'

"Yes." Angus stared into the fire for a few moments. "What really brings you to Ireland? I'll not send my son back to grovel on my behalf. If that's what you're looking for, you've wasted your time."

Leaning back in his chair, Rafe shook his head. "I may have made some noise to his majesty about seeking an apology, but I won't press the matter. I'm here for two reasons. The first is the defense of the border. I am convinced the Goblins who approached you some months ago were in league with the Summer Court."

Angus grunted and stuck his pipe in his mouth, leaning over to extract a coal from the fire and light the tobacco. "Might be that they were. Perhaps we should have given them a hearing, seeing as how your king has served us."

"I understand your feelings," Rafe said. "But the alliance between were-folk and faeries goes back much longer than King Sweordmund's reign. And you know that his heir speaks on your behalf."

Both Rufus and his father laughed at that. Penny sighed. "We all know how far that got her," Rufus said. "With results like that, I think we'd prefer she keep her mouth shut. She hasn't earned us any good will with her little display."

"Not with the king, no," Rafe admitted. "But in the Parliament and among the people, things may be different. If you want the king's favor, you should send people to enter the Tournament."

"Who says we want it?" Rufus said.

Rafe turned to face him. "You should want it. He's got nearly all the power in this situation. Families are separated, businesses are going under. If you can appease him, they can go home and resume their normal lives. Finn has agreed to let the werefolk compete. Now he'll be insulted if you don't. You should expect a formal invitation by this evening. If he doesn't have a favorable reply by morning, he'll take further offense."

"So, we're screwed either way? What jackass set that little opportunity up, you think?"

"I did," Rafe said.

Silence fell over his listeners. They exchanged long glances. Angus sucked on his pipe and stared into the fire, frowning. Rufus growled low in his throat at Rafe, a sound felt more than heard.

Penny sighed. "You should go and fight," she said. Rufus opened his mouth to argue with her, but she held up her hand. "I know, *macushla*, I know. I don't like it any better than you do. But Rafe hasn't set you up in a trap, he's made you a way out of one. We faeries love pomp and circumstance and grand displays. Go and fight. Be gallant and charming. The people will be won over, and the king will have a way clear to forgiving you without seeming to go back on his word. It's best for everyone concerned."

"Let them make me their tame wolf, you mean," Rufus spat. "A pet with ribbons in my hair."

Rafe shook his head. "Never. Come as my honored friend. As a prince of Ireland. I'll seat you beside me at every feast and event. Bring as big a retinue as you like—I still have control of the borders, and I'll grant as many visas as you ask me for, no questions asked." Rafe leaned forward, his eyes meeting Rufus's. "War is coming, Rufus. How soon, I don't know, but I'd guess no later than the end of next year. The Summer Court won't spare your people either. I'll make no excuses for Finn. He deserves none. But," he paused. "I've experienced the Queen's tender mercies firsthand. If you don't want to be made a pet, the Winter Court is still your safest haven."

Rufus stared into Rafe's eyes a moment longer, then ducked his head in a gesture Rafe recognized from contests between Jake and Sam. "Alright," he said. "Why marry a clever woman if you won't take her advice? I'll go, and I'll compete. So will my brothers and cousins. But if this proves to be a trap, I'll never trust your word again."

Rafe stood, extending his hand. "My honor on it," he said.

Chapter Twenty-Six

Rafe returned to Eisteddfod from Ireland to grab Gordie, and, after a quick change into suitable clothes, headed for his club. Rafe stepped out of the carriage and put out his wings, pausing on the sidewalk to adjust his jacket before heading into the club. His dogs followed close at his heels. There was nearly always a junior reporter or three hanging around outside the club looking for small tidbits of society gossip. These days he made it easy for Finn to get word of his activities and whereabouts. No need to have Arthur doing his spying for him when Rafe would happily announce that he was off to the practice yards or the armory or the theater with friends and then make sure others saw him right where he was expected to be.

Forcing a jaunty, devil-may-care lift into his step, he went up the club steps, making sure to tip the doorman. He took up a seat in one of the smaller side parlors meant for private tete-a-tetes between members and ordered a bottle of wine and several glasses. The room was ornamented to seem like a meadow in fall, with a soft green and yellow carpet underfoot like grass, and walls painted in a clever optical illusion of distant maple trees in flaming reds and oranges. The chairs and couches arranged around the room were upholstered in russet with dark polished wood and brass accents.

As his two dogs flopped down on the hearth rug, Rafe paced back and forth, practicing what he was about to say. If the conversation with Rufus had been difficult, this was likely to be worse. Jake and Sam's eyes followed him anxiously as he rolled a sphere of ice back and forth between his fingers, an old swordsman's trick to keep the fingers limber and soothe the nerves.

A few minutes later Rodney and Clarissa, along with Delaney, entered. Rafe turned to his friends, smiling at the sight of them but searching for a fourth.

"Is Genevieve coming?" he said.

"I am indeed," she said, gliding into the room. The other three exchanged glances and hung back.

Genevieve crossed the room to take one of the glasses, sniffed delicately at the vintage, and deigned to sip it before turning back to address Rafe. Her dress was grey shot through with strands of silver and flashes of pink that echoed the wet skies and blossoming trees outside. A spray of apple blossoms adorned her upswept hair, and silver teardrops hung from her ears.

"Let me be the first to say that it is insufferably high handed, and entirely in your character, for you to summon Delaney like this without so much as a please and thank you when you're holding his elderly father prisoner in the Tower." She gestured with the wine glass. "But since we're all here, you might as well speak your mind. Make it quick. We have dinner reservations."

Taking a deep breath, Rafe pressed his hand over his heart and bowed as low as he could to her. "Lady Genevieve, you are entirely right," he said. Blood rushed to his face as he spoke, more from shame at himself than his low position. "I owe you all an apology for my behavior in the last few weeks, and you most of all, lady. I treated you poorly throughout our engagement and put you in an untenable position at Roger's. For all the pain I caused you, I deeply apologize." He held his bow.

"Oh." Genevieve, for once, was at a loss for words. She blinked, looked down at her drink and then around the room, searching for some way to get back her balance. "I suppose..." She shook her head and rolled her eyes. "Oh, do stand up again, Rafe. You're forgiven. Mostly. I still think you deserve a good kick in the pants, but we can at least be civil to one another."

He stood and offered her his hand. "I really am sorry I hurt you. I proposed for all the wrong reasons. You deserve better."

"Yes, I do," she said, taking his hand. "We've known each other for decades. I should have known better than to accept." She granted him a wry smile. "Folly of youth, shall we say?"

"Whatever you like, lady." The two of them laughed awkwardly.

Behind them, Clarissa clapped and cheered. "Hooray. This will make things much less awkward at the Tournament."

Rodney came forward to clap Rafe on the shoulder. "Now that's all settled, why don't you come out to dinner with us? It's been too long." Delaney Overton said nothing, though he did join the others with Rafe.

"I can't, I'm afraid," Rafe said. "The king expects me to attend him."

The mood in the room fell noticeably. Rodney got himself a drink and said, "Keeping you on a short leash, is he?"

"Something like that," Rafe said.

"I'm surprised it's not you in the Tower instead of the Heir," Delaney said. His eyes were unfriendly as he spoke. "After all, she's barely an adult. You on the other hand..."

Rafe took a moment to look down at his toes before answering. "I'd prefer not to discuss a lady who isn't present," he said. "I'll make no defense for myself."

"And what about my father? Any chance you'd do your job and defend him? Or are you too busy locking up dock workers and university students?"

Rodney put a hand on Delaney's shoulder, but Delaney shook him off.

Rafe flinched a bit, but he said, "Before we speak further, may I?" He spread his fingers, encircling the interior of the room with a privacy screen that would block both sound and images. The Junior Flaneur was known for the discretion of its staff, but one couldn't be too careful. He looked around at his friends. "I've been relieved of all duties relative to the Civil Patrol and control of the Tower. That's in Arthur's hands now. I'm sorry, Delaney. There's nothing I can do to get your father out. I can't even visit him. Though I do hear that he is in good health."

Delaney's shoulders slumped a bit as Rafe spoke, and he nodded, rubbing a hand over his forehead. "At least this isn't an elaborate set up to arrest me too."

"No. Never."

Clarissa took a step closer to Rodney. He reached an arm around her waist. Rafe regarded his four friends' sober faces.

"The Summer Court is preparing for some type of offensive against us. All our intelligence points to much greater effort, perhaps even an invasion, than we've seen in the last century, and I believe the Goblins are helping them, or at least will not help us when the attack comes. I need your help, all of you, to convince the king that he has his..." Rafe paused, "his 'boy' back, that things are as they were between us before Deor arrived. I believe if I can do that, he will allow me freer rein to do my duty and protect the kingdom."

Clarissa twined her fingers in Rodney's and said, "And what about Princess Deor? Isn't it your duty to protect her too?" The others nodded as she asked the question.

"The farther I stay away from Princess Deor, the better off she will be." Rafe took a deep, shuddering breath. The image of the cane falling on Deor's back floated before his eyes. "Believe me, all of you, if I could have taken her punishment for her, I would have. I helped bring it on her..." Suddenly his face burned, and his ear tips felt hot. "The best I can do now is appease the king and do my duty as Sword."

Rodney blew out a long breath, nodding slowly. "What part do you expect us to play in that?"

"Genevieve is already helping Astarte organize the Tournament. Thank you for that as well, by the way. I'd like you and Delaney to compete. The more the nobles turn out to participate, the more Finn will feel the Tournament is a success and that he has your loyalty." Delaney grimaced but nodded. Rodney nodded too.

Genevieve leaned her head back, studying Rafe as if assessing a candidate for the Harvest Queen contest. "We'll have to reconcile," she said.

"I... I thought we just did," Rafe said.

She waved him off. "The king wants everything put back the way it was before his turbulent daughter arrived. The good old days. He wants his faithful boy back. Most of all, he wants a happy ending with himself as the benevolent overseer of it all. So, we'll give it to him. Make him feel that his Tournament fixed everything, and all is right with the world again."

"Oh. I see where you're going with this," Clarissa said.

Genevieve nodded at her. "Just so."

"I don't see a thing," Rafe said. "What the hell are you getting at?"

Fixing him with a look that said 'this is why we're no longer engaged,' she said, "At the opening Ball where all the top seeded contestants and preliminary melee winners are feted, you are going to ask me to dance. I will be reluctantly charmed by your penitent longing for my attention. By the night of the concluding ceremonies, we'll have reconciled. You can propose to me after you win the broadsword competition."

"Or better yet," Clarissa said, "right before."

"Yes, I like that." Genevieve pointed to Rafe with her glass. "Go down on one knee in the field and declare you cannot fight without my favor. I'll give it to you. You'll wear it in your helmet. You'll win, or lose, because of the overwhelming force of love. The newspapers will be shrieking with excitement, and no one will give a damn about the princess anymore. If the king doesn't let her out of the Tower on his own, I'll cozy up to him in the days after the Tournament and convince him that I can be her guiding friend and he can safely let her out. He'll be so happy with you that he'll do it."

Rafe's jaw dropped. "I'm not sure...There are consequences to asking someone to marry you..."

Genevieve laughed. "Don't be silly, Rafe. I'm not actually going to marry you." She shot Delaney a sly look that made Rafe's usually unflappable friend blush to the roots of his hair. "In a year or two, Delaney can steal me from you."

Beaming, Clarissa added, "An engagement will give you an excuse to spend nights away from the Palace, Rafe. No one could accuse you of sneaking around when you're clearly just spending time with your fiancée. Besides, the king will be smitten by the whole thing. Remember how proud he was when you proposed the first time? This will convince him you've come to your senses and forgotten all about Deor."

Rodney snickered into his glass. "I'm afraid your duty is clear, Rafe. You'll have to propose to Genevieve. The rest of us will raise a glass in your memory at The Mound." Genevieve shot him a poisonous look, and Clarissa giggled.

Rafe ran his hand through his hair. "I suppose I must make an absolute public spectacle of it?"

Both Clarissa and Genevieve nodded firmly.

"Very well," he said and finished his wine. Glancing out the window to gauge the time, he saw that the sun was setting. "Thank you all. If you'll excuse me, I must attend the king at dinner."

His friends' laughing demeanor faded. Rodney came forward to embrace him with Clarissa. Delaney and Genevieve offered their hands. Rafe whistled to the dogs and headed out into the evening, steeling himself for the hours ahead.

Chapter Twenty-Seven

Though it had been well over a week since the beating, Deor's back was bleeding when she woke. Irritating, and a bit painful, but not surprising. Root had sealed and resealed the wounds, cleaning them, too, every day, but they never held. She would have believed that Root was deliberately not healing her but for the fact that Victor vociferously vouched for him and Root was so distressed that she wasn't healing, Deor found herself talking *him* down and telling him she was going to be fine.

In the bathroom, Deor stood and turned her back to the mirror. It was only half-length, but it showed her back well enough. Indeed, a few places had opened again, and there were thin red dribbles here and there. She was getting better, just not nearly as quickly as expected. According to everyone, the wounds should have been completely scabbed over by now.

She opened her door and Brand scurried out into the parlor.

"Good morning, Brand!" Deor heard Stephen's voice. He came dutifully three times a day, once in the morning, once in the afternoon, and once right before bed, to take Brand out. Often, he brought treats too.

Deor strolled out into the parlor after her dog. "Morning, Stephen," she said with a smile.

He bowed slightly. "Good morning, Your Majesty."

The only other person up was Dell, and he had moved a dining room chair under one of the windows to write.

"Morning, John," Deor said and headed for the dining table. Tea appeared by six o'clock, though breakfast was whenever they got around to it.

Stephen left with Brand, and Deor poured herself a cup. She set it down on an end table next to one of the wingback chairs and headed back for her room to grab a towel. She draped it over the chair, picked up one of the daily newspapers they were permitted.

She skimmed the front page as she settled into her seat. "Preparations for the tournament continue apace." That was pretty much all any of the papers were talking about. None of them mentioned her, or any of those arrested, any trial dates, any new arrests. Nothing that might take attention from the obnoxious omnipresence of Finn's ego parade.

Deor was about to ask where Victor was when a small voice chirped from the fireplace mantle. *The other man was taken. He was returned moments before dawn, when the sky is still dark blue.* Boomie was sitting in the fireplace mantle, crouched down, with his paws just over the edge, like a gargoyle should, apparently unseen by everyone else.

"Is Victor up yet?" She didn't wait for an answer before standing. "I'm going to go check on him." His room was diagonally across from her own. She knocked softly but heard nothing. She stood on her tiptoes and looked in through the small window. He was curled up on the bed, back to the door.

None of the bedroom doors were able to be locked. Well, at least not by the prisoners—privacy was a luxury for the free. The soldiers could lock them in their rooms if they so chose. They rarely did.

Deor pushed the door open as quietly as possible. She almost cried out when Boomie settled himself on her shoulder.

You're hurt. Bleeding.

"*I know. It's fine,*" Deor whispered.

Boomie made a snorting noise, but Deor ignored it.

Victor was asleep on the sheets, and the blanket was in a ball on the floor. It looked like he had come in and collapsed on the bed and passed out. Deor leaned in. "Oh my god," she whispered. Victor's face was covered in small burns. They looked like evenly spaced cigarette burns, raw and red. Flecks of dried blood were scattered across his face.

Deor bolted back out to the parlor. "We need a healer!" She demanded.

The door opened, and Stephen came in, following Brand.

"Get Root. Now!" Deor snapped.

"Are you okay, Your Majesty?" He took a step toward her.

"I'm fine. It's Victor. I—I don't know what they've done to him. Burned him, I think. Please?"

Stephen frowned. "Of course." He left.

Dell was on his feet heading for Victor's bedroom.

"I didn't wake him," Deor said. She winced as she spun around to follow him and Boomie dug his claws into her shoulder to hold on. The movement tugged more of the lashes open, though it was the feel of the blood running down her back rather than the pain that she noticed.

Dell waved at her and Delaney Sr. to stay in the doorway. The rooms were small enough with only one or two people in them.

"Victor?" Dell spoke softly, resting a hand on his shoulder. "Lad? Can you hear me?"

Victor made a noise, a small groan, and stretched himself out of the fetal position. "Dell?" He said, his voice raspy and hoarse.

"Yes, lad." Dell stood up. "Can you sit up?"

Victor nodded and pushed himself into a sitting position. He swung his legs around and sat, leaning back against the wall, eyes closed.

Deor came in. "How do you feel?"

He chuckled and then winced. "Not great."

"Who did this to you?" Deor demanded.

Shield, Shield. Boomie's voice rang into her ear.

Victor opened his eyes. "Arthur."

Deor drew a deep breath and held it for a few seconds before blowing it out again. She wanted to scream and throw things, but there wasn't much to throw, screaming wouldn't help, and having a fit would only make her look, and feel, more childish.

"Why?" Delaney Sr. asked. "You've been here for months. What could you possibly know that they don't already?"

Victor turned his face toward the window. "I have no idea what he wanted."

Liar.

"*I know,*" Deor whispered. "*Shoo.*" She shoved him off her shoulder, and he took flight, darting out of the room.

"What?" Victor said, his eyes still averted. Dell, though, was looking right at her, a curious frown on his face.

"You're lying," Deor said. "Please don't. If you're worried that he'll hurt you more if you say something, then tell us that much. I won't ask you to put yourself at risk."

An uneasy smile crossed his lips, like there was some darkly unfunny joke she wasn't aware of. "He said you'd say that." Victor flicked his gaze to her.

"Say what?" Deor demanded.

He turned his head to stare right at her. "That you wouldn't want people to be hurt because of you." He shook his head. "You've got to get over that, you know. First of all, you will have several people in your service whose job it is to get hurt for you. Closest to you, bodyguards, but soldiers, spies, all manner of folks. Telling them not to do so won't stop them and might even make them feel like you don't think they are capable or devoted."

"That's not what I mean," Deor said dropping her gaze to the ground. "I'm tired of my making mistakes and others suffering from them." She looked back up. "Did this have to do with me?"

"Arthur doesn't need a reason."

Deor covered her face with her hands and fought back tears. She wiped her hands down her face and rested her hands on her hips.

"But no—he wanted to know what I thought my family was planning for the tournament." He dropped his head back against the wall.

Deor glanced around. "Could you two give us a minute?"

Dell nodded and took Delaney Sr. by the arm and led him to the parlor.

Deor sat on the bed next to Victor. "What did he do? How did you get those marks?"

"Iron." Victor closed his eyes again and grimaced. "A small iron cylinder about three inches long." He sat forward and pulled his shirt off over his head. Dots were scattered across his chest too.

"Jesus," Deor said and reached to touch them, only snatching her hand away at the last moment.

He glanced down. "They'll all heal. He said he wouldn't scar my pretty face, or my chest." He looked at Deor. "We dated once, you know? A long time ago. When Rafe was away with the king in the Summer Court battle. Arthur ended it shortly after I accidentally gave Rafe that scar."

"I wondered if he was in love with Rafe," Deor said, letting the rest of it go.

"No." Victor shook his head. "No question he loves Rafe, but not that way. I think that Arthur was messing about with me. I don't think he was really available."

"You mean he was cheating on someone?" Deor snorted. "What a not-surprise."

"No." Victor shook his head. "You misunderstand. I think that he was in love with someone else. Someone far away or unattainable. He was passing time with me." Victor saw her scowl. "Don't get all angry on my behalf over this," he said with a laugh. "We were both passing the time. That's what young soldiers do in their forties. Don't you have a phase like that in the human world? Or do humans live too short of lives?"

Deor barked out a laugh. "I don't think any life is too short for a bit of messing around. But yeah, humans have that too. It is a bit shorter, I think —fifteen years is on the very-long side of it. Some people don't play the field at all."

"Play the field. Good phrase." Victor nodded. "But my point is that Arthur has a certain...familiarity with my anatomy. These marks will heal."

"Good," Deor said. "Is the iron in here still hurting you?"

"Yes," he said. "Being injured, especially iron injuries, makes it worse. I'm planning on sleeping for a few days."

Deor frowned. "Here." Deor turned to face him. "Can I touch you? Can I use magic?"

"Are you going to hurt me?" He asked.

"Not on purpose." She gave a weak smile. "I've been thinking about the iron thing—how it doesn't bother me."

"I trust you." He stared up at her.

Deor concentrated on defensive magic—the part of her power that created showers of silver sparkles to protect her. If she could make a cloud of those, an insulating force designed to secure a bubble of normal space— space that was iron free—then she could help him.

Sparkles blossomed off her in waves, and Victor laughed as they flitted around the two of them. Moments later they were surrounded, caught in a small space at the center of the storm.

Victor drew in a deep breath and stared at her. "I feel better. The iron, I can't even feel it." He flexed his fingers. He laughed as his hands filled with spheres of water he drew from the air. He closed his hands around the spheres, and they hardened, turning into white balls of ice. "Thank you," he said. He opened his hands, and the spheres collapsed into pools of water, running between his fingers and onto the bed. He waved his hand, and the sheet dried, the water evaporating back into the air. He stared at Deor for a moment. "I see why Arthur is so afraid of you."

"Arthur is afraid of anything he can't control."

"Exactly," Victor said. "Can I ask you something personal?"

"Sure." Deor shrugged.

"Are you deliberately opening your wounds? Are you trying to keep from healing? Arthur asked me if you were."

"What?" Deor gasped. "No!" she said with a frown. "I'm a lot of things —a lot of not good things—but masochistic is not one of them. Neither is suicidal. I don't know why I'm not healing." She cocked her head to the side. "Arthur thought you were helping."

Victor nodded. "I have some battle medicine training—all soldiers do. Though it doesn't take any special knowledge to undo flesh-knitting spells, not really. And I'm glad you're not doing it on purpose. It's a bad plan."

"No kidding."

"Um, hello?" A voice called from the doorway.

Deor waved her hands, shooing away the sparkles that had settled around them. Root stood in the doorway, looking puzzled. He reached out to catch a couple of the sparkles, and they burst like bubbles under his touch.

"Lt. Bolton said I was needed here?" he said.

"It's Victor," Deor said and scooted to the edge of the bed so she could stand. "Burns. From torture."

"Ah." Root came closer. "Yes," he said. "I can fix those. Won't take a moment." He set down his bag and opened it. After digging through for a few moments he pulled out a small, flat container. "This salve should stop any pain and encourage healing. They'll be much less sore and then gone in a day or two." He handed it to Victor.

"I'll leave you to it," Deor said, and moved toward the door.

Deor settled back into the wingback chair and thought about what Victor had said, about her not wanting people to get hurt. Maybe she did need to stop thinking that way. She stared at the low fire, at the logs slowly turning to grey ash.

You hurt. Boomie settled on the back of her chair.

Deor nodded but did not reply. She did hurt—she was both in pain and causing pain to others.

"May I?" Dell said, taking a seat across from her.

"Would you take no for an answer?"

"Of course." He studied her for a moment. "You know, you're not like any Aethelwing I've seen. In fact, I had started to believe that creatures like you only existed in faerie stories." He chuckled at his own joke.

"What? Changelings?" Deor asked. If this was going to be some miscegenation argument, she wasn't having it.

"Goodness no. Those are quite common. I mean your little pet there?"

Deor reached down to where Brand was laying next to her chair and scratched him behind the ears. He thumped his tail. "Brand? He was a gift from Rafe," Deor said.

"I wasn't speaking of Brand, either. I am speaking of that adorable friend on your shoulder. The palace's avatar?"

With a gasp, Deor reached up and snatched Boomie off her shoulder and cradled him to her chest protectively in both hands. "You can see him?"

"I am a bard. Of course, I can see him." He waved his hand dismissively. "Don't worry. I mean him no harm. But he talks to you, yes? And you understand him? And he understands you?"

"He speaks ancient faerie. I'm not great at it—the throne just dumped it all in my brain when I sat on it—but yes, we talk."

Dell grinned. "It must think highly of you. Listen to it," he said. "Listen carefully. The more you do, the more it will be able to tell you." He leaned forward. "May I?"

Deor frowned but held out her cupped hands.

"*Hello there,*" Dell said to it. "*Aren't you a cute little thing? Perfect for her, aren't you?*"

Boomie purred under his touch and hopped from Deor to his lap. From there, he looked at her. *Bard friendly!*

Deor wondered if that was always the case.

Dell looked at her. "There's a lot more to your connection to the land than a mental map of the palace and a stone companion."

"Really?" She knew there had to be more to her being heir than just feeling the kingdom. "Can I fix the kingdom? Like Mirrovere?"

"In time, it's likely." Dell nodded. "Probably not from here—even if you weren't in the Tower. You'd have to stand on the land itself. But never forget, princess, this is your home, too, while the king can close some doors to you, you have as much ownership of this place as he does. And as much responsibility to protect it, even if it is from him."

The door opened, and a servant scurried in with breakfast.

"Shall we? I believe it is bacon again. One of the few things I don't tire of having every day." Dell stood and walked over to the table as though he hadn't suggested treason and possibly rebellion.

Chapter Twenty-Eight

The day before the tournament began, the fourteenth of March, the formal guests of the palace arrived. While Roger and Pookie had been at the palace for days, they would still make a formal arrival presentation. Rufus and Penelope, and Vlad Drogos, heir to the vampire nation, and his wife Chloe were all attending.

None of those concerned Rafe as much as did Edgar and Madeline Farringdon. The king believed that since they had caused such a ruckus before, it would make sense to keep them where they could be seen, and guarded, at all times. So, at the palace they stayed.

Rafe drummed his fingers on the table in the Amber Room, waiting for Arthur to arrive. When he did, he sauntered in with all the urgency of a cat after a meal and a nap. "Nice of you to join me."

Arthur sat in the chair across the table from him. "What do you need? Everything is ready."

"I wanted to try one more time to convince you to put my parents somewhere else!" He drove a hand through his hair. "They are dangerous, and dangerous to have here."

"Keep your friends close and your enemies closer." Arthur cocked his head to the side. "I know security, Rafe. I'm also well trained in spying and in self-defense and the defense of others. The Farringdons, like Werewolves and Vampires, are all going to be on the second floor. Three floors below the sealed king's quarters. Roger and Pookie are on the fourth floor. Surely that passes security muster with you?"

"Roger and Pookie are fine, you know I know that," Rafe snapped. "And I'm not worried about the vampires or werewolves, either. Donovan has no reason to do anything that might upset our alliance, and Rufus isn't here for revenge. But my parents will try something. They always do."

"What?" Arthur said. "Do you have any intelligence about this mysterious plan? They are in a house, unarmed, full of armed guards."

"My mother is never unarmed," Rafe cautioned. "One of the traits she has in common with the king." He glanced at the clock on the wall. "They'll be arriving momentarily—unless they are fashionably late, which I expect. Is the king planning on greeting them?"

"Of course." Arthur sighed. "Rafe, everything is fine. You're still smarting from the king's discipline, but you'll rebound. The ball and the tournament are the perfect moment for you to show him what you are— powerful, commanding, clever, and loyal. You have never stopped being the king's favorite—you are his son, regardless of any other children he has."

Rafe gaped at his friend. "Displays of power and authority are not the same thing as having power and authority." Rafe rose. "The king wants to show off how much he is in control, how wonderful the Winter Court is, but he's growing more paranoid by the day. You see it too. This is reckless and stupid."

"Which part? Your parents or—?"

"All of it." Rafe leaned forward, resting his hands on the table so he was eye-to-eye with Arthur. "This is all a farce—our army is weak, our heir is in the Tower along with the Master of the City. This is frivolity, not power. And you know it."

"My job is to keep the nation safe from internal threats, and this includes commanding the Civil Patrol," Arthur said. He rose. "Is that what this is? Are you angry that I am the Shield?"

"What?" Rafe pushed away from the table. "Of course not. Though I do wish I had known about it sometime before you beat the heir in public."

"Your paramour, you mean." Arthur rolled his eyes. "You might, *might,* be fooling the king with whatever song and dance you're doing with Genevieve. Hell, you might even be fooling her—she's arrogant enough to think you'd come crawling back. You're not fooling me. I've seen you glance at the Tower every chance you get when it is in sight. You're obsessed."

Rafe stared at him for a long moment. "You revealed my affair in the worst possible moment, calculated to do the most possible damage to her.

You enjoyed flogging a thirty-year-old, and you shared intimate details about her with the press, all because she challenges your idea of order. And *I'm* obsessed?" He pinched the bridge of his nose. "The king might well try to kill her someday. What are you going to do when that happens?"

"Don't be absurd! He wouldn't kill his heir." Arthur headed for the door.

"Just like his father didn't try to kill him?" Rafe said as Arthur walked by.

Arthur froze and turned his head. "We don't know what happened there."

"Right." Rafe nodded. "Why don't you go up to the library and read the Shield's book and see?"

"I have other things to do, as do you. We need to get to the foyer for the arrival of the guests."

Rafe inclined his head toward the door. "After you."

Arthur glared at him for a moment and led the way.

The men formed an uncomfortable pair in their full regalia of office as the king and his consort, both extravagantly dressed, glided down the stairs to welcome their guests. The four couples watched with varying degrees of attention and appreciation. Madeline stared at the king like he was the only thing in the world, and a small smile curled on her lips.

One by one, they greeted the guests, starting with Roger and Pookie, then the werewolves, the vampires, and finally Rafe's own family.

Madeline gave a deep curtsey, and Edgar bowed. "Your majesties," Madeline said, with a voice like thick honey. No magic in it that Rafe could tell, and the palace safety spells weren't responding either. "I am so pleased to be here at the tournament. I am excited to watch my son compete." She glanced at Rafe, her eyes angry and cold for a flash of a second. "At least my eldest—my youngest is still missing."

Finn held out his hand for hers, "I am sorry, Madeline, about your youngest." He smiled and kissed her hand when she placed it in his own. "But I am certain that Rafe will do us both proud." He shifted his look to Rafe and beamed at him.

"Of course." Madeline flicked her gaze to Astarte and held it for a long moment. "My Lady Consort," she nodded her head in deference. "You, too, are absent your child, are you not? Do you not worry for her?"

Astarte smiled. "I appreciate your concern, Duchess, but I am well."

Madeline turned slightly to the rest of the couples. "Aren't we a happy little band? If you don't mind, Your Majesty," she returned her attention to the king, "the journey from Wellhall is not an easy one, and we have already installed the knights of our region at their lodging in the city today. We would very much like to rest before the ball this evening."

"Of course," Finn nodded. He took Astarte's hand, smiled and nodded at all the company, and led his consort up the stairs. Roger and Pookie followed.

The steward stepped up, a fleet of valets behind him. "Honored guests, dinner will be at six and the ball begins at eight," he said sharply. "These shall be your servants for your stay here. They will show you to your quarters now, if you like, or later, and will see your belongings safely stowed and prepared." He gave a bow and gestured for the servants to approach their guests.

The Farringdons immediately headed for their rooms. Rufus and Penelope stopped to shake Rafe and Arthur's hands and then followed as well. Arthur nodded at the vampires before discreetly following the couples up the stairs.

Finally, Donovan strolled up to him.

"Hello, Vlad Drogos." He held out his hand.

"Donovan, Rafe, please." He took Rafe's hand and then pulled him into a hug. Vampires were notoriously physically intimate creatures, but Rafe hugged him back, tightly. "It's good to see you, my friend." Donovan released him.

"You too." He turned to Chloe, who stepped up for a hug too.

She had always awed Rafe from the first time he met her in his early twenties. She was tall and imposing—not bulky, but muscled like an athlete, and she carried herself as though she feared no one. She had dark brown skin, hair, and eyes, the latter of which could burn red in an instant.

Today her tight spiral curls hung loose around her face just above her shoulders. She moved like liquid with feline grace. She was the most dangerous woman he had met, at least in terms of physical skill.

"How is the Sword these days?" Her voice was low and soft, though not particularly deferential. In fact, it forced him, or anyone, to listen closer.

"Surviving. Trying to make sure the kingdom does too."

She laid a hand on his cheek, stroking it with her thumb. "You'll make it through." She was less flamboyant than her husband, though no less of a presence. She wore a long deep green sheath dress which Rafe knew from experience concealed at least two weapons.

Donovan was in his regular uniform—as much leather as possible and a white, flowy shirt. Rafe knew there was some kind of joke in it, but he wasn't sure what it was. Both of the vampires let their jewelry make a statement. For Donovan, his family ring—a blood red stone the size of his thumb held in a hunk of raw gold. Chloe wore a three-strand choker of diamonds with an emerald the size of a walnut at the center. Subtlety was not their forte. He loved them for it.

"Thank you." He took hold of her hand and kissed it and let it go. So many faeries were nervous around vampires—both feared and looked down on them. Rafe never understood why—or rather he thought the politics of assuming anything not faerie was lower was stupid and unwise. He did understand, though, how their diet of blood might make some folks uncomfortable. Though vampires never feasted on faerie blood if any other option was available. The magic in faeries affected vampires rather like alcohol or drugs, leaving them feeling sick, disoriented, and sometimes weak.

"So, what shall we do to occupy the time between now and dinner?" Donovan asked. "Surely you have some entertainment for us."

"Yes, man," a rough Irish brogue came from the stairs behind him. Rufus and Penny, having quickly changed from traveling clothes, were coming down the stairs toward him. "We're not hanging around in our rooms for hours if we can help it."

Rafe smiled. "The qualifying melee is in about an hour. Would you like to watch?"

"If only I could participate," Donovan said with a fangy grin.

"Aye," Rufus agreed, "but that I can only compete in one event, I'd be in the middle of the melee too. Though I'd skip the qualifier." He gave Rafe a wink. "I'll have more fun beating your stuffing out, I think."

Rafe shrugged. "We'll see." He glanced down at himself. "I'm not going to the melee in all this frippery," he said. "I'll be back in a few minutes, and I'll take you to the field." He nodded to the couples and headed up the stairs. Relieved that Rufus seemed cheerful, Rafe started to have some hope that this tournament might work—that people might be inspired by the Winter Court and that some wounds might be healed. Closing the rift between the Irish wolves and the Winter Court would be a great first step.

Chapter Twenty-Nine

After Rafe had settled the two couples in the box, he headed down to the field himself. He leaned against a fence post and stared out at the field prepared for the qualifying round of the melee. It was impressive what the palace landscapers had done to the Houseboys' practice field in a matter of days.

The once flat, empty field was transformed into a more rugged terrain. There was a narrow river slicing through from the northeast corner to the southwest, winding and twisting. It rushed fairly quickly but was shallow enough to be easily crossed. Ammunition for the water faeries, even if the winter air was dry. There were some low, rolling hills, too, and uneven ground. Loose earth to be manipulated by various earth faeries, some of whom could well shake the ground beneath an opponent's feet and crack it open like an egg. None of the fighters had the Aethelwing earth magic of creating weapons made of pure magic, but many could manipulate metals. He was certain the imported dirt was rich with mineral ore too. There were some plants and trees for those earth faeries. Fire faeries had piles of hay and kindling sticks throughout the field as well. The only elemental group that had nothing in the way of transformable matter were the air faeries. Though with wind one could pick up and fling rocks and sticks, and of course, people. Not to mention the advantages air faeries had in flight. All in all, this would make for an interesting opening melee.

"Everything look good?" A voice behind him called.

He turned to see Stephen approaching in plain clothes, loose but well fitting. Not expensive, but competent, like many of the qualified soldiers and lesser nobles fighting for a spot today. "It does," Rafe said. "So do you. But you're not wearing any Houseboy gear?"

Stephen shook his head. "Nah. I'm going to do this on my own." The man's eyes sparkled with a quiet mischief, and Rafe wondered how many were going to mistake this smart, competent soldier for a Cornwall bumpkin. Whoever did would likely finish watching, not fighting, come the end of the day.

"Good luck," Rafe said and held out his hand.

Stephen grabbed it. "Don't need luck." He smiled. "You're in the broadsword, right?"

"I am," he nodded. "Looking forward to it." He rolled his shoulders. "It's been awhile since I've done any sword swinging outside a practice field." He shrugged. "Hope I can still handle it."

Stephen snorted. "I doubt that will be a problem." He tilted his head to the side and looked Rafe up and down. "Saw quite the uptick in the registrations after you and your friends made a show of it. Smart. Still think you should have let more people in."

"I don't disagree," Rafe said. "The king wanted what he wanted, and, in terms of security, the idea of an open tournament was impossible. It's enough that we've got a thousand armed folks pouring in, at least, all of them carrying their weapons around like proud peacocks with tail feathers. There have already been some minor brawls. Once the ale goes around..." Rafe sighed and shook his head. "But if I had it my way, it would be open to more than just knights and lords."

"And ladies," Stephen added.

"And ladies," Rafe agreed. "There are a few in the broadsword and in the dagger-and-hand to watch out for." He shook his head, and a sly smile crept across his face. "And I'd be wary of the ones in the melee too."

"Oh, I don't underestimate my opponents," Stephen said. "And I've got no problem hitting any opponent. Besides, it's all non-lethal anyway."

"Right." Rafe rolled his eyes. "And that means no one ever gets hurt." He pushed away from the fence post. "It's about time to start. I'll be up in the box watching."

"I'll be one of the few standing at the end," Stephen said. He bowed lightly. "Your lordship." He turned and walked away.

Rafe watched him go. He'd wanted to ask about Deor, but he also knew that any asking might make things worse, and today belonged to Stephen.

Rafe needed to focus on looking like he'd forgotten all about her, like he was back to his old pals, his own haunts, and his old self.

He shifted his gaze upward. He could just see the top of the Tower jutting up behind the trees that surrounded the field. She'd be watching, he knew. There was no way Finn would let her miss a moment of it. The broadsword event would certainly be on mirrors across the land. She'd see Rafe perform with Genevieve's favor dangling from his shoulder. He scowled. He was kidding himself thinking she'd care. She might well hate him—and he'd deserve it—for missing out on the punishment Finn doled out, for being the king's best boy. The term sent a thrill of rage through him, and a cold wind swirled.

"Excuse me, your lordship," a man said.

Rafe looked up. A participant waited in front of him. Rafe touched his forehead with a finger and smiled, stepping out of the way so the competitors could file in. "Have fun," he said, and made his way to the stands and the main box.

Rafe slipped into his seat. The other two couples had settled in behind the seats reserved for the Sword and Shield. The seat in front of Rafe's was occupied as well, by Gordie eagerly leaning forward, hands on his knees, watching the fighters mill about and organize before the first charge.

"Only fifty come out of this, sir?" Gordie asked Rafe without turning to look at him.

"Yes," he answered. "You've signed up for the squire melee?"

"Yes," the kid said, still staring at the field. "If I don't qualify in it, I'm going to do the broadsword. But I really want to make the melee."

Rafe nodded. More glory in beating up several other young men in a chaotic way than efficiently slicing single opponents according to a strict set of rules. He understood—sometimes it was good to go out and hit people. Not any person, per se, but people. Rafe certainly could use a few swings.

As if on cue, Arthur sat down next to him in the seat reserved for the Shield. "Any good prospects?" he asked.

"I don't know." Rafe shrugged. "I don't recognize most of the people, even by name." He scanned the now organized group. "Though a lot of them seem to be wearing similar badges."

Rufus leaned in from behind them. "Are those Sons of London badges?"

"I think they are," Rafe didn't add that he saw more than a few out there with the Aethelwing star on a black background but with an added silver bar, barbed, with a tiny coronet set on it that marked it as supporting the heir, not the king. It warmed his heart, to be sure, but he couldn't help but worry what Finn's reaction might be.

"Damn fools," Arthur said. "They do that in the final, and the king might have them arrested."

"He might," Rafe agreed. "Is there much room left in the Tower?" He hadn't needed to break Finn's commandment against going to the Tower to know that arrests were ongoing. Many of the lesser members of the houses who had come to compete seemed to have been targeted. "Of course," he added, "that's not my concern."

"Nothing unusual," Arthur said. "There's been more street crime and such, so the Civil Patrol is making a small show of force to keep that sort of thing down. Monjoie might be a bit overzealous, but it's nothing to worry about."

Donovan patted Arthur on the shoulder. "Well done. My father is a big fan of zealotry against traitors. Makes things easier." Next to him, Chloe chuckled.

"I believe I have heard that," Rafe said. He had picked out Stephen on the field and watched him. The only way he recognized him was by the cherubic blond curls. He wasn't wearing a helmet, a safety risk balanced out by increased range of vision.

The magic of the competition was thick across the bodies, ready to note hits and alert the fighter with a small pulse. Take enough hits, or one good one, and the magic would light up red, and the fighter would be out—required to leave the playing field to the camp on the far side of it and watch the rest. Or the fighter could stomp off to his dressing stall and disappear, as many, especially the early eliminated, often did. Land enough hits, and the magic would light up green, and the fighter was on to the final round. The first fifty to make enough hits or the last fifty standing were in.

Stephen was on the edge of the field skirting the boundary by a fence. He looked small and a touch unprepared. Rafe focused hard. Stephen had dressed himself in a glamor, one making him look harmless and frightened. Rafe snickered. He couldn't wait to see who fell for it.

"What's funny?" Arthur said, leaning toward him. "I could use a laugh."

"Nothing," Rafe said. "Or it's not important. I was simply taking in the fighters. Stephen is out there, you know."

"He didn't buy in to the final?" Arthur asked. "Strange." He peered out at the gathered crowd, searching. "I don't think he's got much of a chance, honestly. He's bright enough for a Houseboy. That country boy thing is a schtick, but I don't think it is too far off, even if he thinks it is."

"Maybe," Rafe said, non-commitally. "I don't know him well enough to say."

"I read his file over a few times," Arthur said. "It took him twice as long as anyone else before him to be promoted to Caer Eisteddfod, even though it was on his earliest documents as his place of choice. Something's got to be going on there—old Sergeant Rhys is too clever by half to let someone incompetent slip by into the Houseboys."

"True," Rafe said. "I can look into it, if you like. If I'm not overstepping?"

Arthur rolled his eyes. "Stop with that nonsense," he insisted. "It's petulant, and it doesn't suit you."

Rafe tensed. Punching wouldn't do any good—probably wouldn't make him feel better, even. "I'm taking the king's orders very seriously," he said.

"You're not in any danger, Rafe. The king adores you, you know that. Fall in line, and it will be like it used to be. You're his Sword, and I'm his Shield. Isn't this the kind of thing we'd laugh about and hope for when we were first in training?"

Rafe remembered conversations they'd had, imagining powerful political positions that allowed them daring rescues of the king and his lady, and perhaps a few other nobles who would be demonstratively grateful. The memory didn't bring much joy. Everything he'd wanted then had been an ill-conceived fantasy of a boy playing soldier. "You're right," Rafe said. "I have everything I ever said I wanted. You?"

"I suppose." Arthur said.

A whistle went up, and the fighting started. This was a true melee—there were no organized sides. Small explosions of magic blossomed as various fae took aim at each other. The few werefolk rapidly changed into animal form and attacked. Tornado-like swirls, balls of fire, geysers of water, earthquakes, all rocked the field.

Rafe hadn't lost sight of Stephen. He stayed to the edge, ducking and lashing out with magic when he needed to, but mostly staying out of the way. Around him, people pummeled each other. Alliances formed and melted away, as every person was out there for themselves. Rafe settled back in his chair, and Arthur did the same. It was going to be a long fight.

It took over an hour, but most of the three hundred and fifty were gone, a majority beaten, and those who had qualified had stepped back, content to watch as the last few fought to join their ranks. Stephen was one of the last fighters.

His magic had served him well, but now it was down and dirty. A few yards away from him, another man went down—four people remained, and no clue how many spots left. Two of the fighters were strong, sturdy—both in human form, but Rafe was sure they were werebears. The woman stood nearly seven feet tall, as did her companion.

Stephen glanced to his side as a slender redhead probably thirty pounds lighter than Stephen brought his fists up. Stephen spoke, the redhead grinned and nodded. As the two werebears readied to charge, Stephen took three steps back and darted to the side, centering himself behind his new ally. For a second Rafe thought Stephen had pulled a double-cross, leaving the redhead to take the brunt of the fight while Stephen took a moment of rest.

Instead, Stephen lifted his arms, and a swirl of wind picked up. He thrust his hands forward, and the swirl spun around the redhead, lifting him off the ground. In the middle of the whirlwind, the redhead did something with his hands—Rafe couldn't quite make it out through the dust. A burst of white fire shot from the center of the wind, engulfing the two werebears. The magic around them blazed red, and they cursed. There was no way the fire faerie would have had time to make such an impact alone. The whirlwind gave him the moment's distraction he needed.

As fast as he'd lifted the man, Stephen dropped him. The redhead spun to face Stephen, white flames still crackling around his hand. As they squared off, about to strike, both flashed with green magic. The last two spots in the final were filled.

Now that the fight was over, Rafe could see the myriad red spots across Stephen's body. He had one, maybe two more blows left. One touch from the werebear would have knocked him out. The redhead looked as beat up as Stephen. They smiled and shook hands, conversing as they made their way to join the other winners.

The marshals gathered them and formed a line, making sure to magically clean their badges and their crests for display. Many of them had crests that reflected guilds—craftsmen or merchants. Men and women (it was about even on that count) who had earned their knighthoods from being in the military, but whose background was not noble. A few from noble houses fallen on hard times. A field of worthy fighters without the funds to buy their place.

Many of those in the losing crowd had noble crests—younger sons and daughters of noble families. People who had every advantage but had not taken the time to hone their skills. Among them, the younger Overton son, looking annoyed and abashed. He'd performed well enough—he certainly wasn't among the first eliminated—but he wasn't a great fighter, that's for sure.

A whistle sounded, and Rafe and the others stood, applauding as the marshals led the fifty winners past the box, announced their names, and welcomed them to the formal tournament, including the opening ball. The final melee would be the first event on the last day.

Stephen was near the end of the line, chatting with the redhead, but when they passed the center of the box, he looked up and, catching Rafe's eye, saluted with a wide grin. Rafe laughed and returned the salute.

"Not bad," Arthur said. "Smart teamwork there at the end." He finished his applause as the short parade ended and the combatants made their way from the field to their stalls to change.

"Indeed." Rafe turned to the couples behind him. "Was that enough amusement for you?"

"Excellent," Donovan said. "I'm now thoroughly convinced that the vampires would have no trouble taking out faerie knights, even with the disadvantage of daylight on your side."

Rufus laughed and slapped Donovan on the back. "It was a good melee," he said. He nodded at Gordie. "What did you make of it, lad?"

"Oh," he said, fumbling slightly. "I thought it was wonderful. I got some ideas for the squire melee day after tomorrow."

"Smart boy," Chloe said, giving him an appraising and approving look up and down.

Gordie blushed bright red.

"Alright, I think that's enough chatting," Rafe said. "The lad and I need to be getting back to the palace to dress for the ball this evening, don't we Gordie?"

"Yes sir." Gordie straightened and saluted. "We'll see you all later." Rafe nodded at Arthur, "My lord Shield." He turned before Arthur could respond and led Gordie from the stands.

Chapter Thirty

Before the three-sided mirror in his dressing room, Rafe did a half turn, studying the lay of his coattails. The squared tails of his cream-colored satin frock coat flared over a set of matching breeches. Both frock coat and its accompanying waistcoat were embroidered in a free-flowing flower and vine motif in which woody stems twined around periwinkle-colored flowers. The discerning viewer might even spot a tiny wren or baby rabbit stitched into a discreet corner or peeping out from behind a leaf.

"You're sure it's good enough?" he asked Jameson for the third time.

"Perfection, sir. You will be the envy of every heart at the ball."

Rafe grimaced and turned the other way. "That's a bit what I'm afraid of. Don't laugh at me old man—you know what I mean. I'm there as the Sword and one competitor among many. If the king thinks I'm trying to outshine him, he'll be angry."

Jameson put a hand to his mouth until his face resumed its normal somber expression. "Trust me, Lord Farringdon. Or, if you will not trust me, trust my intelligence from His Majesty's valet. Your attire will be entirely suitable, but in no way imply competition or dissension from His Majesty. Now hold still so that I may tie on your garters."

Rafe rolled his eyes but held still as Jameson tied the garters, a historical leftover from an earlier era. There was no earthly way Jameson would let his stockings, woven in cream on cream fan motifs, slide down. The magic that held them in place could probably be used to mortar a building. Rafe slipped on his dancing shoes and took one last look in the mirror. If Deor were here, she would likely laugh at him and call him a walking garden. She would be stunning in her grandmother's jewels and a dress from Wham! and Thorsen.

He shook himself a little, shaking away the fantasy. He hoped she'd at least gotten a chance to enjoy watching the melee from her prison in the Tower. A cold chill ran down his spine. Arthur never did say exactly where Deor was in the Tower. She might well be deep underground in solitary confinement. Stephen had never actually said she wasn't.

"Sir?" Jameson's voice was gentle. "Shouldn't you be getting along soon?"

Startled out of his reverie, Rafe stuttered. "Yes. Yes, of course. I'll be off right now. Thank you, Jameson. You can take the rest of the night off. Enjoy yourself."

Jameson pressed his hands together. "I'll just turn down the bed and lay out your night things then. But I will be within call should you need me, sir."

"Thank you," Rafe said again, heading for the door. He was hardly late yet, but he really ought to be getting to the ball soon.

In the hall, he passed the two night guards with a hasty nod, hardly glancing at the blond man on the left. Then he spun on his heel.

"Bolton!" he barked. "What the devil are you doing here? Why aren't you dressed?"

Stephen looked down at his Houseboy uniform in alarm and up again in confusion. "I'm sorry, sir. I don't see anything amiss with my uniform. I put myself on the roster, sir, so that some of the other lads could celebrate with their friends. Monjoie didn't object, sir."

Throwing his hands in the air, Rafe turned to the other guard. "Get your relief up here immediately. Lt. Bolton is coming with me. Urgent business. He won't be back on the roster tonight."

Wordlessly, the man saluted. Rafe dragged Bolton by the arm back into his quarters, shouting "Jameson! Jameson, where are you?"

"Here, sir." Jameson appeared in the doorway to Rafe's bedroom. "Oh dear." He shook his head in sorrow at the sight of Stephen. "Oh, this will not do. No, no, no. This will not do at all. Come, Lieutenant, let me help you."

Rafe's shoulders relaxed a touch. "I knew you'd save us, Jameson. You see if you can tack him into one of my suits, will you? I'll dig up some jewels for him that won't be too recognizable as mine." He glanced down at Stephen's feet. "Creator blast it, you can't wear boots to a ball! And you'll never fit into my dancing shoes. Maybe we can steal some of Finn's. His feet are smaller than mine."

"Possibly, sir. Need hath no law, they say."

Stephen sputtered, looking in confusion between Rafe and his valet. "I am not stealing the king's shoes. Have you lost your mind?"

"Have you lost yours?" Rafe snapped back. "You're supposed to be at the Tournament Ball in under twenty minutes and you're dressed for combat."

Stephen's jaw sagged. "I am? Flipping hell, nobody told me."

"They announced it at the parade at the qualifier," Rafe said.

"I didn't think they really meant it," Stephen stammered. "I'm not really one for balls."

Rafe glared at him. "You are tonight! Now strip. We don't have much time."

Stephen's normally ruddy pink face flushed with social panic as he ripped off his uniform jacket and sat down on the couch to yank off his boots, muttering the whole time in a string of unintelligible Cornish curses.

All at once, Jameson clapped his hands together like a school master calling the class to attention. "We may yet be saved!" he declared and darted from the room. A moment later he returned carrying with him a garment bag and a shoebox. The box was tied up in a fuschia pink ribbon and the garment bag bore Wham! and Thorsen's unmistakable logo.

"These arrived yesterday, along with a ballgown. My daughter Melanie was deeply distressed by the reminder that the princess would not be joining the ball, so I took it on myself to put them away. My deepest apologies, sirs. I should have investigated them in more detail. I understand that these were intended for you, Lt. Bolton," Jameson said, laying the garment bag reverently across the arms of a chair. He opened the shoebox and drew out a note, reading it aloud.

To our gracious princess,

We are distressed more than we can say that you have not been at liberty to come in for your fittings. In the hopes that you will soon obtain your freedom and return to the happiness of your former state, we have taken it upon ourselves to finish your commission in accordance with the measurements already on file.

The suit of clothes you ordered for Lt. Bolton of the Household Guard have also been finished to the best of our estimation. We have included them, trusting that some member of your retinue may make any needed adjustments. The armor for the melee which you requested is still in the hands of our atelier. We expect to have it finished no later than late morning of the day before the final round.

We have the honor to remain your most devoted servants,
Wham! and Thorsen

"She ordered me clothes?" Stephen's voice couldn't hide his wonder.

"And armor for your final match," Rafe said. His own heart swelled. Of course, she had ordered her guard his armor and dancing clothes. Of course, it was Deor who realized Stephen would have neither the education nor the means to obtain such things for himself. Unlike Monjoie, who let Stephen put himself on the duty roster the night he should be at the ball. It could have been an oversight, but was probably snobbery, and the fact that Deor liked Stephen.

Lovingly, Jameson drew the suit out of its wrappings and held it up for inspection. Stephen put his hand over his mouth, like a child seeing Yule decorations for the first time.

Splendid didn't begin to describe the suit. A silk frock coat the color of new spring grass went over ecru knee breeches and a matching ecru waistcoat. The edges of the coat were embroidered four inches deep in a magenta motif rather like flowering tassels. The magenta embroidery repeated in smaller detail on the waistcoat.

"It's gorgeous," Stephen said. He pulled the skirts of the coat closer. "What is this supposed to be?"

Jameson studied the embroidery for a moment. "Amaranthus blossoms, sir. More popularly known as love-lies-bleeding." He handed the coat to Rafe and said in a more business-like tone, "Now sir, if you would strip down to your small clothes, we can outfit you properly. Promptly now, sir. We mustn't keep the king waiting."

Stephen hastened to obey.

Entering the ballroom with Stephen, Rafe paused long enough for the heralds to announce them, then trotted down the marble stairs into the main ballroom. Overhead the king's banners fluttered, hung on invisible wires of magic, and musicians played from the gallery.

"I take it this is your first ball?" Rafe said.

"Do dances in the village pub's courtyard count?" Stephen answered.

"They do not." Rafe took a glass for himself from a passing tray and another for Stephen. "It's perfectly alright. There's nothing to it. Pace yourself with the food and drink, don't say anything political, and have a good time. Dance if you want to or circulate on the margins if you don't. Stay *away* from tiny crystal goblets full of iridescent green liquid."

"Thank you, sir." Stephen scanned the room. "I don't think I know a single person here except you and the captain." He sipped his drink.

Rafe nodded in agreement and sipped his drink as well. Across the room he spotted his friends clustered around Genevieve. Clarissa waved, and he lifted his glass in greeting to her. "You're more than welcome to stay with me and my crowd," he said. "We're a friendly bunch. Come, let me introduce you."

After much bowing and exchanging of names, Stephen was fully introduced to the group, and they were joined by Donovan and Chloe. Rufus and Penny were on the dance floor bouncing through a lively reel.

"You can practically see his tail wagging from here," Chloe said. Beside her Donovan laughed. Stephen tried, and failed, not to join him.

Even Delaney Overton cracked a smile. "Marriage does seem to suit the Alpha's heir," he agreed.

At the word marriage, Rafe forced himself to cast what he hoped was a suitably heart-stricken look in Genevieve's direction. She responded with a slow flutter of her fan. All around them the noise of the ball swelled, over a hundred voices all chattering at once. The room was so crowded around the edges that most of the guests had pulled their wings in to avoid crushing one another. Only the dance floor was a glorious profusion of fluttering color.

Rafe noted that Stephen had the good sense to keep his hands out of his breeches's pockets, a move that was sure to ruin the hang of his coat, and worse, signal his lack of breeding to anyone with eyes. No doubt he'd had that rule well and truly drilled into him with his first parade dress uniform.

Their shoulders pressed together by the crush of the crowd, Stephen took the opportunity to whisper to Rafe, "Is it normal for so many people to be wearing badges of loyalty at an event like this?"

Before he answered, Rafe scanned the room, taking a slower count of what had only made a brief impression before. Stephen was right—something was amiss. Dozens of Aethelwing house badges were prominently displayed along lapels and sashes, waists and armbands. But far too many of them bore the Heir's insignia. Fewer in number, but just as troubling were the folk who also wore badges representing Wellhall or the Sons of London. Far too many to escape Finn's notice.

Rafe was just about to answer Stephen when a blast of trumpets from the heralds silenced the musicians and brought the dancers to a stop. All eyes turned toward the marble staircase.

"His Majesty Sweordmund Fionnliegh Athelwing VIII, long may he reign. And his Consort, Princess Astarte," the heralds called out. In perfect unison, every head bent in a deep bow as Finn and Astarte entered the room.

Beside him, Genevieve murmured, "Gracious, the Princess Consort knows how to dress for politics."

Rising from his bow, Rafe wondered why Genevive would say that. To his eyes, Astarte looked unaccountably subdued. Where Finn wore a silver brocade coat, subtly embroidered in gold accents, Astarte's dress was an iron grey with only the faintest of opalescent sheen to it. Even her normally golden skin seemed a shade duller than normal. Her neck and shoulders were bare, her translucent wings open behind her, but on her arms, she wore elbow length grey silk gloves. Then he understood. This was Finn's night, his moment of glorious acclaim. Astarte wouldn't think of dressing to compete with the spectacle he presented. She had dressed as if she were his shadow. And if anyone thought that her outfit was just a touch mournful, well that was surely just their imagination.

Slowly the monarch and consort made their way around the room, greeting their guests, stopping every few paces to chat with particular friends or notable people. At last, they reached Rafe and his friends who all bowed again at Finn's approach.

"Rafe, my boy, you look marvelous!" Finn embraced him heartily, and Rafe returned the hug, his heart pounding. "And Genevieve! How delightful to find you here. I would have thought you'd be as far away from this fellow as you could get."

As Finn spoke, Rafe cringed inside, wishing the floor would split open and swallow him alive. But Genevieve merely giggled and shrugged in a manner that managed to convey the slightest hint of embarrassment along with girlish delight. "Well, Your Majesty," she said. "I have spent so much time with your kind wife these past few weeks. Perhaps I've come to understand Rafe's quirks and foibles a little better. And to understand is to forgive."

Little oohs and aahs of excitement ran through the surrounding crowd. The society pages would certainly have plenty to report in the morning.

The look of gratitude Rafe gave Genevieve was, this time, entirely sincere. Finn smiled, chucked Genevieve under the chin, and moved on with Astarte on his arm. Rafe nearly sagged with relief. Donovan took a long drink from his goblet and raised his eyebrows at Rafe over the rim. Rafe pretended not to see him.

Instead, he turned to Stephen, intending to ask him something, anything, about his planned strategy for the melee. But Stephen's eyes were elsewhere. On the dance floor a certain familiar redheaded man was just bowing to his partner at the end of a dance.

Stephen dropped his glass into Delaney's startled hands without looking to see if he caught it and moved toward the redhead, saying as he moved off, "Excuse me. So sorry. I see someone I know."

"Do you know who that is?" Rodney said. "A fellow soldier?"

"Oh that's Charles, Viscount Betancourt," Clarissa said. "I like him. He's the Exchequer's son."

"He was in the melee, wasn't he? One of the top fifty," Delaney said. "Brothers in arms it would seem."

Chloe smirked. "Does that look brotherly to you?"

Out on the dance floor, Stephen was bowing and extending his hand. A moment later, one hand on the redhead's back, the other holding his hand, Stephen spun his new dance partner out onto the floor as the orchestra struck up a waltz. The two men's eyes never left each other even as they wove amongst the other dancers.

Rafe shook his head. Clearly Stephen didn't need his patronage any longer, if he ever had. Turning to Genevieve, he extended a hand. "Does your forgiveness extend so far as granting me a dance?" he asked.

"Why yes, I think it might," she said. "Be a dear and hold this for me, would you Delaney?" She pawned her drink off on the hapless Delaney, who had now begun to look like a waiter, and allowed Rafe to lead her out onto the dance floor.

Chapter Thirty-One

The creak of the door woke Deor from a less than sound sleep—everyone had gone to bed a bit late after watching the red carpet coverage of the opening ball. She bolted upright before remembering the pain in her back and winced, sucking in a deep breath.

"Good, you're up." Monjoie's voice was thick with sarcasm. Before she could respond, he had hold of her arm and was hauling her out of bed.

Brand leapt off her bed and started barking, sharp, high yips interspersed with growls.

"Shut it, you." Monjoie snapped. A yelp followed, along with a thump, as Brand's shadowy form, barely illuminated from the parlor light coming in the bedroom door, hurtled across the room and hit the wall. He dropped to the floor and didn't move.

"Brand!" Deor's voice was a strangled scream and she lunged for the dog, but Monjoie's grip was tight, and he dragged her from the room.

Her eyes blurred with tears when there was no sound, not even a whimper, as she was half-walked half-carried into the brightly lit parlor. Five guards heavily clad in their flexible, iron-resistant armor, waited for her.

Monjoie flung her forward, toward them, and she almost fell, stumbling and catching herself against a guard's chest. He reached out and caught her elbow, steadying her gently. She righted herself. Behind the guards, at the door, was Stephen, watching her, his eyes grave with worry. She glanced over her shoulder at her room and then to him. He nodded.

"Come on," Monjoie said, catching her arm again.

Deor gritted her teeth as he escorted her into the antechamber, laid his hand on the door lintel and mumbled something. The portal opened to a stone room, and he flung her inside.

The room resembled the Tower of human imagination. Stone walls, and a drain in the middle of the stone floor. It wasn't surrounded by iron, and the contrast between it and her previous cell was intense. She hadn't fully understood the oppressive, if ultimately harmless, weight of the iron around her until it was gone. Unlike the interrogation room, there was no table, no chair. He shoved her into the middle of the room.

"Hands!" he demanded.

She blinked at him for a moment. "What?"

"Out in front of you." He pointed at the set of cuffs hanging at about waist height from the ceiling.

"Oh." She pushed the sleeves of her tunic up and held her hands out, palms up. He fixed the cuffs closed around her wrists. Leather-wrapped iron, secured to a chain that ran up through a ring affixed to the ceiling, across the room, and down near where Monjoie now stood. He tugged it, and it yanked Deor's arms up.

She yelped as her hands were jerked above her head and she stood on her toes. The stone was cool, but not cold, under her feet, and it should have been rough. It wasn't. A small tittering noise drew her attention. Boomie was tucked away in the corner, watching. The ground seemed to swell under her feet, cushioning her and rising to keep her steady. If Monjoie noticed her lack of discomfort, he didn't show it.

"Why am I here?" she asked. A cold fear gripped her—perhaps no one else knew she was here. It had not occurred to her that she might be in *that* particular kind of danger, though now it seemed stupid of her to be so naive.

Monjoie did not answer immediately but eased the chain so she was no longer on her toes. She clasped her hands in front of her, feeling the gentle throb of the palace. No iron here, save the cuffs. Her back ached from the jerking around, and she felt the familiar trickle of blood down her back.

Monjoie moved to the wall across from her and touched it. It shimmered like a mirror, and she could see another room. Perhaps it was next door—the mirror could have been a window—but perhaps not.

Deor gasped.

Hanging from a set of cuffs, toes barely touching the floor, was Victor. He wore only a pair of pajama bottoms. He held his head up and stared not at her, but at the other person in the room—no, other people. There were more than one. Arthur, shirtless and waiting at parade rest a few feet away. Next to him a small table with a series of not-quite-identifiable, but gleaming tools. Off to the side, in a stately chair, sat Finn.

Like her first experience with Arthur in the Tower, Deor could see another figure in the room—blurry, almost like a ghost, standing in the far corner of the room. Perhaps a trick of the light, except that Finn's gaze flicked over to it and back a few times. Finn likely thought he was the only one who could see whomever that was. Deor focused hard and tried to make out a person, but Monjoie spoke, jolting her out of her concentration.

Monjoie touched the glass. "Your Majesty? We're ready."

"Ah." Finn turned to look at Deor and smiled. "Excellent."

Deor swallowed hard. The king looked cheerful, pleased even, like he had a surprise for her.

"Welcome, my most beloved-by-the-people daughter," he said. "Did you watch the tournament today? I'm certain it was to be broadcast on the mirror. Both Arthur and Monjoie did quite well."

"Yes," Deor said cautiously. "I assumed that you wanted me to."

"Indeed, I did!" The perkiness in his voice was strained. He was eager to say something to her, she could see it on his face, but he held it back and would continue to do so while it suited him. "Do you know why?"

Deor blinked. "So I could see what I was missing by being in the Tower?" Perhaps it was a gesture of goodwill on his part, an attempt to include her, but she found that thought absurd.

"Again, yes!" He glanced at Arthur. "She really is clever, you know?"

"Yes, sire," he answered calmly. If any of this performance unsettled or surprised him, he didn't show it. If anything, he sounded vaguely bored.

"Let's see if she can get this last one—it's a bit harder, you know." The king stood and approached the glass, hands behind his back, reminding her of a college professor about to ask a question he was sure no one could answer. "Now then, can you tell me what I wanted you to see there? The important thing—most important—for you to notice. If you're going to be a good queen, you'll need to see things like this clearly."

He was crazy. She could see it in his eyes. Whatever he wanted might not have been real and certainly was out of her capacity to guess, strung up as she was, throbbing pain running through every lash and deep into her wings. "All of the people in your household performed well," she said, taking a stab, knowing it was wrong.

"Indeed, they did. I am particularly proud of them and expect them to make the finals—I rather think that Arthur and Monjoie will ultimately face off. Won't that be exciting?"

"It's a win-win," Deor said, trying to keep sarcasm from creeping in—though certainly if one humiliated the other, or perhaps desperately wounded the other, it would be.

"Yes." He nodded at her. "A win-win. I like that phrase. But that's not what I had hoped you observed. Arthur?"

Panic swelled in Deor as Arthur reached for this table and chose something for the king. Deor blew out her held breath when she saw it was a mirror. Finn touched the glass between them, and it melted away. He stepped through and held the mirror up in front of her. A sweeping view of the crowds in the stands rolled by, like a long pan shot in a film. Crowds of folks in various attire cheered and waved. Most of them had some sort of badge pinned to their clothing. As the mirror panned back and forth, she saw a lot of similar ones—none meant much to her. There were two that were prominent. One was a navy blue background with a fountain, and the other the eight-pointed star of the Aethelwing house, but several badges bore an addition—the heir's crown above the star.

"They're all wearing different badges. I see a lot of fountains, and a lot of your stars. More of those than anything else. That's a good thing, right?" She would not, she imagined, be chained in a room with a drain if it were.

"The fountains are the badge of Wellhall, the badge of your Farringdon friend here." He flicked his hand at Victor behind him, without turning. "But the different Aethwing badges, well that is something else entirely. The extra detail? That signifies that this is the badge of the heir." Finn held the mirror up again. "Look how popular you are."

He was right. Deor swallowed hard as she scanned the crowd. There were few Aethwing badges—maybe none—that were the star alone. "I see."

"You see?" He turned back and slammed the mirror down on Arthur's table. The Shield did not move a muscle, but Victor flinched away from the sound, closing his eyes. Finn turned back. "I do not think you truly see— not what I see. They are supporting you. Following you!" His voice was rising, and silver was bleeding into his irises. "Those are *my* people, not yours! You have been conspiring against me! Planning on humiliating me like this!"

"No, Finn," Deor shook her head. "Absolutely not! How could I? I've been in the Tower the whole time. I haven't spoken to anyone but the guards!"

"Oh?" He said. "That's strange. I heard that you and Victor have grown quite close in your short time in the Tower."

"Not really," Deor said. "But I didn't talk to him more than to anyone else in the cell." It was mostly true, when she thought about it. She'd visited with Delaney about the economics of the city, Dell about Winter Court history—

"Ah, but he's been giving you lessons, has he not?" He glanced back at Victor who also looked at her.

"What do you want me to say, Finn?" Deor asked. Her heartbeat rose as he refocused on her, pounding against her ribs. A chill tore through her, and she wanted to believe it was from Victor, and not her own fear. Hadn't Finn hurt her, hurt them both, enough already?

"The truth," Finn said with a smile.

Someday, I will see that smile disappear, even if I have to cut it off myself. The thought streaked through her mind and underneath her feet the floor quivered. Had Finn thought something similar about his own father? Was this always how it always went? Only a suspicious dance until he got too old or careless and she grew too tired of waiting—

His smile shifted to a frown. "What are you thinking?"

The words almost leapt from her lips, but she bit her tongue and held still. His magic filled the air in between them and crawled across her skin. A flurry of silver sparkles spun off from her, and the king waved them away.

"That I don't understand," she said. "If you hate me, just exile me. Banish me. Un-heir me." She shrugged and spoke aloud her fear. "Or, if you're going to kill me—"

"No!" His voice was sharp with shock. "Kill my own heir?" He seemed, for a moment, genuinely appalled. "The Winter Court must have an heir." He shook his head. "No. You are my child. It is my job to make you suitable."

Deor nodded. "I want that too." Her eyes darted back to Victor, his back arched, his breath ragged. His toes couldn't support his weight, and who knew how long he had hung that way, the pressure on his chest. "Please," Deor added, her eyes snapping back to Finn's face. "Don't hurt him anymore."

"Aha!" Finn stood. "Why do you care so much for him?" He stalked closer to Victor and Deor's stomach dropped. "Is it his resemblance to Rafe?" He caught Victor's chin and jerked him forward. "Or is it about hurting me?" He released Victor and turned back to face her.

"I don't want to hurt anyone," she said. That didn't matter, though—

what she wanted. People kept getting hurt. "I don't want you to hurt anyone."

"I don't." He glanced at Arthur and nodded.

Arthur stepped forward and picked up a fine scalpel.

"Just because you're not the one with the blade—" She cut herself off when Arthur brought the blade around and Victor yelped. A few crimson drops rolled down from a thin slice below his left nipple. "Stop it!" Her voice echoed through the room, making Arthur flinch.

"It's fine," Victor's voice was shaky, rough. "He's not doing any life-threatening damage."

"Yes, Deor," Finn mocked. "No damage." His eyes glittered, the silver iris alight with glee.

"Victor has been teaching me how to use a knife," Deor said flatly, trying to keep her eyes on Finn. It didn't work. She kept glancing at the slow drops of blood oozing down Victor's stomach. Arthur was, if nothing else, an expert. Pain but not lasting harm—Victor was right, she hoped.

"And?" Finn asked. He glanced back at Arthur. "Pick one of your favorites. I want my daughter to see how much my Shield loves his work."

Arthur nodded but didn't speak. He scanned the tray, musing.

"And what?" Deor said, panic rising. "We talk about stuff—nothing, anything."

Finn nodded at Arthur, who had chosen a small flail. He flicked it back and forth, the tails snapping in the air. Each one had a small, wicked hook at the end. Something that would catch and snag the skin.

"Arthur, how can you do that?" Deor snapped, her voice trembling. The tears were pooling and would spill out soon. There was no chance, she knew, that her tears would persuade Finn to stop.

Arthur started slightly at his name and for the first time met her gaze. He glanced at the king, who shrugged. "It is my job. I serve at—"

"The king's pleasure, yes, I've heard," Deor said. The dam broke, and tears fell out of her eyes. Finn's smile widened. The tears, though, weren't pity, though she ached for Victor's hurt. It was rage, burning so hot that she was surprised the room had not filled with her sparks.

A glance at Monjoie told Deor that he was enjoying the show too—and her tears all the more.

"In your own time, Arthur," the king said. "We're in no rush." Finn glanced behind him, and the figure moved forward, crossed into her room, and took a place in the corner opposite of Monjoie. There was no way any of them, save Finn, had seen it.

The first hiss of the tails through the air and the crack of them connecting with flesh made Deor jerk her gaze back to Victor. She kept her eyes open, blinking the tears away, and watched the blow rip Victor's skin, each lash mark punctuated with the small holes in the flesh, a drop of blood welling against pale blue skin.

"Specifically, what has he said to you?" Finn asked.

"I don't know" Deor said. "We have talked about his childhood, Wellhall—"

"Ah, and what of interest there?"

"Mostly that his mother is a psychotic bitch, but I think you already knew that," Deor snapped. "He's not a traitor, and he hasn't said anything to indicate as much to me. He's been here for months, what more could he possibly know?"

"Excellent question. But it seems that the Tower isn't so secure as we thought, is it Monjoie?"

"No sir." The slimy man stepped forward and bowed.

"Monjoie intercepted letters being snuck in and out between him and his mother."

"What?" Deor said and looked at Victor. "I never heard anything about that. I never saw anything." The look of shock, followed by utter fear, flashed across Victor's face. "I don't believe it."

"Show her." Finn said.

Monjoie took papers from inside his jacket and held them in front of her eye.

Deor skimmed them. They were damning. A strong but feminine handwriting about how she and her people could disrupt the tournament, raise anger against the king. She looked up. "If you let him go, she can't go around telling people you have her son, which, by the way, is the truth. But this doesn't prove that Victor ever wrote back."

Monjoie showed her another couple letters. These were in Victor's handwriting—she'd seen some of his writing on his tablet. And they discussed her. Teaching her to fight. A few of the conversations they'd had about Madeline and his own assurances that he wanted nothing more than to use her. One comment delighting in how much Deor seemed to like him —and that maybe there was something there to take advantage of, like his brother had...

"No." Deor dropped them and shook her head. "He didn't write these."

"Did you write them, Victor?" Finn asked.

"No." His voice was a rough whisper.

"You ask him, Arthur," Finn said. "Pointedly."

The lash came down once, twice, a third time.

"What was that you said, Victor?" Arthur asked.

"I didn't write those. I swear." His voice was shaking, and Deor could hear the tears.

"Please," Deor said. "I believe him."

Monjoie stepped back to the wall and hauled the chain so that it jerked her hands above her head again.

She yelped in pain as she was hauled again to her tiptoes.

"Fair enough," Finn said. "If you believe him," he said, stepping through, "then stand in for him." He waved at Arthur who followed, lash in hand.

Finn stalked up to her. He grabbed her by the back of her shirt with both hands and shredded it.

Deor shrieked and grabbed at the cloth, trying to keep the shirt from falling off of her.

"Don't!" Victor shouted. "Leave her alone!"

Finn turned back to face Victor, as did Arthur. Monjoie kept his eyes on her. "How gallant," the king said. "I see why she likes you." He turned back to Deor. "I'll leave it up to you," he said. "Do you want to be lashed?"

"No," Deor said, almost no sound coming out. Her whole body shook, and tears streaked down her face.

Monjoie came forward, and she screamed, sure he was going to touch her, or worse, strip the shirt from her. Instead, he stood close behind her, his breath on her neck.

"Touch her, and I'll kill you!" Victor hollered.

Behind Deor, Monjoie chuckled. "Treasonous wretch," he called to Victor. "You'll get yours for your betrayals soon enough." He grabbed the remains of her shirt and tore it away.

She cried out again and twisted, pulling against the chains, struggling to find some way to cover herself. There was none.

"Where should the Shield start, princess?" Monjoie whispered, lurking behind her, his mouth close to her ear.

Deor swallowed hard. She drew a deep breath and focused on the king, his face close to hers.

"Five more lashes, for lying," the king said. "Him or you? Choose."

Her eyes darted to Arthur, who stared at a fixed point behind her.

"He won't help you." Finn said.

Deor's whole body trembled. Finn's face filled her whole vision, and the magic, the hate, and the rage, poured off him and rolled over her, like she was a rock in the face of a tsunami. There was no right answer. He'd see her flogged again, or she would watch other people suffer.

"I can't...," she said. "Don't make me choose, please."

Finn laid his hand on her cheek, and she flinched away. *"Daughter,"* he said in Faerie, *"there is no escape from this. I will wait on your choice, and the longer you take to decide, the higher the number will be. Him or you. Eventually it will be enough to kill, and that, of course, will not happen to you. So, six now?"*

She shuddered, the cold air chilling the blood running down her back. He caught the other side of her face with his other hand and held it steady, forcing her to look him in the eye. *"Seven?"*

"Him," Deor blurted out the word.

"What?" Finn said, still cupping her face. "Who?"

"Victor," she said. Her gaze dropped to the floor. "Not me."

"Excellent choice," he said. "Arthur?"

Arthur nodded and moved back toward Victor.

"And Arthur?" the king asked. Arthur paused and turned his head slightly back toward the king. "Use the flail with the iron tips. And spread it around—front and back. Was it eight?" He asked.

"Seven," Deor said, pleading.

Finn smiled at her. "If you ask nicely," he said.

"Please, Your Majesty," Deor whimpered.

"Please what?" he asked.

Her mind raced. If she asked for fewer, would it make it worse? Would it rebound on her? "Please, Your Majesty, I'm begging you, no more than seven lashes for Victor." She swallowed hard and fought to keep her eyes down. If she met the king's gaze, would he see the hate there?

He pulled her face forward, and she gasped. His lips pressed against her forehead. "How could I refuse my own child's humble request?" He let go and stepped away from her. "Monjoie," he snapped, "let her down."

Monjoie hurried to the side of the room and released the chain.

Deor dropped to the floor, collapsing onto her hands and knees.

Finn caught her arm and lifted her to her feet, gently, like he actually cared that she did not suffer. It only made it worse. She clutched her still-bound hands to her chest, covering herself as much as possible. "Go fetch Root," he commanded Monjoie, "bring him here and wait outside until you are summoned."

Monjoie frowned, frustration visible, but he did as commanded.

Finn's eyes darted from her to Victor as Arthur began the lashes. Each strike brought a cry from Victor and a small whimper from Deor. Her chest tightened more with guilt as each new array of lash-marks and bloody gashes blossomed on his body. By the time Arthur finished and lowered Victor to the ground, where he collapsed, Deor was sobbing, swaying.

"Leave him, Arthur. Join us." He waved Arthur to the corner where Monjoie had been.

Arthur replaced the flail on the table and stepped through the mirror. With a wave of Finn's hand, the stone wall returned. The king shifted and looked to the other corner, cocked his head to the side. Suddenly the figure was crystal clear to Deor. A man, a faerie maybe, dressed in Victorian finery. Blond hair tumbled down loose over his shoulders in waves. His hands rested on a mahogany walking stick, silver tipped, though she could not make out the silver figure at the top. He nodded to Finn, who returned his attention to Deor.

The blonde man's gaze followed Finn's, and he started slightly when caught her staring. He smiled. Compassion, empathy, and understanding radiated off him with more power than anything she had ever felt. He tried to comfort her, she was sure of that, his magic reaching out, even as he stood stone still, to her, washing over her body, down her back, easing her pain. Deor's whole being recoiled at the magic, healing as it seemed. Her faerie and human side joined in rare agreement, and her stomach roiled. She clamped her mouth shut and tried not to vomit. Whatever that thing was, it was pure power. Her fists balled, nails sharpening, as she stared him down. *Kill it*, every fiber of her being screamed.

"Daughter?" Finn's voice brought her back.

She snapped her gaze to him, and when she glanced back, the creature was gone. Deor looked between Finn and the now vacant space. He gave no sign of anything at all, and Arthur remained unmoved at parade rest. Pain rolled back as the magic dissipated, as though it had never been there at all.

With a few whispered words, he released her from the cuffs, and they tumbled to the ground.

Deor crossed her arms over her chest.

Finn reached for her, and she flinched away. "There, there," he said, cupping her cheek and wiping away a few tears with his thumb. "I know this is hard, daughter." He looked at her with something that resembled loving care, though she was certain he had no idea what that really was. "Do you feel guilty? Responsible for his suffering?"

Deor nodded, not trusting her own voice.

"Perhaps I could ease your guilt," he said.

She looked up at him, her heart fluttering with fear.

"Kings and queens," he said with another glance to the corner, "we are special. We command the very land itself, the air, and the magic that fills it. Our weakness becomes our nation's; our strengths too. We mete justice with only a word, a thought." He stepped back from her, crossing his arms. "I fear that this demonstration is not enough to move you to be better."

Deor said nothing.

"*You displease me,*" he said in ancient Faerie, his voice hollow and rough. "*Learn the consequence of my displeasure.*"

Deor screamed as the wounds on her back tore open at his voice. His magic, driven by will, dug into each slice across her back, like a scalpel. Deor collapsed again, on her hands and knees, blood splattering on the ground around her. She drew sharp, short breaths, not noticing the whimpering squeaks that accompanied each one. Tears blurred her vision.

He crouched down in front of her. "I know it hurts—I know how much discipline hurts." He lifted her chin with a finger and waited until she looked at him. "My father could be a hard man," he said. "His lessons were often sharp. But I learned."

Well enough to put the bastard down yourself when the time came, a traitorous voice whispered in her head.

"You'll learn too," he said. "And you will be a great queen for it, when your time comes." He caught her arm and helped her to her feet. She cried out and swayed, falling against him. He steadied her, letting her lean on his arm. Looking down at her, he sighed. "Attachments and affections bind you and impair your judgement. Tonight has freed you even if you don't see it now. Being the monarch means that sometimes others must bear pain for you and that you cause pain for the good of the kingdom. Do you understand?"

Deor clamped her eyes shut, hoping he didn't see the silver flash of rage that edged her vision. She swallowed and nodded again. She deserved this —all of it, whatever he said or did. She let someone else suffer for her. She let another person take punishment she herself should have borne.

She drew deep breaths until her eyes were clear and then opened them to stare into her father's. "I don't think I understood, really understood, before this moment. But I do now."

He beamed at her, like all was forgiven. "That's my smart daughter!"

In the corner of the room, Boomie stretched his wings and called to her, a sound that rippled through the ground under her feet.

"I promise, father, I will never, ever forget the lesson."

"Arthur?" Finn said, calling to him. Deor had forgotten he was even in the room. He lurked on the other side.

"Yes, Your Majesty?" His gaze flicked back and forth between him and Deor.

"See to it that Deor makes it back to her room in the Tower. Victor as well." He scanned her back. "See that a healer makes a visit to her too." He took her hand from his arm, leaving her to steady herself, and walked to the door. "Goodnight, daughter," he said, and left.

Root hurried in, along with Monjoie.

"Get some people to clean this room up," Arthur snapped. "As soon as Victor is able, see him to the Tower." He frowned for a moment at Monjoie whose eyes seemed to glitter with repressed glee. "No more pain or damage. Understand?"

"Absolutely," he saluted. "Come with me," he said to Root who, after a glance at the princess, followed him from the room.

She wondered if Arthur would know if Monjoie hurt Victor again, if he would check, or if he really cared at all.

Arthur gathered his shirt and jacket and headed for her. When he reached for her, she stiffened, a flare of small sparkles surrounding his hand.

"Ouch!" He snatched his hand back. He glared at her. "There's no need for that. I'm not going to hurt you."

Deor shrugged. "Can't help it." Her voice quavered, and she swallowed hard. She wanted to show him no fear, but there was nothing she could do to hide the pain as thick drops of blood soaked her pajama bottoms.

"Here," he said, holding out his shirt to her. "It might be easier for you to put it on backwards." He shook it a bit and held it out in front of him. After she didn't move, he tilted his head back to the ceiling and closed his eyes.

Deor stepped forward and slipped her arms into the shirt. Arthur let go of it, and she tugged it all the way on, tucking the folded collar under her chin.

"Here," Arthur said. "Turn around."

She did as she was told.

He fastened one of the top buttons. "Now it won't fall," he said.

"Thank you." She turned to face him.

"Can you walk?" he asked, dragging his jacket on but not bothering to button it.

Deor took a couple of unsteady steps toward the door. "I think so."

"Good." He opened the door and led her into the hallway. "We'll take the portal at the end of the hall." He offered her his arm, and she took it. With his free hand, he took his mirror from his jacket pocket. "Asphodel?" he said. A few moments later, the mirror cleared.

"What?" The red-headed healer blinked blearily at him. It wasn't yet dawn, Deor guessed.

"Come to the Tower. The princess needs your care."

That woke her up. "Emergency?" She asked.

"Of a sort. Bring material to repair someone from flogging injuries. She seems to have opened her wounds."

Deor snorted.

Asphodel nodded. "I'll be right there."

Arthur led Deor down the hall then portaled them to the entryway of her cell. He let her in and stepped inside.

Lt. Bolton stood, waiting for her. In his arms was an unmoving Brand.

Deor gave a muffled cry and hurried toward them, even as her whole body shuddered with pain. She got to him and reached for Brand but paused. She looked up into Lt. Bolton's eyes. "Is he...?"

"He's asleep." He glanced past her to Arthur and then back to her. "I'm not an earth faerie, but I learned some animal magic when I was a shepherd back home. He's got a concussion, maybe, and a broken rib or two, but he's going to be fine—we'll get him a healer."

"Thank you," Deor said, ignoring the tears on her face. She took Brand from him and cuddled him close, burying her face in his warm fur. She could feel the rise and fall of his breath, hear the soft beating of his heart.

"I'm here," Asphodel called from the entryway. "What is the emergency?"

"Let her in," Arthur said to the guards outside.

"It's four o'clock in the morning," she said, irritation thick in her voice, "what could possibly—dear creator! What happened to your back?" She rushed forward to Deor.

"The wounds reopened," Deor said.

"I say, what is going on out here?" A bleary-eyed and gruff looking Delaney Sr. stood in the doorway between the parlor and the bedrooms.

"Nothing—" Arthur started.

"Most certainly not nothing!" Asphodel snapped. She glanced at Arthur, a frown pulling at the corners of her mouth.

"What is the matter?" Dell said, looking rather perky for the hour. "I was at prayer, and I heard the commotion."

"I'm fine!" Deor snapped. "Both of you, please, go back to bed."

Both men shared a glance and nodded at Deor before retreating down the hall.

Deor turned to face Asphodel. "Here." She shoved Brand at her. "Help him."

Asphodel stared down at the dog proffered to her. "Of course, but first, Your Majesty, we need to see to you."

"No." Deor shook her head. "You look at Brand, or you don't look at me at all."

Asphodel looked about to object but merely shook her head and took the puppy. She sat on the couch with him on her lap. After a few minutes of soft mutters, she looked up. "Mild concussion. Two broken ribs. A few bruises." She focused her gaze on the puppy for a moment, and a swirl of magic blurred her hands. "There. He's mostly healed up now. He should take it easy for the rest of the day."

"What happened to him?" Arthur asked.

Deor turned on him, despite the still oozing slashes on her back. "Monjoie kicked him across the room."

His eyes narrowed. "Monjoie should not have done that."

For a moment, Deor was silenced by the hard anger in Arthur's eyes.

"Asphodel," he said suddenly, "I will leave you to the princess. I will be back to check on her later. Lt. Bolton, stay and keep an eye on things—someone should be returning with Victor soon. Make sure he gets safely to his room."

"Yes, sir," Bolton saluted.

"Alright," Asphodel passed Brand off to Lt. Bolton and waved Deor over to a chair. "Sit, facing the back, so I can see what has happened here."

Deor did as she was told.

Asphodel clucked and muttered under her breath as she examined Deor. Her touch was soft, gentle, and, except that Deor already hurt all over, would have been near painless. "Tell me again what happened," she said patiently. "Did you strain yourself physically?"

Deor snorted, then winced. "I displeased my father." She shifted uncomfortably in the chair.

"Ah. I understand," Asphodel said. Her voice was soft, yet firm, shutting off the need for further explanation. Deor remembered now—Asphodel was Astarte's personal healer. "Okay, well, I'm going to have a go at closing these back up."

"Great."

Asphodel hummed while she worked, and Deor imagined she would have a lovely, tender singing voice. Every now and again, she'd stop abruptly and seem to concentrate, and then go back to the humming. "All set," she said after about ten minutes. "I think those should stay closed, but I will come back tomorrow and check. If they split open again before then, have the guards call me."

"Thank you." Deor pushed back from the chair and stood. "Can I take a shower? Or will that reopen the wounds?"

"I'd stay away from anything banging on your back, but a sponge bath should be fine." Asphodel gave her one last smile, more sad than reassuring, and left.

Deor moved to the couch where she perched on the edge and waved at Bolton to pass her Brand. He did. She settled the dog in her lap, his soft snores bringing a smile to her face. "Thank you," she said, looking up to make eye contact with Bolton. "I don't know what I would have done if I had lost him." She sniffed hard and managed to keep back the tears. She couldn't lose something else she was supposed to protect, to care for. And what would she ever tell Rafe?

The door opened, and Victor came in, followed by Arthur.

Deor swallowed hard.

Victor froze when he saw her on the couch.

Deor gently set Brand down on the couch next to her and stood. She hurried forward to Victor. "I'm so sorry," she said, forcing herself not to cry. "Are you okay?"

Victor gave a small bow. "I am well," he said stiffly. "Thank you for asking after my health, Your Majesty."

"Victor, please," Deor moved toward him but stopped when he stepped to avoid her. "You have every right to be furious at me," she said. "I'm furious at me." She wanted to reach out to him, to touch him. "I was a coward. I'm so—"

"Sorry. Yes. You've said." He stared at her for a long moment before fixing a polite smile on his face. "If you will excuse me, Your Majesty, I think I will go lie down."

As he moved to pass her, Deor caught his arm. "Victor, is there anything I can do? You're my friend—"

"No, Your Majesty. There is nothing you can do." He drew his arm away from her. "Forgive me for being so blunt, but I do believe it is my best interest—and yours—if we keep as far away from each other as possible. So, if you could find it in your heart to not speak to me, and certainly not touch me, I would be eternally grateful."

Deor gaped. She closed her mouth. A hundred things flew through her mind. She wanted to beg him not to be that way. She wanted to tell him he had every right to be that way. She wanted to curse her father to the stars and back. Instead, she was polite. "Of course, Lord Farringdon." She nodded and stepped back.

He moved past her and down the hall toward his room. She heard the door close.

She glanced at Arthur, who headed for the cell door. He paused, turned toward her. "You would do well to take a lesson from today, princess. Be careful to whom you show your affection, lest the king have others chosen to bear what should be your punishment." He sighed, like a disappointed parent. "I told you that you would hurt people." He left, closing the door behind him.

Deor dropped onto the couch.

There was nothing she could do here to help anyone. The best she could hope to do was stay as far out of Finn's mind as possible and speak to as few people as she could. What if Finn went after Delaney next? He was older than she or Victor—who knows what damage could be done? She cuddled Brand close to her, and a terrifying thought took hold of her. Arthur knew, and so Finn had to know, how much the dog meant to her, and what was to keep Finn from taking him away? Or worse, putting him down.

Deor gathered Brand into her arms and hurried to her room, shutting the door behind her.

Chapter Thirty-Two

For days after, Deor stuck to the same routine. She would let Stephen in whenever he knocked, not bothering to get up, so that he could take Brand out. He would return with her meal, which she took in her room. Except for quiet trips to the bathroom, Deor hadn't left her cell since she'd been brought back that night. She assumed the tournament was going on as planned but hadn't watched any of it nor read any of the papers.

Once again, Deor awoke to the soft rapping on her door. She winced as any movement pulled and tugged at the wounds on her back. They didn't bleed much, if at all, but they hurt like hell. A constant stab of pain every time she shifted position, stood, or stretched.

Pangs of guilt shot through her again, and she wondered if Victor had healed yet, or, if like her, his wounds still ached. The look on his face—so stiff, so formal, asking her to keep her distance. He didn't look angry, or even disappointed. No. His expression was carefully schooled neutrality, a blanket politeness that stabbed her to the core. Disdain, anger, hate—those all would have been genuine, and genuinely deserved. What he gave her was fake, civilized ceremony.

She tugged the door open, and Brand trotted out, wagging his tail.

"Who's a good boy?" Stephen cooed, and Brand dropped into a play bow before barking. "Go wait by the door," he said, and Brand scurried off.

"He likes you a lot," Deor said.

Stephen shrugged. "I'm a reasonable brief substitute for you. May I come in?"

"Sure," Deor said. She shifted slightly and propped herself up on her elbow, tugging the blankets around her modestly, though she sensed that Stephen was more like a brother than anything and would laugh at the thought of sneaking some kind of glance. "How are you? You look cheerful!"

Stephen's face spread into a wide grin. "Today is the last day of the tournament. I won the melee this morning! And thank you for the ball clothes and the armor. They were amazing."

"You're welcome." Deor sat up and hauled herself out of bed, doing her best to ignore the searing pain. She flung her arms around his neck. "That is awesome!" She stepped back. "I'm not surprised," she said. She patted him on the shoulder. "Let me put on some proper clothes, and we can go out, and you can tell me all about it. I want to hear everything about the fight."

"And Charles," Stephen added as she turned away to grab a proper tunic.

"Charles?" She dug through a pile of clothes on the chair at her desk. "Who is he?"

"A young man I met in the quals and then met again and the ball. And that I beat again today." He couldn't seem to shake his smile. "We're going out for a beer next week."

Deor glanced over her shoulder. "I definitely want to hear all about this Charles. What's he like?"

"He's tall and thin, not skinny, but thin, and has flaming red hair, and—holy creator in heaven! What happened to your back?" Stephen hurried forward to her and placed his hands on the top of her shoulders. She winced. "Stand still," he said.

As soon as his finger touched her, even with a small amount of pressure, pain shot through her. She drew a sharp breath in between her teeth. "What did you do, stab one of my wounds?"

"No." He poked again and again, eliciting the same response. "I haven't touched the wounds, just the space in between. You've got a serious infection. There's pus, but no blood." He flipped the blanket back up over her. "I'm going to get a healer."

"Wait—" Deor clutched her shirt to her chest and turned to face him. "Do you really think it is serious?"

He was already halfway out the door. "I've seen things like this before, princess. You're no lamb, but I've lost a few to what looked like normal cuts. Infection gets in, it's hard to get out."

Deor nodded. "I'll get dressed and ask Dell if it is that bad."

"I'm getting a healer, regardless."

"You'll have to get through Arthur for that," Deor said.

"Not a problem." Stephen nodded at her and left, shutting the door behind him.

By the time Deor got dressed and out into the parlor, Stephen was gone with Brand. Dell, Delaney, and Victor were sitting around the table, looking vaguely concerned.

"Come sit with us," Dell said and gestured at the fourth chair.

Deor flicked her gaze to Victor.

"Yes," Victor said. "Come sit."

Deor made her way to the table and sat, careful not to lean back against the tall chair. "So, how are you?" She glanced around the table. A newspaper sat in the middle, its headline praising the tournament. "Oh," she said. "Stephen won the melee this morning. What's left?"

"Arthur and Monjoie are in the dagger-and-hand finals, while Rafe is in the final round of the broadsword against Rufus."

"That's nice?" Deor asked.

"It is," Overton jumped in. "It might just mean that there will be a reconciliation—that the king might lift the ban, given how well Rufus has performed."

"Rafe should beat him senseless," Victor insisted. "What?" he said when the others gaped at him. "Rafe is the best swordsman in the Winter Court. He's one of the best in all of Fae. The Summer Court Sword might still be better, but it would be a hell of a fight."

"True," Delaney nodded. "But you're quite good."

"Passable," Victor corrected. "I'm more a dagger fighter—you know, down and dirty, hand-to-hand, that sort of thing. Like Arthur, actually."

"What about me?" Arthur said, strolling into the cell. He was in his tournament clothes. Stephen followed him, Brand tucked under one arm. "I hear you're not feeling well, princess. I hope you're not wasting my time—I need to get to the final."

"You wouldn't be in it if I were able to compete," Victor said. "You know I'm better than you are."

Arthur snorted. "Pity we can't find out in the tournament. You always leave your left side undefended."

"I'll keep that in mind." Victor nodded at Deor. "The princess needs you."

"Yes, I've heard." He looked at her. "You're ill?"

Deor opened her mouth to offer a pert answer but thought better of it. "I feel alright," she said. "Stephen suggested I see a healer."

"He did." Arthur waved at her. "Well, come here and let me see what the fuss is about."

Deor stood. "Where?"

"Come over by the window." He stood next to it, glaring at her impatiently as she stood up, trying to hide the wince.

She knew he'd think she was acting. Stephen set Brand down on the floor and followed him over to Deor.

"Need a hand?" Stephen offered her his arm.

Arthur rolled his eyes.

"Nah, I'm fine," she smiled at him and at the others around the table. None of them seemed to buy it.

She got to the window and turned her back to Arthur. She let her loose robe slip off her shoulders, fighting the urge to clutch the front of the robe to her chest. No one here was interested in a show, and she didn't need to broadcast her growing discomfort at the way her body seemed now to be something separate from herself. Something that all of the people around her—all men—felt perfectly comfortable commenting on, speaking about her, but not directly to her. She heard Arthur's sharp intake of breath.

"I told you," Stephen said, face serious.

"How long?" Arthur asked.

"She was fine when she got back here, as far as I know," Stephen answered. "Right, princess?"

Deor shrugged and immediately regretted it. She hauled the robe back over her shoulders and turned to face the Shield. "It hurt when I got back from the king, and it hurts more now, I guess. I've spent most of my time in bed sleeping."

"Not out here, then?" Arthur frowned at her, peering, like he was trying to see through her, into her, and work out whether she was up to something.

"Come on," Deor said, "You saw what the king did. I am not making up my wounds. He opened them again."

"I was there," Arthur snapped. "Asphodel saw to you?"

"Yes, she closed them, I thought, and said they'd be knitting again in a couple days. Then they didn't." She pursed her lips. They stared at each other for a long few moments before Deor spoke again. "I think it is like with the makeup glamours and trying to use magic to secure jewels in my hair. The magic slides off. I'm not healing as fast because of the human. It isn't Asphodel's fault."

Arthur crossed his arms. "Asphodel is an excellent healer, and I'm certain she wouldn't do anything that would result in an infection on purpose." He looked her up and down. "Your wounds seem like they are open, but they aren't bleeding."

"Okay," Deor said. "I can't see them, but I can feel them. They're hot, and they hurt like hell. Sometimes I get chills, sometimes I break out in a sweat."

"I'll get the healers," Arthur said, "after the finals tonight. They're busy right now in the lists. The final rounds are the most dangerous. You can hold on a few hours, I'm sure."

"Of course." Deor nodded.

"Excellent!" He turned on his heel and left, Stephen shaking his head, but following behind.

When the door slammed shut, Deor flipped it off with both hands. "Brown-nosing toadie," she muttered.

Deor looked at the three men. They were still seated at the table but had given up any pretense of being interested in anything but her. Delaney looked worried—laugh lines on his face creased and intensified with distress. Victor had paled. Dell's face was a serious mask. He studied her, she was certain, but if he had anything to say, he was keeping it to himself.

Finally, she broke the silence. "Are you healing, Victor?" she asked. She crossed back to the table and resumed her seat.

"I'm fine," he said with a nod. "Totally healed—not even a scar."

Deor sighed, relieved. "Thank God. I'm so, so sorry," she said, forcing herself to stop instead of spiraling into a repeated litany of apologies and explanations. "I'm a coward," she added and looked down at the table.

"I don't know about that," Victor said. "I doubt you'd been in that position before."

"I still should have known better." She pulled the paper toward her and stared at the picture on the front page. The finals of the tournament were being held on the palace grounds, the open space below the second floor balcony converted into a field. She'd have given anything to be able to watch the people joust and sword fight. It would have fulfilled a childhood dream of medieval tournaments being real—not the fake kind with huge turkey-leg dinners and actors on horses, but real men and women, with true liveries and weapons that had seen real battles.

She dragged her gaze up to meet Victor's. "He was always going to hurt me," she said. "I don't know if that's true for you. I could have at least tried to help you."

Victor leaned back in his chair, eyes fixed on her. "That's true," he said. "The bit about always hurting you. He was always going to hurt me, too, though. He'd made that clear before you arrived. He was curious to see how far you would go to try to protect me."

Deor dropped her head into her hands. "I hate that man," she said, her voice barely a whisper.

"Careful," Delaney said. "The walls have ears, child."

She looked up. "I know they do. But it's the truth."

"The truth or falsity of it doesn't matter at all," Dell said. "Don't say it aloud again. You need to decide what you are going to do with all that emotion."

"Right now?" Deor asked. She gave a bitter laugh. "Try not to cry."

Chapter Thirty-Three

The final day of the tournament had arrived, and all around the Palace grounds, cheers echoed. Thousands shouted from inside the Palace walls, and thousands more around the city cheered and shouted as the final events of the Tournament were broadcast.

Inside his dressing booth, Rafe sat quietly on a stool, his head resting on his hands, which grasped the hilt of his sword, point down toward the earth. He concentrated on his breathing, letting air and magic flow through him in easy lines. Carefully, methodically, he placed all the cares and anxieties of the current days in the back of his mind. Deor's pain. His missing brother. Finn's growing paranoia. Robbie. Astarte. They could wait for another day. Now there was only the breath and the sword.

"Sir?" Gordie said. "Are you alright, sir?"

Rafe raised his head with a smile. "Quite alright, young squire. I haven't yet taught you how to prepare for battle, have I? Remind me to do so when this is all over. You can dress me now." He laid aside the sword, blunted for the Tournament, and held out his arms.

With his armor strapped on and his helmet tucked under his arm, Rafe strode out to the final event of the Tournament. Behind him came Gordie bearing his banner, the Aethelwing star *argent* on a ground *sable* under an unsheathed sword, *argent*. Today he fought as the Sword, representative of the King and all the Winter Court.

Along with Gordie came other members of his household along with his friends and supporters. Delaney and Rodney had both finished their events and, still in armor, they fell into step behind Jameson and Melanie. Jameson bore Rafe's sword and Melanie his shield. Stephen, bathed and refreshed from his win in the melee this morning, joined them with a jaunty grin to Rafe. Even Delaney's brother, George, came along. And of course, Jake and Sam, brushed to within an inch of their lives and wearing black and silver harnesses pranced alongside Rafe as his honor guard, their heads held high. He could not have asked for two better knight supporters.

From the opposite side of the grounds came Rufus, similarly armored. A sash of his family's tartan, pinned with a golden wolf's head, crossed his breastplate. Beside him Penny bore his shield, a wolf's head *or* upon a field *vert*. A retinue of his friends and family, all wearing the Irish Alpha's tartan came with him. Rafe counted at least twenty followers. More than a couple had pinned on the Heir's badge as well. Inwardly, Rafe winced to see it, but kept his face composed. Perhaps Finn would be too focused on him and Rufus to notice.

The two contestants met at the royal stand as heralds' trumpets blared. They bowed to one another and shook hands before turning to bow deeply to Finn. At Finn's side, Astarte smiled back at them. Genevieve sat beside her wearing a white dress sewn all over with tiny eight-pointed stars in Wellhall blue. A large black and silver king's badge rested on her shoulder.

Finn acknowledged their bows with a gracious smile and wave of his hand, but his eyes flicked over Rufus's entourage, and his smile hardened. "You may proceed with the event," he called out, his steward's air faerie magic amplifying his voice to reach even the farthest viewers.

Rufus began to turn toward the fighting ground, but Rafe stepped forward, beckoning Stephen to join him. "Make me louder," he hissed.

Stephen blinked for a second but nodded and blew a puff of magic at him that ringed his throat. In front of Genevieve, Rafe went down on one knee and held out his hand, trying to remember the words he had hastily memorized out of chivalric romance found in the library. If the words were good enough for the Knight of the Broken Garter, they were good enough for him.

"My lady Genevieve. I most humbly beg your succor for my pitiful estate. My days have been dark and my paths winding without your favor. Take me back into your heart again and there let me reside forever."

Genevieve blushed, gasped, and covered her face. Beside her Finn and Astarte clapped and hugged each other. *Ooohs* and *aaahs* broke out all over the assembled crowd. Just as Rafe began to wonder just how long he was going to have to hold out his hand to her, Genevieve rose, brushing real tears off her face and took his hand. She leaned down over the stands' edge to kiss him. Her honey blond hair fell all around their faces.

"Well done. Who wrote that for you?" she whispered under the cover of her hair. The watching crowd broke out in thunderous applause. She kissed him again for good measure and stood up. More applause and cheering.

"Well, well," Rufus said. "You've certainly found the way into the people's hearts."

Hot prickles of embarrassment broke out along Rafe's back and hairline. Up in the stands Genevieve was taking off one of her sleeves, conveniently detachable for just such an occasion, and proffering it to Rafe to wear as her favor. Gordie helped him tuck it into the shoulder latch of his armor. Rafe blew Genevieve a kiss.

"Fighters to your places!" a herald shouted. "At the Marshal of the Lists command, begin!"

Side by side, Rafe and Rufus walked into the square laid out for them. Plenty of room to circle and dodge around each other. No room to run from the thousands of eyes. Rafe saw that Rufus intended to fight bareheaded and handed his own helmet to Gordie.

"Begin!"

Swords up, the two fighters circled each other, grinning. Ah, this was what got the blood pounding through his veins. Just him and his opponent.

"Come on, then," Rufus grunted, beckoning to Rafe with his blade, and Rafe obliged with a quick slash across Rufus's upper arm. Rufus parried with his shield and dodged to the left, his backswing nearly catching Rafe in the knee.

In his back, his wings twitched, eager to come out for their role in the fight. But Rafe's armor was solid in back, not that he would have deigned to cheat even if he could. In a life or death battle he would have happily swooped down on Rufus from above, but this was pure swordplay—no wings, no magic, no transformations.

They circled more, trading quick, almost tentative blows, each feeling out the other's style. Ah yes, Rafe saw it. Rufus wanted to close with Rafe, to make up the advantage Rafe's height and longer reach gave him. Keep him at arm's distance then. Rafe slashed and backed, slashed and backed, hammering down Rufus's shield arm while dancing just out of reach of a return blow. Chips and chunks of Rufus's shield flew in all directions. Soon he wouldn't have a shield at all.

Though Rafe had the advantage of size, Rufus was quicker. Lightning fast on his feet, he sliced and carved, darting in past the edge of Rafe's shield and dancing away again. Rafe planted his feet like stone and drove his shield full weight against Rufus, intending to knock the other man down.

But Rufus did not fall. Rufus attacked, a quick upstroke of the blade that caught Rafe's hauberk, slicing the cloth's edge before Rafe beat down on Rufus's arm with his pommel. He heard a gasp of pain as the heavy pommel connected with his opponent's wrist. For a few seconds, Rufus retreated, wringing his sword arm and sheltering behind his broken shield. Rafe lowered his own shield a fraction to give them both breathing room. No reason to rush this.

Their eyes met. Rufus grinned and Rafe returned the smile wholeheartedly. "Now to it!" Rafe shouted. Rufus answered him with a joyful howl, and they rushed together. Shields, swords, armor clanging in a messy, harried tangle of blows. Feet scrabbled for purchase. Their shield edges locked, and they pushed and shoved against each other, teeth clenched, whacking at each other's heads. Rufus's fist caught Rafe square in the eye, and he spun away, blinking with the pain.

Roaring, Rufus followed up as Rafe brought his hand up to his tear-blinded eye. But Rafe could still see just fine from his other eye, thank you, and he caught Rufus's blade on his own, driving the Irishman back and back across the field with a rain of blows so fast they blurred the air.

Ten feet down the field, Rufus regained his balance and struck back. His blade sliced Genevieve's favor from Rafe's shoulder. Rafe kicked him in the knee. Rufus caught himself, driving his shield point into the ground and using the force to propel himself up inside Rafe's guard. Rafe brought his sword hand down, and their hilts locked, their sweat-grimed faces inches from each other. Panting they strove, neither losing an inch, blade edges scraping against each other.

Hold hard. Retreat to return, but never fail. Rafe's old swordmaster's words came back to him as they always did in such moments. Rufus was panting just a fraction harder than he was. If he held on just that much longer, he could win. He knew he could. He saw his opening, and he took it. He let his back heel slip on the damp grass, just the merest sliver of an inch.

Rufus bore him to the ground, his sword point at Rafe's throat. "Yield!"

"I yield me," Rafe said. His arms fell at his side, open to Rufus's mercy.

Easing away slowly, Rufus lifted his blade from Rafe's throat and drove it into the sod. "Well fought," he said and offered Rafe his arm up.

"An honor to cross swords with you," Rafe said. He grasped Rufus's arm and the two embraced, pounding each other on the back.

Their shields and weapons left on the field, they marched back together to receive their prizes from the king. On every side the people stood and cheered, chanting their names.

But Finn did not receive them so joyfully. He stood at the front of the royal box, his eyes edged with silver and his face grim. A golden laurel wreath studded with pearl dewdrops was in his hands. Beside him stood Astarte carrying a gilded sword no bigger than a letter opener for the second prize winner.

"Rufus, son of Angus, heir to the Irish pack," Finn said. "We congratulate you on your win." No congratulations had ever been so cold or bereft of favor. All around them the cheering hushed. "Take this laurel wreath in token of your prowess."

Rufus cast an alarmed glance at Rafe before stepping forward and inclining his head to receive the wreath. But instead of placing the wreath on Rufus's head, Finn handed it off to a page girl and jerked his hand in Rufus's direction. Confused and trembling, the girl placed the wreath on Rufus's auburn curls.

"Congratulations, Sir Wolf," she said in a tiny voice before stepping back.

When Rufus rose from his bow, his face was red with fury. Before he could speak, Finn held up his hand. "You have won your prize. Did you think our royal eyes were blind to your insolence? Did you think you could trespass so far upon our favor without penalty?" He waved his hand at Rufus's retinue.

Too late, Rafe realized that the Household guards and Civil patrol members standing around the box had more than doubled since the beginning of the fight.

"Finn, what are you doing?" he shouted.

"Arrest them!" Finn gestured to Rufus's people. "Every person in this rabble who wears a badge of sedition."

Astarte was shaking her head, her hand on Finn's arm. Beside her, Genevieve threw up her hands in a pleading gesture. Rafe couldn't hear the two women, but they were pleading with Finn.

Rafe ran forward, interposing himself between Rufus and the king. "Sire, you cannot do this! The Tournament is a place of peace. The Irish are here under my aegis. I promised them safe passage. I gave them my word."

"Then your word is forfeit." Finn turned away, shaking off Astarte's hand before taking her firmly by the elbow and leading her away from the royal box. All around him, Houseboys and Civil Patrol members were casting shackling spells on Rufus's people, his siblings and cousins, as well as anyone else in the crowd who wore the Heir's badge.

Rafe spun toward Rufus just in time to see Rufus draw back a fist aimed at Monjoie who was laying hands on Penny. The man wore a Wellhall badge next to his unit insignia, Rafe noted, but dimly, as if it didn't matter. He'd figure out what it meant later. Rafe chopped Monjoie in the neck before Rufus's blow could fall. Monjoie buckled, gagging.

"This way," Rafe shouted. He shoved both Penny and Rufus toward his own retinue. The Irish wolf pack's banner fell in the scrum and was trampled underfoot. No time. He had no time to save symbols, there were people to protect.

From the king's stand, Ama Nefasta hurried toward them, her ceremonial sickle held in a distinctly offensive posture. Genevieve came close behind her, holding up her long skirt as she ran. Rafe, Ama, and the rest of his retinue closed ranks around Rufus and Penny, driving a wedge between the crowd full of panicking people. Rafe cast a hasty glamour over both Rufus and Penny, blurring their faces and dulling Rufus's distinctive shock of hair.

"Don't ask, just hurry," he barked at his little group, and they complied.

All the way to the great gate they ran in tight formation, dodging Houseboys and the Civil Patrol. At the gate, Rafe bull-rushed his way past the guards and opened the portal to the gates of the university.

"Go! Now!" he shouted. Without a word or look to anyone else, Rufus helped Penny over the threshold and stepped through after her. Ama gave Rafe a curt nod and followed. Rafe closed the portal behind the bard and werewolves, now safe at Eisteddfod for the moment.

In the arena the little group stood panting, surrounded by confused guards, some of whom were calling for their superior officers and Arthur on their mirrors. One stepped in front of Rafe, his hand held out. At Rafe's side, Jameson staggered, gasping too hard for air and clutching at his chest. Melanie and Gordie caught him by the arms and held him up.

"Medic!" Rafe shouted. He yanked the mirror out of the nearest gate guard's hand and said, "Can't you see this man is ill? He's old and frail. Open a portal to my quarters at once so that I can send for my healer."

"I... yes, sir?" The confused guard, a corporal, opened the portal and let them all step through. Rafe stepped through last of all, locking down the portal so that no one except the Shield and King could follow. It would take more power than he had to lock them out of any part of the Palace.

He turned toward Jameson, who was now sitting on the couch, fanning himself a bit with his hand. Melanie sat beside him, her face wrung with worry. Genevieve was pouring him a glass of water.

"Hang in there, Jameson. I'll get a healer right now," Rafe said.

"No need, sir," Jameson said. "Merely a little shortness of breath after exercise." He shrugged modestly. "I may perhaps have overplayed my distress for the benefit of the guards."

"Father!" Melanie smacked her father in the shoulder and then flung her arms around him.

"Now, now, my dear. I'm quite alright," Jameson said, patting her on the back. He gently extracted himself from her arms and stood, brushing out the creases in his trousers. "If you'll permit me, sir, I will prepare us all some tea. Old and frail, indeed. Pshaw." He glided out of the room as the others looked after him with open mouths.

His hands shaking more than he wanted anyone else to see, Rafe flopped into the nearest chair and hugged his dogs.

Chapter Thirty-Four

The cell door swung open again, and Asphodel charged through, Root and Mac—the king's personal healer—following. Arthur and Stephen trailed behind.

"The Shield says you're not well," Asphodel said, coming up to her. "That you've gotten worse?" She reached to touch Deor's forehead and stopped, glancing at the princess for permission. When Deor nodded, Asphodel rested her cool, soft hand against her forehead. After a few moments pause she pulled her hand away, a deep frown lining her face. "Fever." She glanced over her shoulder, "Mac?"

The old healer came to her. "Let me take a look at your back, lass." He reminded Deor of her grandfather. A gruff, sharp man, hunched over and ailing even before she was born. It hadn't stopped him being sharp with his tongue. Several strokes and heart attacks hadn't ended his enjoyment of cigars either. She could still feel the rough scruff of his beard against her cheek when she hugged him. He scared some folks, but she had always laughed, delighted by his fierce frowns and gravelly voice. And for her, at least, he softened.

"Sure." Deor returned to the window and slipped the robe off her shoulders.

Mac whistled. "Definitely an infection." He glanced past her to Arthur. "How did you let it get this bad?"

Asphodel touched Deor's shoulder. "I'm going to examine you, alright?"

Deor swallowed hard and nodded.

As usual, Asphodel's touch was soft and gentle. The magic exploring her wounds hurt enough to make Deor whimper. Every tendril of magic Asphodel sent forth, even those Deor could tell were meant to sooth, were sharp, stabbing. After a couple of minutes, Asphodel stopped and blew out a sigh.

"I don't know what that is," she said. "Something is both stopping you from bleeding and keeping the wounds open. That's got to be how you got the infection. But I can't get whatever it is out of the way. No matter what I do, it won't budge. At least as far as I can tell, the infection hasn't spread to your wings. If it does," she shook her head, "it can go anywhere in the body —lungs, kidneys, heart, brain. Or you could lose the function of your wings."

Deor swallowed hard—for a long time she'd have been happy as a clam if the wings had vanished. Now all she could think was that Rafe never had a chance to touch them.

"It's magic," Dell said, standing. "The king's magic."

When Arthur glared at him, Dell shrugged. "Glare all you want, Arthur."

Victor jumped in. He looked to the healers. "The king reopened her wounds. All of them. With his voice. I didn't see it, but I felt the magic surge. I thought that king's voice thing was myth."

"He could kill with it, if he wanted it enough," Dell said, matter-of-factly. When the others gaped at him, he added, "I've been alive a long time, and I've studied faeries, all of fae. That kind of power is possible, though rare. Interesting that he's got it now, though."

Mac shook his head, anger sharpening his gaze. "Nasty stuff," he said. "But looking at this, I can't disagree. It's hard to make out, but I've been taking care of the King since he was in leading strings, and I know his magic when I see it."

"So?" Deor said. "How do you fix it? Like, do I take an antibiotic."

"A killer of living things?" Root asked, looking appalled.

"Human medicine, for, well, yes, killing bacterial infections."

"Oh," Root nodded. "That makes sense—and sounds less barbaric." He shuddered. "Everything I've heard about human medicine—cutting people open, poisoning their blood so that it almost kills them—I don't know how humans survive."

"We don't," Deor said flatly.

"I think," Asphodel said, "that Mac is right about the cause of the problem. We have a couple of options. If this is a magical curse of some kind, we could go to the king and ask him to lift it."

"Next!" Deor said. "We're not saying a word about this to him." She met Arthur's gaze. "The king doesn't find out about this, not yet."

Arthur nodded. "I see no reason to trouble his majesty with a minor infection."

Asphodel lunged forward like she might slap him but held herself short. "Wonderful," she managed through gritted teeth. "The other option is a healer that understands the situation better. We need someone who studies bimorphs. And the best person is—"

"Lady Penelope," Arthur finished for her. The now-wife of Rufus, son to the Alpha werewolf.

"Yes." Asphodel crossed her arms. "Do you think she'd be willing to come?"

"There isn't anyone else?" Arthur scanned the faces of the three healers.

"I'm afraid not, lad," Mac said. "I've been at this a long time, but I've never worked much with changelings of any kind. That young lady is one of the best healers I've ever heard tell of."

Arthur frowned. "After the final, the king dismissed the werewolf and his wife without reconciliation. They might be back in Ireland by now."

Asphodel raised her eyebrows at him. "I'm not sure how that is our problem, *Arthur*. The princess needs medical attention—now."

"Captain, or Lord Shield," Arthur corrected. He glanced around the room. "I believe they have retreated to Eisteddfod. I will speak to Lady Penelope. Until then, let's leave the princess and her court to their rest." Arthur opened the cell door and gestured for the healers to leave.

Asphodel caught Deor's hand and squeezed it. "I'm sorry that I haven't helped."

"It's not your fault. It's the half-human thing." She squeezed back. "Thank you for all you've done."

Asphodel nodded and let Arthur wave her out of the room.

Chapter Thirty-Five

Rafe rolled his shoulders. Thanks to Mac, there wasn't much pain from the beating he'd taken from Rufus—his own ego hurt far more than his body. He was furious at the king—any chance at reconciliation was gone, and at this point, the Irish wolves might well leave the Winter Court formally, or try to. His own reputation as a man of his word had taken just as much a beating as his body.

On the mantle in the parlor sat the small golden sword, the second place for the Broadsword competition. He'd managed, barely, not to fling it into the fire as soon as he'd walked through the door. Genevieve had helped, reminding him that the king would likely come to see him, and it, later.

Genevieve sat across the coffee table from him, eyeing him curiously. He made certain to keep his own magic under control and not chill the room, at least for her sake. She was the perfect excuse to beg off the celebratory party after the Tournament—some private time with his lady to help him nurse his wounds. The king had practically waggled his eyebrows in innuendo when Rafe had told him.

He picked up his wine glass and noticed it was empty. Genevieve's was too. "Do you want another glass?" Rafe asked. "I'm having one." He poured wine in his glass and held the bottle out to her.

She held her glass toward him. "I believe I do."

He finished off the bottle into her glass and set it aside with the other two empty ones. She'd matched him glass for glass. A good vintage, too, so they'd taken their time. Not the best, but good. Rangley, as usual, and not just because they gifted Rafe dozens of bottles a year. Their vintages, even from the worst part of the king's illness, were decent, which said a lot considering how bad many of the crops were. He took another sip and caught her staring. "What?" he asked.

"It is odd, don't you think, that we get along better now, pretending to be a perfect couple, than we ever were *being* it." She set her glass down and leaned forward a bit. "Why do you think that is?"

He pretended it was the wine that made him blunt, honest, but it wasn't. "We were always pretending, Genevieve. Weren't we?"

She gaped, about to protest. "I—" She cut herself off. "I wouldn't put it that way. I certainly cared about you. And I certainly was *not* title hunting."

"Ah." Rafe laughed. "I know you weren't. And I wasn't trying to marry up by snagging the Harvest Queen." He nodded sagely. "Be careful, though, what she says has a tendency to stick in your mind."

"I don't know what you mean."

"Okay," he said with a shrug. "She had it coming, though, at Roger's. What you said. You do make her insecure."

"Why?" Genevieve took another drink. "She's the princess."

"You're the one who looks like one. You are perfect-seeming. And I made a huge mistake by asking you to help her. If I'd been in any way not a complete fool, I'd have seen that blowup coming a mile away."

Genevieve rolled her eyes. "I learned the hard way that she isn't a child." She quirked the edge of her mouth into a smile. "Especially when she stole my fiancé."

"She didn't steal me." Rafe barely managed to reign in the flush of anger, the snap in his voice. She was teasing him, and he deserved it. They'd known each other a long time, and long before they were a couple, she knew him well. He returned her smile. "You didn't mourn my loss long, Gen." He knew she didn't like the nickname but that she could take the joke.

"Indeed," she admitted with a gracious nod. "Delaney escorted me home that day. Though we waited a week to be seen in public together."

"If I remember correctly, he escorted you home on more than one occasion when I had to leave you somewhere."

"He did," she smiled a soft, tender expression that he rarely saw. "He is, I think, the most gentle man I've ever known. This has been hard on him, with his father in the Tower. The title hasn't passed formally, so there are those who don't listen to him. His brother George doesn't make it any easier, either, saying ridiculous things to the press." Her dreamy gaze sharpened, and she locked eyes with him. "How long after that night were you and the princess together?"

"Forty-eight hours," he said flatly.

"You didn't wait long to go after her."

Rafe laughed again. "I did not seduce her. I don't know that I could have. And by that, I mean, had she not wanted me, I certainly could not have convinced her, and I don't know that I would have ever given myself permission. We were at MacIntyre's Inn. She simply asked me if I would like to have sex with her."

Genevieve's eyes widened. "That's one approach, I suppose."

"I appreciated her bluntness," he said. "But now she's the one getting hurt, and I'm the one sitting here, engaged to the most eligible woman in all of the Winter Court. I'm the apple of the king's eye." His own bitterness made him flinch.

"Are you afraid she'll think you've thrown her over?"

"No." He shook his head. "She was very insistent that we were friends enjoying each other's company, not lovers."

"And you? What did you think?"

"I thought I'd leave when she told me she didn't want me anymore and not a moment earlier." He finished his wine.

Genevieve set her wine glass down and crossed the space between them. She took his hand, the one with the engagement ring, and kissed the back of it. "You are a good man, Rafe. Don't ever let anyone tell you otherwise." She squeezed his hand. "Shall I stay the night?"

"What?" He started. "I don't think—"

She laughed. "Rafe, I am *not* asking to have sex with you. I was asking if you think I should stay, for the sake of appearances."

"Oh." He chuckled. "You know, I would like for you to." He hung his head, avoiding her gaze. "I'd rather not be alone."

She nodded. "Well, why don't we plan something. Some sort of small party perhaps? Or a trip together? Planning it will give your mind something to do and going will get you out of here for a while. Perhaps back in the north? Or even out of the Winter Court? I find the vampires a bit... disturbing, but I know you get on well with them. It might be a good political move."

Rafe nodded. "That's a splendid idea." He stood.

The knock at the door was rough, sharp, and followed by Arthur coming in, once again without permission.

"I swear, Arthur, why do I even bother to lock the door?"

He glanced down at the doorknob still in his hand. "Oh." He looked up at Rafe. "I'm sorry. I forget that because I'm Shield, doors don't stay locked—not without some heavy-duty spells." Before Rafe could object, he held up his hand. "I'll make sure that I put some on this door immediately."

"How nice. What do you want?"

Arthur glanced at Genevieve, and down at their hands, still clasped together.

Rafe raised Genevieve's hand to his lips. "Will you excuse me?" he said.

"Of course, darling." She kissed him on the cheek and moved toward his bedroom.

"Wait," Arthur said suddenly. "Perhaps Genevieve might help—she might have insight into this problem."

Rafe raised his eyebrows and exchanged glances with Genevieve. "I don't want her involved in anything that might put her in harm's way. And you are most certainly not questioning her."

"That's not what I meant!" Arthur snapped. He was shaky too. Not normal. "Please," he said, softer than usual, "sit."

Rafe gestured to Genevieve who took a seat on the parlor's small couch, nearest to Rafe's chair, where he took a seat. Arthur sat across from Rafe in the other chair. "So?" Rafe said.

Arthur looked back and forth between the two of them for a moment before settling his gaze on a spot between them. If he couldn't look Rafe in the eye, it was bad. "The princess," Arthur said. "On the eve of the first day of the tournament, the king was angry. He came to see her in the Tower and," Arthur licked his lips and finally met Rafe's gaze, "he opened all her wounds again. I don't know how. He literally did it with his voice—his own command of magic. They split open like I had just struck her."

"Oh my god!" Genevieve said and covered her mouth with her hand. She was no wilting flower, but the image of Deor's back splitting in ten places certainly turned Rafe's stomach.

Arthur ignored her outburst and continued. "The wounds won't close. All three—Mac, Asphodel, and Root—agree that it is the king's magic keeping them from healing. They've gotten infected." Arthur drove a hand through his hair. "And now the infection might have spread to her wings."

"What do you want me to do about it?" Rafe wanted to demand to see her, to go and hold her, tell her it was going to be fine. It would be a lie.

"The king's wrath is legendary—or at least I thought it was only a legend. If he won't listen to you, why would he listen to me? It might hurt her worse if I advocate for her."

Arthur shook his head. "That's not what I want. I need," he stopped and swallowed hard, "she needs a healer, a bimorph healer."

"Lady Penelope." Rafe frowned in disgust. "Who is, as we speak, at Eisteddfod with her humiliated husband."

"You could get on campus. You could talk to them."

"Me?" Rafe bolted to his feet. "Rufus won't let me near Penny. Not after today. I'm certain he believes I knew what was coming—what the king was going to do." Cold blasted off him, rimming the wine glasses and bottles with frost. He drew a deep breath and hauled the magic back. "I'm sorry Genevieve," he said, glancing down at her. Goosebumps had raised all along her arms.

"It's fine, Rafe." Her eyes were fixed on Arthur. Rafe had been on the receiving end of that gaze a few times. It had made a number of people cry. "Perhaps I could help?" she said. "I could speak to Ama—she will probably still take my calls—and see if I could get her to agree to let us on campus. If I can tell her the truth—"

"Out of the question," Arthur snapped. "The bards will have a fit if they think the princess is being tortured."

"She is being tortured, isn't she?" Rafe demanded. He stepped away from Genevieve and paced in front of the fire, trying to let out some of the anger, the pent-up magic swelling inside him. He wanted to freeze the room—freeze Arthur—solid.

"Not at the moment," Arthur said.

Rafe managed not to hit him, only because Genevieve flung her hand out in front him as a distraction. She didn't have to say anything—of course punching Arthur was a stupid thing to do. Rafe sighed. He tugged at his jacket, making sure it was back in place. "So? What do we do? I'm not sneaking onto campus."

Arthur stared at both of them, his gaze flicking back and forth, for a long while. "Let's call Ama. If you can get her to agree without telling her the details, Genevieve, that would be best."

"I'll do my best." Genevieve closed her eyes and drew a deep breath, which she blew out through her nose. She settled a serene expression on her face and opened her eyes. "Alright," she said, her lips sliding into a polite, genteel smile, "let's get Ama on the mirror."

An hour later, an unmarked carriage rumbled along the city streets, Rafe, Genevieve and Arthur tucked inside. On top rode Monjoie and Stephen, both disguised to look like ordinary cab drivers. It had taken Genevieve only fifteen minutes to convince Ama it was necessary to come onto campus—once she had told the bard that Deor was suffering, she needed to say nothing more.

The carriage slowed at the entrance to the university's west gates. They didn't stop but were waved inside by the large werebear guarding the gate. Ama had, apparently, paved their way. Again, they met no resistance at the edge of faculty housing. Penny, despite being married to the Irish heir, still maintained a flat on campus, so she could have access to the University's healer labs and libraries.

The carriage stopped in front of the three-story townhouse.

Rafe heard and felt the soldiers drop down and straightened his jacket. He was wearing his own colors and crest—Wellhall, not the eight-pointed star of the king. He also hadn't glamoured the colorful shiner that Rufus had given him in the final bout. Reminding Rufus he had won might make him a bit more sympathetic. Rafe rather hoped the large werewolf wouldn't try to punch him again. Although if that was what it took to get Penny to Deor, he'd hold still and let Rufus swing.

Rafe nodded at the soldiers as he got out of the carriage and offered his hand to Genevieve. When Arthur moved to exit, Rafe put up his hand. "We'll mirror you if we need you," he said. "But it is best if you stay in the carriage and wait. Let's not immediately make them think they're going to be arrested."

Arthur slumped back into the carriage, a sullen expression on his face. "Fine," he said. "I'll send you the pictures from the healers—if Penelope needs some convincing, they should do it."

"I hate that we're preying on her empathy and compassion," Rafe said.

"Manipulation is a weapon of war," Arthur shrugged.

"We are not at war!" Rafe snapped and slammed the carriage door shut.

Genevieve watched him from a few steps away, about half-way to the front door. Certainly, by now Penny and Rufus knew they were there. He schooled his face into a neutral expression and smiled at Genevieve as he offered her his arm, and they made their way up to the front door. Rafe reached for the bell, but the door was yanked open.

"What do you want?" Rufus's voice was a low growl, filled with the kind of menace that made Rafe's muscles tense and sent him reaching, almost unconsciously, for a weapon. But once again he had none, a precaution and a sign of good intent that he hoped would work again.

"Good evening, Rufus," Genevieve beamed at him. "We were hoping we might have a word with you and Lady Penelope."

Rufus's attention snapped to Genevieve, whose serene smile was fixed in place. He frowned, confusion replacing anger. "A social call?"

"Of a sort." She stepped toward him, and decades of social graces moved him out of her way as she led Rafe past him and into the flat. She drew them both into the parlor and sat on the couch, pulling Rafe down with her. "Would you mind if we spoke to Penny?" she asked.

"What about?" Penny stepped into the room.

"I need your help," Rafe said suddenly. "Please—"

"Your face looks fine to me," she said, voice flat.

"It's the princess. It's Deor," Genevieve said. "She is quite ill. The palace healers insist that only an expert bimorph healer can help her."

"Flattery won't get you anywhere," Penny said. "Though I appreciate the implication that I'm an expert."

"No implication," Genevieve said. "It's a fact. Please, even if you won't come to the palace—"

"You mean the Tower," Rufus cut in.

Genevieve ignored him. "If you won't come with us, at least take a look at the images that the healers have sent with us." She gestured at Rafe.

He took out his mirror and tapped it a few times, then held it out to Penny.

She took it. She stared at it for a moment, looking this way and that. "Have these pictures been altered in any way?" she asked, not looking up.

"Not so far as I know," Rafe said.

Penny's frown deepened as she flicked from image to image, and a small gasp escaped her lips. "This is terrible. That's a horrible infection." She looked up. "How are her wings?"

Rafe shrugged. "They aren't sure. Her human side is making it hard for her to heal. Magic is interfering." He was careful not to specify the king's deliberate magic.

She studied them for a few more moments and handed the mirror back to Rafe. "Let me get my bag," she said.

"Penny," Rufus objected, reaching for her arm.

"I have to go," she said, heading for the stairs. "If I can help, I have to go."

Rufus rolled his eyes. "Of course, you do," he said, though Rafe could hear the love and admiration there. "Let me get my things." He glanced at Rafe. "You're not goin' into that Tower alone." His gaze seemed to dare Rafe to disagree.

"Of course, you are welcome, Rufus," Rafe nodded. "Thank you both so much."

CHAPTER THIRTY-SIX

When the door creaked open to Deor's cell, she was already awake. Unlike the last time Monjoie had crept in, he had made noise in the outer parlor. She sat in the middle of her bed, legs crossed, Brand tucked behind her. She drew in a deep breath and blew it out, willing magic into her hand where a blade formed. She didn't much care what would happen to her—it would be worth it—but that man would never lay a hand on her dog again.

"Princess?" The voice was soft, plaintive. "Lights on."

Deor blinked in the bright light for a moment as Stephen's form came into view. He was staring at the blade in her hand.

"Is that for me?"

"No." She squeezed her hand closed until the blade dispersed into a small shower of sparks. "I thought you were Monjoie again."

"Ah. No." He held his hand out her. "I know it is late—or early—but Arthur has brought Lady Penelope to see you."

Deor uncurled her legs and let Stephen help her to her feet. She grabbed her robe and flung it around her shoulders. The air was cold, Winter still, at least in the Tower. "Is everyone else up?"

"Yes," Stephen said. "Arthur wasn't particularly quiet coming in, and there's quite a troop—Asphodel, Mac, and Root came too."

With a roll of her eyes, Deor sighed. "They might as well just take out the wall and replace it with a glass door. Then people could come stare at me all the time, and I wouldn't have to get up." Deor stepped forward. "Hold Brand, okay?"

"Sure." He scooped up the dog.

In the parlor, the gang was all gathered—including Rufus. The other three prisoners were dressed in their night clothes, too, all standing, arms crossed, near the table, opposite Arthur, by the door.

"Princess," Arthur said with a nod. "Lady Penelope is here to look at your injury."

"Great," Deor said. "Where do you want me, Penny?"

Penny frowned, scanning the room. "I wish there was somewhere more private," she said. "But your cell is too small, I'm sure." She looked at the table and shook her head. "One of those chairs will have to do."

Root dutifully grabbed one of the tall-backed chairs from the table and brought it to Penny.

Penny turned it so that the back faced the fireplace.

Deor dropped the robe from her shoulders.

"Remember, Lady Penelope and Rufus," Arthur said as Deor settled on the chair facing the fireplace, "anything you see here is classified. If you speak about anything you see here," he stole a glance at the other three prisoners, "that amounts to treason, and you will be prosecuted."

Rufus glared at Arthur, anger and loathing etched in his features, and for a moment Deor thought he would take a swing at him. Rufus wore an open shirt, and Deor saw a series of bruises. The tournament, of course. She didn't ask how it went. The tension between the two men suggested not well.

"Of course, Captain," Penny said in a soothing tone. She turned her attention to Deor's back. "Okay," she said, her voice the essence of calm. "I saw some pictures earlier, and they seem to have been quite accurate. This is definitely an infection, I can see that immediately. Princess?" she said.

"Penny, please, call me Deor," Deor said momentarily turning toward her.

Penny smiled and nodded. "Is it alright if I touch you—if I use some magic to examine the wounds?"

Deor nodded. Tears welled in the corners of her eyes, but she struggled to keep them from falling. The small gesture from Penny, like Asphodel, of asking before touching her, it made her feel almost human.

Penny's touch was gentle, but the magic, like Asphodel's, stung, and Deor winced.

"That hurts?" Penny asked.

"Yeah." Deor sniffed and closed her eyes. "But it's okay. Do what you have to do." She took deep breaths in through her nose and out through her mouth as tendrils of magic ran through her. Penny was skilled—the pain wasn't enough to make her cry out.

Penny withdrew her hand and shook her head. "I can feel the infection, but I can't tell how far it has spread. There is magic there—it's blocking my exploration and it's likely what is blocking the healing, keeping the wound open, but keeping the blood out too. So, you're not losing blood, but you're not healing either. But before I do anything, I need to know what's going on with your wings, so I'm going to need you to put them out."

"What?" Deor shuddered. "Won't that tear open my wounds? They'll cut out right across them."

"The wounds are already open. And wings are part magic—there's a good chance that no, they won't affect the wound at all."

"But not a 100% chance?" Deor swallowed hard.

"Correct."

Deor nodded. "Okay, but I don't know if I can. Ever since the...," she paused for a split second, "the flogging, I've made sure to keep them in. I thought they'd do more damage. They're so tight, I don't know if I can put them out."

"I can help," Penny said. With a soft smile she added, "I helped you with them once already, remember?"

Deor had seen cranky Penny, fiery Penny, even concerned Penny. Never Penny the healer, until now. Everything about her made Deor feel better, safe, cared for. Just her hand on Deor's shoulder calmed her, made Deor certain things were going to be alright. It wasn't magic, some spell, Penny used—it was her gift, plain and simple.

"Let's do it," Deor said. She closed her eyes again and focused on her wings. They were tight in her back, tamped down, almost withered. She drew her magic to them, filling them, at least trying to, but they were too tight. Pushing harder sent shivers of pain rolling through them, and she clenched her fists.

Penny's magic joined her own, like a cool, gentle river. It filled her wings, but even that couldn't release the hold on her wings. Deor pushed her magic at the thing blocking her—black, inky tendrils of thick oil spread across each of her wounds, wrapped around her wings, binding them. Every time her magic prodded at them, pain shot through her.

"Okay, let's take a step back," Penny said, withdrawing her magic, lifting her hand off Deor.

"No." Deor said through clenched teeth, or she thought she did. Maybe she hadn't said it out loud. Either way, the sentiment shot through her system. No, she would not stop, not until this thing, whatever it was, was out of her body. How had she not noticed it before? How long had it been there?

In her mind's eye she gathered her magic, a growing mass of her sparkles, shining silver. Her heart pounded in her ears, rabbit-fast, and her breath came in shallow, desperate gulps.

"Princess!" Other voices had joined Penny's now—so much concern, but their touches weren't going to heal her, no matter how much skill or power they had.

She shoved, releasing the mass of magic like a wave, crashing through the oily black magic and slamming it out, through her wings.

Suddenly, Deor was flung forward, and she landed on the floor, on her hands and knees. Her eyes were still closed. The ground, the stone floor of the palace, felt cool and soft beneath her. Her face was wet and drops fell onto her hands and ran down her arms. The soft whisper of metal on silk rustled in her ears.

She opened her eyes.

Silver blurred her vision, but she could make out her hands, and there was something different about them—she could see the clear drops, tears. They were tears. The wetness on her face: she was crying, softly but steadily, tears in rivers down her cheeks. That wasn't all, though, splattered across her hands, her arms, red, too. Blood on the shiny surface.

"Everybody, stay back!" A voice commanded. It came from next to her, and the sound of it made her shoulders tense, her nerves ablaze, a flash of panic through her gut. She turned her head. The silver aura was like tunnel vision, a man, standing in front of her. Arthur. Reaching for her.

"Don't touch me." Her voice, scratchy and rough, came out a croak.

He didn't stop, didn't even pause.

More soft whispering of metal, a series of *snick*, one after the other.

"Gah!" He flung himself backward, almost falling.

Deor sat back on her heels, resting her hands on her thighs, and looked down at herself. Every inch of her skin was silver, the rise and fall of her chest as she gasped rippling with reflected light. She slowly raised her right hand and stroked the back of her left. She was still flesh but magic too. Lining her arms from her wrist to her shoulder, a perfect inch apart, wicked, curved blades. Two on her shoulder glistened with drops of red.

Deor returned her gaze to Arthur, who clutched his hand and gaped at her. She swiveled her head, taking in the people around her. Eyes wide. Mouths agape.

She rolled her shoulders against the weight on them. Her wings. She breathed a sigh of relief. They were out, she could feel them. She straightened her back, arching it slightly and fluttered them.

"Gah!" Arthur said again and raised his hands to shield his face, as did everyone else. Red drops splattered across him, across the floor, across everyone and everything. Blood. Her blood. Now that she saw it, she could feel it, dripping down her wings, down her back.

Panic built in her chest, and her breath, already short, quickened. Hysteria was building, and more blades snicked into place on her arms, spread across her chest.

"Everybody, back!" A different voice this time, afraid too. Rufus lunged forward toward Deor.

"Stop!" A commanding voice, and Rufus froze.

Deor turned her head to see Penny next to her, less than a foot away, her hand flung out against Rufus.

"Don't come any closer. She might … she might…"

"Shoot off blades like a wet dog shakes off water." A wry voice behind her: Victor. "And I doubt any of us are wearing anything that could keep them out. I know I'm not."

"We're in an iron box!" Arthur insisted. "How the fuck is she…?"

"Her house, my boy," an old, smug voice. Dell. "Even in the Tower."

"Her humanity, too, I'd wager." Rufus's voice was a forced calm. "Iron resistant."

"I can hear you, you know?" Deor said. "It's rude to talk about me like I'm not here."

"Sorry," Victor stepped into her line of vision. "Are you okay?"

"I'm bleeding," Deor said.

"A bit, yes." Victor said, wiping a few drops from his face. "Splattered quite a bit when you flexed your wings there." He crouched next to her. "You don't need to be afraid. No one here is going to hurt you." He held his hand out, palm up, toward her. "Can I help you up?"

"My eyes are silver, aren't they?" Deor asked, not reaching for him. She flicked one of the blades sprouting from her arm. It vibrated with a soft *twang*.

"Yes," he said. "Solid through. All of you is, as far as I can see, except your wings."

"Still red like fresh blood, Captain?" Deor said, throwing a glance at Arthur.

"Yep." he said, not moving.

Deor nodded. "Okay." She turned back to Victor and took his hand. He stood and helped her up. "So," she turned to Penny, "my wings are out. Now what?"

"Well, why don't we see if we can get the blades to go away, and the armor with them. Then I can look at your wings and see how they are."

"Right." Deor looked for the chair. It had launched forward and was laying on its back, the top of it in the fire.

"I've got it." Victor grabbed it and hauled it out. There were some scorch marks, but it hadn't actually caught fire. He settled it back on its legs.

Deor sat. She opened and closed her fist several times, splaying out her fingers. First, she placed her right hand on her left shoulder and slid it down to her wrist, wiping away each of the spikes. She repeated it with the left. Then her front. "You know," she said, staring at her armor-clad body. "I seem to have lost my clothes."

"Right," Penny said.

"I'll get them." Stephen didn't wait for an answer but darted back to her room, Brand still tucked under his arm, squirming all the way, and returned with another open-backed shirt and pajama bottoms. "Here."

Deor leaned in and caught Brand's face in her hands. She kissed him on the top of the head as he whined. "We're almost done. Good boy." She took the clothes. "Thanks."

After pulling them on, she sat again, and after a few deep breaths, the silver receded.

"Just a reminder," Arthur said, wrapping a piece of her shredded shirt around his bloody hand, "nothing anyone has seen here leaves here."

Penny ignored him. "Can I inspect your wings?"

"Yes." Deor held still. The release of her wings had done nothing for the pain in her back. Though the adrenaline had dulled it for a while, now that she was calming down again, the pain flooded back with a vengeance. The wings didn't seem to matter either way, making it neither worse nor better.

"Well," Penny said, "Good news is that they aren't infected. I think whatever was holding them in, you pretty well obliterated."

"I think it was my father's magic," she said. "Bad news?"

"Speaking of your father's magic, it's still wedged in your flogging wounds. So long as they are open, they won't heal, obviously, and are in real danger of further infection. So, we need to get his magic out."

"And how do we do that?" Deor asked. "Magical force?"

"Maybe," Penny said. "But my guess is that if your little burst didn't do it, none of us can. We could go to the king...?"

"Nope." Deor shook her head.

"Thought so," Penny frowned. "I've got a way, but it will hurt."

"Shocking," Deor said. "What is it?"

Penny opened one of her bags and dug through it. She withdrew a cloth bundle tied with a string. She opened it and unrolled it to reveal a set of gleaming steel scalpels. She drew on a pair of gloves, and picked up one, about the size and length of a number two pencil, with a wicked slashed blade at the top.

"You're going to cut it out." Deor said flatly.

"Yes," Penny said. "You're not allergic to iron, but the king is, like the rest of us faeries. Iron works against faerie magic, so it should work against this. I had these made special. Sometimes werefolk get hurt by faerie magic."

"So, how does this work?" Deor asked, fearing she knew the answer.

"Well, I'm going to sterilize it, and then have you pull in your wings. I'll numb you up the best I can. Then I'm going to slice out the magic bits while trying very hard not to nick your skin."

"You're going to physically carve the magic from her body?" Mac said. "That's barbaric!"

"Got a better idea?" Penny asked.

"No," he admitted. "We could treat the infection killers—antibiotics, the girl mentioned?"

"We'll do that, too," Penny said. "But you know as well as I do, if those wounds stay open..."

"Yes. Open, plus the lack of blood flow. She'll be septic within hours. You're right."

"Let's do this!" Deor said. She drew her wings back in and stood. "Where do you want me?"

Penny rested her hands on her hips. "We'll use the dining room table. We'll put some blankets on it, and that will let me reach you easily. Okay?"

Deor nodded and waited while Rufus and Victor reordered the room to suit Penny's needs.

Deor climbed on the table and lay down on her stomach. "All set."

"Okay," Arthur said. "Let's give them privacy." He shooed the people toward either their cells or the door.

"No. I don't mind," Deor said. "They can stay if they want."

Dell and Delaney exchanged glances. "I think we shall retire, my dear," Delaney said. He and Dell left.

"Staying," Victor said and sat in a chair by the fire facing Deor. He offered Deor his hand, and she took it.

"Me too," Rufus said, and took up residence in the other chair.

Brand whined frantically and put his paws up on the table to lick Deor's nose. Stephen scooped up the puppy and sat on the couch.

"Fine," Arthur said. "I'll leave you to it."

"Stop right there, you cronie!" Deor snapped at Arthur. "If you can split my back open, and you can stand there while Finn opens my back like Ziploc bags, you sure as hell can stand and watch it be fixed."

Arthur looked about to protest but relented. He came over and took a position, almost exactly like the one he took when she was tortured by Finn and stood still.

"Great," Penny said. "Asphodel, could you help me with the disinfectant for the wounds, first?"

The stinging of the disinfectant was mild compared to what was going to follow, Deor knew, but she couldn't help but wince just a bit.

Penny settled in and raised her scalpel. The fact that Deor couldn't see it coming made it worse. She tensed, bracing for the feel of the blade. It came. Deor buried her face in the pillow someone had brought from her room and tried not to scream.

As gently as she could, Deor knew, Penny slid the blade into the top wound on her back. She dragged it along the full length of the slash and back. She took steel tweezers and snatched hold of the edge of the king's magic. She tugged, and Deor yelped. The magic came away from her body like a particularly clingy scab, tearing away from her flesh.

Asphodel followed Penny, gently stopping the bleeding and using magic to close the wounds.

Deor heard Victor inhale sharply as she clutched his hand. "Sorry," Deor mumbled into the pillow and tried to let go of his hand.

"It's fine. I'm fine." He clutched her hand and laid his other hand on top of hers. "Hold on all you like."

She did.

The pillow was wet with tears when Penny finally stopped. "There," she said, stepping back around to where Deor could see her. "But don't get up just yet. I got a majority of the magic, but there are little bits. And unfortunately, magic is not holding those wounds together. I think it is a combination of the king's magic, and your own human resistance that makes it difficult."

"So, what do we do?" Deor asked. "Wait for them to close on their own?"

"Couldn't that leave awful scars?" Victor asked.

Deor snorted. "I assumed we were way past that."

Penny went back to her bag and drew something out of it. Whatever it was, it was in a plastic bag—the kind that doctors and dentists keep their tools in to ensure they are sterile. "Have you ever been to a human hospital?" She ripped open the packet and what came out looked like it came from Office Depot.

Something in Deor's brain clicked. "You're going to staple them shut."

"Yes."

"Wait, what?" Root asked.

"She means," Mac said, his voice a rough growl, "that she is going to use iron brads to hold the skin together until it heals on its own."

"I think it will leave fewer scars than stitching, in part because any thread that has iron in it is going to be much thicker than the medical thread or staples. But I could stitch it, if the princess would rather."

"Like you do clothes, only with skin?" Root asked, face turning slightly green.

"Yes." Deor said. "They are easier to get out too?"

"Yes. Again, under normal human circumstances, I'd use dissolvable thread, but I can't guarantee that would work against the magic. Many of these staples may well fall out as you heal up. The rest, they aren't hard—or particularly painful—to remove."

"Let's do that, then," Deor said.

"Root," Penny said, "Do you want to help—if it is okay with the princess?"

"Fine by me," Deor said. "I've been a patient at a teaching hospital before."

Root nodded and shakily joined Penny.

With every pop of the stapler as it pinched closed her flesh, Deor winced slightly. Arthur, who dutifully stood watching, grew increasingly uncomfortable, each wince more visible than the last, until he looked like he might vomit.

As the sun rose and peeked through the window, Penny finished. "Here," she said, handing Deor two bottles. "The first is pain medication— that's got magic in it. Take it when you need it. The other is human antibiotics. Three a day for a week, then two a day for a week, then one a day for a week. Got it?"

"Yes ma'am." Deor said, taking the antibiotics.

"And even if you feel completely well—"

"Don't stop taking them until they are gone." She grinned. "I know the drill."

She smiled and gently patted Deor's shoulder. "I forget that you grew up with all this." She leaned down. "I will always come if you need me. Send a message, and I'll be here as fast as I can."

"Thanks, doc." Deor sat up. "I feel better already. Really." She got off the table and gave Penny a hug, moving slowly.

"Okay," Arthur said. "Time to go." He shooed the healers, along with Stephen, Penny and Rufus toward the door and held it for them as they left. He returned his gaze to Deor. "Let me know if it is not healing," he said. He left and shut the door before she could answer.

At the sound of the door closing, Delaney and Dell came into the room. "All done?" Dell asked.

"Yes," Deor nodded. "I do feel better, actually." She set the bottles of pills on a side table "I'll take my first dose with breakfast," she said. "Then I'll have a nap."

Victor rose from the chair and began to clear off the make-shift operating table and return it to its status as dining room furniture. Deor joined in. "I can do this," Victor said. "You sit."

"Nah," Deor said. "I feel better than I have in a long while. Let me help a little. It's blankets and pillows, not concrete blocks." She pulled a blanket off and folded it to return it to her room. As she moved, she could feel the slight tug on the staples in her back, but they weren't overly painful—in fact, there was something comfortingly heavy about them, as though they were protecting her from the magic around her.

For the first time since she came to the Tower, her body didn't feel like Finn's hands were on her. Even in the iron box of the cell, she felt free. Under her feet, the palace thrummed, and in the corner of the room, Boomie chittered cheerfully at her. The castle itself seemed better, too. She wondered if Finn could feel the difference, and if he knew what it meant.

She wondered what she would say the next time they spoke.

For a split second, her eyes flashed silver and blades edged the tips of her nails. Her hand curled slightly at the thought of facing the king, as though she was about to grip the hilt of a broadsword made for her and, quite possibly, for him too.

CHAPTER THIRTY-SEVEN

Standing beside Genevieve in the throne room of the Palace, Rafe no longer struggled to hold in his anger. Instead, the feeling, and the cold that went with it, had settled into a leaden blanket that weighed down his shoulders. Weapons weren't allowed in the throne room, and he felt the absence of his sword across his back. Still, he didn't want to fight anyone at the moment, not even Finn. He just wanted this charade to be over. From the subdued posture and lack of gaiety among the rest of the assembled nobles, his attitude was widely shared. Donovan and Chloe stood together near the wall, a little back from the rest of the crowd, their crossed arms and sardonic expressions making it clear they were not present to cheer for the king.

Only Monjoie, standing with Arthur on the opposite side of the room from Rafe seemed in a cheerful mood. He smiled to himself and bounced on his toes, looking around the room.

Odd behavior. Rafe roused himself a bit, scanning the crowd as they awaited Finn and Astarte's arrival. His parents, Madeline and Edgar stood close by, practically at the foot of the throne. Even odder. Given their position and Finn's penchant for locking people up on the merest pretense these days, he would have stayed as far back and as close to the doors as possible.

Roger and Pookie stood just a stone's throw from Rafe, Rodney and Lord Rangley beside them, though Rafe couldn't see Clarissa. Genevieve's parents stood at the back of the room with close friends and allies. Gordie was somewhere in his rooms, assisting Jameson. By rights a squire should have been present for an event like this, but since Rafe didn't trust him not to glare ferociously at the king, he'd instructed him to stay away. The lad hadn't argued. Penny and Rufus were absent, of course, as well as all the bards save Ama, but nearly every other member of Parliament was present and accounted for. If no one wanted to be there under the king's eye, neither did they want to be conspicuous by their absence. Delaney Overton was the most notable exception. Rafe reviewed the crowd again, looking for his normally punctual friend and wondering.

Just as the heralds began to raise their trumpets for the king's fanfare, Delaney slipped into place beside Rafe. His face was creased by worry and his hair was unbrushed. He hastily buttoned up his court coat as he stood.

"What's wrong?" Rafe whispered without taking his eyes off the door through which Finn would enter.

"They took George," Delaney hissed back. "I've been up half the night trying to find him and up again at dawn arguing with Arthur, Monjoie, the Palace Steward, anybody who could possibly grant me an interview with the king to get him released from the Tower. They won't even tell me which level he's on. Monjoie laughed in my face."

"Why didn't you call me?"

"I didn't think you could help."

Rafe lowered his head in shame. The flat truth of it weighed him down even further.

Finn entered, Astarte on his arm, and the only sound in the room was the rustle of clothing as hundreds of nobles bowed. In silence, Finn approached the throne.

He did not reach it. As his foot touched the first step of the dais, Madeline stepped in front of him, her hand held out. Power rippled up and down her arms, pooling in her outstretched hand. Behind her Edgar dropped the glamour that had hidden his sword.

All around the room, nobles gasped and drew back. Rafe dropped Genevieve's arm and started forward, daggers of ice forming in his hands.

"I wouldn't, if I were you." Monjoie, a naked blade already in his hands interposed himself between the little group at the foot of the throne and Rafe and Arthur. A knife slid out of Arthur's sleeve into his hand. Two more Houseboys slid into position, flanking Monjoie and isolating Finn and Astarte from help. All through the room retainers with Wellhall badges drew out weapons. The Houseboys at the main doors slammed them shut and drew their weapons, too, but any hope of help died when they nodded to the others wearing the Wellhall insignia.

Madeline's voice rose above the gasps and shouts of the crowd. "Nobles of the Winter Court, my esteemed Peers. It is time we were done with this incompetent farce of a king." She stepped further up the dais so that everyone could see her. "Do not make any hasty decisions. My people have already secured the quarters where your household knights and other champions are staying. They will not be coming to save you. My people have also secured the Tower of London. The king, his Consort, and the Heir are in my hands. As are the heirs of many of your houses, given the events of last night."

Ripples of shock and horror ran through the room. Rafe risked a glance to his left. Chloe and Donovan stood to one side, looks of mild boredom on their faces. Donovan had his arms crossed, one leg bent, his foot propped on the wall behind him. Chloe was studying her nails, though Rafe knew perfectly well she had excellent peripheral vision as well as other senses that allowed her to see what was going on around her. The message was clear enough—the vampires would not break their pact with the Aethelwings, but neither would they involve themselves in a civil war.

Madeline was pacing back and forth at the top of the dais. "Let me be brief. The Parliament cannot unmake a king, but they can render him powerless. So, I call for a Parliamentary motion. Right now. Strip this man of his power. Make me Regent until such time as he dies and then crown me as Queen. Give me the throne, and I will restore this nation to its former glory. Your imprisoned children will go free. The land will flourish once again. And no bastard human will trouble you." She spread her arms wide, a benevolent smile rather like that of a shark upon her face. "Your decision is simple. I call for an immediate vote."

All around Rafe the murmurs and mutters grew louder. People huddled together, clearly panicking. Chloe nudged Donovan and said something that made him laugh behind his hand.

"This is treason!" Finn roared. "You cannot do this! If you so much as entertain this insane proposal—"

"Seconded," Delaney said. "I second Duchess Farringdon's motion and vote for immediate passage." He dropped his voice lower. "I'm sorry, Rafe. She has my father and my brother."

Rafe nodded, understanding. Of their two captors, only Madeline had offered the Overtons a way out of prison.

"What about the Princess?" Genevieve shouted. "She is a legitimate

Heir. If we must have a Regent, let it be her." Shock rippled through the crowd. Some nodded, warming to the idea. Others booed, shouting that Madeline was a true faerie and a descendant of the Aethelwing line. "She'll learn," Genevieve said, pleading. "Anyone can learn. You're trading one tyrant for another."

"Silence!" The full force of Madeline's will crashed into Genevieve with the word. Genevieve staggered, doubled over and fell to her hands and knees. Water had condensed out of the air around her, leaving her a draggled, gasping mess, unable to stand.

"Come now." Madeline's voice was a warm purr, no less laden with power than before. "Let me see your hands. Show me which ones of you have sense."

Lord and Lady Rangley, too shame-faced to look up, raised their hands in consent. In one corner, Roger and Rodney argued ferociously, their air faerie magic blurring their lips and concealing the sound of their words. Around the room, hands began to go up. "Aye," sounded from one faerie noble after another.

Chapter Thirty-Eight

Deor sat on the couch in her cell, jaw hanging open. The people had voted... "Did she... did Madeline just—" She spun to look at Victor, who seemed as bewildered as she did. "Did your mother just become queen?" Deor forced her legs to work and stood.

"No." Dell rose too. "She can't do that, not yet. Not if the king lives, if you live."

"She said the Farringdons are part of the royal line. Is that true?"

Dell frowned. "Yes, but it isn't that simple. She's from the non-heir line. Her ancestor was not chosen by the first of the Aethelwings, and they left to found the duchy of Wellhall. History is unclear as to whether or not they were from that point on estranged and hostile, but that certainly became the situation."

"It's the reason I can't inherit Wellhall so long as Rafe is alive." Victor stood, too, and crossed his arms in front of him. "That first Farringdon Duchess made magical pact with the land that the eldest, and only the eldest, can inherit Wellhall. A rather severe correction to someone else's mistake, if you ask me."

"So, she has a legitimate claim?" Deor asked. "She can really be appointed by Parliament?"

"Yes." Dell nodded. "The choice of monarch can be made by Parliament in the case of a lack of an heir, or an unsuitable one."

"That's how your father almost lost the crown." Delaney said from his seat on the couch. "When Prince Sweordmund killed his father in self-defense, he was jailed and put on trial. The Farringdons then tried to force a vote of no-confidence and install themselves. The jury found him not guilty of murder, and Parliament voted to install him as king. With a few dissenting votes."

"That sounds horrible." Deor shuddered at the thought that perhaps he had been guilty, and, as a powerful prince, gotten away with murder.

Dell seemed to read her thoughts. "I was there, princess. His father had gone mad and thought Finn was trying to kill him. He wasn't. The king had already murdered his wife, and then came after his only child." Dell shook his head sadly. "I was helping the lad study when he was called to the throne room. I went with him, unasked, of course. The king attacked him, and he did everything he could to fight back without killing or even harming his father. It was his life or his father's."

Deor stared at Dell for a long while. "Thank you." A vision of the king's eyes, flat silver with rage, rose in her mind. Could she kill Finn if she had to? Would she take the chance if it came? And did she have her own madness to look forward to?

Sharp spikes of pain tore through Deor's chest, and she crumpled to the floor. She pressed her eyes closed and tried to breathe, but the pain made her gasp for air. A heart attack? The pain seemed to radiate from her core through her whole body until every inch of her ached. She clenched her teeth and forced her wings to stay in, unsure if they would rip out her staples, or possibly be ripped apart on them.

The men were gathered around her—she could feel their presence. Brand had pressed himself against her body, and his whines vibrated against her. Under her the floor was smooth, soft, and she pressed her free hand against it.

Another wave struck her—not physical pain, but agony of another sort. Rage, and close behind, fear. She sucked in another breath, her whole body shaking. Her nails sharpened, digging into her flesh. Not cutting her, but the magic stung, like it wasn't her own.

Don't leave us! Boomie's voice sounded from somewhere above her.

"*I'm trapped in the Tower! I'm not leaving you!*" she muttered in reply. "*I swear to God, to anything and everything, to the very bedrock of the land, I will not abandon you!*" Her voice rose, and she was shouting. "*I am yours, and you are mine. I swear!*"

The pain and anger flooded out of her, like a dam bursting, leaving her panting and spent on the floor. She gathered Brand up into her arms and clung to him, his steady heartbeat comforting against her own.

Behind her she could feel Dell, Delaney, and Victor. They were near panic. When her vision cleared, she saw why. Boomie was in front of her. Not the small, travel-size gargoyle she knew, but a full version, as big as a tiger, with his broad bat wings out behind him and his stone tail scraping the floor as it whipped back and forth. Solid platinum orbs stared at her.

"You see that," she said over her shoulder, "right?"

"Yes," Victor managed, his voice a whisper.

Boomie was fixated on her. She gently set Brand down, and he ran to the stone monster before she could stop him. Fearless he sniffed the creature up and down, and barked, dropping into a play bow in front of it. The cat-headed creature cocked its head and leaned down, gently bumping his nose into the dog's. When he lifted his head, Brand barked again and ran around him in circles, expecting to play.

"Boomie?" Deor asked.

The cat turned its pupil-less eyes to her. "*Your job. You promised.*"

Deor struggled to her feet, toes curling against the stone floor, warm and soft as plush carpet. She walked toward him, hand outstretched. "*I did promise. You are mine, the whole of you.*" She reached for him, and he inclined his head, allowing her to pet him. "*Everyone.*" Deor ducked down wrapping her arms around the great creature's neck, resting its head on her shoulder. She clung to him. "*He's gone, isn't he?*"

"*Yes. There is someone else at the throne...?*"

Deor stood straight. "*Yeah,*" she said. "*Let's go fix that.*"

She turned to the men behind him. "*The king is gone.*"

"Dead?" Dell asked.

Deor glanced back at Boomie, who seemed to shrug.

"*I don't know, and I don't think it matters. But it's my kingdom now.*"

Victor and Delaney both gasped, but Dell smiled. "I believe it is, my lady regent."

Deor shook her head slightly to clear it. She'd been speaking high faerie again. "We've got to get to Madeline. The palace doesn't want her, it wants me."

Victor pointed at Boomie. "What is that?"

Deor glanced over her shoulder. Boomie twitched his tail back and forth, watching Brand leaping after it, catching it and chewing on it—to little effect, given it was stone. "It's the palace," she said. "Normally he's not that big. He's usually about the size of a housecat."

"Huh." Victor looked around. "We'll pound on the doors until they open them, saying you're ill, and then we'll jump the guards—"

"There aren't any guards," Dell said. "They've all left to join Madeline."

"Right," Victor said. "Then we'll break the dining room table legs and bind them together as a battering ram for the door."

Deor looked to Boomie. "*This is my house now, right?*"

"*Your job. Yes.*"

Deor laid her hand on the cell door and closed her eyes. Five huge iron bolts in the stone held the door shut. "*Open.*"

They slid back with an audible *thunk*. The two other sets of doors cracked open at the same time as well.

"Let's go," she said.

After a small pause of shock, the three men followed her into the hall.

"Could you always do that?" Victor asked.

"I don't know." Deor headed for the portal at the end of the hall. They were on the top floor of the North tower. The portal would take them to the palace and the throne room. The magic of the palace thrummed through her, through her back and wings, dulling the pain to a distant throb.

The portal rippled, and a few armed men came though, a motley retinue behind them. The first one froze when he saw her. "Princess?" Stephen said.

"Stephen!" Deor ran to him and hugged him.

"I came to get you out...?" He looked past her at the men behind her and the open door. "What the hell is that?"

"That's Boomie," Deor said. "My palace."

"Your invisible friend," Stephen nodded.

Victor scooted slightly away as the creature came up next to him. "It seems mostly friendly."

"We've got to get her to the throne room," Delaney said. "Immediately."

Stephen nodded. Gordie was with him, as were a few other young soldiers and squires she recognized. Her heart ached at the thought of asking these kids to fight trained soldiers.

"Come on," Stephen said. "We'll portal."

"No, wait," Deor said. "The others, in the prison. Where are they keeping Robbie?"

"The main wing, top floor," Stephen said.

"Show me." She moved toward the portal. "How many guards do you expect we'll face?" she asked. "We need weapons."

"Not so long as we're in the Tower we don't," Stephen said. "Madeline thinks that she has the Tower locked down, so there were only a couple of her men guarding it. All the rest are gone, 'keeping order' in the throne room."

"When I saw what happened on the mirror, I called some other squires and came here—ran into Stephen on the way," Gordie added.

"Excellent." Deor couldn't help but smile at how proud the young man seemed—and as far as she was concerned, if they all survived, he should tell everyone he'd saved the princess.

Stephen hit the portal, and it opened in the hall of the main prison. Deor drew a deep breath as she stepped in. "How bad is it?" she asked.

"Not too bad. There was not much interrogation of most of these prisoners. Arthur was quite firm on that point."

"Great. Maybe I'll only break one of his kneecaps. Maybe." She stepped to the first door in line.

"The keys are in the guardroom downstairs." Stephen looked to Gordie. "Go get them." The squire nodded and took off.

"We don't need keys," Victor said with a smile. "We've got the ultimate lockpick."

"I can do it, but it will take forever—I have to do each one separately. Keys would be great, but until Gordie gets back, yeah, I can handle it." Deor laid her hand on the first door. Compared to the Tower cell, this was easy. With barely a push of her will, the door sprang open. She swung back the door. "Robbie!" Deor's voice cracked with relief. She flung herself inside and nearly tackled the girl with a hug.

Robbie clung to her. "Is it true?" Her eyes were rimmed red, her face splotchy with tears. "Is the king dead? Is my mother..." she trailed off.

"I don't know," Deor said. "But what's important is that right now you're free. We've got to get everyone else." Deor let go and stepped back. "Okay?"

Robbie wiped her nose with the back of her hand and straightened. "Right."

Deor walked down the hall, opening doors on either side. Aiden, Redfern, and the others rounded up in the first arrest were there, as were Tess, Ian, and MacIntyre.

"How many people have been arrested?"

"There are probably a couple hundred—maybe more." Stephen said. "The last few days of the tournament, the king saw to it that almost anyone with a badge he didn't like was at least questioned."

"Tosh!" A voice from further back in the crowd rang out. George

Delaney, a lanky and rather fussy young man, moved his way through the crowd. "Father!" he said when he reached Deor. He rushed into his arms and hugged him. "You're okay," he said, pulling back.

"What do you mean, tosh?" Deor asked.

"I certainly never wore a Wellhall badge or anything with those Sons of London riffraff." Behind him, Redfern arched an eyebrow, but said nothing. "After the finals last night, there was a huge sweep of people—several of my friends from the best families."

Deor scowled. "That's how she got the Parliament members' families."

Gordie, panting, burst through the portal, several rings of keys in his hand.

She put her hand on Gordie's shoulder. "You and the other lads open all the doors. Get everybody out. I'm going to have a chat with Madeline."

"I'm coming, too," Tess shouted. A general chorus of agreement rang out.

"Alright," she said, quietly relieved at the rag-tag army that would be at her back. "Those who want to, follow me. The rest, help the squires free the people."

Deor waved her hand, and Boomie joined her by the portal, everyone gaping. "It's weird that people can see you now," she said to him. He merely looked at her. She laid her hand on the lintel of the portal, and beneath it the whole palace thrummed in anticipation. "Throne room."

Chapter Thirty-Nine

No, mother!" Rafe hurled both his ice daggers straight at her along with every drop of water he could summon from the room around him. A gale of stinging sleet-like razors battered her defenses. For a second, she staggered backwards.

Chaos erupted around the room as the king's partisans, or at least those who did not support Madeline, grappled with her retainers and those caught in the middle crowded to get out of the way. Rafe had eyes only for his goal. He dodged past Monjoie's swing and hurled himself straight at Edgar.

Edgar's sword was just descending toward Finn's head when Rafe rammed headfirst into him. They rolled, struggling and grunting, onto the floor. Edgar held tight to his sword, bashing Rafe in the face with the hilt. Rafe kneed him in the groin. Edgar hissed and curled in on himself but didn't lose his grip on either Rafe or the sword.

Somewhere nearby, Arthur was shouting. "Get the king out!"

A flash of golden light and Edgar howled, blinded by Astarte's magic. Rafe punched him in the jaw. He seized his father's sword hand and slammed it into the stone floor, bashing the weapon free. He scrambled to his feet, sword in hand.

Screams came from the dais. Astarte and Madeline were locked in battle, their magics a swirling maelstrom between them. Hail and snow battered at Astarte and thorned vines grew from the floor, entangling

Madeline's feet. Behind Astarte, Finn, gleaming silver sword in his hand, hacked and slashed at two Wellhall retainers while Arthur and Monjoie rolled on the floor, punching and biting at each other. All around the room, screams, explosions and flashes of magic erupted.

Rafe ran straight at Monjoie and kicked him hard in the ribs, hard enough to allow Arthur to scoot out from under his grip. Faeries in glittering court apparel lay on the floor as Wellhall retainers stepped over them. More people in Wellhall badges were streaming in through the far doors, pushing up toward the throne.

"Behind you!" Arthur shouted. Rafe whirled just in time to catch Edgar's attack on the edge of the sword. Edgar howled and fell back, his arm bleeding from a deep slash.

"Get the King and Consort out!" Rafe shouted at Arthur. He dodged past Edgar and kicked off from the ground, wings erupting from his back. From the air he rained blows down on Madeline, but her defensive magic shielded her. "Run!" he shouted at Astarte.

Madeline turned her attention toward Rafe, and Astarte renewed her attack. Arthur seized her arm. "Run!" he shouted.

Arthur pushed Finn and Astarte out the side door through which they had come as Pookie and Roger held off the Wellhall retainers. Roger might be an old man, his footwork slowed by years, but his rapier, supposedly blunted and worn only for ceremony, was still lighting quick. Pookie lashed out with a foot, kicking a Wellhall soldier in the knee.

Rafe dodged and rolled through the air, evading his mother's blasts of magic. He dove for the doorway just as Roger shoved Pookie through it. Together they slammed the door shut and pressed their bodies against it.

"Finn! Seal the doors!" Rafe shouted.

Finn put out his hands to the walls, calling to the Palace in Ancient Faerie, and the lock fused shut under Rafe's hand. Together, Roger and Rafe dashed after the royal party, already hurrying down the halls.

At the first portal point they came to, Arthur opened a door directly into the Household. Finn tried to leap through, but Arthur put out a hand. "Me first, sire. We don't know how far they've infiltrated." He stepped through and looked from side to side before beckoning Finn and Astarte to follow. Rafe waited until Roger and Pookie went through before closing the portal behind him.

"I can put a minor lock on it," he said, "but I don't have the Shield's magic."

Arthur nodded grimly and closed his eyes, his hands held up above his head as magic gathered around his fingertips and flowed down the length of his body. He struggled mutely, his breath becoming labored. "Sire," he gasped. "I can't do it. Madeline...something is stopping me from sealing off the Household entirely. I can hold it, but not forever. We've got to get out of here, or we'll be trapped."

"Then this is where we fight," Astarte said. She walked to the window where a garden of potted plants grew and dug her fingers deep into the soil. The plants stretched and grew, twining themselves up her arms and planting their roots all along her body until she looked like the walking embodiment of summer in full bloom. Vines trailed behind her as she walked, and blossoms nodded in her hair. Every leaf was razor sharp, and every bloom had teeth.

Rafe nodded and took a sword from a display on the wall, examining the edge. It wasn't in perfect condition, but it would do. Roger flexed the blade of his trusty rapier. Pookie picked up a fire poker.

Finn shook his head. "We still have one way out." He beckoned to them all with the sword in his hand. "This way."

He led them back through the household to his bedroom. When he led them further into his closet and began hurling clothes away from the back wall, the others exchanged worried glances. Finn began hammering on the walls at the back of the closet.

"Let. Me. In." he shouted. "Dammit, I am your king! You belong to me!"

Rafe moved to stand between Finn and Astarte. Roger put out a hand to Finn's shoulder. "Sire? Who are you talking to?"

Outside, dimly, they could hear Madeline and her followers breaking through the Household's outer doors.

"The Palace!" Finn shouted, kicking the wall. "It's not listening to me." He drew himself up, calling the royal magic around him. "I command you to show me the way!" The floor vibrated underfoot with the force of his command. Slowly, with creaks and groans, the back wall of the closet split open into a rough doorway, a dark passage leading downward into the dark. Faint lights dotted the walls.

"This way," Finn commanded. He strode forward into the passage. Astarte followed him. Arthur and Rafe came last, glancing over their shoulders. Once they were through the door, it did not close behind them.

Arthur jerked his head in the direction Finn had gone. "You follow them. I'll be with you in a minute." He began weaving a glamour over the opening. Rafe hurried downward into the glimmering dark.

Their footsteps echoed and scraped in the dark as the king's party hurried downward. Once the glamour was in place, Arthur pushed forward to the head of the group to take point. Rafe brought up the rear. He trusted Arthur's glamours the way he trusted the ground not to shift under his feet, but still his hyper-alert ears brought him the sound of other footsteps following them from far above.

He caught up to Roger and whispered, "You're an air faerie. Can you hear anything coming behind us?"

Roger paused on the stairs, letting the others get a little ahead. Magic glowed faintly toward his head, undulating in waves that reached his ears. Slowly he nodded. "I think they found their way through."

"Do you have any idea where this is leading us?" Rafe breathed.

Roger shook his head.

His eyes focused on the dark stairs above him, Rafe said, "When they catch up to us, you get Astarte out. Let me hold them off."

Their eyes met in silent agreement and without a word, both men hurried to catch up with the others. Far below, Rafe could sense the presence of a large body of moving water. More water to work with was always a good thing. He smiled and picked up his pace.

CHAPTER FORTY

The portal opened, and Deor stepped through. She was slightly to the side and behind the throne, entering the same portal she had exited on the night she found out she was the heir to the Winter Court.

The room was bustling with activity—Madeline was at the center, smoothing her skirts and talking with her husband, who was securing a cloth around his forearm. Ama was nearby, hovering, looking cross. The Speaker of Parliament stood near the throne, too, looking like she might be sick. In the back of the room, looking like they were enjoying a day at the races, Donovan and Chloe watched with mild interest.

Around the room were various nobles, many of whom Deor recognized from her trip to Parliament. They were huddled in groups, and some were in tears. Soldiers, all with Wellhall badges despite their palace uniforms, patrolled with cheerful smiles and hands on their swords. Everyone was suitably cowed.

Deor moved out of the way to let others follow her in, Stephen and Victor following close behind. Victor had acquired a sword from one of the squires still freeing people from the Tower, and Stephen still had his own.

Deor straightened her shoulders and strode toward the center of the room. *"Madeline Farringdon! As I live and breathe! What a not-at-all-shock it is to find you here in the throne room as though it were your own."*

She hadn't yelled, not even raised her voice, but the crystal-clear words, in perfect Faerie, rang through like she had used a microphone.

Madeline spun toward her and smiled. "Lady Deor," she said. "I am glad to see you well. And you have returned my dear son to me! He was a prisoner in the Tower, I take it." Madeline looked her up and down, her eyebrow quirked. "Interesting prison attire," she said.

Deor looked down at herself. She was barefoot, no surprise there. She was also in her pajamas. Flannel pants with a drawstring and a long loose tunic. Her hair was up in a ratty bun, and she wasn't wearing a bra. Perhaps, she mused, she should have paused to put on something more appropriate. Too late now.

Deor shrugged, fixing an indifferent expression on her face. *"I'm sorry I didn't have time to change. Honestly, I don't know what one wears to stop a coronation—last time I was in a pantsuit. Perhaps I'll start a new trend."* She took another step toward her. *"Now step away from my throne."* She quivered a bit as she said it, half expecting the palace to rumble and drop huge chunks of itself on top of her.

From behind the throne Boomie sauntered out, tail flicking. Several people screamed and backed away, even guards. Boomie ignored them and took a seat next to the throne, gaze swiveling back and forth, as though he were about to judge a fight.

For the first time, Deor wasn't sure Boomie would choose her.

"The palace." Madeline stared at Boomie. She took a step toward the giant stone cat, but it flattened its ears at her approach. Madeline stopped and returned her attention to Deor. She cleared her throat, *"Your father abandoned the palace. You know it to be true. He left it and his nation without a king. I claimed the throne. Parliament has voted. It is done. I am Queen."*

Deor snorted. *"You can't be Queen, even if Parliament did pick you freely, which I doubt. I, the real heir, am alive. So, for your brief regency, I and the palace,"* she gestured at Boomie, *"thank you. Now move."*

Madeline shook her head and gazed at Deor like a pitying mother might a misguided child. Deor flexed her fingers and thought about clawing her face off but stayed still.

"You do live, child, but you are so young, so inexperienced. Do you think you have the skill, the diplomacy, the knowledge to run this nation? War is coming—there are whispers of it everywhere. Can you keep your nation safe? If we put a child on the throne," she waved at the throne with a sweeping gesture that spun her to face the whole of Parliament, *"we know the result. The Winter Court will fall to the Summer Court, the end of our nation."*

"When you voted," Deor said, addressing the audience, *"I believe you did not know I was an option. I would like to propose that there be another vote—"*

"NO!" Madeline's voice rang out, enough to make everyone flinch. Even the palace itself trembled—and Deor felt its allegiance slip.

"Your father abandoned the palace—it was free and unclaimed, and I claimed it. Perhaps in a century or two, you might be a fit heir, but now, today, I am what the Winter Court needs. I am what it has chosen. Everyone here knows it." She gestured at her soldiers—so many armed soldiers. *Take her back to her cell, and anyone who might wish to go with her. She will speak no more."*

"Try it, mother," Victor said as he and Stephen drew their swords.

For a moment everyone froze, staring at each other. From next to the throne, Boomie yawned and stretched his paws out in front of him. Brand trotted over and sat next to him, happily wagging his tail.

The doors at the end of the hall burst open, and Gordie rushed in. The crowd parted slightly at his entrance; behind him trailed a number of people, including several Houseboys, without Wellhall badges.

"Your Majesty," Gordie said and bowed. "I'm sorry it took us so long." He jerked his thumb over his shoulder. "These men were locked in one of the cells—they wanted to stop and pick up some weapons on our way."

Deor grinned. A few of the Houseboys were a bit roughed up, but that only seemed to add to their eagerness to engage with Madeline's group.

Delaney Overton, Junior stepped forward. "I move that we vote again for regent."

"I second that," his father said, coming to stand next to his son.

There wasn't even a pause for the Speaker, relief clear on her face as she hugged her wife who had arrived with the other freed prisoners, to call the vote before most of the people chimed in with "aye" and "yay."

"Revote!" The Parliamentary Speaker said, glaring at Madeline.

"Let's see if they'll support you when they no longer fear you," Deor said.

"All in favor of the regency falling to Princess Deor?" the Speaker called out.

The support was overwhelming.

Boomie rose from his place next to the throne and strolled over to Deor. He sat next to her and knocked her hand with his head until she stroked him between the ears.

"Fine!" Madeline said, silencing the murmuring crowd. *"Then prove you're fit. There's no proof your pet there is anything but an illusion. If you are so sure you are the true regent, sit on the throne! If you're unwilling, I will."*

The massive chair loomed behind her, the raised mound of stone from which it was carved seeming to grow. She swallowed hard. The first time she sat on it, it inspected her inside and out, body and soul. It recognized her as the daughter, the heir. It also was quite clear that its response to traitors and usurpers was swift and pointed—literally.

"It's enough that we choose her," Delaney Overton Sr. said. "As the Master of the City, I can think of none better."

"Sit on the throne!" someone called. Several voices joined in chorus.

A hand on her shoulder made Deor start. Dell moved in front of her and leaned in to whisper, "You must, child. Without that, they will not really believe in you. The situation of the Winter Court is perilous enough. The official regent can call upon the promises made—those of other nations like the Goblins and the Vampires. Without their aid..." He raised his eyebrows.

Deor cast another glance at the throne. "I'm afraid," she whispered, almost inaudible.

"Of course, you are," he said. "If you weren't, you wouldn't be fit to be regent." He glanced at Madeline. "That," he said, pointing with a jerk of the head, "is what a total absence of fear looks like. Your father, too, is supremely confident in his abilities and ideas."

Behind her were all the freed prisoners. Students, merchants, farmers, nobles. If she concentrated, she could feel the beating of their hearts, of the entire nation. "Alright," she said. She took a step toward the throne, and the crowd parted in front of her. On one side, Brand fell into step and Boomie on the other.

The closer she got, the more the throne seemed to normalize. One small step up onto the dais, and she was in front of it. She sat.

CHAPTER FORTY-ONE

At last, the long, uneven stone steps ended. The tunnel through which they had passed opened up into a broad shelf beside a rushing river. Daylight glimmered at the far end of the tunnel. Best of all, a narrow wooden pier led out to a boat just big enough to hold their party. Its design was so old as to be quaint, but from what Rafe could see the rigging and single sail were intact. No doubt they were covered in preserving magic.

The water was choked with ice floes all jostling and creaking against each other, but enough open water remained to allow a skillful sailor to navigate. Oars lay in the sides of the boat, but with Roger's magic and the strong current they wouldn't be necessary.

"Good thing we have the Admiral of the Navy with us, eh?" he said to Pookie as Arthur helped Finn into the boat.

"I swear we have a bigger toy boat in our bathtub," Pookie said. "Still, it's better than swimming to Northfalls."

From the end of the pier, Roger beckoned. "Hurry, my love."

Pookie moved to join Roger, pulling Rafe along. But Rafe hung back, one ear cocked. The footsteps from up the stairs had stopped, but he didn't trust that. There were all sorts of ways to cover one's approach. Behind him the air from the stairs moved and he turned, sword raised.

Roger was in the boat now, casting off the lines and giving instructions on how to raise the sail. Still Rafe hesitated at the base of the pier. He waved at Roger. "Go. Go. I'll catch up."

Astarte called from the boat, a note of desperation in her voice. "Rafe! Get in the boat! Right. Now!"

Wellhall soldiers swooped out of the darkness on silent wings. Before he could kick off the ground, one had tackled him. Rafe's head hit the ground, and he saw stars. His sword hand slackened, and his sword fell into the water. Monjoie was on top of him, beating his face in. He called a rush of water up from the river and hurled it at Monjoie. The freezing water poured over both of them, and Rafe squirmed out from under him. He kicked and shot backwards, ice slicking his path.

Rafe turned his back on Monjoie. Nothing mattered except getting to the boat and the soldiers attacking it. Astarte's vines whipped and slashed, snagging one soldier around the ankle, but he cut off the vine with his sword. In the prow, Finn threw silver daggers as fast as he could make them, but the soldiers flitted and danced aside. Arthur swung an oar.

Behind him, Monjoie was laughing. "Do you think you're the only water faerie in the world?" he shouted. Great shards of ice shot up through the pier's boards, blocking his way. Rafe put out his wings to leap over them and an ice floe the size of a sofa rose out of the river and slammed him down.

He landed painfully on the pier, his upper body hanging over the water. At least two ribs cracked, and a wing bent under him. Raising himself up on one arm, he gasped out "Go! Go now! Roger, get them out of here!"

A great gust of wind whooshed through the tunnel and filled the sail. Rafe struggled to sit up and unbend his wing, but its outer half was numb from the impact. As the boat moved away from the pier, Astarte lunged for the side. Vines shot out from her arms, tethering the boat to the pier.

"We can't leave Rafe!"

Rafe tried to shout "go" at her, but the cracks in his ribs kept him from filling his lungs. Astarte scrambled over the boat's side, her plants freezing on to the ice that stood between her and Rafe. In the boat, Finn shouted for her to not be a fool.

Monjoie was coming. Raised up on one elbow, Rafe sent a sheet of ice under his feet, but the man only laughed and sailed forward on it, his wings lending him extra balance. Rafe's head spun where it had struck the ground. He put up a hand. Warm blood trickled from his temple.

"Astarte! I order you to get in the boat!" Finn shouted. He raised his sword and hacked at the vines tethering the boat to the pier. She didn't even turn around. Roger's wind rushed through the tunnel, pushing the boat out of the cavern and into the Thames.

Rafe managed to scoot himself further onto the pier. Monjoie kicked him, and he went down flat again. Thorns from Astarte flew at Monjoie, striking him in the face, but he ignored her.

Sword in hand, Monjoie stood with a foot planted on Rafe's sternum. "Do you have any idea how long I've wanted to do this?"

Grunting with the pain in his ribs, Rafe said, "What did I ever do to you?" Not that he cared, but if Monjoie was talking he wasn't stabbing.

"Not to me, personally," Monjoie said. "To Wellhall. To your mother. Did you know she fostered me? Not as a hostage like you, you pathetic lick-spittle. A real foster, chosen and freely given. All through Finn's reign she preserved the safety of Wellhall and its people. She kept us whole while he poisoned the rest of the country. And you followed him." He raised the sword high. "And now I'm going to bring her your head. And the Consort's too."

"Not while the river is here," Rafe gasped. "Not while I can help it." He called on every ounce of magic he could, every drop of water and shard of ice. With a great roar, the river rose up and swept them both away.

Ice floes and pieces of pier battered Rafe from side to side. The force of the river bore him down, tumbled him over, destroyed his sense of direction. His lungs burned, spasmed. There was no up. He tried to pull air from the surrounding water, but pain and confusion scattered the magic before he could form it. The turbulent water bore him downward, beating and tumbling his body against the riverbed. And then something hard struck him in the head and there was nothing. Nothing at all.

LIKE THE FIRST time she sat on the throne, a swirl of images overtook her senses. She was whisked away to a void where space and time were irrelevant. A tiny roar came from next to her. Boomie, his normal size, looked up at her. She scooped him up and sat him on her shoulder.

She turned around and around, peering into the darkness surrounding her—the same space where she attacked Rafe during the adoption and where they connected through this massive, ancient chair, the focal point of all the magic of the kingdom.

"Hello?" She said. "If you're going to reject me, could we get on with it? The suspense is killing me—well not literally, but you get the idea."

A man appeared. Tall, older, probably Finn's age, with a bald head and great, red wings spread behind him. *"Hello little one,"* his voice was gravelly, like he hadn't spoken in ages, like it pained him to do so. The tone was gentle, his address not mocking, but affectionate. *"I wish I had lived to see you,"* he said, *"in person."*

"I don't know who you are."

"You do, even if you don't." He stepped forward until he was in arms reach. Deor didn't move. *"So, you want to be regent, eh? That other woman wants it, too—I can feel it from here. We all can."*

Deor remembered the kaleidoscope of visions she had on the throne, scene after scene of interactions between her kin, going all the way back. She hadn't understood at first, they spoke in Faerie, but then she had. The important moments of her ancestors, recorded forever, in the hunk of stone on which she sat.

This man in front of her, in her vision he had been sprawled out on the black and white tiles of the throne room, blood pooling beneath him, a sword through his belly melting into mist. A young man with ebony wings and tear-filled silver eyes stood over him.

"You're my grandfather." She swallowed hard. *"My father killed you."*

He nodded. *"Yes. Though my mind had long been lost to madness, he allowed my body to follow. You are here to take his place?"*

"Yes." She reached up and put her hand on Boomie. *"It's my job."*

"Your job," Boomie echoed.

"Indeed, it is," the man said. *"And you accept it?"*

"I do." She braced herself for some rush of something, wind, power, light, but there was nothing. *"So, that's it then?"*

"It is." He turned to leave.

"Wait!" Deor said. *"You're not really my grandfather, are you? He's not trapped in the throne. Those were pictures of the past. So, what are you?"*

The creature turned back, its face and body blurring as it rolled through dozens, maybe hundreds, of other forms, until it stopped, a figure of a middle-aged woman. She wore a white bardic robe made of some kind of fur lined with cloth, a belt woven of silver and gold, and a somewhat self-satisfied expression. Her arms were crossed. *"You know,"* she said. *"You're the first one to know—or perhaps to care—that I was not what I seemed to be. I have been here from the beginning."*

"Are you the first Aethelwing?"

"Some things never change." She laughed, the derision of it stinging Deor. *"Do you think your family is the beginning?"* She shook her head, her long

brown hair loose down her back flowing with the movement. "*I am not a queen,*" she said. "*I was—am—a bard.*"

"*Like the books in the library?*" Deor asked.

"*Those are my kin,*" she said, "*though they are much younger.*" She sighed. "*You are such a little one.*"

Deor frowned. "*I hate it when—*" The glare from the woman silenced her. "*Sorry.*"

"*Thank you.*" Her frown softened. "*I mean younger, not small. You don't strike me as particularly different from any other monarch.*" She peered at her, and then chuckled. "*I am mistaken. You remind me of one other—a long time ago.*" She shook her head. "*I was beginning to think you'd never show up. A half-breed.*"

Deor rolled her eyes. She curled her fingers and swirling magic formed in her cupped hand. A small push of will, and Deor would have a sword. If this woman was going to tell her she wasn't fit because she was only half faerie...

"*Again,*" she said, eyeing the forming sword, "*this is not an insult. It is a fact. Though you are more than half faerie. That much I can see in you. You have a long road ahead of you, Aethelwing. War is coming—*"

"*With the Summer Court.*"

The woman furrowed her brow, confused. "*I do not mean civil war—though your kind are inclined to that.*" She snorted. "*Long slumbering enemies you have awoken.*"

"*What are you talking about?*" Deor's stomach dropped. "*What enemy?*"

The woman looked up, past Deor, like she was listening to someone else. She flicked her gaze back to Deor. "*Be ready to stand alone, though you may find allies, if you can win them to your cause.*" She reached for Deor, laying a hand on her cheek. Her touch was faint and warm, like a ghost. "*I am sorry,*" she said.

"*For what?*" Panic filled Deor—the woman's words sounded like heaven-sent prophecy.

"*That we left the problem to you to solve. You are the cause; you are the solution.*" She laughed again, but it was gentle, and pulled away her hand. "*It's time for you to go. When the time comes, when you need it, remember this conversation. Until then, always know Faerie belongs to you.*"

Deor gasped and opened her eyes. She was sitting on the throne, staring out at the people, and all around her, a shower of her silver sparkles was floating through the air. They spun lazily, coming together in a circlet that settled on her brow for a few seconds before fading away.

The crowd gaped at her until Ama strode forward. "Parliament and the throne have spoken, Deor Smithfield Aethelwing is Regent of the Winter Court."

"Hail to the regent!" Victor cried. Around him, cries of "hail the regent" echoed through the room.

A few yards away, Madeline glared at her, furious. Before either woman could act, Madeline's husband Edgar grabbed her arm and walked her from the room, surrounded by her own retinue of guards.

Deor let them go. Wellhall would need to withstand an onslaught of the Summer Court, and without Madeline there, it might fall, and with it, the Winter Court. She would deal with Madeline later.

In the meantime, Deor felt like she had woken from a dream, and there was something in it she needed, desperately, to remember. The important thing was to focus on the Winter Court.

The people looked up at her expectantly.

"Tess MacIntyre," Deor called. The room, a buzz with excitement, quieted. "Come forward."

Tess made her way through the crowd, a slight line of worry creasing her brow. She curtsied. "How may I serve the regent of the Winter Court?" she asked.

Deor shook her head. "No, Tess," she said. "It is the regent who must serve you. *From henceforth I declare Mirrovere your land. I restore to you the title of your father and call you Countess of Mirrovere.* When you are ready, return to your home and heal your land. Whatever aid I can provide, you have but to ask."

Tess's jaw dropped, and she gaped at Deor for a moment. Finally, she managed, "Thank you, Your Majesty," and curtsied again before running into the arms of her brother and uncle.

Toward the back of the room the werewolves Finn had arrested waited, their expressions grim.

"I hereby lift the ban on all werefolk. They are restored to full citizens, with all rights and privileges thereof. I apologize for the monarch's cruelty and behavior toward them, both those who are citizens or residents in the Winter Court, and to Rufus and the entire werewolf clan of Ireland. I deeply hope that the previous friendship between our people can be rekindled." She inclined her head toward the group.

One stepped forward, tall, broad shouldered, and a near twin to Rufus. "I will take the message to my brother and father."

"Thank you." Deor looked out at the people watching her. At her feet Brand sat, wagging his tail. Behind her, perched on the throne, was Boomie, back to his regular size. She wasn't sure if everyone could still see him or if, job done, he had returned to obscurity. She cleared her throat. "Thank you all. I am afraid that I haven't got much time. War is coming. Madeline was correct about that. We need to prepare." She looked to one side. "Lieutenant Stephen Bolton," she said. He snapped to attention. "You are now my Shield. I will take some time and counsel before I name a Sword." She scanned the room. "Delaney Overton Sr., will you and your son gather such people as you see fit for a meeting with me two days from now, about the state of the Winter Court?"

The Overtons bowed deeply. "Of course, Your Majesty."

"Thank you again," Deor stood. "In the coming days I will come to address Parliament with plans going forward. Until then, you are dismissed." Deor rose and stepped off the dais, waiting for some sense of her connection to the land to wane, but it did not. Now that the adrenaline was fading, the pain in her back flared again. She winced and did her best to ignore it.

The Houseboys and squires gathered around her. "Gordie, will you gather the squires and help these people. Call the healers—get anyone anything they need. You're in charge, okay?"

"Yes, Your Majesty." Gordie bowed and rose, beaming. "Alright, lads," he called to the other squires. "You heard her majesty. Let's help these people." He moved away with the group, sending some off to get healers and servants with supplies.

"Ama, Dell," Deor said. "Would you stay here, too, and make sure that everyone is okay, and gets home? Please, also," Deor said, leaning close to Ama, "make sure Genevieve is okay—and tell her I said thank you for standing up for me. I'll be in touch with her as soon as I can." She turned to Robbie. "Robbie," Deor said, "would you stay with me?"

Relief flooded the girl's features, and she nodded. "My mother—"

"We'll find her," Deor said. "Now that Madeline's gone, they should be fine." She glanced up, past the crowd, to the two vampires, still standing next to the wall, looking amused and impressed. She looked back at Robbie. "Stay here for a moment, please."

She stepped away and headed for Donovan who straightened from his reclined posture against the wall. His wife did as well. "Hello, Donovan," Deor said. She turned to the woman, "You must be Lady Chloe Rodzevrah." Deor held out her hand. "I'm thrilled to get to meet you. I'm sorry it wasn't under better circumstances." She glanced down at her outfit again. "And in appropriate attire."

"Oh, I love your choice in loungewear." Chloe took her hand. "And I can't think of a better, or at least more interesting, circumstance."

"I know you two are lodged here in the palace," Deor said. "Would you mind staying a little longer—I would love your counsel."

Donovan eyed her for a few moments. "Why not? We've got nothing more interesting planned."

"Thank you. If you'll excuse me?" She turned to Victor, Stephen, and Robbie. "Let's go to my rooms and talk."

Chapter Forty-Two

Finally, as the sun began to set over the western wall, Deor returned to her old rooms in the Household. In what turned out to be the shortest meeting ever, Deor, Victor, and Stephen agreed that they were safe for now. The remaining Houseboys and soldiers were on guard, and others would be called in from other garrisons as needed. Everyone, save those invited and those who lived there, had left the palace—most eager to be home with family nearly lost or recently regained.

She'd briefly considered asking the Steward to find her a place to stay elsewhere in the Palace—rooms that wouldn't remind her of Rafe and Finn and everything else that had happened—but Stephen had pointed out that the Household was the most readily defensible part of the Palace should anyone come after her. And her books were there.

She flopped down on the couch in the parlor, trying not to let herself stare at the closed door to Rafe's rooms, and sent Melanie for tea. Deor let her head flop back on the couch arm and closed her eyes.

Boomie landed heavily on her stomach, just below her ribcage. She coughed and opened her eyes. "Now what?"

"*Do job! Consort!*"

Deor groaned and put her head back down. "Not now, Boomie. You can't expect me to find a Consort on my first day of being Regent. Besides, Astarte is the Consort."

"*Yes! Consort. Consort now now now!*" Boomie pounced on her ribs like a cat on a toy and then leaped backwards, zooming into the air and heading for her bedroom. Deor groaned. She levered herself off the couch and went to see what the persistent little cat-gargoyle wanted. Brand trotted at her heels.

Just inside her bedroom door, Boomie hovered. As soon as Deor entered, Boomie headed for her walk-in closet. Remembering what lay at the back of her closet, Deor picked up the pace. The passageway down was already open and waiting for her.

"Oh no," Deor said. "I've read too many adventure books to do this alone. Wait just a second."

Boomie flailed and looped the loop in frustration, but he waited until Deor returned with Stephen in tow. He pointed at the passageway and said, "Your once-again-invisible pet have something to do with this?"

Deor nodded and beckoned for him to follow her. Sighing, he unsheathed his sword and came along as Boomie chittered and urged them to hurry.

At the very bottom of the steps, they found Astarte soaking wet and unmoving. She was covered in a drapery of crushed and broken rose canes that grew down from her body and into the stone floor. Deor could see a faint golden light pulsing where the plants met the stone, but the leaves were brown and withered. Even as Deor watched, black rot crept up the vines.

Deor and Stephen ran over to the Consort, Deor putting her hand on Astarte's head to brush the hair out of her face. An unhealthy smell, like mildewed earth hung about her. Deor pulled out her mirror and held it in front of Astarte's face. Only the faintest fog showed on the glass. Beside Deor, Brand crouched and whined, his eyes worried. He crept forward on his belly and stuck out a tongue tip to lick Astarte's forehead.

"I think she's dying. Stephen, pick her up," Deor said. "We've got to get her out of here."

Stephen hesitated for a second, glancing back up the stairs and then at the open end of the tunnel through which the river flowed. He crouched beside Astarte and brushed away the leaves and vines. "You really shouldn't move a wounded person," he muttered. "Could be internal bleeding."

Boomie landed on Deor's shoulder. "*No more Consort.*"

Deor peered at the golden light. If she watched closely enough, she could see it moving, a slow seep of power into the black stone on which Astarte lay. She wriggled her bare feet on the stone, feeling the land beneath. The more she connected to it, the more powerful she felt. The land itself was pouring into her. The connection in her mind clicked.

"Stephen, we have to risk it. I think the land...I think it's killing her."

Stephen scooped her up in his arms and ran back up the steps two at a time. Clutching her skirts, Deor hurried after him with Boomie and Brand at her heels. As she pushed herself up the stairs, the wounds in her back ached and pulled with the effort.

"Go. Go ahead," she panted, stopping to lean on a wall. "I've got Brand." She pulled out her mirror between gasps for breath, calling "Asphodel. I... Astarte needs you. Come to the Heir's quarters."

It took Asphodel and Mac an hour to stabilize Astarte. Even then, the best they could do was settle her into a deep coma. Robbie never left her mother's side, except to direct servants bringing up healing plants from Astarte's greenhouse. They turned the entire bedroom into a hanging jungle, full of the smell of green, growing things and flowery perfumes.

Finally, with Astarte settled and Robbie tucked in by her side, Deor made her way to her room, stripped off her clothes, and collapsed into bed. Within moments, she was fast asleep.

CHAPTER FORTY-THREE

Deor startled awake. The sun was bright in the window, and Stephen stood next to her bed.

"What time is it? Did something happen? Is Finn back?"

"It's almost noon," Stephen said with a smile. "Victor and I decided you should sleep until you woke, unless there was reason to wake you. And no. There has been no word from the king, or anyone in his retinue."

"I thought sure I'd wake up to find Finn back in the palace, safe and well as you please." She sat up. "So, what happened? How bad is it? Is it Astarte?" Sorrow swelled in her chest. The thought of Robbie losing her mother was too much to bear.

"Astarte is unchanged. Asphodel isn't certain she's much better, but she is stable, and certainly not worse. It's nothing bad—just curious. Take some time getting up and ready, and I'll be waiting for you in the parlor." He bowed slightly and left the room.

Deor sighed in relief. She trusted Stephen to tell her the truth—he wasn't the type to put off bad news. She got up and headed for the bathroom and a not-too-quick shower. As Deor put on the clothes Melanie had laid out for her, a halter tunic and light cardigan over loose pants, her mind drifted. She wanted to go home—pack up and leave the whole of Faerie to someone else and try to forget everything that happened. There were particularly clever, wise, strong people in the Winter Court, it would be fine, and her grandmother would make that wonderful apple pie...

DON'T LEAVE US!

Wincing, Deor held out her arm. Boomie landed on it and stalked up to sit on her shoulder. His paws were warm against her shoulder, and he didn't claw through her light sweater.

"You shouldn't read my mind. It's invasive and impolite. And I'm not leaving. I'm just fantasizing about leaving."

Boomie chuffed.

The makeshift halter top Melanie had produced worked well, including the bra. It left her back open to the air, to the ambient magic, even wearing a light sweater. With the metal staples and the magic around her, she seemed to actually be healing.

Deor knew that home wasn't home anymore. She could try to go, but the thought of stepping into the human world made her shudder. The faerie in her wouldn't be bothered by the iron and steel, but the separation from the kingdom? The void would be unfillable.

Anger at Finn flooded her again. She was furious at his abandoning Astarte, abandoning the kingdom, and abandoning her. As much as she wanted to punch him, she also resented him fleeing and leaving them all behind.

Asshat.

Deor giggled. Boomie had picked up a few words from her and seemed to like that one. *Well, might as well go and see what curious thing Stephen has for me.* Boomie leaped into the air and whirled to the ceiling where he vanished.

Deor came into the parlor. "Okay, so, what's going on?"

"Someone weird showed up and asked for you, so I brought him here. He's right outside." Stephen opened the door and waved the mysterious visitor in.

In walked a tall, thin, bewildered-looking man, with unfashionably torn jeans, a tattered sweatshirt, shaggy brown hair, and crooked glasses. He carried a ratty backpack, an army duffle, and a small black gym bag.

"Bill!" Deor flung herself across the room and hugged him. He dropped his bag and embraced her, too, and they stood there for a long while. Deor let tears fall—the first of any kind of happiness in so long—against his shoulder. His body had been lean when she left, but now it felt frail. She pulled away and wiped the tears from her eyes. "What are you doing here?"

He wiped away a few tears too. "I was so worried about you—we hadn't heard from you. You weren't answering your mirror. So, I came." He put his hands on her shoulders. "You look well," he said. "Tired, though. I can see it."

"Tired," Deor agreed. "You look rough—more than twenty-four hours of travel rough. How did you get into the Winter Court? Were they mean to you at immigration?"

"What?" Bill shook his head. "No. I told them I was looking for my friend who had arrived a few months earlier—she was at the University. Then I told them your name. Then they put me in a room, and Stephen came and got me. We talked a bit, and he gave me a bite of lunch and brought me here." He looked panicked for a moment. "The food doesn't mean I'm trapped here, does it?"

"No," Deor shook her head. "Did you take the ferry?"

"Yes," he said. "Your grandmother kept copies of your mom's letters. I can follow directions as well as you can—maybe even better." He grinned at her. He was clearly happy to see her, and relieved. She could see that much. But there was a lot of pain in him too. Lines at the corners of his eyes and mouth.

From near their feet, Deor heard Brand growl. She glanced down—his ears were up, and he was crouched down, a low, menacing rumble from the back of his throat. He was pointing at Bill's gym bag.

"Get back!" Stephen said, darting between her and the bag. "It moved." He drew his sword and leveled it at Bill. "What did you bring?"

The bag twitched again, a low hiss seeping out what Deor now noticed were the mesh sides.

Stephen lunged forward.

"Wait!" Deor shoved him and he stumbled.

"It is moving, and your dog is growling at it. I've never seen Brand do that before." Stephen tentatively kicked the bag, resulting in more hissing.

"Don't hurt him!" Bill said.

Deor shook her head and leaned down to unzip the bag. "You brought him?"

"I couldn't leave him behind." He furrowed his brow. "Is it a problem?"

"Nah." Deor flipped the unzipped panel back. "Hey there, Killer."

A white cat sat up and glared at the room around it. Pale green eyes settled on Brand. Killer was a huge, fluffy white tom cat—clearly some kind of Main Coon, as he weighed thirty-five pounds. Chunks of his ears were missing around the edges from fights he'd won in the neighborhood, mostly against racoons and the occasional possum, before being adopted and converted into a housecat.

Brand trotted closer to sniff Killer.

"Careful," Stephen said. "Malossians are hunters—if that cat runs, he might chase it."

"He'd be sorry if he caught Killer," Bill said.

Thankfully, violence didn't seem to be in the cards. Killer jumped out of his bag and sauntered over to Brand. He hissed once. Brand barked and ran a lap around all of them before skidding to a stop in front of Killer, barking again, and dropping into a play bow.

Killer looked up at Bill, and back at the dog. He reached out a paw and bopped Brand on the nose. No claws. Brand barked again and took another lap around the room. Killer made his way to the fire and laid down, where he endured a good sniffing by Brand, who then flopped down next to him.

"That went well," Deor said. "Sorry for scaring you, Stephen. He should have warned you about Killer."

"No problem." Stephen put his sword away and knelt down to pet Killer. The cat endured the touch with mild disdain and began to purr.

Animals settled, Deor turned to Bill. "I'm sorry I was unavailable," she said. "It's been an odd few months."

Behind Bill, Stephen rolled his eyes.

Bill frowned. "You need to stop with the lies. I'm here in front of you. Whatever story you made up to keep us from worrying didn't work anyway."

"Long story short?" Deor chewed her lip. "My father turned out to be king, I've stopped three coups, but he fled the palace in the face of the last one yesterday, and so I'm regent now."

"That sounds about right." Bill opened his backpack and pulled out a newspaper. "I picked this up waiting in line at Immigration." He handed her the daily *Times*. The story was front page news. It summarized the past few months since she had arrived better than she ever could have. It even had pictures. "So," he peered at her. "You have wings?"

"I do," she said. "I'm not putting them out."

Bill nodded. "You never had them before."

"I did. They just never came out—because of the iron and the human side and all that. How about you? You don't look well, Bill. Worse than when I left."

"It's been a hard few months for me too. When you left I did get worse. I don't know why. I saw a lot more ..." He paused and glanced at Stephen, "things."

"We'll get someone here to look at you. There are lots of good healers." She turned to Stephen. "Is Penny still in town?"

"No," he shook his head. "When you lifted the ban on the werewolves, she and Rufus went back to help organize folks there—the ones that are coming back."

"Which isn't many, is it?"

Stephen shrugged. "It's hard to tell yet. I think some are waiting to see how this goes. If it lasts. Some of them don't have the money to rebuild their homes or businesses."

Deor pinched the bridge of her nose. "Add that to the list of stuff I need to deal with. We need to set up some sort of fund to help them come back if they want to."

"Yes. But Summer Court first."

Deor grabbed her mirror and called Melanie, asking for some food and for a room on the fourth floor to be made up for Bill and Killer. "Okay," Deor turned back to Bill. "I cannot tell you how happy I am to see you! I've been missing home so much. Lately it feels like it is gone—like I could never go back."

Bill paled some. "Really?"

"Yeah." Deor crossed her arms. "I think it is that I've been a bit ill—fighting an infection—but I'm getting better."

"That's good," Bill said, but he didn't sound like it was good. In fact, he looked like he was about to cry.

"What is it?" She reached out and put her hand on his arm. "Whatever it is, I'll help. We can deal with it together."

He closed his eyes tight, and tears slipped out, running down his cheeks. He opened them and caught her hands in his. "I'm so sorry," he said. "Your grandmother...she died. A sudden heart attack one evening." He seemed to struggle for something to say but shook his head. "I'm so, so sorry."

Deor pressed her hands over her mouth. She could only stare at him, frozen. She braced herself for the pain. Her chest tightened, but no overwhelming emotion hit her. Instead, her shoulders curled, and she shivered, feeling more like being reminded of something she already knew, not hearing it for the first time.

He reached for her but paused. "I'm sorry," he mumbled again.

She scanned the room. Brand was still on the floor next to Killer. The fire still crackled. The room was warm and quiet. Beyond the palace, across the Winter Court, people moved—they laughed and cried, worked and rested, doing whatever their lives required. The world went its way, as though the clenching pain in Deor's heart didn't exist.

Deor collapsed onto the couch, hands still pressed against her lips, and rocked back and forth. The tears burst from her, and she drew a deep breath that nearly choked her. She gasped, small squeaks coming from the center of her chest. Finally, the sob broke free and shook her, body and soul. Bill was at her side, his arm around her, and she leaned into him, weeping in deep, shuddering gulps of air. She clung to him, and he told her to cry, to let it out, that he had her, that she was safe. He stroked her hair and rocked her.

Something bumped her leg, and she looked down. Brand has his paws on her thigh and whined softly. She picked him up and settled him in her lap. To the other side, on the back of the couch, Boomie sat, his round eyes focused on her.

You grieve. For family. So sorry.

Deor sniffled. *"Thank you, Boomie."*

"What is that?" Bill said. He hadn't let go of one of her hands, and he sat very still. By the fire, Killer had perked up and watched it with interest and a flick of his tail.

"That's Boomie," Deor said. "He's the avatar of the palace, and sort of the Winter Court. It's the way the palace—the magic—talks to the rulers. Most people can't see him most of the time."

"It's a stone cat gargoyle with bat wings."

"Yes. He is." Deor wiped at her face. "He speaks Ancient Faerie," she said, glad for something else to talk about.

"And so do you?" Bill asked. "I mean, you're good with language, but...?"

"Long story. Remember all those cyberpunk stories where folks got stuff uploaded right into their brains? The throne did that to me when I sat on it. I can speak and understand Faerie, though I'm still learning to read and write it."

"Could it do that with me?" Bill asked, giving her a smile.

"No. Sorry." She sniffed again. The first wave of grief had passed, and her body felt wrung out from it. For now, though, she wasn't crying. She would focus on the business part of this. "So," she said, "funeral arrangements? Will? Estate?"

"All handled." Bill leaned back. "You know she gave me power of attorney when you left. So, it's all done. I spoke to the lawyer, the money is in trust, the houses are being cared for until you decide what to do with them."

"Wow." Deor squeezed his hand. "Thank you so much. And you got your part of the estate settled?"

Bill ducked his head. She knew he hated talking about money, and frankly, so did she. Bill's family hadn't had much, which was another in the litany of reasons they didn't seem to care when he disappeared to Deor's for days at a time.

"It's all settled," he said. "You know she took care of me," he said, not meeting her eyes.

"Good." Deor leaned forward and kissed Bill on the cheek. "I love you like a brother, and she loved you too." Deor frowned; he hadn't answered her first question. "So, when is the funeral? I know she has a plot--"

"Yeah, that's handled," Bill said again. "She had a plot and the service all paid for." He looked her in the face. "The funeral was two days ago." When Deor gaped, he plunged on. "I couldn't find you; I hadn't heard from you. It was arranged, and I couldn't just leave her in some mortuary's fridge while I came to look for you—"

"Of course," Deor cut him off, politeness taking over. "Right. You're right. She wouldn't have wanted that. I wouldn't...didn't...don't want that." She sat back and pressed her hand to her chest. Her heart rate was spiraling upward again, and her breath coming in short gasps.

She wasn't getting a goodbye. No viewing—not that they were great, but one last glimpse. A chance to touch her hand, even though Deor knew her grandmother wasn't there anymore. When Deor touched her mother's hand at the viewing—one Deor insisted on attending—it reminded her of wax,it didn't feel real. Deor searched her memory for images of her grandmother, for moments they shared, panicked for a moment that she wouldn't remember, that her grandmother would be utterly gone. Ridiculous, she knew, but she couldn't shake the fear that she would forget, especially in Faerie, where the real world already seemed like it didn't exist.

"When you can come back," Bill said, "we'll go to the grave, you and me, and we'll stay as long as you need, our own kind of service."

Deor nodded, not trusting her voice. She couldn't force a weak platitude out of her mouth, and that was probably for the best. Her grandmother hated things like that. Honestly, she'd prefer that Deor and Bill tell ridiculous stories about her and laugh until they couldn't anymore. "I want to say goodbye."

There was a knock at the door, and it opened a crack.

Deor wiped at her eyes and straightened. "Come in?"

"It's me." Victor came in with Stephen. "I heard there was someone I should meet." His eyes flicked toward Bill and then back to her. "You're crying." He stepped toward her, glaring at Bill. "What happened?"

Deor stood. "Victor, this is my friend Bill." She waved at Bill to stand, and he did. "Bill, this is Victor."

Bill held out his hand. "Hello."

"Bill and I grew up together. He's my oldest friend." Deor sniffed hard and wiped at her eyes. "He came to tell me that my grandmother passed away. The funeral has already happened."

"Oh, by the creator," Victor crossed the room. "I'm so sorry."

Stephen followed suit, putting an arm around Deor's shoulder gently. "As if you didn't already have enough shit to deal with."

Deor's tears started again. "I don't have time to go back now, but Bill is going to be staying for a while." She reached out and took his hand. "Here with me."

Victor's gaze darted to Bill. "Are you sure that's wise?" His brow furrowed. "Now might not be the best, or safest, time for a lover...?"

Deor gasped and then laughed, with Bill joining in. "Oh, no. No no no." She leaned her head against Bill's shoulder. "My grandmother basically adopted him. Like fostering. He's my brother more than anything."

"Wait!" Bill said as a look of recognition crossed his face. "You're the one in the paper."

"Me?" Victor asked.

"Yes! You're the one Deor got in trouble for having sex with, right? Dark hair, blue skin, blue eyes."

Deor winced. "Bill—"

"No," Victor said, glaring at Bill. "That would be my brother, Rafe, who is currently missing in action."

"Oh...oh my." Bill shoved a hand through his hair. "Sorry. I—I have a tendency to blurt things out."

"And you're friends with Deor? How shocking." He sighed and looked at her. "Parliament sent a formal letter this morning requesting your attendance with an update on your regency—things like who will be filling the position of Sword and Shield.

"Right. Still no word from Finn? I haven't heard anything." She looked to both Stephen and Victor.

"No," Stephen said. "We need to start planning in case he doesn't contact you. There is a possibility that your father is dead."

"No." Deor shook her head firmly. "He's not. I can feel it. And not because I'm particularly excited to see him again. The palace would know; it would tell me. It feels abandoned—and still conflicted about a regent. There would be none of that if Finn were dead." She rested her hands on her hips and looked at the three men. "Victor, send word back to Parliament that I will be there tomorrow, at the start of the afternoon session, with an update."

"Yes, Your Majesty," Victor said.

"What if the king doesn't contact you?" Stephen asked.

"I'll tell them the truth. I'm still regent, I'm working on putting measures in place, we're looking for Finn, and that I've been moving forward with my own cabinet just in case, and then I'll stall for more time." She turned to Bill. "Why don't you get settled? Maybe rest, eat something, and then come back here, and we can talk some more."

Bill nodded and, at Deor's gesture, followed a servant with his luggage out, carrying Killer with him.

"Security risk?" Victor asked.

"None," Deor insisted. "Who's he going to talk to? No one knows who he is or that he's here. And he's loyal to me, I know that." Deor smiled softly. "He's also someone that will tell me right to my face when I'm being an asshole. So that's a plus." She rubbed her hands over her face. "Okay, so as of right now, Sword," she pointed to Victor, "and Shield," she pointed to Stephen. "We'll deal with Consort later."

Both men's eyes widened, but neither objected.

"Great," Deor said. "Both of you go get to work in the offices below and get some handle on the state of the nation. Anything I can give to Parliament tomorrow will be helpful. You'll both stand with me tomorrow?" Deor asked.

"Absolutely," Stephen said.

"Of course," Victor added, though he seemed worried. Deor ignored it for the moment.

"Right. I'm going to shove all the emotions I'm wallowing in down into a little pit in my soul and lock them away so that I can go write some kind of speech. Send me anything I can use as soon as you know it."

Both men bowed and left the room.

Deor, with the help of Victor and Stephen, and with Bill watching, spent the rest of the day and most of the night trying to figure out how to say that

she was learning as fast as she could, that she was aware of the Summer
Court threat, and that everything was fine and was going to be fine, even if
they had no idea where the king was. It was three in the morning before
they finished—no one was happy, but it was done. Good enough would
have to do.

Chapter Forty-Four

Deor sat in Finn's spot at the breakfast table. She wore a plain grey dress, and her hair was loose, still short from Arthur's shears. All around the table she saw nervous glances, worry lines on faces, and the dark puffy eyes of sleepless nights. People kept looking to her as if she would tell them what to do next. Victor sat where Rafe would have, and Stephen in place of Arthur. Robbie sat next to Deor, as Astarte would have, and Bill had taken up Deor's old seat. It felt both right and wrong—she trusted everyone around her, but they were as lost as she was.

Deor hadn't managed to eat much. The last thing she wanted was to vomit all over Parliament. She scanned the table—everyone except Bill had a similar lack of appetite. At least a half a night's sleep and some good food had improved him. He looked much better than he did when he arrived. That, at least, was a small comfort.

"Your Majesty?" A servant—one of the king's secretaries—came into the room. "There is an urgent call for you. From Northfalls."

Deor bolted to her feet, and the others followed suit. "I'll take it in my parlor." She looked around the table. "Come with me, all of you, but stay out of sight, please. Except for you, Stephen. You stand by me."

In her parlor, she settled into a wingback chair. Servants had moved the sofa so that it was in front of the fire, out of the view of the mirror. She had a glass of water on the table next to her, and Brand lay at her feet while Jake and Sam were in front of the fire. At her right side, standing, was Stephen.

Everyone else was out of sight on the couch. She tucked an errant piece of hair behind her ear and rolled her shoulders—and didn't even wince.

She drew a deep breath and waved at the mirror. It went black and cleared, and Finn looked at her.

"Daughter!" He said, relief washing over his face. He looked fine—perky even. His eyes were clear and his clothes he wore were clean and pressed—and well fitted. "You are alive and well." He beamed at her.

"I am." Deor swallowed. "I see you are as well. You are at Northfalls?"

"Yes." He waved at someone and Arthur stepped into the frame, flanking him as Stephen flanked her. "With the help of Arthur, Pookie, and Roger, we made our way up to Northfalls." He shook his head. "We only arrived last night and were too exhausted to call."

Deor nodded. She couldn't keep her eyes from flicking back to focus on Arthur. He stood at parade rest, as always, but his eyes kept roaming around, sometimes meeting her gaze, other times searching her parlor.

"I saw what happened—some of it—on the mirror. I came to the throne room and found you gone."

"I know," Finn said. "The papers have been very detailed." He seemed cautious. "You have proven yourself quite the Winter Court hero." He smiled again. "The regent who saved the Aethelwing line and the Winter Court."

Deor managed not to snort at him.

"Can you, or Arthur, tell me what happened at the dock below the palace?" she said.

Finn's smile wavered at being asked for an explanation, but Arthur cleared his throat. "We were outnumbered. I got his majesty into the boat, with Roger and Pookie. Rafe and Astarte were fighting the Wellhall men. His majesty called for Astarte, but she would not come. When Rafe told me to leave, I did." His glance dropped, a corner of his mouth twisting with what might be shame.

Deor nodded. "Rafe is with you?"

"No," Arthur said. "He's not with you?"

"No." Deor shook her head. She drew a deep breath. "We haven't seen any trace of him.".

"I'm sure he survived," Finn declared. "My boy is a water faerie—we were at the docks…"

"Are you not," she asked, "going to inquire about your consort, whom you left for dead?"

Finn shuddered.

"She's alive, by the way," Deor said. "I found her at the docks later that night. She was near dead from the loss of power."

"Oh, thank the heavens," Finn said. "Can I see her?"

"Astarte is in a coma—the healers were able to stabilize her, barely. Now we wait and see. Robbie is with her."

Finn opened his mouth and then closed it again. He considered her for a moment. "I am sorry. If I had stayed, I would have died, and the kingdom would be kingless." He shook his head. "That would have been chaos."

Deor sat forward in her chair, anger stiffening her shoulders. "You abandoned the palace and the kingdom. I was able to open the doors in the Tower, to free not only myself, but everyone else. I sat on the throne again. The palace had to choose someone, and it chose me instead of Madeline— barely." Deor drew a breath and tried to rein in the anger. "The palace is angry, too, at you."

"Yes." He looked contrite. "And I can make it up to you, to the palace, to everyone."

"You desperately want to come back."

"I do." He smiled. "I knew you would understand. The kingdom needs me."

"Okay," Deor said. She sat back in her chair, chin lifted. "So, come back."

"It's more complicated than that," he said. Next to him, Arthur looked toward the floor. "Go down to the main portal and open it for me. Open a portal to Northfalls, and I will come home."

Deor blinked. "Why can't you open the portals yourself?"

His smile faltered a bit. "I'm proud of you for all you've done. Now restore the kingdom and open the portal."

Deor trembled. Her chest tightened as she said, "You can't open them."

"I'm weak from the attack—"

"No, you're not. You're fine. You can't lie to me about the palace, Finn. It won't open to you anymore, will it? It's done with you. The throne, the land, they chose me."

"As regent." He said, voice low. His eyes had grown cold, and his jaw was set in the same way it had been after her speech.

"I gave up my job, my dream, to find you, and gave it up again to stay. It was nothing to you, my career, but everything to me. Then I was the princess, and I took the job seriously. I said no to you."

"You did," Finn said hurriedly. "You were so brave." He nodded. "When I return, you will be one of my main advisors—"

"I wasn't finished." Deor cut him off. He gaped a bit and closed his mouth. "While I was in the Tower, my grandmother died. My last blood connection to home, to the human world. I didn't find out until yesterday. I missed her funeral, Finn."

He shook his head sadly. "I told you that you must be very careful with the attachments you form. That is a lesson you must learn. I had to leave Astarte behind, and Rafe. The kingdom matters above all else. You had to leave the human world behind. I told you that night. It is a hard lesson, but one I had to teach you."

"Wait," Deor shook her head. Her fingers tightened on the chair's arms, and she swallowed hard. The night in the Tower when he ripped open her wounds. She counted the days back. She counted the hours. Assuming that Bakersfield time was as far away from Faerie as it was from London time, Finn reopened her wounds when her grandmother and Bill were finishing dinner. "Did you have something to do with my grandmother's death?"

He crossed his arms. "You needed to learn."

"Stop saying that and answer the question."

"I did it for you."

Deor's gaze flicked to Arthur who looked shocked. As soon as he met her eyes, he looked away. "Did what, exactly?"

Finn uncrossed his arms and took up his lecture posture. "You are connected to her—through your mother. I knew that you were not merely half faerie. You couldn't have been, because your mother wasn't fully human. She couldn't have seen me if she were." He shifted, uncomfortable. "A mere human woman would not have died from pining."

In her bones, in the bones of the palace, Deor knew her grandmother's death wasn't a tragic accident. It was murder. "Is killing her what hurt me?" She tried to keep her voice even.

"The opposite actually," he said, still in lecture mode. "The power of the king worked through you to her—to help her, and you, let go of each other. The opening of your wounds was more about my displeasure."

"Did you know your magic stayed in my body? Kept the wounds open and allowed them to get infected?"

"I'd never done that particular thing before." The same cruel expression from that night was back. "But I suspected it might. The king's displeasure is a mark that does not fade quickly. You needed the reminder of the order of things." He glanced at Arthur. "Right, Captain?"

Arthur jerked like he'd been poked. "Order is important," he said, voice a harsh whisper. He couldn't meet Deor's eyes.

"I could have died," Deor said.

"I trusted my healers, and they healed you," Finn said. "I was right. You are not split between human and faerie. Now you are free to live here and let your past go. I will come back, and everything will be as it should be."

Deor stared at him as her heart beat in her chest, the blood thudding in her ears. Nothing in him had changed—nothing would change. He was cruel, petty, and vengeful to the bone. He was the most important thing in the world.

Slowly, her mouth dry, she spoke. "That night, you asked if I understood. I thought I did, but I was wrong." She stood. "Open the portals, Finn."

"What?"

"Open them. You're the king—or you claim to be—the palace itself cannot ignore you. Open them."

"I can't." He stood too, eyes silvering in an instant. "The palace has locked me out. Treasonous piece of rock." He pointed at the mirror, fingernails long and silver. "Open the portal right now lest I name you a traitor!"

Deor snorted. "Name me a traitor. Like, what? Call the press? Or curse me to the air and hope it drifts south?" She shook her head. "I will not open the kingdom to you. You forsook the palace, and it has returned the favor. And you, Arthur," Deor said, suddenly noticing him again. "Look at me." He did. "Your job is to protect the king. You're not my Shield, but you are his, so stay there and do it." He swallowed hard and nodded.

"I created you! You owe me your life!" Finn yelled. "You belong to me. You all belong to me!" He gestured at her, at Stephen. "The whole of the Winter Court belongs to me! I can destroy you if I will it! I am his majesty Sweordmund Fionnleigh Aethelwing the Eighth. King of the Winter Court. Who the hell do you think you are?"

The king flung a blade at the mirror, which bowed and rippled. An instant later the knife tore through the mirror, driving at her heart. Deor raised her hands to protect herself, but before she could get them up, the *ching* of metal hitting stone echoed through the room. Boomie hovered in front of her, and all that remained of the blade was a cloud of silver sparkles dissipating into the air.

From the mirror, Finn gaped, bewildered. Arthur stared at him, his surprise hardening into open loathing.

Deor rolled her shoulders and braced herself for the pain. She shoved her wings out, though her staples, sending them flying, and they fanned out behind her. Power coursed through her, adrenaline dulling the pain.

"I am Deor Smithfield Aethwing, first of her name, and until the palace and the land will otherwise, I am the Regent of the Winter Court. You," she said, "are through." She flicked her hand at the mirror, and it went dark.

"So," she looked at the people around her. She softened her expression. "Does anyone have a problem with this?" She scanned the room. "I need to know—I need you here for me, and that means telling me if and when I've done wrong."

"All hail the Regent!" Victor said.

"Amen," Bill followed.

Deor looked to Stephen. "You?"

Stephen seemed to consider it. "He's a horrible king. With him here, we'll lose a war to the Summer Court in the blink of an eye. Especially without Rafe. Maybe someday he can come back, but not today."

"Thank you—all of you. We'll get through this. We'll keep the kingdom safe. Together."

"And Parliament?" Victor asked. "You've got to address them."

"I do." Deor looked down at the plain grey dress she had intended to wear. "Melanie! Jameson!" she called, and they hurried in from the servant's door. "Melanie," she said. "I can't wear this dress. Go fetch me the Wham! And Thorsen I was going to wear to the ball." The girl beamed at her, curtsied, and hurried off. "And Jameson," she said. "I need you to find me the crown I wore when I gave my speech—the one with all the spikes— and the jewelry that goes with it."

"Of course, Your Majesty." He bowed and hurried away, a smile on his face.

"What are you going to say?" Bill asked, worry creasing his brow.

"We've got sixty minutes to figure that out."

"What about the king?"

Deor answered. "I will tell them the truth: I am the Regent, and the king is not coming back."

Coda

Slowly, painfully, Rafe awoke. His face was pressed against the rocky shingle, his lower half still washed in the freezing ocean water. He shuddered, gasping to pull air into his lungs. Then his whole body convulsed, vomiting up the sea water he had swallowed.

After a long time, the coughing and spewing stopped, and he could breathe again. He eased himself up into a sitting position on the pebbles, feeling his ribs. Definitely broken. His head throbbed too. The rest of his body hurt too much for him to tell where there might be specific injuries. He wiggled his hands—might have a broken finger too from the way one of them moved, but he was too numb from the cold water to tell yet.

Looking around, he muttered, "Where am I? And how did I get here?" Wherever he was, the magic was thin, damn near inaccessible. Even sitting with his feet in the Atlantic Ocean, he felt weak, as if his magical abilities were muffled or blocked.

He peered out over the choppy, grey water. Just offshore, three heads like rounded stones bobbed up and down in the swell. As they came closer, Rafe saw their large, dark eyes, their snouts and whiskers. A fourth face, gilled and hung around with hair like strands of branching seaweed joined them, popping up head and shoulders above the waves. Behind the merperson, the kelpies hung back, huddling together.

"Hail, faerie," the mer said.

"Hail," Rafe managed. He raised one hand in greeting.

"My friends saved you from the water and the boats," the mer said. Xe's double rows of teeth showed as xe talked. "They are kind creatures—without them, you would be food for the minnows and crabs. But they fear men. They wish to keep their skins."

Rafe nodded, understanding. Too many kelpies over the centuries had had their skins stolen by men seeking a slave-bride for them to approach him. "Tell them I am eternally grateful," he said. "And to you too."

The mer shrugged and flipped xe's tail. "You are known to us. My hatch-kin have swum in warmer waters with you on the other side of the veil."

"The other side? What do you mean?"

The mer pointed out to the open water, and Rafe's stomach sank. Ships like moving cliffs, but made entirely of iron, sailed across the horizon, dozens of them. Somehow, he had crossed a broken place in the borders between the Winter Court and the magic-starved human world.

"How?"

The mer shrugged again.

"Can you take me back?" Rafe asked.

The mer shook xe's head. "We found you. We did not bring you. The ways back are..." Xe gargled something, xe's hair moving around xe's face as xe tried to find the words in Rafe's language. "...they come and go? Not like the tides that can be relied on."

"They're erratic. Unpredictable," Rafe said.

"Maybe that is the word. They are spawning too much. Not like in the days of our ancestors." Xe ducked under the waves suddenly and Rafe waited patiently for the mer to re-wet xeself. When the mer reappeared, xe said, "The holes in the veil are happening. Being made to happen. Like the poisons that come from the ships." Xe ducked under the water again and reappeared. "I must go to deeper waters. Good luck, faerie." The kelpies soon followed.

Left alone on the darkening beach, Rafe hauled himself to his feet. A quick check of his pockets confirmed that his mirror was smashed to bits and its magic gone. Limping, he made his way up the strand until he found a footpath. The thought of dealing with humans made him shudder, but there wasn't an inch of him that wasn't bruised, scraped, or broken. He drew in another shuddering breath and shivered. He needed shelter, he needed food, he needed a safe place to heal.

The adrenaline rush of finding himself alive was wearing off, and the aches and pains grew more intense. His hands throbbed, as did his temples.

The moon was high in the sky above him, but there didn't seem to be any light but that and the stars. He must have been farther from a human city than he thought.

In the moonlight he could make out a large stone building, rising like an island just off the beach. It looked old, and stately, but not a castle. He pressed onward, up sand until he reached a stone road—more a path than anything, that led out from the beach to the building. From the damp and the seaweed covering it, the road would be underwater when the full tide came in. Every step hurt a bit more than the last, and he was certain more than just his ribs were broken.

He arrived in front of the building and gazed up at it. It had a spire, though he couldn't quite see the top. Half a dozen shallow steps led up to the massive arched doors. He rested a hand on one and closed his eyes. The wood was old, and it wasn't devoid of magic. Whatever this place was, there was some kind of magic in it, though it did not feel faerie. He tentatively touched the handle, aware that humans often used iron, but it didn't burn—perhaps it was brass. He pulled—the door was heavy, but the hinges were well oiled and it opened smoothly. He stumbled inside.

The large room was empty, the air heavy and still, and lined with tall windows of colored glass. At the far end was some kind of dais. He stumbled forward and dropped to his knees.

"It is a bit late for visitors," a cheerful voice rang out. "Oh, my lord!"

Rafe looked up and saw a man striding toward him down the center aisle. He wore a brown robe tied with some kind of rope, a cowl thrown back. He looked like a bard, perhaps. He hurried forward, ducking under Rafe and settling Rafe's arm over his shoulder. "Evelyn!" he hollered in a way that made Rafe wince. "Come! Quickly."

Rafe grunted as the man maneuvered him up the aisle.

"I am Caedmon," he said. "Easy now. It's not far to the dormitory, and my brother will be here soon to help."

"You called?" Another voice, Evelyn.

Rafe looked up to see another man, similarly dressed but with an eyepatch too, rushing toward him. He slung Rafe's other arm over his shoulder and together both men helped him to his feet.

The two bustled him through a door to the right of the dais and down another hall. Finally, they led him to a room with a bed and eased him down onto it.

"Thank you," Rafe said. He looked back and forth between the two men, who regarded him carefully. "Where am I? What is this place?"

Caedmon smiled. "You are at Mount Saint Michael. This is a holy place." He and Evelyn gently pulled off his coat and shirt, what were left of them. "Come now, lay down. You are safe with us." He helped Rafe into the bed.

"A church?" Rafe said. Dell had spoken of them—they mattered to the human religion he came from, but that was as far as Rafe could make his brain work. "Sanctuary?" he mumbled.

"Of course," Caedmon said. "You are safe and protected here."

"And you'll be healed too," Evelyn added.

Rafe blinked up at the two men with their kind faces, and he believed them. "Thank you," he managed before he let himself drop into a dreamless sleep.

The End

About the Authors

Sarah Joy Adams is co-author with Emily Lavin Leverett of the Eisteddfod Chronicles. She is also the author of the Kinslayer Winter series, about modern day berserkers in Buffalo, NY, from Falstaff Books. When she is not writing about faeries, vampires, and Norse warriors, Sarah teaches medieval literature and creative writing. She can be found on Facebook or http://sarahjoyadams.blogspot.com/.

Emily Lavin Leverett is a writer, editor, and English professor. She is the co-editor of *Lawless Lands: Tales from the Weird Frontier* and *The Weird Wild West* with Misty Massey and Margaret McGraw. Her first novel *Changeling's Fall*, co-written with Sarah Joy Adams will be followed in 2018 with *Winter's Heir*, the second novel in their contemporary fantasy faerie tale series *The Eisteddfod Chronicles*. She is currently working on another urban fantasy novel set in Raleigh, NC. Her scholarship focuses on the connection between Medieval English Romance and the *Discworld* novels of Terry Pratchett. She lives in North Carolina with her spouse and their three cats, where they remain stalwart Carolina Hurricanes fans.

MORE BY THESE AUTHORS

Sarah Joy Adams & Emily Lavin Leverett

The Eisteddfod Chronicles

Changeling's Fall

Winter's Heir

Sarah Joy Adams

The Kinslayer Saga

Steel Mill Vikings

Emily Lavin Leverett

The Wolf & The Nun

The Wolf in the Cloister

The Enchanted Rose

The Song of the Black Wolf

Emily Lavin Leverett (editor)

The Big Bad

The Big Bad II

The Weird Wild West

Lawless Lands

Predators in Petticoats

FALSTAFF BOOKS

**Want to know what's new
And coming soon from
Falstaff Books?**

Try This Free Ebook Sampler

https://www.instafreebie.com/free/bsZnl

**Follow the link.
Download the file.
Transfer to your e-reader, phone, tablet, watch, computer, whatever.
Enjoy.**

www.ingramcontent.com/pod-product-compliance
Lightning Source LLC
Chambersburg PA
CBHW021502110726
47899CB00001BA/262